Praise for *A Tale of T*

"Maxted succeeds in capturing the ways people can talk past each other and miss connections with even those they need most in the world. . . . [She has a] sure grasp of intimate relationships." —*The New York Times Book Review*

"Maxted is a terrific writer with a droll comedic voice. She excels at creating vivid, believable protagonists, and even her minor characters are full of life." —*The Washington Post Book World*

"With her winning combination of honesty and warmth, Maxted has ensured herself another triumph." —*Glamour*

"Compelling and heartfelt while still displaying Maxted's trademark humor. If you have a sister, you'll want to share this book with her, and if you don't, you'll wish you did." —*Library Journal*

Praise for *Being Committed*

"Maxted's cheekiness and intelligence help this tale transcend the genre." —*People*

"It's refreshing to find a protagonist who questions whether marriage really means happily ever after." —*Entertainment Weekly*

"Deliciously snarky . . . Maxted tosses barbs like a champion darts player, and she paints a scathingly hilarious picture of her misguided but appealingly frank heroine." —*Publishers Weekly*

"A lively, romantic romp." —*US Weekly*

heroine may well prove habit-forming. *Get Getting Over It*, and then see if you can."

—Gregory Maguire, *New York Times* bestselling author of *Wicked* and *A Lion Among Men*

"Breezy and subversive, but with a heart of vulnerability. *Getting Over It* never loses its humor or its warmth—a great achievement. I loved it!"

—Marian Keyes, internationally bestselling author of *This Charming Man*

"A charming and compelling debut."

—Suzanne Finnamore, author of *Otherwise Engaged*

RICH AGAIN

Anna Maxted

St. Martin's Griffin
New York

To the boys: don't ever behave like this.

RICH AGAIN. Copyright © 2009 by The Parallax Corporation. All rights reserved. Printed in the United States of America. For information, address St. Martin's Press, 175 Fifth Avenue, New York, N.Y. 10010.

www.stmartins.com

Library of Congress Cataloging-in-Publication Data

Maxted, Anna.
    Rich again / Anna Maxted. — 1st U.S. ed.
        p. cm.
    ISBN 978-0-312-57028-6
    1. Upper class families—England—Fiction. 2. Rich people—England—Fiction. 3. Sisters—Fiction. 4. Parent and adult child—Fiction. 5. Domestic fiction. I. Title.
    PR6063.A8665R53 2010
    823'.914—dc22

                                                                    2009033711

First published as *Betrayal* by Sasha Blake in Great Britain by Transworld Publishers

First U.S. Edition: January 2010

10 9 8 7 6 5 4 3 2 1

BOOK ONE

LOS ANGELES, 1996

Emily

It was 10.30 a.m. and Emily lay naked on the lilo, using her mother's favourite suede coat as a towel, and let the gentle breeze waft her around the infinity pool. In one hand she held a pint glass of chilled Baileys. Her first to-do on arrival at the mansion had been to order Quintin to freeze three ice-cube trays of her favourite drink, because there was nothing worse than a warm Baileys or a dilute Baileys. She drew on her fifth Silk Cut Light of the day, and gazed at the forever-blue sky of LA.

Everything: perfect.

She liked the world upside down, especially when it was so prettily fringed by those pink and red flowers that smothered any suggestion of ugliness – wall, pole, fence and, possibly, person – in the Hollywood Hills. She liked that there were invisible teams slaving night and day to keep all she saw gorgeous. She liked the quiet. The only noise was the buzz of helicopters, either the paparazzi harassing stars or privately owned by the stars themselves. She liked that it was summer and that Mummy had complied with the annual lie that Emily 'work' as an intern at the Beverly Grand.

It was lucky that Mummy adored Emily more in theory than in person, and seized on any chance to put oceans between them. Mummy wasn't interested in people under eighteen. By the time Emily was old enough to come to her attention, it would be too late.

To Mummy, this was just another one of Emily's LA jaunts, where she could drink and smoke and do coke and trash the 26,000-square-foot mansion off Mulholland, while pretending to work at her father's hotel. As long as Mummy didn't *witness* a felony and wasn't forced to make a show of responsible parenting, as long as someone was paid to delete all evidence of wrongdoing, Mummy was just grateful to have a fourteen-year-old with the wit to entertain herself.

It was annoying to be underestimated, but she wouldn't be for much longer. Meantime, her parents' lack of interest was useful. The pinnacle of her life plan – to seduce her best friend, Timmy – would be accomplished that day without interference.

Timothy Rupert Peregrine Giles, heir to the Fifteenth Earl of Fortelyne, was seventeen and Gordonstoun was shaping him up nicely for a lifelong stay in the warm embrace of the Establishment. He was charming, witty, able to acquit himself admirably in any social situation; he was a good rower, a fine rugby player, and – having been removed from his mother at seven and only briefly reunited with her after puberty – he knew nothing about women.

Tim had no idea that if a girl recommended Lanikai Beach in Hawaii for the best surfing – several times, over several months, in passing, until he became convinced that the idea was *his* – that she might have an ulterior motive. He was one of those nice but frustrating guys, blind to who was a saint and who was a bitch, because he imagined that wicked must show on a girl's face.

However, his naivety and good nature were great assets to Emily. She'd waited until he booked Hawaii, and then she'd said, 'I'll be in LA around then. Come for the weekend. I'll send the jet.'

She knew that while a seventeen-year-old boy could (bizarrely) resist *her*, he couldn't resist 'the jet'.

Tim's family had pots of money but, to Emily's disdain, they had no idea how to spend it. That crappy old Land-Rover they bumped about in! Those hideous saggy green cords his mother Pat – a *countess!* – was always tramping around in! If they flew, they flew *commercial!* All that dreary centuries-old furniture! And their parties! Never happy unless a great big draughty marquee was involved; only satisfied if their guests were squelching up to their waists in mud; curiously cavalier about the quality and quantity of the food.

So, the private jet was winging its way to Hawaii and the Maserati would collect him at the airstrip. As far as he knew, he was staying for the 'weekend', a concept familiar to him, as most posh people she knew spent every weekend filling their castles with braying guests, who were expected to kill birds and bunnies, take endless walks, play charades and take part in any number of life-sapping activities from dawn to dusk. God forbid they had a quiet couple of days lolling around to music and watching the box.

This weekend – *her* LA house party weekend – would be different. LA was made for parties, unlike England. In England, throwing a party was an imposition: against you stood the weather, the traffic and your guests' prior commitment to staying home and sniping about next door.

Emily smiled to herself. She'd found her own event planners, people who were clued in to *now*. They'd sorted the valet parking and the street-use permit. They'd notified the neighbours, with enormous bouquets – she didn't want the LAPD wading in. They'd organized the bartenders, security guards, caterers, decorators, insurance, bonded storage for the art and antiques – like she cared, but *they* did – and they'd even offered to supply a couple of dozen fashion models paid to chuck themselves naked into the pool at midnight.

Like, talk about your worst *nightmare!* But the limo service into the Hills was a good idea, as most of her guests couldn't drive. The party would set Mummy back nine hundred

11

thousand pounds, plus another ton when Emily flew out all her mates from London. She was embarrassed at having them slum it in Virgin Upper Class (she hated to appear budget) but there was no way that they'd all fit in the family jet. Anyway, it was reserved for Timmy and, short of appropriating Air Force One, there was no alternative.

She'd chosen the guest list with care. Her own crowd was pretty cool, and Leonardo was invited, and Johnny – she prayed he wouldn't drag along his girlfriend. It was a great bore that the bar had to be officially virgin, but she didn't want Quintin busted for serving liquor to minors. Anyway, there was a secret alcohol den for the chosen few and, in *hommage* to Johnny, she'd ordered the Jacuzzi to be filled with vintage champagne. She had to invite *some* A-list females, so she'd chosen Alicia and the Ricci girl – no one too distracting.

The DJs, Sasha and John Digweed – oh my God, their gigs were *so* cool! She *loved* how trance let you *be*, and it made her *so* horny. They were going to blow everyone away. And *she* was going to blow Timmy away.

'Quintin!'

'It's eleven, Emily, a selection of drop-dead outfits await your inspection.'

She'd picked them out a week ago, leafing quickly through *Vogue*: 'Get me that, and that, and that.'

'Thanks, Quintin!'

She loved Quintin. She wondered if his mother had just *known* he was gay, setting eyes on him. It was quite cool to have gay friends. Well, to be acquainted with an actual gay person. Officially, it was 'his' party, and he'd done everything in his power to ensure its success. He knew the best beauticians; her eyebrows and bikini line were immaculate, and the hot-stone massage – 'You'll feel like you've just had sex, darling,' he'd said, then clapped a hand over his mouth. She'd smiled; she loved that he thought of her as an adult.

She'd been body-brushed and seaweed-wrapped and Pilates-stretched to within an inch of her life. She disliked the underground gym – she felt it gave the house a whiff of the Hyatt – but she'd done ten miles on the running machine. Her teeth were virgin white, and her tan was café crème (poor Mummy thought that 'sexy' was to fry yourself the colour of a hot dog). She'd gone for an early hike up Runyon every morning, *and* she could now swim the entire length of the pool underwater.

Emily was ready to bet that no one in the history of the world had prepared quite so thoroughly for a blow job.

She drained the last of the Baileys, swam to the side and jogged up the steps. The Mexican gardener fought against nature to look the other way. 'Feast your eyes,' she cried as she skipped past.

Quintin had laid out the clothes on her bed. Amid the tiny gorgeous scraps of material passing for dresses was a black mini kimono from Galliano. Perhaps she could wear it with the Wonderbra, black fishnet stockings, suspenders and red and black lace knickers from Topshop? And you couldn't beat black patent Prada heels. To hell with heroin chic – she preferred prostitute chic. Seventeen-year-old boys weren't complex, so why confuse them?

Here was the plan. She'd have the driver take the Merc and grab her a Fatburger with chilli cheese fries. She'd eat, doze and watch MTV while they tarted up the house. Quintin could deal with questions and Timmy wasn't due till eight. Bang on four, she'd shower, do her hair and make-up. The air con would have to be polar – happily, Mummy wasn't here to scream, 'Shut the fucking *doors!*' Mummy loved a professional make-up artist, although they invariably made her look like a drag artist. No way was one of those clowns going *near* Emily's face!

She ate, slept, woke, looked in the mirror; FUCK, her eyelids were PUFFY. Puffy as HELL.

'Quintin! Quintin, Oh my God, come now, help!'

To his great credit, Quintin staggered into her bedroom wielding a seventeenth-century stone Buddha.

An emergency application of ice cubes and cucumber limited the damage, 'and it's imperative that you remain vertical from this moment on, and whatever you do, don't cry.' By six o clock she felt sufficiently calm to dress to *The Immaculate Collection*. She flossed, brushed, blinked through the sting of the mint mouthwash. Then she had a fag. Sod it, that was what gum was for.

'Very *Pretty Woman*,' murmured Quintin when she did a twirl.

Stupidly, she felt nervous. Tim hadn't called – did he have the house number? He had her mobile, but reception was shit in the Hills. Oh, these boys, they never called – they just arrived. She scurried back to her bedroom, quick snort; *now* she felt good. She poured herself another Baileys, then wandered to the upper deck, threw herself on a sun lounger and gazed through Chanel shades at the amazing sprawl of the San Fernando Valley and the San Gabriel Mountains, almost purple on the dimming horizon. The ocean was a thin serene line. It was hard to stay still, so she jumped up, lit a fag, went to say hi to Sasha and John.

'I enjoy your work,' she said coolly, tossing her hair.

John winked at her and said, 'Thanks, little girl.'

He was cute in a rough sort of way, like a builder. She couldn't decide whether to be offended or flattered, so she purred, 'See you later,' and sashayed off.

The house looked wild. They'd set up tacky-but-cool fluorescent palm-tree lights at the front gates, and the word *Believe* in huge curly white script was projected to the bottom of the pool. Later, the pool would become a monster bubble bath (the bubbles, colour of your choice, were guaranteed to vanish, leaving no trace, by dawn). They'd managed – how, in the dusk, she had no idea – to refract light into its composite colours; as a result, the entire house was a mass of rainbows. The pagoda had been cleared of furniture and was now an open-air dance floor. The lemon, fig, peach and grapefruit trees were hung with crystals, all sparkling, amid the fruit. And there were white flowers everywhere.

Oh, and they'd turned the tennis court into an ice rink.

She peered into the open-air Jacuzzi, then knelt, like a cat before a saucer of cream, and lapped at it. Fucking A, man! If you hadn't drunk Krug from a Jacuzzi, you hadn't *lived*. Emily sat up, tilted her head and laughed aloud. Although . . .

'Quintin!'

'My lady?'

'Please bring ten bottles of crème de cassis.'

She emptied them into the Jacuzzi, giggling, and watched as it turned a hot pink. *This* was the spot, oh my God! And don't think she wouldn't turf out Johnny to get close and personal with Tim. Although, it was kind of gross. She didn't mind immersing herself in Depp's bodily fluids, but *the girl-friend's*? No *way*.

The Jacuzzi needed to be roped off with some of that yellow police-crime-scene-do-not-cross tape. She asked Quintin to organize it, and went to check out the bar. Virgin everything. Americans were so bloody terrified of booze that it was illegal to drink until you were *twenty-one*, but if you wanted a gun licence: you're *so* welcome! Her guests would get high on drugs instead.

The food was lush: sushi from Katsu-ya – their tempura prawns were to die for; fish and chips from Ford's – *love* that Oo-ee Sauce, but, sigh, no garlic *tonight*; chocolate fountains; candy-floss stalls; milkshakes from Fosselman's – unbeatable, especially the cookies and cream; and, of course, cupcakes from Dainties. She'd have to resist, she had more important business and – oh my *God*, the limos were arriving. She screamed with joy to see her girls, who screamed back. Her parties always merited a good scream. The British guys walked around, hands in pockets, trying not to look impressed. The American guys were all, like, 'Man, this is *awesome*!' There was lots of air kissing, and the music was at full blast. It was going to be a *bad* night.

But where was Tim?

Leonardo showed, with an entourage of fifteen. He was cute, not as squat as on-screen, but spent a tedious amount of time huddled in a remote scrum, or fiddling with his mobile. She'd shrugged prettily and said, 'Guess you should find a party downtown.'

Tram lines improved her mood, and she had to test a glass of Jacuzzi booze to make sure it was drinkable, and those tempura prawns, what an addiction! Hey, and there was her favourite boy, Barney: middle posh, cheerfully sleazy, loyal as a red setter, *always* randy (he'd tried it on with her mother and she really, *really* didn't want to know how far he'd got). Barney insisted she try the chocolate fountain. Instead of dipping in a pink marshmallow, he dipped in his cock.

She shrieked with laughter. 'Fuck *off*, Barney, I don't know where it's been – or rather I do!'

But, suddenly, more than anything, she wanted to suck him off. Girls like her didn't send jets for just anyone. How *dare* Tim reject her. She'd spent months of preparation, not to mention nine hundred thousand quid on his blow job!

Fine. Well. She'd give it to someone else, someone who *deserved* it. She turned to Barney with her best pout, and—

'Hi there, Em. Cool party.'

She swung around, eyes glittering, and Barney faded tactfully into the shadows.

'Tim.' She *had* to laugh. 'Tim, you must be *boiling*!' He was wearing black faded jeans, cowboy boots, a pink shirt under a white wool tank top, and a great red pashmina with gold thread wrapped around his neck. 'This is LA, Tim, not Edinburgh.' She grinned and walked around him, unravelling the pashmina. 'You need to show me some skin.'

'I don't know,' he said. 'There appears to be a skating rink.'

'Well, it is Hollywood. Someone's got to break a leg.' *Shit.* She must be nervous. That joke *sucked*.

She waved over Quintin, who was booze marshal, and pressed an illicit Jack 'n' Coke into Tim's hand. 'By the way,' he said. 'Thanks awfully for the ride. It rocked.'

'Do you mean there was turbulence?' she teased. 'Because I simply don't allow it.'

He blushed, letting his hair fall over his eyes. 'Only in my heart.'

She felt her heart crinkle like a tissue. Poor baby, he was so inept. 'Oh, Tim,' she said, and stroked his hair. 'You are just . . . beautiful.' She took his hand. 'Come with me. I have something to show you.'

They crept down to the lower deck, where the Jacuzzi was cordoned off. The whole of downtown LA spread below them like a magic carpet.

'Nice view,' she said.

'I prefer this one,' he replied, gazing into her eyes. Oh Jesus. On no account must she laugh.

Somehow, Quintin had found a sign that read 'DANGER OF DEATH' above an illustration of a prone stick figure, a lightning bolt pointing at his neck. Em booted it to one side. Then, slinkily, she sat on the ground, and said, 'I don't want to get my shoes wet.'

Slowly, Tim knelt, like a knight before his queen, and slipped off her shoes. It was OK – she'd deodorized her feet to hell. He was breathing hard. She necked her Kir Royale; she tipped her head back too fast and her vision swam. She felt odd, wired, but not in a good way. Fried prawns and white powder didn't go – remember *that* for next time. She was about to take off Tim's shoes, when she saw that he'd whipped off *all* his clothes, except for his boxer shorts.

He grinned. 'Let's Jacuzzi.'

She stood up and, silently, he pulled at her obi-style sash. The black mini kimono fell open, and she shrugged it off. Tim's mouth actually fell open at the sight of her in her tiny knickers, stockings and Wonderbra. He pulled her on to his lap, and their lips met in a hard clash. To her surprise he took the lead.

'You kiss good,' she gasped, and he replied, 'I fuck better.'

17

His dick pressed hard into her stomach, and she felt a lurch of desire. 'Oh, baby,' she sighed, wrapping her legs around him. 'I'm just a girl.'

She should really go down on him *now* . . . now would be a good time, but she had to let her stomach settle. She leant back as he leant forward, chasing the kiss, and, screaming, they toppled into the Jacuzzi.

'My hair,' she shrieked, and got a mouthful of Kir Royale.

'Far *out*!' gargled Tim, surfacing, and then he pulled her under. But she couldn't kiss for laughing, and then got Krug up her nose. She surfaced, spluttering, and so did he. Her eyes stung, but she was so wasted she couldn't stop laughing, and nor could he.

'Stop laughing,' she gasped as he grazed his lips to her nipples. *Zing!* Every sensation was magnified and it wasn't entirely pleasant. 'I'm going to . . .' It was quite hard to focus. She wasn't sure she could hold her breath that long – she tried a sexy smoulder. 'I'm going to give you the chew of your life.'

He shouted with laughter. 'Emily, Emily,' he muttered, as his mouth found hers. 'You dirty girl.'

He stood up and she pulled off his boxers. Oh my. Basically, in the cold light of day, these things weren't the *prettiest*. In fact, a penis was, like, gross. But right now, she was *so* in the mood, and to her, it looked good enough to eat. She licked and sucked, and he shuddered and groaned and thrust. It was fine, except when he thrust. When it hit the back of her throat it made her stomach heave. But she writhed, and sighed, and gave him the coy looks for about a thousand years, and he rolled his eyes, half comatose with bliss, but showed no sign of approaching the finish line. Bloody hell, hurry *up*, she wasn't exactly having fun here. She should really do the deep throat thing now, the grand finale, and he would never *look* at another girl. He would dream of marriage – he was an old-fashioned boy, he'd be digging through his mother's jewellery box, ferreting out the great-grandmother's engagement ring in no time. The thought spurred her on and she could feel – thank God, her lips were totally numb – it was near the end. 'Yes, I'm going to come.' She squeezed her eyes shut tight as he jerked violently. Come on, Em, keep going, think of castles. God, she felt rough. Her head ached, as if it was being crushed, and he was pushing her hard, down and – 'OH YES!' Oh *no* – rearing back in horror, she puked a great stinking fountain of pink champagne and half-digested fried prawns all over him.

LONDON, A YEAR EARLIER, 1995

Claudia

'One large tea, please. Can you put two teabags in there, please? And cold milk – it must be cold, *not* hot – just to the colour of a St-Tropez tan. Or, um, pine wood! A caramel slice – yes, the exact colour of a caramel slice. *Please* don't put too much milk in there, it mustn't taste milky. And one latte, medium-sized, can you put extra cinnamon on the top, please? Not too much froth, the froth mustn't exceed one-third of the cup. And the milk must be semi-skimmed. Oh, sorry, I forgot to say, the milk for the tea must be full fat. Yes. And a triple espresso, with an extra two inches of hot water. And one slice of peanut butter on toast – brown toast, not *too* well done, and absolutely *no* butter. Smooth peanut butter – on no account crunchy. Sorry. A fried-egg sandwich, still runny yolk, with butter, *not* margarine, on white bread – bread, not toast. Could you – I'm so sorry about this – cut off the crusts? Thank you! And, finally, you'll be pleased to hear, a low-fat blueberry muffin. Oh God. Is there anywhere else, do you know? Oh, really? Are you sure? She won't be able to tell? I'll risk it! Well, thank you, *thank you*.'

It was hard work, being a journalist.

Claudia pressed the button for the twenty-seventh floor and tried not to drop three hot drinks on the red carpet. She also tried not to think of JR wreaking terrible dog vengeance in her flat.

According to Upstairs – who'd given the information with remarkably gentle reproach – JR had howled at teeth-gritting pitch for seven hours straight every day this week. For a senior citizen, he was remarkably spry. She suspected that he'd also pissed in her black Prada bag. She'd left it on the floor by mistake and every time she passed it, she got a *whiff*. She'd have to organize a dog-sitter, one who could fend off bites. JR knew who was leader of the pack, and it wasn't Claudia. He slept *in* – not *on* – her bed, his long haughty snout resting on her cream pillow. His breath was foul, he snored, and he had fleas.

She suspected her grandmother was looking down and laughing.

Still, Claudia was happy. She was twenty years old and she was *free*.

She had a home of her own, a tiny, one-bedroom flat, allegedly in 'Highgate' but nearer to the A1, which mostly belonged to the bank. Ruth had left her no money – everything had gone to the RSPCA – and she'd choke before she took a penny from her father.

When Claudia brushed her teeth, she could hear the *ping!* as her upstairs neighbour switched on his bathroom light. At night, in bed, she could hear him cough (or worse). He had a cheap sports car and a second wife, and he was always smiling. The people on the ground floor had three little boys, one in a wheelchair – MD, she thought – and the mother was always smiling, too.

It was a happy house, not exactly the high life.

Truth was, people expected her to be loaded because of Dad, even since his disgrace – which was not that he'd been ruined by the Lloyd's crash, but that he *hadn't*. He'd lost millions but he'd managed to keep *enough*. The lawsuit had failed to prove that Jack had knowingly transferred funds and properties; he'd won his case but lost his reputation. *The Times*'s Financial Editor had written, 'Everyone is bankrupt, but some are more bankrupt than others,' and a letter signed by forty destitute Names had been printed the next day; 'Some are more corrupt than others.' She'd felt sick reading it, but she agreed.

Jack hadn't always been like this. Once, he'd been a good man.

Claudia's colleagues had discovered who she was, despite the fact that she'd taken Ruth's last name – Mayer – and they didn't like her for it. She spent her day fetching dry cleaning and precisely ordered snacks, endlessly yo-yoing in the silver lifts of Canary Wharf's Tower, and trying to set up exclusives with reclusive, press-hating stars for the writers. And she knew that when she wasn't looking, Linda, the frumpy secretary, mimicked her walk.

She didn't care. She had a *job*, unconnected to the family, and she had her pen friend Lucy to thank for it.

It had been Lucy who'd suggested that Claudia call the deputy editor of *UK Sunday*, Martin Freshwater. 'My stepdad works on the publishing side,' she'd written, 'although *don't* mention his name. I know that Martin is looking for people.'

Lucy had even written down Martin's direct line. It was incredibly kind of her. Odd that when Claudia called, Martin said he *wasn't* looking. But he'd said he liked the sound of her voice, and she was welcome to come in for a week on work experience.

She'd been so excited that she'd wanted to ring Lucy and hear her voice – they'd never even spoken on the phone. But Lucy's response had been disappointing. Lucy's stepfather was moving the family abroad: a business opportunity in South Africa. Lucy was to join the family firm and train as an accountant. She'd promised to send her new address in Cape Town but never had. Claudia guessed that it was to do with the stepfather. She tried not to be hurt.

She succeeded.

This had nothing to do with inner strength and everything to do with Martin Freshwater.

Martin Freshwater was unfairly gorgeous. He had blue-green eyes and a hint of stubble. He had sharp cheekbones and blond floppy hair with a touch of grey. He typed like a demon, using two fingers. Usually, a lit cigarette rested between his ring finger (unadorned) and his middle finger as he tapped away. He was a brilliant editor, so . . . *masterful* and his shirts were a little crumpled, suggesting he needed a woman to – oh God, shut *up*! No, what she meant was, Martin Freshwater needed a woman who could recommend a good dry cleaner.

Martin Freshwater was the reason she was eating again.

According to her shrink, who was a nice person but made her feel mad, an eating disorder was a form of depression. She had all this anger, but she didn't dare show it, so it had festered inside.

She supposed the shrink was right. At first it had been a way of snatching back some control from her parents. But bulimia was such an ugly way of trying to be beautiful. It made you hate yourself even more than you did when you were fat. After four years of it, she wanted to be *normal*.

She'd tried. It was the same as other people quitting smoking. You did it a million times but then you suffered one miserable day, no, *two* miserable days, and you craved the delicious comfort of a nice poisonous lung-clagging fag. And then you thought, Sod it, bought a pack, smoked the lot.

She wanted to love herself but she needed *verification* from a respected source. There were a few boys who 'liked' her. But she didn't like them, and not just because of their two-ply personalities, or designs on her father's money. She'd know, after one minute, that these boys didn't *get* her. To them she was no more than a slot machine: good to stick something in, or get money out of.

Martin Freshwater liked Claudia for *herself*. He had given

her the strength to kick her habit. She wasn't going to be eating pastry anytime soon, but she was doing all right. He wasn't a boy, he was a man. He was thirty-seven. Martin Freshwater made Claudia feel happy. There was a connection there: when she looked into his eyes, there was *recognition*. They were kindred souls. Her attraction to him was primal, something not experienced before, and she felt sure – the feeling was so strong – that he felt the same way.

They hadn't even kissed.

But they were going to.

She placed his triple espresso on his desk. He glanced up. Everyone was crowded around the picture desk, squinting over the light box, no doubt to cackle over stills of young female celebrities as yet un-airbrushed and revealing some happy human flaw such as facial hair.

'Claudia, busy tonight?'

She took a breath. 'Well, er, I need to take my dog out . . . a quick walk . . . he has to go to the toilet . . .' *Yes, mention 'toilet'.* 'But otherwise . . .'

'I'm meeting Meg Ryan's PR at the Connaught. Come along. See how it works. Might have to run a puff piece on some nobody before we get Meg.'

'Oh, yes. That would be great.'

'Good. See you there. Eight thirty.'

She was stupidly happy. She left the office dot on five thirty, sped home and spent two hours beautifying. JR (who had ripped up three cushions) got the briefest toilet break of his life. When she put down his freshly made pasta and chicken – JR famously had a weak stomach which you ignored at your peril – he turned coldly away from the bowl.

'JR, I *beg* you!'

He sat down with a thump on the carpet, and rested his head on his paws. He was pining for Ruth. She crouched beside him and stroked his silky head. 'I'm sorry, Mr.'

She glanced covertly at her watch. Time to go. She looked hopefully at JR's tail – not a twitch. Ah, crap.

'I'm sorry, madam. Dogs are not allowed in the hotel unless—'

'He's a guide dog!' *Claudia, you idiot.* She stared into the middle distance. 'I'm partially sighted.'

'I see. I mean . . . I wasn't aware that collies were . . .'

She considered the response, A collie? I was told an Alsatian! but she said, 'I'm meeting someone in the bar. Could you . . . ?'

The woman firmly took her arm. This gave new meaning to the term blind date. Why, *why*?

As they approached, she saw Martin. He stood up. She sensed a double-take.

'Martin?' she said, feeling her face purple with embarrassment.

'Claudia!'

The woman was still regarding her suspiciously. Miserably, Claudia patted the back of the sofa and pretended to feel her way to a seat. Meanwhile, that bloody JR wasn't behaving like a guide dog. His tail waved wildly and he jumped at Martin and licked his wrist.

'Oh dear,' said Martin. 'This dog is going to fail his seeing-eye training.' He smiled at the woman. 'Thank you.'

She scurried off.

Claudia couldn't meet Martin's gaze. 'The PR cancelled,' he said.

'Good. I mean . . . because I . . .'

'Not at all. She would have been impressed to find that *UK Sunday* is an equal-opportunities employer,' he replied.

'Are you laughing at me?'

'I am.'

She giggled. 'Fair enough.'

'What will you have?' he asked.

She tried to think of an impressive drink. 'Campari and lemonade.'

Martin ordered, and she blurted, 'Do you have any pets?' It

was as if her brain had been hijacked by a really stupid person.

'I do. Keith. He's a Siamese cat. He chose me.'

'*Keith?*'

'Keith Moon. Same personality.'

'I love cats, but I inherited JR and he'd never tolerate the competition. He barely tolerates *me*. I suspect he disapproves.'

'Then he is a dog of poor taste.'

She looked up. She wanted to kiss him. She wasn't afraid. A kiss didn't have to mean sex. She could put him off for . . . a year? Anyway, she didn't have to worry about *that*. All she had to think about right now was a kiss. And she knew, in her heart, that when she kissed this man, there would be no panic, no constricting throat. She knew that she would sink into that kiss like a feather pillow. Everything about him was desirable: the scent of him; the way he spoke. It was like an invisible force drawing her to him.

It was *fate*.

Of all the billions of people who had passed through the world, Martin Freshwater and Claudia Mayer were, by chance, on the planet at the same time, in the same country, in the same city, sharing the same 20 square feet of office – gosh. He could have been born five hundred years ago, and she could have lived her life in miserable isolation, her soulmate dead and buried before she was even born! Or she could have grown up on a sheep farm in New Zealand, unaware that the love of her life was on the other side of the world! But there was a God, and here he was, smiling at her, their knees not quite touching. He was also her boss. Well, if it got serious she could quit. Talk about jumping ahead. You haven't even—

Oh. Oh! *Oh*.

After a long, long while, she drew away, bit her lip. No inhaler!

'I've wanted to do that ever since I first saw you,' he murmured. He shook his head. 'This sounds like a line but I don't do this. Hit on colleagues. Or girls as young as you.

When I was younger . . .' He grimaced. 'It doesn't matter. I'm an anti-social old git. But' – shrugging – 'something about you, Claudia, I find' – he leaned towards her again – 'magnetic.'

She looked down. 'I find you . . . also,' she finished.

'So,' he said, raising an eyebrow, 'Claudia Mayer, what would you like to *do* about it?'

PARIS, LATE SUMMER 1996

Jack

The place had no address worth mentioning. He felt so tense he was *fizzing*. He couldn't pop any more pills. And that fifth coffee had been a mistake.

It was so mortifying. What was he *doing* here? It was going to be a disaster. He was hated in Britain by the press, by the Establishment – people who had been his *friends*.

Only Harry remained constant, but Jack was so cynical now, so paranoid, he couldn't believe that Harry liked him for *him*; he felt sure that Harry must get some kick out of consorting with a poorer, humiliated Jack, that he must feel smug and good about himself: Ah, I'm clever and rich, but *you* did everything wrong, no more jets and 'copters for you, my friend, and serve you right!

The worst thing was to have the world know that Innocence was the boss of Élite Retreats. The world *had* to know – and see for itself – that his wife truly owned and ran the empire, or Lloyd's would seize every brick and coin of the business he'd worked so hard to build.

He could still barely believe that the unscrupulous bitch had stolen the last fifteen years of his life's work shortly before the Lloyd's crash – fraudulently signed over millions and millions of pounds' worth of his properties and assets to herself – but that he couldn't grass her to the police, because if *she* lost everything, *he'd* lose everything, which was a lot worse than losing nearly everything.

As it was, he was only able to start over – with a business that was legitimately his – because following the desperate, aggressive litigation, Lloyd's had agreed to cap his losses earlier this year. He was one of the 'lucky' ones; the 40 per cent of Names who would share an £800 million settlement fund – as they bloody should, having sustained 65 per cent of the firm's liabilities!

It hurt Jack that he remained ostracized because that evil cow Innocence had stolen his empire wholesale to 'preserve' it – and no one believed he wasn't complicit. It hurt him because, despite Innocence's fraudulent precautions, Jack had still lost so much: what she hadn't taken, Lloyd's had. He had paid through the nose with possessions and property. Other Names hated him because he wasn't destitute. How dare they make a moral judgement: Jack was destitute *for him*.

Now he was in the humiliating position of having to beg her for pocket money to buy this ugly little wreck of a hotel.

Vanity Fair had wanted to do a New Year's cover with him prostrate on the snowy ground in a skimpy toga and a crown of thorns and her stepping across his back in gold stilettos, a gold chain-mail bikini and a crown, wielding a *mace*. A fucking can of mace, more like.

'Over my dead body,' he'd said, and she'd snarled, 'That can be arranged.'

In the end he'd done it to shut her up. In return, she'd lent him the equivalent of a fiver to buy *this* place.

It was a shack.

He had been avoiding calls from the manager all week. He knew the place was jinxed, that any message would bring news of disaster. And the Hôtel Belle Époque opened to guests in four days.

He was filled with gloom, but you could always shoe in a little extra squeeze of additional despair. The hotel – *his* hotel

27

– had changed hands at least seven times in the last ten years, and there had been a piece in one of the gossip columns about the last owner holding an exorcism in the basement, to try and rid the site of its ill fortune. Jack didn't believe in the evil dead – as far as he could tell, people liked to expend their share of evil while still alive – but it was useful that others did. He'd ripped out the page and kept it.

Beggars couldn't be choosers, he thought. The act of tearing out a piece of the newspaper reminded him of his mother, a long time ago, ripping coupons out of the *Daily Express* to get money off a jar of instant coffee. He felt as if he'd travelled in a large, pointless circle. He felt as if he'd been successful, *once*. It was a shock to realize that success could leave you, like a lover. He had striven for success all his life, and it had been natural to assume that once he'd *got* success, success was his to keep.

To fail, and to fail in front of a worldwide audience, was devastating.

But – his hands squeezed into fists – he would be back. He would show everyone, make them eat *shit*; all the people who had felt a shiver of pleasure at his misery and shame would choke on their fucking Cornflakes as they read of his second coming. He'd rise like a ghost from the earth, and he would rule again.

In particular, Innocence would be in for a shock. She had him by the balls now, but that would change.

That said, right now he was fighting a persistent urge to fall on the ground and sob. He didn't dare to *look* – to look properly – at the lobby of his newly renovated hotel. He was too frightened. This project had been like no other.

Eighteen months ago, when he'd seen the first investment of the rest of his life, he'd felt sick. It was impressive that the owner had done so much to make it *this* ugly. Every panelled door had been boarded over; every original feature had been ripped out and cheaply replaced. It was a small hotel, only twelve rooms, but that was the point. It had potential: high ceilings, huge windows, an underground pool. The broker had made a great fuss about the 'subterranean' pool, but of course, when Jack saw it, it smelled of drains and the water was grimy with green and black algae, like a stagnant pond.

He'd bought the hotel, having no better option, knowing that he was being charged more than it was worth. The banks wouldn't invest, and he would die before he asked Harry. They hadn't done business since going their separate ways after getting out of the City, and he knew it was one reason that their friendship had lasted.

Innocence had made him beg.

They'd had fast, hateful sex – she'd *bitten* him, like a black widow, on the shoulder. He'd rammed it into her, rough and hard, exorcising his anger with every thrust. Trouble was, although the message was 'I despise you', she'd mis-interpreted it as 'I desire you'; it had been annoyingly good.

Then she'd summoned her solicitor to draw up a strangle-hold contract.

So the Hôtel Belle Époque had been completed on a meek budget of make do and humble pie, and Jack had worked closely with the builders, the architect, the interior designer, and interviewed the staff himself. Before he would have delegated, careless of the cost, but now he was like an old spinster carefully counting pennies out of her purse. Splashing money around was no longer in vogue.

It had surprised him how much he had enjoyed his involve-ment. He was also shocked at how much cash he saved himself by being on the spot to veto extravagance: they didn't need to buy new chairs, the old ones were rather beautiful and unique, they just required reupholstering. It made him realize that other people were never going to be as smart with your money as you were – another lesson learned so late.

It had been a thrill to see that sad, neglected hotel's glorious rebirth, and to be such an essential part of it. He knew that this hotel would be different from the others in the Élite Retreat stable, now masterminded by the Cow. They were cool, fresh, stark and modern, a spring clean for the mind, but Hôtel Belle Époque would be an expression of old-school glamour. It would hark back to happier times, although there would be twenty-first-century touches (those chairs were reupholstered in bubblegum pink). It would have an old-fashioned aura and eccentricities: sixties sputnik lights; sparkly chandeliers; excessive comfort – the curly-armed sofas would be soft and sink-into-able, hard furniture was banned. It would incorporate the feel of his aunt's country cottage, with a higgledy-piggledy line of blue and green glass bottles on the shelf of every white bathroom with its clawfoot bath. All his best memories would be crammed into this hotel: an ornate palazzo ceiling in the restaurant (to serve good French country food, not fussy prissy Parisian nonsense); decorative lace ironwork gates. What this hotel would say was: Stuff you all and your minimalist pretensions, we are going to look after you in the old-fashioned way, we are going to spoil you rotten, indulge ourselves and you. *We know best.*

The empire of Élite Retreats had been a creation of cold calculation; the Hôtel Belle Époque came from the heart.

Clients knew what to expect with an Élite Retreat hotel; what they wanted and what they were going to get. In that sense, checking into an Élite Retreat was like buying a KitKat. While styles and quirks varied with each location, there was a list of unconscious desires always fulfilled: all-white interiors; bathrooms with Carrara marble surfaces and massive square baths; mood lighting; huge shuttered windows; beds with neutral linen covers, Frette sheets; Shiseido cosmetics; fresh lilac for a splash of colour (guests were asked about allergies at check-in); dark wood oval table instead of a desk; organic chocolate and Cristal champagne in the mini-bar.

But the Hôtel Belle Époque was one big quirk. Normally, a costing was made for the contents of every room; Innocence had loved the feel of a cashmere throw she'd been given one January evening in Malibu, so, for the LA project, his people had investigated the cost of 820 throws, two for each room. It had added $287,000 to the budget, but it was so – as

Innocence would say – *luxe*. Each room in the Belle Époque, however, was unique and personal. There was no ubiquitous cashmere throw, no *autopilot*; each room had a subtle theme, and was named. He hoped that eventually guests would find a favourite and ask for it.

Over those fast, frenzied months, he'd felt bullish, excited, certain he was creating something great, with a small, select team of inspired, devoted people – but now, as the opening night grew close, his confidence had vanished. Every night brought a hideous nightmare, his mind taunting him that his success had been a fluke, that his great secret was he was weak, a hollow man. A few times he'd actually woken feeling faint with terror.

He had no one to turn to. He'd cut himself off from those he loved, because he knew no other way of being strong. He couldn't care – not since the death of his first wife Felicia. Caring made you vulnerable. He'd told himself that all he had to do was work, and once he was successful again, *then* he'd apply himself to his family, and *then* they would all be happy. But sometimes, like today, he couldn't imagine ever being happy again.

After a lifetime of taking her for granted, he realized he missed his mother. *Pathetic*. Once people were buried, you were free to idolize them, love them with abandon. When they were dead you could admit the full extent of your affection, secure in the knowledge that you would get zero back. Being loved frightened him. This was the safe way of loving, something he could no longer manage with the living.

He should look up now. He should really look up, leave the mad prison of his own head and pray that, for once, reality would be a little kinder.

Slowly, with dread heavy in his gut, he lifted his head and looked around the lobby. His heart pounded and his hands were slick with sweat. His legs were rubber. He breathed carefully so that his stomach wouldn't hurl up its contents. Briefly, he went blind with fright. And then he blinked, stood tall to face his final fate – and it *was* his final fate, because if this project failed it would kill him.

His vision cleared and he fixed on his new obsession, and as he stared with amazed disbelief, his eyes prickled with emotion and he felt a shifting sensation in his chest. He imagined it as the two grey stones of his heart grinding slowly towards each other, still apart, but moving closer to recovery.

The lobby of his Last Chance Saloon was just as he had imagined, but a thousand times more beautiful. The delicate wall chandeliers twinkled and the warm red walls seemed to enclose you like a womb. It was intimate but friendly, funky, not intimidating. It wasn't cool and it wasn't grand; it was perfect. The dark antique-wood floor shone in the flickering light of the fire; the logs crackled and reminded him of Christmas. It was a curious sensation to have, at 9 a.m. on a Tuesday in August, but it relaxed him. He felt the long frozen muscles in his shoulders and neck trying, failing, to shed their rigidity and hang loose.

The woman stepped like a brisk angel from the gentle shadows of the concierge desk. She had glorious curves, waves of blond hair and a mischievous smile (he always noticed when a female was devoid of straight lines). '*Bonjour, monsieur, et bienvenu.* Welcome!' She looked him up and down without apology. 'I'm glad you're here,' she added, her London accent faint but distinct. 'I'm Maria, head of housekeeping. I offered to show you round. I'm the one staff member you haven't met – you asked to meet every employee, so I thought it was a good opportunity and the manager agreed.'

She smiled at him with a slightly defiant jut of the chin. But he noticed the tremor in her voice, that she smoothed her already smooth skirt and tucked an imaginary strand of hair behind her ear. Well, it was natural to be nervous of the boss, even if you could present a confident front.

He couldn't help the automatic calculation in his head, though: another decision reflecting his reduced status. *Before* the Lloyd's disaster, when he was master of all he surveyed, no one would dare to suggest that Jack Kent be shown around his new project by a *servant*. Mind you, in those days everyone was a servant ... Now, he always compared: before, it would have been like *this* but now, in my crappy cut-price life, it's like *this*. It was a compulsion, torturing himself with the curious emptiness of his own heart.

His instinct was to be petulant, but then that too was a sign of weakness. It would make her despise him; feel that he deserved his fall. Anyway, if assigning him to a maid was a sign of disrespect from top management, for once he didn't mind. There was something he recognized in the woman's smile – or was it her eyes? He wanted to be near her.

'I'd be delighted to have you show me round, Maria,' he said, hearing his voice boom in the hail-fellow-well-met manner that the slickest captains of industry employed these days. 'Have we met? You seem familiar.' Instantly, he regretted asking. The world was littered with people he had pissed off.

'Oh,' she said, and laughed, 'not exactly, no.'

Later that night, he sat at a pavement café and drank a cold beer, his mind almost relaxed. Odd, he was musing, that northern France was exactly like Cornwall, but Paris was utterly Mediterranean – and look at those monochrome mademoiselles gliding past! *Robo-chic*. So elegant in their high heels, unlike English women: the slightest heel and they walked at a slant, as if hiking into a stiff wind. Not Maria, though. Sensible kitten heels. He thought about her response.

He supposed it was true, what people said, that he was a bad listener. He'd developed the arrogant habit of only hearing what he wanted to hear. It had got him into deep shit. Now, in leaner times, he paid more attention. He analysed every word spoken to him, ready to pick up on the slightest hint of disdain.

But it wasn't disdain he was searching for with Maria. He found her intriguing and he didn't quite know why. He'd asked if they'd met before. And when he played back her words in his head – 'Oh [*laugh*], not exactly, no' – they made him wonder. 'Oh, not exactly, no' didn't mean, 'No, I don't think so', which was just a polite way of saying 'No'.

But he couldn't for the life of him imagine what her words *did* mean.

LONDON, 1997

Claudia

She was fast running out of excuses for not having sex with her fiancé.

Who would think a man could be so persistent? He reminded her of JR, whining for a walk. Her whole evening was ruined before it began because she was panicking about what would happen *after*.

The ballet had been stunning. Sylvie Guillem was her favourite dancer – so strong, so haughty, you didn't *worry*. Even when she watched Darcey Bussell, Claudia always left stiff from the tension of willing her not to wobble. But sitting in the gorgeous Opera House watching Sylvie dance Odette/Odile, and holding hands with Martin, was heaven. You felt safe. Also, classical ballet was perfect in being entirely sexless. If only *Swan Lake*, a paltry three and a bit hours, could have lasted a little longer.

Now they were sitting in a cosy corner at Christopher's, and she was refusing a second glass of wine. He wasn't getting her into bed *that* way. She could feel her shoulders tense and it riled her. He should respect her wishes. Instead, he got angry with her.

She should explain, about what had happened when she was a child, but she was too ashamed. She loved Martin and she planned to marry him and live happily for ever, and she would not risk messing that up by telling him the truth.

He'd ordered the chicken breast – *breast!* Even the menu taunted her with the sex they weren't having. She'd ordered the salmon fishcakes with buttered spinach, creamed potato – *creamed* potato, like the disgusting line in that song, 'Greased Lightning': 'the chicks'll cream'. She was so obsessed with not having sex that she was obsessed with sex.

She ate slowly, and she'd order dessert if she had to – better to be fat than be laid. Her eyes pricked with tears.

'Hey, Mouse. What's up?'

'I'm fine. I've just got a . . .' She knew if she said 'headache' his mood would dive. '. . . something in my eye.'

He peered closely at her face, pretending to inspect it. 'My God, yes, so you have, it's an . . . eyeball!'

She smiled, despite herself.

'That is the saddest smile I've ever seen. Anyone would think you weren't happy to be engaged to an old fart like me.'

She liked him like this, handsome, amusing, in a social setting that ruled out a lunge. She smiled a real smile, grabbed his hand and kissed it. 'Martin, there's no old fart in the world I'd rather be engaged to.'

'I'm going to test you,' he said, teasing. Casually, gently, so she didn't realize it was happening, he held her hand in his and lowered it to his lap, which was under cover of the elegant white tablecloth. She felt her fingers alight on a hard, warm, now slippery surface, it felt like a snooker ball but—

She screamed, loudly, before she could stop herself, and jumped up, knocking over her chair.

Every waiter in the room raced to their table – it was the kind of action you saw in a hospital when a patient flatlined. 'Madam! What is the matter? What is the problem?' Her breath was coming in short, airless bursts, and she fumbled for her inhaler. She was so furious that if she *had* been able to speak she would have probably said, 'The food is delicious, only I caught a fright when my boyfriend here tricked me into touching his erect dick.'

In a fast, angry movement, Martin retrieved the inhaler

from her bag and thrust it under her nose. In a low, calm voice, he addressed the anguished waiters. 'Everything is fine. Sorry to have alarmed you. My fiancée has this irrational' – he spat the word 'irrational' – 'fear of . . .' He paused. '. . . custard.'

Custard? She could see that the waiters were having similar problems suspending disbelief.

'Stupidly, I thought that she might *enjoy* some *custard* tart with spiced summer fruits, but of course, *foolishly*, I had forgotten her total *aversion* to it. You know' – there was a bitter, yet conversational edge to his tone – 'she can't bear the *feel* of custard, let alone the *taste* of it, and even the mere idea of it gives her a panic attack.'

She couldn't help herself, she was sobbing, and she knew her face was ugly, crumpled, red.

The head waiter's expression was granite. 'It seems to me, sir,' he said in a voice of ice, 'that your companion is extremely upset and needs to be taken care of. Please, madam' – he turned to her with a gentle understanding that made her want to fall on him and cling – 'the meal is on the house, and I apologize for any unintentional upset. Please try to enjoy the rest of your evening.'

With a final muted glare at Martin, and a sharp nod, he retreated, and his staff with him.

'Thank you so much,' she whispered, and steeled herself to walk steadily out of the room. But once she was out of their sight she fled down the sweeping stone spiral staircase and when she hit the spikily chill air of an English winter, she kept running.

'Wait, *wait!*'

She ignored him, until he grabbed her shoulder and forced her to stop. Then she hit him across the face. 'How *dare* you! Say sorry, *say* sorry!' She knew she sounded like a brat, but she couldn't help it. But he would say sorry for being so . . . *vulgar*, and they'd kiss, and make up, and go home to their separate beds.

It was their normal routine.

'No,' he said, in quiet, cold fury. 'No, Claudia, I *won't* say sorry. And don't slap me again because I will slap you harder. We have been seeing each other for two years, and we have been engaged for a fucking year, and you still won't let me *near you*! I am so fucking *sick* of being made to feel like a dirty old man by you. I've got nothing to lose by acting like one. I am so tired of being lied to, of you and your many headaches, migraines, stomach cramps. It's all *shit*, Claudia. It is *not* my style to trick a woman into groping my cock at dinner but I said I'd test you and I did, and you know what, you fucking failed! And I ask myself, why the hell are we engaged to be married because you clearly find me repulsive!' He turned and walked away.

She stared after him.

It was an utter disaster, and it was all her fault.

She wanted to run after him, beg forgiveness – but what would be the point? No excuse but the real one would do, and the real excuse would blow their relationship to bits.

All her shit, getting in the way.

The relationship was over, even before anyone else knew they were engaged. Wait till Jim, associate editor, Martin's immediate junior, found out. Jim, an arrogant, talent-free misogynist, hated Claudia. He could barely contain the curl of his lip on sight of her. He probably imagined she was shagging Martin senseless every night, and why wasn't she shagging *him*?

If Jim found out, a flood of malice would burst its banks. He'd leak it to *Private Eye* and make her look like a slag. And then the papers would pick it up – her own included – because it's news if a supposed heiress marries a *civilian*, especially if he is seventeen years her senior.

And then Daddy and Innocence would explode with rage. Daddy, because he'd hate the idea of Claudia doing . . . what she wasn't doing. Also, *he* liked to be the man with the youngest wife.

Innocence would find something to snipe at. When

Claudia was fifteen, Innocence had returned, drunk, from a break in rehab. Swaying across the ballroom swigging lager from a can, trailing fag smoke and fox furs, her stepmother had warned Claudia against 'diluting the bloodline'. These days, Innocence had pink hair and talked less about bloodlines, but Claudia knew she'd disapprove of Martin. He was gorgeous – she'd want him for herself. But of course, none of this mattered *now* – her dreams of irate parents and twisted colleagues were mere fantasies because *now* her relationship with Martin Freshwater was doomed.

She took a cab home, put on her softest, oldest, frumpiest pyjamas. Months ago, in a mad burst of optimism, Martin had bought her a pink La Perla baby-doll nightdress. It silently reproached her from inside its box on a high shelf. She sighed, and heaved on a puffy coat. 'JR. Piddle. Let's go.'

Then she noticed a white envelope, no stamp, shoved under the front door. Not *another* house party. These people were impossibly jolly. She ripped open the envelope. Then she read the contents. A chill crept up her spine like an insect, and she froze where she stood.

Claudia,
*   I write as a friend. You need to end your relationship with*
Martin Freshwater now. Nothing good will come of it, only agony
and misery.
*   I am sorry.*

PARIS, WINTER 1997

Jack

'Meet me under the Eiffel Tower,' she had said to him, as a joke. It was a dangerous joke. This wasn't the plan. Maria had one mission to accomplish with Jack Kent, and could not be distracted by *lust*. She'd been surprised and horrified to find him so sexy. It made her feel like a predator. It was crazy to get involved. She had to do the job and remain detached: there was a higher purpose here. All those furtive years of spying, the elaborate effort made to train in the hotel business, had been for one reason only, and finally the time had come.

She was required.

She had questioned the morality of what she was doing, many times. But she had justified it to herself more often. The sequence of terrible, incredible, possibly inevitable events that she had covertly witnessed over the last year had proven her right.

And she was risking it all for a bit of sex.

A bit of sex would have been excusable, but she knew it would be more. There was a fierce and undeniable attraction. It was hard when they were together *not* to touch. She would not lay a finger on him, but he was always finding an excuse to put a hand on her shoulder, or arm, and when he did, she felt a bolt of desire ricochet through her, and she knew it was mutual. She had pushed him away, like a prim little miss, more than once. But it was only a matter of time. She *was* that saucy minx who said 'no' when she meant 'yes'; she was a tease, and when she was rejecting his attempts to kiss her in the linen closet, her breath quick and shallow, it was nothing but a long, slow seduction. He knew it, she knew it, and it filled them both with a fire of passion that would have to be expended . . . soon.

But worse than this, she *liked* him. He had this hard shell, but she could see that he hid inside it, because he was scared of his capacity for love.

It could get in the way of achieving her goal. It didn't have to, but it might, and she was mad to take the chance.

She sighed, lit a cigarette and gazed up from beneath a huge arch at the iron latticework. The tower itself gave off a golden glow against the night sky. It was truly romantic, and bizarrely beautiful.

She knew it would be tonight. The beginning – and possibly the end.

'Close your eyes and come with me,' said the voice that thrilled her, and she felt him propel her firmly through the crowds. 'Trust me,' Jack whispered, and she felt his cheek brush hers as he pressed her into a cab. She breathed in the heady scent of his aftershave, lemony, musky, potent; she relished the feel of his hands on her arms. She allowed herself a quick peek at his hands, imagined the feel of his strong, tanned fingers inside her . . . He was wearing a baseball cap – the papers loved slapping him on the cover, he was an easy hate figure and had a lot of enemies. The media would pay big to catch him out, and every reader understood the code of a married man pictured with 'a close female friend'.

They didn't know the *half* of it.

She wondered if they'd find out.

It was an amazing turn-on, letting him guide her.

'*Merci,*' she heard him say to the driver. They walked on gravel for a time and then he lifted her into a seat. 'Don't open your eyes,' he murmured, and she didn't. She knew exactly where they were, but it didn't matter. This evening had a momentum all to itself, and she would let it carry her. She felt the whoosh of cold air on her face as they rose higher.

'Now kiss me,' he breathed, and he leaned over her, strong and tall, and she let him dominate – just for a few wicked, indulgent hours, she would let him control *her*. She was glad she was sitting down because her knees felt like water. His kiss was music; it was poetry. She was a practical girl who did what she had to do to get by, but now her head was a whirl of dizzy rapture and she vaguely recalled out of nowhere a shard of verse from her schooldays – Shakespeare, or that other bloke – something about a kiss that would suck out your soul. Oh God, she would give hers gladly. Perhaps she already had.

When they finally, reluctantly broke apart, and she opened her eyes, they were rising over the glorious spectacle of the

Champs-Élysées and the Arc de Triomphe, over the City of Lights itself. She felt that if she leaned forward, she could touch the Obélisque de Louxor. It was both curious and bewitching, an enormous and unashamed phallic symbol, proudly bestowed on one country by another. Oh, Maria. She had one thing on her mind tonight – and it was the wrong thing.

He was stroking her face. She couldn't meet his eye and he gently lifted her chin and made her look at him.

'Would I be right', she said in a teasing voice, 'to say this is the first time in a while you've been on a Ferris wheel?' Right now, joking around was the only way she could cover herself.

'It's strange,' he said. 'I look at you, and I want to take you on every Ferris wheel in every city in the world.'

She attempted a feeble joke, but the words stuck. She shivered, and he pulled her closer. She huddled up against his shirt. It was the quality of the shirt, the luxurious feel of its butter-soft cotton that did it. She felt a brief stab of hate, so fleeting it was gone before she could chase it away, a reflex to his *comfortable* life. Oh, she knew he had suffered, yet it didn't matter: he could buy anything he wanted, he *had* bought anything he wanted, anything and anyone. He had no clue of the struggle and fear that were a daily part of so many normal people's lives.

Most of his ill fortune had been self-inflicted. She was an expert on the subject of Jack Kent. He had worked for his money and his power and success, but there was the flipside. He had lied, cheated and – most pertinent to *her* – he *stole*. And he felt hard done by! Jack didn't know he was *born*.

He was holding her hand. She could feel his fingers stroking the underside of her wrist and it was making her crazy.

'Please,' she said, and she was almost begging.

They barely made it to the suite. The sex was desperate and loud and animalistic; she was sobbing with pleasure and pain – 'More,' she gasped, 'more' – and he was almost delirious with lust, groaning her name over and over; oh God, he was a work of art, and he was so *fucking* good, it was as if he was worshipping her with his dick. She wanted him everywhere at once, she wanted to say the words but she was too delirious, too greedy for his lips, his hands, his tongue, the feel of his firm, powerful body underneath her, on top of her, behind her. Oh God, let it never end.

Maria was a chaste sort of person, at heart.

It was just the other places . . .

The fifth time, just before dawn, they did it on the stone balcony. 'I want to fuck you before the whole of Paris,' he snarled in her ear, and she purred with delight, rubbing her pert behind against him and feeling his dick harden. She let him screw her from behind – a good metaphor for their relationship, *once*, she thought – and then she gently eased herself off him, turned around, wrapped her legs around his and, while he could easily bear her weight, pushed him inside and to the floor, writhing around on him as he gazed up at her, a sloppy, sex-sated grin on his handsome face.

'What', he murmured, 'would you do if my wife walked in?'

She arched an eyebrow. 'You mean,' she said, 'what would *you* do?'

She was bloody exhausted. But she couldn't get enough. And this wouldn't last for ever. Who knew if it would last the day?

At 9 a.m., they collapsed on the high bed. Her whole body throbbed and she felt soft and bruised and rubbery, as if she'd been deboned.

They drank red wine, gazing into each other's eyes, and fed each other roast chicken. She was starving. She felt like a savage. Fuck, eat, sleep, fuck again.

Jack dropped a chicken bone on the silver plate and it landed with a *tink*. He rolled over, until he was pinning her to the bed. 'Maria,' he said, his eyes full of laughter. 'My God! Have my children!'

With supreme effort, she pushed up and rolled over, so that he lay on his back and she pressed down on *him*. 'Jack,' she said. 'My darling Jack. I *have.*' She paused. Her heart was hammering so fast she could hear it reverberate around the room like a drum roll. 'At least, I have had *one* of your children.'

She leaned back on her heels and turned her face this way and that. 'Can't you see *any* resemblance?'

NEW YORK, FEBRUARY 1998

Emily

A lot of teenagers who ran away hadn't a clue. They nicked the keys to their dad's Rover, chucked a change of underwear in the back and invariably drove the car into a ditch. Emily had the maid pack six Louis Vuitton suitcases, ordered her driver to take her to the airport in the Bentley, and borrowed her mother's pilot who took her in the Learjet to a private airstrip in Manhattan. You had to keep it glamorous. There was no point running away to somewhere *less* fabulous than home.

She checked into the Paramount. It always amused her *not* to stay in one of her mother's hotels. She quite liked the brownstone on the Upper West Side, but not the white grand piano, or the exact replica on the ballroom ceiling of Michelangelo's frescoes in the Sistine Chapel. Mummy was *so* proud, having commissioned it herself, and Emily didn't have the heart to tell her that the 1993 version of 'The Last Judgement', with Innocence as the Virgin Mary, was widely agreed in New York to be the most vulgar piece of interior décor in the city. Also, if she'd run away to the brownstone, she'd be *found*, which was not her object.

She wanted to have some fun. Also, Timmy was in New York. He was working on Wall Street, JPMorgan Chase. She thought it sweet that he wanted to make his own money when he was going to inherit Scotland. Well, more or less.

She hadn't seen him since the blow-chunks job, almost a year and a half ago. Oh my God, that was, like, the most embarrassing moment of her *life*. She'd fled to her bedroom, passed out on the floor and woken fifteen hours later. Quintin had taken care of all the mess – later, she understood that Élite Retreats had picked up the bills for two busted arms and one fractured leg *and* settled five lawsuits. Ice rinks and alcohol were *so* not a good mix.

Actually, Timmy had written to her since. Obviously *he* was cool with her – she'd been right to refuse him sex. The blow job, up to the point of final impact, must have been exceptional. She hadn't replied to his letters, unlike all the other girls he was no doubt writing to. There was nothing the upper classes loved more than a good letter – you couldn't pass one in the street without receiving a thank-you note. She'd been mortified by their last encounter – throwing up was so *childish* – but now, she had recovered her composure, she was a year older, a year more alluring. It was time to hook up.

He wasn't going to get laid this time round either. *Nearly*, but not quite. And she wasn't going to call him, they were going to bump into each other, purely by chance, as he left his office. Century 21 was close by. Apart from Topshop, Emily did not care to shop at a store which had fewer than two assistants per customer, and the idea of a sort of *jumble* sale store with *bargains* made her want to leap in a hot shower. Still, Timmy wasn't to know that, and it was a fine excuse for running into him.

She held her breath, burst into Century 21, grabbed the first item nearest the door, paid for it, secured a bag, and left, purple in the face. She then disinfected her hands with a spray. Then, still shaking the invisible dirt out of her hair, she summoned her driver. It was freezing, and her black suede red-soled Christian Louboutin boots with the six-inch heels weren't made for walking.

Sixty Wall Street, aka the world headquarters of JPMorgan

Chase, was a great big cock of a building. It towered into the crisp blue sky, tall, thick and self-important. God, she loved New York. She loved New York and she loved New Yorkers. *Rude?* They were city people! Smart fast busy city people who spoke up for themselves. Not like Londoners, God bless them. She was absurdly fond of London but compared to New York's bigger, brasher, shinier skyline, it was a little old lady, and as for rudeness, Londoners beat New Yorkers by *miles*. They didn't shout, they muttered, which was worse. Emily had never actually been on the London Underground but according to Quintin – who regularly visited his mother in Acton – people did not give up their seat for a pregnant woman, pretending instead to be engrossed in their news-papers. The London tube system was full of standing, tearful, pregnant women. Well, that was just sick. Emily hadn't ridden the subway in New York, either, but she liked to imagine that if any commuter tried to pull off that kind of crap here, no pregnant New Yorker would stand for it. Papers would be ripped from faces with a bellow of, 'Hello! I'm standing here!'

New York was like an adrenalin shot to the butt, it made you feel you could accomplish anything. It lifted you up, it loved life, it was the city that said, 'Sleep when you're dead.' Emily winced in pain and snapped the heel off a boot. It was OK, she told herself; she had seven more pairs at home. Then she hobbled over to one of the great black square pillars and pretended to inspect the damage. Guys like Timmy were hypnotized by a damsel in distress. They liked their strong women incapacitated; it made domination less of a struggle.

Although there were worse ways to pass her time than staring at an endless stream of men in suits, she did not enjoy standing on one leg for over an hour in the biting cold, and cursed Timmy for not appearing. She'd grab a hot chocolate and come back tomorrow. She looked in her compact mirror – her nose was pink and numb with the cold. You have *no* idea, Tim, she thought to herself, how far I'd go to get you.

On day three, her patience was rewarded.

'*Em?* Hello! What a gorgeous surprise! What brings you to this neck of the woods?'

She waved the slightly dog-eared Century 21 bag, and waggled the snapped heel in his face.

'So good to see you! Emily, this is James Claudderaugh – James, Emily, Emily, James – and Toby McIntosh-Forbes – Toby, Emily, Emily, Toby – and Rahdirahblahblahblah.'

'*Hi there!*' She showed her teeth and assessed his colleagues, discounting each as mating material in seconds: prematurely balding . . . eyes too close together . . . short like a tree stump . . . you have to be kidding me . . . end of message.

'So what are you up to? Would you like to join us for dinner at Elaine's? She's a total star.'

Emily liked fast food, or health food; she did not enjoy wasting time in restaurants, nor was she interested in some fat old woman. Oh God, could it be that banking had turned Tim into a wanker?

'Darling, there's nothing I'd love more, but I have an engagement. And I have to fix this shoe. Although . . . I'm going to be at the Grand Central Oyster Bar around eight thirty.' She smiled winningly around. 'When you feel like eating clams, nothing else will do.' She was a great believer in subliminal (or not so subliminal) suggestion.

Now we'd see. Would he ditch fat old Elaine and his ugly boy crew and haul ass across town on the vague non-promise of some horizontal action?

A thoughtful look crossed Tim's face. 'That would be splendid! You were saying, weren't you, Toby, you were going to try and see a film' – Toby's face was fantastically blank – 'er, you know, that one I've already seen?' Still blank. 'Elaine's was as a matter of fact a mere suggestion . . . our plans were still vague . . .' Light slowly dawning on the dim, rugby-crushed face . . .

'Oh, *absolutely!*'

Emily winked. 'Well, great. Goodbye, gentlemen. Tim, later!'

*

She lovingly prepared herself – a perfect parcel of temptation in a Dolce & Gabbana leopard-print silk baby-doll top with spaghetti strap halterneck, hotpants, a Christian Lacroix skirted trenchcoat, and black suede knee-high boots from Voyage – in her 'deluxe' room at the Paramount. She wouldn't stay here again. The room, smart, stylish, modern, yada yada, was the size of a matchbox. She actually felt claustrophobic. Worse than that, she felt *poor*. My God, this must be what it was like to live in a council flat. Just hideous. How did people *cope*? The lack of *air*, it just about choked you. She kept bumping into *furniture*, it made her feel *fat*. A hotel that made you feel poor and fat – what a total failure of marketing. Mummy and Daddy's hotels were palatial and stunning by comparison – presumably, people booked the Paramount only because the doormen were hot. There could be no other reason. Next time she'd stay at the Four Seasons: big rooms, onyx ceilings – the Four Seasons knew how to treat guests.

She arrived at the Oyster Bar early to arrange herself as she wished to be seen. Tim's first glimpse of his future wife would be a classic pose, a 1950s starlet, perhaps, enjoying a cigarette, sipping a milkshake through a straw. Milkshake, not alcohol, even though she felt like a glass of red, because when Emily was up to something particularly devious, she liked to offset her behaviour with an outward show of innocence.

Tim arrived on the dot of eight thirty-five – she noted that he'd been home to shower and change. Cute.

He slid into the seat beside her and smiled. 'How are you?'

'Good,' she said.

'You're never good,' he said, grinning.

She gazed at him from beneath her lashes. 'Today I am,' she said in what she hoped was a demure voice. 'It's too cold to misbehave. I am going to eat some clams, catch up with my old friend Tim, and be at home in bed by ten thirty.' She smiled. 'Shall we order?'

The bugger was, Emily hated clams, but wanted to tease Timmy into a froth of desire that she would then frustrate. A goodnight kiss, then he would be primly turned away. She looked at the 'raw' section of the menu. 'Raw' was sexier than 'cooked'. And 'cherrystone' – yeah, that would do it. Raw cherrystone clams, I mean, come *on* – if that didn't suggest eating pussy then she might as well give up and go home. But . . . popcorn shrimp . . . mmm.

'That tequila lime oyster shooter is calling my name,' said Tim.

Willpower was just a positive spin on 'self-denial' and Emily was not a fan. 'Would it be rude not to join you?' she said.

'Very,' replied Tim.

One tequila lime oyster shooter led to another. 'You know,' Emily said with a sloppy grin, sprawling on the counter and gazing up at Tim – he was super cute, with his scruffy hair, and he was *lean* now, not skinny. 'I do like the *sound* of raw cherrystone clams, and I will definitely order them *one* day, but right this second I think I should have a jumbo lump Maryland crab cake to soak up this booze. Because I . . .'

'No indeed,' agreed Tim.

She blushed. He thought he was getting some.

She ate half the crab cake; he ate the other half. At one point, she got some on her chin, and he reached out, wiped her chin, and sucked *her* bit of crab cake off his finger. She nearly fell off her chair – oh my God, *how* horny? OK, two years ago, it would have been disgusting, but now, now she was fifteen, it was *totally* hot.

It was annoying: in theory, Tim wasn't that sexy. But in person, he just was, which made him difficult to resist.

'Their dessert menu *rocks*,' she said, clanking her bottle of Goose Island 'Honker' Ale (you had to order it, for the name, Tim said) against his. 'Listen to this: honey pecan pumpkin pie . . . black plum almond cream tart . . . Florida key lime pie . . . New York cheesecake . . . chocolate mouse . . .

I mean, chocolate mousse ... chocolate mocha layer cake.' She threw up her hands. 'How the hell are you meant to decide?'

'Order them all.'

Very 'first date' in theory, but in practice piggish and unattractive. 'I will order *one*.'

Tim sighed. 'You're very monkish today. But OK. I say chocolate mouse.'

She refused to let him feed her even a spoonful. 'I like to be in control,' she explained. He was looking at her in *that* way. 'What?'

He shook his head. 'I need a cigarette.' She watched him, tipping his head back to blow the smoke up towards the cavernous white-tiled ceiling. She wanted to lick his neck. Yes, she was prettily driving him to distraction. He smacked down a wodge of cash. 'Babe, can we get out of here?'

'You can see me home, if you like.'

His eyes said *I'll do more than that*, and he let out a stifled groan and leaned towards her. She allowed his lips to brush hers. 'No, you won't, naughty boy,' she breathed.

Exactly twelve minutes later, despite a wind-chill factor of minus three, Emily allowed Tim to fuck her up against a wall. It was her first time and it was *glorious*. She had known that sex would be amazing, but the feeling was beyond anything. It was heaven. She heard herself whimper and squeal with pleasure. After, she clutched him, trembling. He scooped her up and whispered, 'Come on, girl, let's do this *properly*.' He paused. 'All that clam talk just made me *crazy*.'

She giggled and hung on his arm.

And so, it turned out that, unwittingly, Emily had told the truth. She *was* at home in bed at ten thirty. She and Tim shagged like dogs until they fell asleep at four. And when Emily woke the next morning, she rolled on top of him and they started again. 'You are *very* bad,' she told him, 'you have led me astray.'

If the sex hadn't been so totally delicious and he wasn't

such a *god*, she would have hated him. She hated herself for being so weak, and even as Tim brought her off with his tongue and she screamed with bliss, she was raging inside: *You idiot, Em, this wasn't the plan.*

Nor did she know it, but by midday she was pregnant – and that wasn't the plan either.

PARIS, WINTER 1997

Jack

Maria watched as six degrees of confusion, disbelief, fear, amazement, shock and, finally, recognition passed over Jack's features. Then, to her surprise – oh, this man always surprised her – he gently took her hand and kissed it. She had the feeling that it wasn't enough and he wanted to slide off the bed and kneel before her.

'Claudia's real mother,' he gasped, and then he buried his face in her chest and cried. She hadn't expected this reaction – she didn't know what she had expected – and because she needed him to help her, she worried that he'd think the sex was a means to an end. It wasn't. God help her, she was in love with him.

As a child, Maria had seen her three older cousins get engaged, one after the other, and imagined that each proposal was a grand surprise. Then, as little children often are, she had been horribly sexist, assuming that the decision to marry was entirely the man's, that the woman's only say in the matter was 'yes'. More than that, she had assumed that the decision to *love* was entirely the man's, and only if *he* said it was OK could the woman open her mind and heart to dresses and bouquets, confetti and cake.

She was stunned to discover when *she* met the man of her

dreams that the love she felt was immediate, that there was no doubt of it being mutual, that of course she would be proposed to. Marriage was a certainty, not a surprise!

It hadn't quite turned out like that.

But while a romantic heart can be crushed, it is almost impossible to kill, and now, over two decades later, Maria felt that long-forgotten emotion, strangely close to madness, consume her. It was unmistakably love.

The first time around, she had ruined it, and the reason was sex. She feared that history would repeat itself and the fact that she'd fucked him before revealing the truth, and what she required from him, would ruin it again.

She blurted, 'I love you, you know. I didn't mean to, but I can't help it.'

He smiled at her. His eyes were still red. 'I know you do. It's OK. I love you.'

'I didn't mean it to happen this way,' she said. He lit a cigarette and passed it to her. 'I didn't set out with this in mind.'

'What', he said, '*did* you have in mind? And' – a harsher note entered his tone, as if some doubt had just occurred, or maybe it was her paranoia – 'how did you know that Claudia was yours?'

She blushed, pulling the white silk robe around her. Suddenly, like Eve, she needed to cover her nakedness. 'When you give up a baby,' she began softly, 'you are always looking. You never stop looking for your lost baby. I didn't want to give up my baby but I had no choice. It was the seventies – it was the *worst* thing you could possibly do. I came from a proud family. They'd call themselves a *good* family . . . I was in love for the first time and I knew nothing, I was sixteen years old. I did what I was told and so I did . . . *that*. I didn't even know that you could get pregnant the first time. I thought you had to have practised for it to . . . take. I let it happen, because I knew, on my mother's life, that this was my man, that we were going to marry and live together loving each other for the rest of our lives. I was a very simple girl then. But teenagers think in absolutes. It's all absolutely wonderful or bloody terrible. It got terrible. He got scared. I think he was scared of my father. He denied it was his. He was sixteen too. He had plans for his life, he wanted to be free, and it was so, so shameful. He just melted away, out of my life, and there I was, this big ball of disgrace. My own mother stopped speaking to me. I got sent away, to a relative, and when I had the baby, she was sped away. I didn't even get to hold her. The doctors were cold, disapproving, but the women were worse. There was one kind nurse – *one*. I wanted to give my baby something of myself, and the only thing I had was the gold chain with a gold heart on it that my parents had given me for my sixteenth birthday. It's very distinctive: my uncle was a jeweller, he had it made. I kept the gold chain, and the nurse pinned the heart to the baby's vest. When you give up a baby, and you're little more than a child yourself, you have no idea of what you've done, of the life-destroying enormity of your error. It's only later that you realize, and of course by then it's too late. I wasn't allowed to know where my baby had gone, who she was with. I had no official way of finding her. But all through my twenties, I looked for my girl. On the street, on the bus, everywhere I went, I looked.'

'But' – she jumped as Jack spoke. She was no longer really addressing him, she was lost in her own world – 'but, Maria, how would you even know if you'd seen her?'

'I would have known,' she said. 'A mother . . . knows.' She paused. 'But, day after day, I saw babies and girls, everywhere, but not mine. And then' – she shook her head, as if she still couldn't believe it – 'ten years after her birth, *to the day*, I was flicking through the *Daily Mail*, and there was a photograph on the gossip page, the one written by Nigel Dempster. It was a photo of you, and your . . . wife, and Claudia, and the caption said, "The Hon. Innocence Ashford and her multi-millionaire husband, Jack Kent, take Claudia, their adopted daughter from his first marriage, to see *The Nutcracker* at the Royal Albert Hall to celebrate her tenth birthday." ' Maria looked at him and smiled. 'It could have been a coincidence,' she said. 'But Claudia was wearing a necklace. And on it was my heart.'

Jack shook his head. 'That's an amazing story,' he said. 'So what did you do? Did you try and make contact?' He frowned. 'I can't remember but . . .'

'No,' she said. She smiled again. 'Can you imagine what you'd have thought, if I *had*?'

He gazed into her eyes. 'I'd have thought that you were a mother who wanted *my* baby back.'

'And?'

'I'd have thought you were a gold-digger.' He paused. 'Are you? Is . . . is that what this is about?'

'Oh please,' she said. 'So I got all the information I possibly could, on you, and on Claudia. And, from that day on, I watched her.' Maria looked down and picked at the gold embroidery on the bedcover. 'She never looked happy.' She looked up. 'None of you did.' She shook her head. 'It was a lesson, to see a family, riding in the latest Rolls, dressed so beautifully, off to the airport to New York, or Bermuda, or Fiji' – she grinned – 'good old Nigel reported everything – looking so miserable. I wanted to rescue her, but I was terrified that she might reject me. It was better, it was safer, to watch and admire and love her from a distance. I told myself that it was too late to be her mother, but I could be her guardian angel. I mean' – Maria laughed, and it was a bitter sound – 'I just told myself that to make myself feel better. I knew I could do nothing for her, ever. I had nothing. I was in a world of pain, of my own making. It was torture. It still is.'

Jack squeezed her hand.

She cleared her throat. 'Jack,' she said. 'I *thought* there was nothing I could do for my girl. But, oh God, it turns out there is. A couple of years ago, she got a job, didn't she, at a newspaper. And then . . .' Maria swallowed. 'When I saw, I just . . .

53

But I suppose in a horrible way . . . it's natural. I've heard of it before. You're just drawn . . . you don't even know why. I couldn't stop myself – I just wrote. I never have before, but it was a mistake. I need *you*, Jack. You have to stop this. Don't tell her the truth. It would be too much. Just find a way.'

He was staring at her, incredulous. 'Maria. I don't understand. Find a way to stop *what*?'

She realized, with a lurch of nausea, that the whole business was so repellent to her, she had been circling it, like a frightened animal. So she told him. Then she watched as he ran to the bathroom and was sick.

LONDON, WINTER 1997

Claudia

Claudia walked into the office and gave Martin a crisp nod. She would remain professional. She would remain *dignified*. When your own thoughts were eating you alive, this was no easy task. For the last twelve hours, the words of the hand-delivered note had been circling her mind like a serpent.

Could it be from Innocence? Innocence had a violent dislike of other people being happy in their relationships; it made her feel inferior. If she saw a couple kissing it would ruin her day. Claudia hadn't told Innocence but then her stepmother regularly had people followed. Innocence probably knew more about Martin than Claudia did herself.

Whoever it was from, the letter was a lie, a spiteful attempt at sabotage. But what if there *was* something Claudia didn't know about Martin? He didn't talk about his past, but he'd hinted that there was something in it that he wasn't proud of. A sex change? A sex change! No. She'd seen his particulars, there was no *way* they'd been fashioned out of a woo-woo.

Claudia put a hand to her forehead. It was extremely hot. She should take a moment. She was becoming hysterical.

She gulped down her double espresso and snapped on her computer. She was a *journalist*, not some pathetic wimp. She would not condemn Martin without hard evidence. She would consider the *facts*. *She* was the one behaving badly: refusing to sleep with him for no apparent reason, forcing him to trust her, to believe that one miracle day in the vague future, they'd start bonking for Britain and never stop. If Claudia wanted to marry Martin – and she did, *desperately* – she must ignore the letter, and be patient, kind, loving in every *other* sense to show him that she adored him *and* wanted him, that she'd forgiven him for last night, was sorry for her own behaviour, and please don't break up with her, because the day they married, she'd put the past behind her and snap into being the perfect wife. She couldn't quite bring herself to go over to his desk, but she wrote him an email: 'Forgive me, darling, I was horrible. It was all my fault – you are not to blame in the slightest. I overreacted and I totally understand your frustration. The truth is, every bit of you is desirable and gorgeous, I want you so badly, I have never loved anyone like I love you, and I did just want us to wait a little bit longer . . . until we are married, but I hate to make you sad, and hate you to think that I don't utterly lust after you . . . so how about we meet tonight at my place? We could have a drink, then see what happens . . .'

Then she deleted that and emailed 'Hi' instead.

No response. Then, *three* hours later, he came over to her desk, where she was briskly inputting copy.

'Hi,' he said. 'I have a job for you. Could be fun.'

She looked at him. He met her gaze directly, and she tried to smile. It was harder than she imagined, this lavish exhibition of lust and adoration. 'What is it?' she said.

'Well. Here it is. We want an exclusive with Meg Ryan. What we have on our side is a huge circulation, and the right demographic: three million layabouts who like to eat crap and watch rubbish.'

She allowed herself a tiny smile. His voice grew a shade warmer.

'However, two years ago, we did a cuts job on her, which they didn't like. You know, assembling an "interview" from previous interviews, stuff like, "Ryan says, 'Dennis and I have an amazing bond, we'll be together for eternity,'" which she may have said a while back to the *Sunday Times* or the *Daily Mail*, but she sure as hell didn't say it to us. But she *said* it, so, in theory, it's still the truth.'

He grinned at her, expecting her to grin back. She remained po-faced. He was maintaining, to her face, that a jumble of quotes taken out of context and jammed together was the truth. This man didn't know the difference between the truth and a lie!

With the words of the letter still writhing around inside her head, this didn't instil her with confidence.

Martin shrugged. 'Anyway, if we want some face time, we have to jump through hoops. Her PR firm represents one or two newbs who they—'

'Two *what*?'

'New bloods: young actors nobody's heard of who they need us to promote. If we want half an hour with Meg, we have to run interviews with *three* newbs. A double page spread each.' He sighed. 'We're talking about a girl, Mollie Tomkinson, starring in some Mike Leigh miseryfest. She's the spit of a tomato frog and it's *Mike Leigh* – I think they're trying to close the paper. So, we'll leave that for last, and there's always the chance we'll get Meg if we make a big fuss of the first two. So here's the first tape. At least it's Hollywood, it's called *Vengeance*. The guy you're looking at is Ethan Summers. No, I've never heard of him either. He's got the F-factor, which is the only reason he'll make it. At least in five years when more than six people have heard of him, we'll be able to say "We got him first." Ring Der Führer, I mean, the

PR, get her to bike over his biog – they should have already done it. Watch the film tonight and set up the interview for next week. The guy lives in LA but he's in London promoting.'

'Fine. All right. Thanks.'

Martin raised an eyebrow. 'I thought you'd be pleased. Your first interview with a big star.'

Claudia glared at him. 'Make up your mind. You've spent the last ten minutes telling me he's a nobody. Why don't you decide on a version of the truth and stick to it?'

He stared at her. 'In this office,' he said quietly, 'please remember that I am your boss, and you are being paid to work here. So I suggest you try and behave accordingly.' She watched as he snatched the video off her desk. 'Carry on with your typing. There are plenty of other people here who'd appreciate the chance of a byline.' He stalked off.

She turned back to her screen, cold-faced. She loved him, but she was not a sap. She wanted him to love her, but she couldn't smile and make nice when she was bloody furious.

She would have loved to have done the interview with Ethan Summers. Now the fat secretary would get to do it.

Claudia was stupid, letting her emotions get in the way of her career. Soon enough, her career could be all she had. But that was not going to happen. She wasn't letting Martin go that easy. Look, if he did have some dark secret, she could find out. She'd spy on him: think of it as investigative journalism. He wouldn't notice, he wasn't observant with *people*, only with cars. He could spot a nice car.

She'd have to convince him that she was out of town, so that he'd feel safe to engage in his deceit ... dressing in women's clothes? She'd tail him in a cab. She'd wear a head-scarf and dark glasses – it would be very Jackie O. She'd bring a camera – black-and-white film? And then she'd con-front him with the evidence at a French café. She'd throw down the stills on the table – she might have to practise that bit – and he'd be *mortified*, but there would be a simple explanation! He was in a play! And they would laugh and—

'Claudia, I need you to nip downstairs, get me a coffee. And you can pick up my dry cleaning. Fuck knows where the ticket is. Cheers.'

She jumped, and blushed. 'Yes, Jim.'

Her Harlequin romances were giving her slightly unrealistic expectations; she'd have to cut down. She sighed, and smiled at Jim. He returned her gaze, unsmiling. She looked down. She didn't think he'd sent the letter: her instinct told her it wasn't him. If he had, he wouldn't have been able to resist a knowing smirk. God, he made her uncomfortable.

She did Jim's errands, and was rewarded with a pat on the lower back. Martin was out, otherwise he wouldn't have dared. She lurched away as he sniggered, and scurried back to her desk. She tried to work but she couldn't. She needed to know about Martin *now*, but realistically, she was going to have to wait. He was going to be away over the holiday, visiting his sister in Canada. Oh my goodness, was that a *lie*? Now she was seriously depressed, too depressed even to be cheered by the image of herself as Jackie O. It wasn't a game. If Martin *was* deceiving her, it would break her heart.

Her phone rang, and she picked it up.

'Claudia Kent?'

'No, Ms Green, it's Claudia Mayer, if you don't mind.' She gritted her teeth. Only her father's secretary persisted in calling her by *his* name.

'I have your father on the phone. He needs to speak to you immediately.'

Claudia suddenly felt like a small plastic doll being toyed with by an endless succession of men – Martin, Jim, Jack – and she'd had enough. 'If my father wants to speak to me, he can pick up the phone and call me himself,' she snapped.

'I believe it concerns your engagement to Martin Freshwater.'

A great fireball of rage ballooned in Claudia's stomach. 'Tell him to mind his own bloody busi—'

'Claudia! Be quiet and listen!'

She jumped with nerves – her father sounded even more on edge than usual. 'No,' she whispered, her voice weak with fear. She couldn't bear confrontation, it terrified her, she hated a fight. 'I will not listen. I'm not ten years old! Stop talking to me like I'm a child. I'm marrying him! We've set a date!'

'Claudia, I forbid it. I—'

'What are you talking about? You can't forbid it – I'm not asking permission, I'm telling you!'

'Claudia, wait. Please. I have my reasons. I'd p-p-prefer not to tell you over the phone. I suggest we—'

He was astonishing. He genuinely expected her to break off her engagement for no other reason than because he said so. Even he knew this was some nerve – she'd never heard him stutter in her life.

'The phone is fine,' she said. 'So tell me,' she added, trembling. 'What exactly do you have against him?'

Could it be that her father knew that Martin was married? No. It was a business thing, she bet it was. Jack hesitated and she knew she was right.

'I don't have anything against the man himself,' said her father, and Claudia's lip curled with disgust.

'Then leave me to my joy,' she said coldly, and put the phone down.

PARIS, WINTER 1997

Jack

The bloody Valium bottle – *open*, for God's sake! You'd think they'd realize that in times of real desperation you got the shakes, you just ... Finally, at *last*. Jack tipped the bottle upside down in his mouth and gulped down a few pills with a vodka chaser. He lit a cigarette and lay under the bedcovers with a black shirt wrapped around his head to dull the light and noise. Every sense was throbbing; it was as if his skin had been flayed off and his nerves were exposed to the cold winter air.

And he was freezing. He could see from the thermostat that in fact it was twenty-two degrees in the room, but he was so cold that his teeth chattered. He was desperate to see Maria – he felt as if his body was flying apart and only her arms around him could keep him together – but he was also desperate *not* to see her, because he knew that she'd burst into the room, breathless with excitement, and the first thing she'd say would be . . .

'Did you tell her?'

Painfully, he unwrapped the black shirt from his head, and the piercing light from the lamps and the buzz from the plasma TV and DVD player – that torturous drone – threatened to split his skull in half. He could see her peering at him in alarm. She scurried over to the bed and felt his forehead. It occurred to him that no woman had felt his forehead in twenty years.

'Darling, oh my God, what's wrong! Did she take it . . . badly?'

He could hear the wobble in her voice, and he didn't think he could stand it if she cried. He had no emotional reserves, nothing to give, he was barely holding himself together. 'No,' he said. 'I told her everything. It's fine.'

'Well, thank God. I can't believe it took you a week, Jack, I know it was a shock but . . . Never mind, no harm done. Wait a minute. She's *fine*?'

'Well,' he corrected himself hastily. His brain was muddled and he was having difficulty finding the right words. 'Obviously not *fine*, but she's all right. Considering.'

'So she's ended it?'

'Yeah.' Just leave me alone now, please.

'And had they . . . had they . . . I mean, she wasn't . . . ?'

'No.'

'Sweet Jesus.' She put her hand on her heart and flopped backwards on to the bed. Her voice was like a loudspeaker booming in his ear. She wiped away tears and sat up again. 'So how was she in *herself*?'

Ah, Christ. It was done – well, no, it *wasn't* done, but she thought it was done, so why wasn't that enough? Why was your success never enough, why did women have to know every tiny detail that *led* to your success? If you brought down the moon for a woman, she'd hold it in her hand, and get a thoughtful look on her face, and start quizzing you: 'So, did *you* bring down this moon – how exactly? Or did you get a man to do it? Were you thinking of me when you did it? Was it easy to bring down the moon, easier than it sounds, because if it was easy then maybe I need you to bring down a slightly heavier planet . . .'

He took a slow breath. You had to fight the bad thoughts with good thoughts. It was that simple. 'Darling,' he said in a surprisingly reassuring voice, 'she will survive.'

Maria's hands trembled at her throat. 'And . . . do you think . . . Will you tell her about *me*? I know she's had a hideous shock but I so want to meet her. I've waited so long . . . physically, it's so hard not to be able to . . . make contact. It might take her mind off what she's been through . . .'

Her weakness gave him strength. 'Maria,' he was able to say, in a plausible manner, 'it's not a good idea. Not right now. It's too much, too soon. Give her time to get over this, and I will introduce you when the time is right. I've been thinking of throwing a party to mark the opening of the hotel. You can meet then.'

She nodded stiffly, her lips pressed tight together, unable to mask her wretched disappointment. A double tear rolled down her cheek.

'Hey, sweetheart,' he said. 'Don't be sad. I have a surprise for you. You and I are going on a trip.'

'What, business?' she said.

'Oh no,' he said. 'Pleasure – purely.'

SURREY, EARLY SUMMER 1998

Emily

Emily looked at the wire coat hanger with dislike. 'You have got to be kidding me.' She blamed Tim. *He* had screwed her, totally. She should have stuck to blow jobs. But no. She had given it up for *free* – and now look. It was a nightmare to have a problem which couldn't be delegated.

The shit was going to hit the fan, and she'd been delaying the moment of impact. She'd gone back to school and Tim had gone back to work, and he'd written to her, 'Excellent to see you.' Perhaps that was some kind of jovial shorthand for 'Excellent to see you bouncing on top of me.'

Or was he pretending that it had never happened?

The trouble: it was easy to pretend. You had a hot shower, you wore school uniform, you no longer reeked of the musk of passion, you tied your hair in a prim ponytail, you had early, girly nights with your room-mate – a teenager who slept with a pink bunny and was in love with all of Take That, you felt sick all the time and lost weight, you deleted the memory of that night.

Under those circumstances, surely pregnancy was impossible?

She hadn't had a period since, but apart from that, there was no sign, so she'd done nothing.

She'd always imagined that she'd have an abortion in a snap. And she'd told herself, all through those long months, that she *would* have an abortion: there was still time. But she couldn't bring herself to ring Nanny or Quintin and say,

'Darling, book me an abortion!' The truth was, she didn't want a baby, but she didn't want an abortion. Ideally, the baby would go away by itself. But it hadn't. In fact, she was strangely amazed by the baby – she was touched that it wanted to stay. It *wanted* to be born. It was *her* baby . . . oh God. She stroked her stomach. You are clever, Emily. You are stupid, but you *are* clever, Emily.

Emily chucked the murderous coat hanger to the back of the wardrobe and walked to the bay window. It was a beautiful view: feathery yew trees bordered the vast lawn that led down to the lake. The swans on the lake had two cygnets – ugly little grey things, but the swan parents were amusingly proud. They fussed around their offspring and hissed and flapped at any other bird if it came too close.

How hard could it be if a swan could do it?

Anyway, she was sixteen, like, *just*.

She would see the headmistress Mrs Priddy tomorrow and calmly confess. Mrs Priddy would be wowed out by her maturity, and grant her permission to stay on at school to take her exams. Mrs Priddy was a maternal woman, with young children of her own, and she was kind of cool.

Mrs Priddy would pass on the news to Mummy and Daddy. Mrs Priddy would sanction the baby. And if a top private school took a stand, Mummy and Daddy would unite behind her, and the Earl and Countess would be under great pressure to give their blessing. It would be a boy, and they'd submit to the lure of an heir's heir. And if it wasn't, what woman or man could turn against a cute baby granddaughter in a pink dress and frilly pants? Tim might not wish to marry immediately, but he was a stand-up guy. He would want his kid to be legit.

Yeah. She was quietly optimistic.

Nanny was bored of being a glorified secretary and yearned for dirty nappies and sleepless nights. She would look after it with pleasure, while Emily continued her education. A baby wouldn't make *that* much difference – it was only tiny. It would be fun. Like a really expensive cuddly toy.

Having a kid early was only a problem if you craved freedom and couldn't afford staff. *She* had money, and her final destination had always been Tim. Emily breathed a sigh of relief. It would work out after all.

THE SOUTH COAST OF ENGLAND, THREE DAYS LATER

UK SUNDAY – YOUR BEST READ, YOUR BEST FRIEND, EVERY SUNDAY!

CELEBUTANTE EMILY PREGNANT AT SIXTEEN – WHO'S THE DADDY?

Expecting baby
Emily Kent, 16, younger daughter of the disgraced hotel tycoon, was last night expelled from her exclusive £8,000-a-term private school, after admitting that she is expecting a baby.

£53,000,000 fortune
The father is Viscount Chateston, 18, Emily claims, eldest son of the Earl and Countess of Fortelyne, and heir to the title and an estimated fortune of £53,000,000 in land, property, art and bonds.

'Deeply in love'
A source close to Emily told *UK Sunday*, 'Emily and Tim are deeply in love and he is over the moon at becoming a father. They are young but they both love kids and cannot wait to have their own.'

'Gold cot'
'Yes, the child will be rich and privileged but that makes no difference to them – they are very excited at starting their own family. Emily has already picked out a gold cot from Harrods!'

Earl denies allegations
But Viscount Chateston's father was furious last night and denied

the allegations. 'Emily is well known for her love of partying,' said His Lordship, the Earl of Fortelyne, 54, speaking exclusively to *UK Sunday* from his £20-million castle residence in Scotland.

'Highly popular'

'She is a highly popular young lady with an impressive circle of male friends. She may have arrived at what she considers the most favourable conclusion regarding her child's paternity. Perhaps, in the cold light of the lawyer's letter, she may wish to reconsider.'

Refused to answer

Viscount Chateston, 18 – who is working on Wall Street for a year before attending Cambridge University – refused to speak to reporters at his $500,000 Upper West Side apartment last night.

£200,000 supercar

Ms Kent, who is thought to be four months pregnant, was driven away at 93 m.p.h. from the school at 8 p.m. last night in a £200,000 canary-yellow Lamborghini Murciélago by her mother, the Hon. Innocence Ashford.

'Dodgy' deal worth billions

The self-styled Miss Ashford – who was born Sharon Marshall and grew up on a council estate – is worth billions, after her husband signed over his hotel empire to her in what many financial experts term a 'dodgy' deal, shortly before the Lloyd's crash, which would have ruined him.

Family newspaper

Her response to questions from reporters last night is not fit to print in a family newspaper.

Close friend

Her father, seen here pictured with a close friend, was not available for comment.

Claudia had ordered the paper out of spite – she hoped that the secretary had botched the interview with Ethan Summers and that it was reduced to a tag line. The hostess brought it in with breakfast – 'Thank you, how lovely' (she was still awkward about being *served*) – and she'd put it to one side without even looking at it. She forced herself to eat the porridge and drink the orange juice, which was freshly squeezed. She smiled despite herself. It was her father's bugbear: hotels that served metallic orange juice. Well, he'd approve of this one, even though it was a tiny b. & b. in remote Cornwall.

She'd asked for a few days off, and on Thursday had driven down to the coast with JR to the Old Vicarage. It was in a field in the middle of nowhere, and if you walked to the end of the field, the land stopped and you found yourself teetering on the edge of a cliff that looked down on to a stony beach and miles of blue sea. The sheep were like blobs of cotton wool dotted around, and the owners of the b. & b. had a broad-faced English tabby, who liked to jump in your car and go for a drive – JR had been assessed as no threat.

Claudia had spent half of Friday wandering on the beach and the other half in the graveyard. She never tired of reading the names, imagining these people's lives, what they'd looked like, and whom they were loved by. It had been so peaceful. It was just so heavenly to have *quiet*. The reception on her mobile was zero, but she'd turned it off just to be sure.

Since their argument – and the mysterious letter – she and Martin had recovered. Without a word spoken, they had agreed to gloss over the cracks in their relationship. She had discovered nothing, nor had she slept with him. Little had changed. It appeared that despite their suspicions and frustrations, they so wanted to love each other. Yet on occasion, those silent undercurrents surfaced, knocking her off balance. She'd had to get away.

By Saturday night, she was missing him dreadfully, and couldn't resist checking her mobile. Oh my *God*! Twenty-seven messages. He really must love her, but a promise was a promise. Cornwall was a break from Martin, and so she would not listen to his mournful messages of love until she returned to London.

But the next morning, she'd finished breakfast, showered,

wandered back into the room and unfolded the paper, and then, as her hair dripped on to *UK Sunday* until the words 'Pregnant at sixteen' grew soggy, it had all become clear. Oh, Emily. The poor, poor thing. She must be feeling so frightened, helpless and lost. It was horrible. She'd call her to offer support. *Poor* Emily.

LONDON, SUMMER 1998

Emily

'Fuck *OFF* you arseholes and leave me *ALONE*! I'm wearing headphones and I can't even *HEAR* you!'

If it was possible to be born without parents, Emily would have done it. What bastards. How dare they? Fine for *them* to tramp around the world, screwing around like a pair of cheap tarts, and yet when she had sex *once* – three times – with *one* person, whom *she* at least *intended* to marry, they freaked out!

She was, like, over sixteen at the time – if you counted her age from her date of conception. And she'd refused to bitch about Tim to the press – she wasn't going to blow her chances that way.

He didn't deserve her loyalty. What a scumbag.

Now he didn't write! No doubt he'd used up all his stupid monogrammed notepaper.

He didn't phone.

No *way* was she calling him, and if he *did* ring – not that she *cared*, or picked up the receiver every five minutes just to make sure the phone was, like, even *working* – she was going to be out.

And his father the Earl was a total wanker. It was *so* embarrassing. The whole country must be laughing at her. Telling Claudia's crappy paper – *implying* it, which was worse – that she was a crack ho who'd slept with a million men! How *dare* he! But fine, if he wanted to get into a libel war, her mother was worth *loads* more than a pissy fifty-three million. Bring it on!

Emily stamped into her closet. It was a cool closet with a leather floor and controlled thermostat, but none of her clothes fitted. That didn't *totally* matter, as she rarely wore anything twice. She was going to enjoy being big. Not *fat* – people who called pregnant women 'fat' were morons and, Emily noted, always fat middle-aged men. She was going to have the time of her life, throwing her weight around, sucking up space. She felt *special*, and she felt *superior*, and everyone else who was *not* pregnant (including that stuck up two-faced bitch headmistress Mrs I'm Not Getting Any Priddy) could fuck off. As for her *father* . . . my God! He'd stormed back from Paris, where he was obsessed with that dumb hotel, Belle Époque – he was planning this opening-night party, except it wasn't an opening-night party as the hotel was already open, it was an ostentatious, superfluous celebration, planned for this autumn, to trumpet the fact that the crooked old phoenix had risen from the ashes. Invitations had gone out to the rich and famous: Tom Cruise, Mel Gibson, Bruce Willis, Julia Roberts, the Duran boys, Prince, Puff Daddy, Elton John, Linda Evangelista, Cindy Crawford, Cindy Lauper, Naomi Campbell, Helena Christensen, Bono. Would all those egos fit in one building?

It was an impressive list of old people, Emily thought, and she wondered if any of them would show up. She couldn't imagine that this bunch wanted to be associated with her father. Then again, a free party, with Bvlgari gift bags . . .

Dad had been furious at being dragged away from his pet project for something as trivial as his daughter getting knocked up at an age when she should still be playing with dolls, and he'd screamed at her, and sworn. It was horrible because she'd rarely heard him do either. Innocence had stood by, flicking her pink bouffant and checking her nail varnish for cracks, and smoking a fag – a fine grandma *she* was going to be. The point of all the screaming and swearing was that Emily was a stupid tart who should have kept her legs shut, or used 'protection'. She liked the bit where she'd been accused of dragging 'the family name' through the mud.

He'd really upset her. He made her feel *small*. Because of him, she was suddenly terrified. She'd get him for that.

Emily sat in her closet, arranging her five hundred pairs of shoes. It was comforting; it made her feel in control.

He'd been out of control. She wondered if he was on something, he was so *wired*. At one point – shortly before zooming off in his new red Ferrari Testarossa (mid-life crisis alert!) – he'd shouted, 'You and your bloody sister, the pair of you are killing me, I am going to slit my *throat* because of you two!'

'Pay no attention,' Innocence had muttered, flicking ash.

He'd turned on her, snarling, 'You don't know the *half* of it!'

'I know everything,' her mother had snapped. 'Some old git's asked Claudia to marry him and she's said yes, and you've got the hump because he didn't ask *you* for her *hand*!' Innocence had burst out laughing.

'You're kidding me,' Emily had said, forgetting her own misery. 'Claudia's *engaged*?'

'Yes,' her mother had replied. 'Only we don't care because he's a nobody. She's *wasting* herself, when she could have made an alliance.'

'We're not the Tudors, Mother,' Emily had said.

Innocence had glanced at her daughter's stomach, and smiled.

LONDON, SUMMER 1998

Claudia

'Emily? Hello, it's Claudia. I hope you don't mind my ringing. I know we haven't spoken for a while but . . . I saw the paper and I wondered if you were OK.'

'You saw *your* paper. I'll give you an exclusive if you like.'

Claudia hated it when Emily was sarcastic. Their relationship had been strained since they were children. Emily seemed to dislike her for a whole host of reasons.

'I'm going to resign, Emily.'

'Don't be mad. I need you, seriously, to write a piece on me! You know, put across *my* side of the story. I'm going to charge *UK Sunday* two hundred Gs.'

'Emily! Have they been posting envelopes through the door offering cash?'

'Yes.'

'Ignore it – all. You don't need the money – and for that amount, they'll write what they like. They'll want to describe what Tim was like in bed, and they'll want to say stuff like "He watched the cricket over my shoulder while pumping away and he got six innings before he was out. He could bat for England, he's got a *huge* bat and big red balls!" And *you* won't have a say. They don't give copy approval. *And* they'll make you pose in a thong. And even if I write the copy, they'll rewrite it. You'll come out of it looking *awful.*'

'Oh. Right.'

Claudia knew it was bad of her, but she felt pleased to be in a position where she could give Emily advice. Emily was always so self-sufficient, so scornful of Claudia.

'Em, would you like to come over? I'm staying at St Martin's Lane. Make sure you're not followed. Get Charlie to drive Nanny out of the gates in *your* favourite car – it helps if it's got tinted windows – she'll have to wear a blond wig and dark glasses. They'll all take off after her, then you can sneak off here.'

She felt Emily hesitate. 'I'm not scared, Claudia.'

'I know. But . . . it would be nice to talk. I have a problem too. By the way, I'm signed in under the name Freshwater.'

'I'll see you in an hour.'

'Oh, and Em?'

'Yes?'

'A – a baby is always special.'

Claudia put down the phone and fanned her face. She walked to the window, and looked out over Leicester Square. It was a beautiful sight. Nelson's Column looked to be in arm's reach. It was as if London and its landmarks had been squashed and squeezed to fit into her own private viewing gallery. New York was new and brash and modern, but she preferred London. London was truly beautiful, it was *stately*, it had a long and distinguished history. Perhaps, because she had no idea where she came from, who her blood parents were, the past – *any* past – was precious to her, and London had an awe-inspiring past. It was a kick, to be a tourist in your own city – a *paying* tourist, not a guest in one of Daddy's hotels where you served at *his* pleasure. It was a joy to be anonymous.

There was a bang on the door. 'Yes?'

'Me.'

Emily breezed in and went straight for the mini-bar. 'Ooh, jelly beans. Yum.' She tore open the pack. 'So,' she said, cracking open a can of Coke. 'You're shacked up with some coffin-dodger.'

Emily had a way of putting things. 'Well,' she said. 'He's not *that* old. Only—' Claudia stopped.

'What?'

Oh damn. She was going to cry. 'I think . . . I'm not sure . . . quite a few months ago I got this letter. And then, last week, another one . . . saying the same thing. I should end the

71

relationship because it will only lead to "agony and misery".
I don't know who's sending them. It might be Dad – I think
Martin might have crossed him in business. He's trying to
forbid it, but I just . . . I'm not speaking to Dad, he's so insulting. Or it might be someone else. I either have a friend or an
. . . enemy. I . . . I know Martin loves me but I think he's
deceiving me.'

Emily burst out laughing. 'Oh *please*! You're deceiving
yourself more like.'

The tears dried up. 'Thanks for your support,' she said
stiffly.

'Oh, Claudia, what's the big deal? Show him the letters, ask
him if he's hiding something. *Then* you'll know. Christ, if you
think you've got problems, look at me!'

Claudia did look at Emily. She looked scared witless. 'I'm
sorry. How . . . are you feeling?'

'I am *enraged*. You saw what that cunt said about me in that
shit rag.'

'Emily! Don't . . .! But, yes. I know it's not true.' She *hoped*
it wasn't true. She had no idea what her little sister got up to.
Well, some idea.

'Of course it isn't true! Tim was my first shag! And my
last!'

'Oh, Em! I wish you had waited. Oh dear.'

'I need to *prove it*. To the world. And to Tim. That prick. I'm
going to get a paternity test.'

'Oh! Are you sure? Don't you have to wait till the baby's
born?'

'No. You can do it any time. I just have to get a sample of
Tim's DNA.'

'How will you do that?'

'I'll find a way. Quintin says there are about a zillion
companies who do it for you in like a *day*. They'll even collect
the evidence from your house. Only thing is – and there's a
tiny, tiny risk for the baby, like, *one* per cent – I get a needle
up the—'

'Yes, OK. I get it. It seems rather drastic.'

'What about my situation *isn't* drastic?'

'True. Oh, I have an idea! I know. You can do an interview with *Hello!* For free.'

'Are you insane?'

'Emily, *Hello!* will print exactly what you want, and if you ask them to donate your fee to a charity, they'll say that, then you remain pure. If it's for money, then people can say nasty things, even if it's proven that Timmy *is* the father.'

'He fucking is! Great, even you don't believe me.'

'I do, I do. Listen, Emily. I think it's a great idea, the paternity test, but how will you get Tim to cooperate?'

Emily smiled. 'He just called. He's flying in from New York. He wants to "talk". We're meeting tonight at his father's club.' She grinned. 'Every fourth Tuesday they let in women and dogs. I'm going to start a fight in the Cigar Room and pull out some of his hair.'

In spite of everything, Claudia wanted to giggle. 'Isn't there a *kinder* way?'

Emily raised an eyebrow. 'He's not getting a chew, if that's what you mean.'

'It really wasn't.' Claudia cleared her throat. 'If you want,' she said, 'I'll speak to *Hello!* for you. I'm sure Innocence would let you use her PR, but refuse. And I'm surprised that Max Clifford hasn't called. But I think you should be very careful. Max is probably not the person for you. He's great but if you have Max, it makes you seem so . . . media *savvy*. Em, are you listening?'

Emily was picking the cashews out of the nut jar and wiping her hands on the white linen bedcover. 'Mm.'

'Emily,' Claudia went on. 'I wonder if you would do something for *me*?'

Her sister looked up sharply. 'What is it?'

'Would you mind if Martin came up to this room, for a . . . drink?'

'He's from the paper, right? Oh my God. This is a set-up!'

'*Of course* it isn't!' She paused. 'I . . . just want you to meet him. I thought maybe . . . you might be able to *sense* if he . . .'

'. . . is a gay serial killer who's already spoken for?'

Claudia sighed. 'It was just an idea. You should go. He'll be here in a minute.'

'*God*, Claudia. You are *such* a martyr! I'll meet the guy! But if he dares write a *word* about me, then I swear—'

'He won't. I promise. Oh my! That must be him!' She scurried to the door, checking her reflection en route. Emily was already sprawled on the bed, flicking through the cable channels.

'Hi,' Claudia said shyly, and allowed herself to be kissed. 'Come and meet my sister. She's . . . resting.'

She led Martin by the hand into the room. 'Emily, this is Martin. Martin . . . *Emily?* Oh my gosh, she's choking on a nut! Martin!'

They both rushed forward; Emily held up a hand. 'Chill,' she gasped. 'I'm fine. It was a cashew.'

'You don't look fine, Emily. You look terribly pale. Let me get you a drink of water. Here. Don't *shock* us! We should all have a drink. Martin? What will you have?' She smiled awkwardly at Martin. He smiled back.

'Whatever's there.'

'We could order some coffee?' She glanced at Emily, who was staring – so *rudely* – at Martin.

Martin grinned at Emily. 'What? I'm not *that* old!'

'No,' said Emily, backing away. 'How old are you exactly?'

'Emily!'

'It's fine, Claudia. She's just looking out for you, and I am an old git. I'm forty.'

'That figures. *Fuck*. I have . . . morning sickness. Claudia . . . I might need you.'

'I'll order the coffee, love. You see to your sister.'

Claudia hurried after Emily to the bathroom and shut the door. 'Jesus, Emily!' she hissed. 'You were *so* rude!' And she was *still* staring! Oh, God. It was true then. Emily could *tell* he was deceiving her. Or, worse, she must have seen him in a strip club or something. 'You ... you recognize him, don't you?'

To her surprise, Emily took her hand, so softly. 'Claudia,' she said. 'I do recognize him. And I think you must too.' Claudia saw with shock that her sister's eyes were full of tears. 'And I know now why Dad wants you to end the relationship. It's not business. He knows. Oh, Claudia. This is *sick*. I just ... wonder what evil spirit led you to this man. I think you're right. I think you do have an enemy ...' Emily stopped.

'What?' whispered Claudia. She gripped Emily's shoulders and shook her. 'I don't understand you. "Evil spirit"? You're scaring me to death. What are you saying?' She felt half hysterical with fear.

Emily swallowed. 'Claudia,' she said. 'It's not just me and Tim. I think that you and Martin need to take a paternity test.'

For a moment, a blessed moment, Claudia didn't get it. 'Why?' she said in her stupid innocence. 'I'm not pregnant!'

Then, finally, she got it, and her world crashed around her.

SCOTLAND, LATE SUMMER 1998

Emily

Emily didn't like it like that, but he did, and she didn't want the baby poked around, so she let him.

'Pull my skirt back down when you're finished,' she murmured, but he seemed to be in a zone all of his own. Her face was digging into the cream leather upholstery of the Land-Rover. It smelt of animal – or maybe that was *them*. When her mother's car no longer smelled of new leather, her mother bought a new car. No doubt this Land-Rover had been in Tim's family for generations and hailed back to Cromwell's time. God knows how many people had sat on this seat. Technically her face was in someone's *arse*. Ugh, Emily. Think nice thoughts. Could the driver see through the screen? It gave her a thrill to think that he might. She liked to create desire – Emily was a tease and proud of it.

'Oh my *GOD*,' gasped her husband as he shuddered into her. She sighed, and passed him a tissue. This way, it did nothing for her. It was uncomfortable; it was a charitable act. Also, her olive-green maternity dress was Chloé – you had to dress smart for the in-laws – and any visible sign of bodily fluid would spoil the effect.

'All done now,' she announced, rolling over and sitting up, but he shook his head, and pressed her gently down until she was sprawled on her back.

'Tim-Tim wants to give Em-Em a special kiss.'

She sighed as his head disappeared between her legs. 'Knock yourself out.' He was, oh, *what*, just, like, *whoa!* at going down on a girl, but she didn't like all this baby talk. Baby talk and sex didn't go together, as far as Emily was concerned. Gross or what? Next thing she'd discover, her husband slept with a teddy bear. She preferred to talk dirty.

That said, Tim was a *very* good boy and he deserved his little treats. Emily grinned to herself.

At first, meeting at the club, he'd been all stern and serious. 'Was this a *trap*, Emily? Is this monstrous hullabaloo about cash?' he'd asked, lounging in the huge overstuffed armchair, sipping brandy and puffing on a fat Cuban cigar. His feet didn't quite touch the polished wood floor. He looked like a ten-year-old smoking a sugar cigarette.

She'd wanted to throw her glass of flat ginger ale in his stupid privileged face. 'Yes, that's right. It was my grand plan to land myself with a kid when I'm too young to drive it to the park. What happened to you, Tim?' she'd said slowly, shaking her head. 'You were my *first*. I haven't been with anyone since. I loved you, once. I have your baby in here. And we don't deserve to be insulted. I'll make my own money, thanks. I don't need a hand-me-down fortune off *you*.' She'd stood up. 'I'm going now. Don't expect to see me, or your son, again.'

Then she'd leaned her face right into his and stroked his hair gently, ending in a sharp yank, making him yelp with pain. She'd placed the handful of hairs in a little plastic sandwich bag. 'The results of the paternity test will be published in *Hello!* Goodbye.'

She'd stalked out. Once she was in the street, the tears had run down her face and she'd brushed them angrily away. She wasn't a *weeper*. Crying was pathetic, it made you feel crap and it totally destroyed your make-up. OK, there had been a few small fibs, but basically, it was the truth. She *had* wanted to trap him, and it *was* for money – no, security. 'Security' was excusable. But the baby wasn't the trap! The blow job was the trap. The baby *ruined* the trap! And . . . well . . . she *felt* that the baby was a boy.

'Oh, it's a boy,' Nanny had said, touching a finger to her stomach. 'Girls take away your beauty.' Nanny knew best!

Tim had come legging it out of the club, smelling like his father. He'd whirled her round to face him. The stink of cigar smoke made her gag. 'Marry me!' he'd cried. He'd fallen to his knees on the pavement of SW1. He'd grabbed her hand and kissed it. 'I'm sorry, babes,' he'd said. 'I love you – I always have. I was afraid – my father – I'm my own man. I'm going to have a son! I want you as my bride. Will you' – he smiled – 'do me the honour of becoming my wife?'

The vision of a turreted castle rising out of the gentle morning mist, a young princess in a dress of spun gold sweeping across the drawbridge, the jewels in her yellow hair sparkling in the sunlight, fair Emily was her name . . . And Timmy *was* a very fine fuck. A little weak in personality, perhaps, but he was only nineteen and girls matured faster than boys. Also, while honour was something she could work with, Emily did not obey, and planned to start never. Better weak than domineering.

'I have two words for you, Viscount,' she'd said, and his smile had drooped. She'd giggled and shaken her head. Then she'd crouched, until they were both sitting on the pavement, and purred in his ear, 'Las Vegas!'

Forty-eight hours later, they were man and wife.

To be honest, no fairy-tale princess that *she* knew of had married in a drive-thru, even if it was named A Little White Chapel Tunnel of Love, but it had been cool to screech up to her wedding on a Harley. The heat was impossible and the traffic on the Strip was insane – like a parking lot – so the Harley had been the sensible option, *and* it had allowed her to fondle the groom en route. Her dress was Vera Wang (hence the delay), and Quintin had flown in from LA to be a witness.

Afterwards, she and Timmy had shagged each other senseless on one of the huge revolving beds in their 15,000-square-foot Sky Villa at the Medici. 'Do you know how much I had to lose at the tables to keep this suite?' gasped Tim as he ground into her.

'Whatever it was I'm worth it,' she'd gasped back, 'and anyway, we saved on the wedding!'

They'd stopped screwing long enough to check out the topless showgirls at the MGM Grand. Then they'd staggered back to their suite, and he'd shagged her from behind in the outdoor pool so they could both admire the *un*believable view. It had a glass end wall and with every thrust she felt as though she was going to burst out of the water on to the Strip below. She was used to excess but this was crazy: the bronze statues, indoor waterfall, the marble floors, the butlers . . . kind of like home. And sex was too *fun*! She made Tim do it in the glass elevator too, and on the poker table. '*Poker* table,' she'd said. 'Get it?'

'You're going to,' he'd replied.

'Oh, *yes*!' Emily squealed now. 'Wow. At least I'll be relaxed when we tell your parents.'

Tim sat up, wiped his chin, straightened his tie.

She smiled. 'You reek of sex, and the tie is not going to fool anyone.' She was acting cool, but she was jumpy as a cat. The Earl was not going to be thrilled to find that his son had tied the knot. But the fact she was providing his son with a male heir should soften the blow. He'd get over it. He had no choice. She had the marriage certificate in her green Hermès snakeskin suitcase, and a copy of the DNA test results – only to be brandished if he became abusive. The laboratory notepaper was, she thought, preferable to an issue of *Hello!*

'We're here,' Tim said. Emily had wondered if people *could* look green. Now she knew they could. 'Now, remember. He'll want to know that I'll be free to continue my education, and pursue my career. He'll also want to know that *you* intend to be a supportive and obedient spouse.'

Spouse?! 'You're kidding me, right?' The words popped out before she could stop them, and a chill curled around her heart.

Tim looked harassed. 'He's old school. He's like *his* father. He'll want to know that you'll raise the baby as a Fortelyne. Nanny Margaret will be only too pleased to come out of retirement, and the likelihood is, you'll live at the castle, so they can keep an eye.'

He could not be serious. 'So,' she said, 'your parents won't . . . vacate the castle?'

He laughed. 'Would you? Hey. Chin up, buttercup. You'll barely set eyes on the kid if you don't want to. That's got to be a bonus. You can spend all day riding, get your figure back.'

'Fuck *riding*,' said Emily. 'And screw my figure. It will be back to its former glory in, like, a *week*. Look to your own figure, Fat Boy. I'm having a baby, what's your excuse? *I* want to play mother.'

Now she was bricking it. To Emily, 'mother' was a verb. Maybe it came from having parents with better things to do than parent. Emily was one big ball of rebellion. But inside, she was traditional – well, *kinda*. She ached to be part of a happy family, a loud, jolly family who ate Sunday lunch together, who played ball games on their extensive lawns, who curled up together in front of a roaring fire. Cook would make the lunch. A gardener would keep the lawns, and a housekeeper would stoke the fire. But *Emily* would read stories to her kid at bedtime, she would play soldiers or dolls, she would kiss better grazed knees, she would *know* this person, she would love and be loved because there was love in her heart, but she'd got this far in life with nowhere for it to *go*.

When you were little, your parents were your sun and moon, and only *they* could fuck that up. She wasn't going to.

She half expected a slap, but Tim ruffled her hair. 'Easy, Tiger,' he said. 'The old man will give you a hard time, but he'll come round. I suspect if you make a scene, he'll permit you to live in London with your parents, for the first few years at least.'

Her head was swirling. This guy was like two different people. In the US, he was sexy, suave, he could spin a line. In the UK, he was a scared little boy. *Not* hot.

'Let's get it over with,' she said, and took his hand.

The car was parked in the courtyard, and together they walked over the drawbridge.

'Maybe your dad's crouched underneath, like a troll,' she whispered.

Tim's mouth was a straight line.

The portcullis was up. Emily imagined the Earl ordering his steward to let it drop as she passed, its great iron teeth slicing her in two from head to foot, like a salami.

They walked across the internal courtyard and Tim rapped on the heavy iron knocker of the main door. A man in a black uniform let them in without smiling; Emily didn't recognize him.

'The Earl and Countess are in the Tower Room, my Lord.'

'Thank you,' said Tim. Emily's kitten heels echoed on the

flagstones. Jesus, a carpet wouldn't hurt. Slowly, in silence, they walked up the curling staircase. Ancient worn tapestries depicting battle scenes hung from the walls like a warning, and the eyes of a thousand haughty ancestors gazed down at her with disgust from their framed splendour. Everything was fabulous about a castle when you were nine, but at the grand old age of sixteen, Emily saw that they'd done the bare minimum in terms of interior décor. Would a red velvet drape go amiss? She wanted candelabras dripping wax; here were electric light bulbs in nasty little green fringed lamp-shades. Were those curtains *Laura Ashley*? Also, despite the warm weather, it was *freezing* in here. Tim knocked on a door.

'Enter!' barked a voice.

They tiptoed into a room where the thousands and thousands of books that lined the walls seemed to close in on you. Emily hunched her shoulders; the slightest move and she'd be buried in an avalanche of first editions. The Earl was sitting behind a large desk, and his wife was perched on an aged sofa. At knee level the material was worn to string by generations of passing Labradors. The windows were arrow-slits, and it was dimly lit. The ancient rug was so threadbare, Emily's heel caught, and there was a clear ripping sound as she yanked it free.

'Good morning, Father,' said Tim. 'Hello, Mother, you're looking . . . well. I suppose you've heard the news. I did the honourable thing—'

'You did an appalling thing, you blasted idiot. Your mother is *far* from well, she is *beside* herself. The lawyers would have taken care of everything, but you've made a laughing stock of us all. Has your education taught you *nothing*? Have you no sense of duty?'

Emily imagined that the Earl would like her to be looking at her feet, so she didn't take her eyes off his cold, furious face. He was wearing the grossest pair of saggy birdshit-green cords she'd ever seen, and a jacket with patches on the sleeves, like her old geography teacher.

'I do indeed have a sense of duty, Father, and it's a boy, which is why—'

'Not to little Miss Kent from Hampstead and her bastard, you moron, I am talking about your loyalty to your family name, your heritage. Does the Fortelyne crest mean nothing to you? Did you not consider that your idiocy brings into disrepute *generations*? You are bred from a distinguished bloodline, from a succession of men who have cherished and valued the Fortelyne name for the last six hundred years, who have sacrificed their lives to protect and promote its unique legacy and unblemished reputation. And you have disgraced every last one of them!'

The Countess, Emily noted, wasn't crying. She was staring, blank-faced, at a point behind her son's head. *Say something*, she thought. He's your *son*.

Nothing.

'You're fortunate, though. This thing isn't legal. We'll pay her off. Though you can forget Kitty Fotheringhaugh – a week ago, the daughter of a senior peer would have given her eye teeth to write *Fortelyne* after her name. You've thrown all that away, along with the best part of your future. We'll salvage what we can.'

'It *is* legal!' Emily burst out. She couldn't believe this man.

'As I am reliably informed, the legal age required of one to marry in' – the Earl's bony nose twitched – '*Nevada* is eighteen.'

Emily beamed. 'Yes, we know. If you're sixteen you need consent. And that's why Mummy gave her permission with a notarized affidavit.' She scrunched her left hand into a fist, and gave the Earl the finger – the *third* finger, on which shone a thick gold band. 'It's as if we'd been married in Westminster Abbey by the Archbishop of Canterbury himself! And isn't this ring just *too* cute?'

She could feel Tim, beside her, shrivelling in his shoes. She stuck her stomach out.

'Then,' said the Earl, sighing deeply, 'I'm afraid you leave me no choice.' His steel gaze locked on to his son. 'I shall instruct my solicitors. You will inherit nothing. No title, no castle, no land, not a stick of furniture, not a penny, not a pound.'

'But—'

She felt frozen in time and space, as if trapped in a nightmare. Was she, *this*, so bad that he would *do* such a thing? She hadn't even considered it. She hadn't realized it was possible in *1998*. Nor, by the look of him, had Tim. His face was ashen. It was as if his soul had slipped away with the news and left a shell. Tears ran down his face, and she shuddered.

'You have chosen to make your own way in life, and by doing so, you have turned your back on your family.'

'Please, Father—'

'Family is the most important thing,' interrupted the Earl. He waved a dismissive hand. 'Console yourself with its motto: *Semper fortis existo*. You may go. Derek will drive.'

'May I . . . kiss Mother goodbye?' gulped Tim.

Emily watched. The woman sat like a statue. Emily turned and followed Tim out of the room. He was sobbing, his shoulders shaking. She knew she should comfort him but she couldn't say a word.

So many dreams. So many years of planning a precise, perfect future, and who could have known it would turn out like this? She was bound to a weak, penniless, castle-free prince . . . with a *baby* to raise. Why was it always the bloody princess who had to pick up the pieces?

LONDON, SUMMER 1998

Claudia

Claudia couldn't cry. She couldn't eat, and she couldn't cry. She didn't know if she could *live*. Each moment was torment.

When she gazed at her reflection, a pale ghost stared back. She turned on the shower, and let the hot water cascade over her. She stood, scrubbing at her skin with a rough flannel, until her legs no longer had the strength to hold her upright, and then she curled up on the floor, her mouth open in a silent howl, until the water ran cold.

She hadn't seen Martin since he'd come to the hotel. She'd managed, God knew how, to tell him that Emily needed 'privacy'. He had assumed that her odd behaviour was down to anxiety over her sister; she had managed not to throw up as he'd kissed her mouth. The second she heard the lift *ping*, she'd fallen to the floor, 'Oh God, oh God . . . no . . . no . . .'

Emily had emerged from the bathroom and placed Martin's beer bottle in a plastic bag. 'I could be wrong. Wait for the DNA test results.'

And Claudia had screamed, 'Fuck the DNA test results! He's my real father. My real father! I know it, I see it . . . and so do you! I was going to marry him! Oh God, I was going to sleep with him! I was going to sleep with my real *father*!'

And then she'd stood up and screamed and screamed until Emily had slapped her face.

A week had gone by, and she hadn't left the hotel room. The DNA test results had confirmed what she already knew. When Martin rang, she'd told him she had the flu, and not to come round. She felt so weak she could barely end the call. She thought of kissing him, the feel of his arms around her, and retched.

She hated him – she hated *him* for not seeing, not realizing, not knowing. She was a forgotten mistake of his youth – the biggest mistake he'd ever made and now he was going to reap what he'd sown. She shuddered. At least they hadn't *done* it. What they had done was bad enough but if they had done *it* . . . She'd have found a gun and shot herself in the head.

She couldn't face telling him the truth. She just couldn't do it. She didn't want to speak to or see him ever again.

She wanted to hurt him. It was his fault. He had betrayed her. He had betrayed her, nearly twenty-three years ago, when he'd rolled out of bed and promised her blood mother, not meeting her eyes, 'I'll call you.' He had been betraying her ever since. Every moment of unhappiness that she'd suffered in her life was *his* fault.

But she didn't want to hurt him *that* much, not enough to tell him that he'd come close to screwing his own daughter. That kind of knowledge tore a person apart from the inside. It made you dirty; it was the kind of stain that didn't wash out. It hung over you, clinging and filthy, like a shroud, making you feel as though you had no place in the world, and that you were a vile aberration and didn't deserve to live.

She would spare him that.

She would be cruel to be kind. She would hurt him just enough so that he would be glad to have escaped with his freedom. He would hate and despise her and, most importantly, he would *run* from her. But he'd recover, and eventually he would look back on their relationship with a wrinkle of the nose and mild relief. He would never ever seek her out, and one day he would meet another woman and the unpleasant memory of Claudia Mayer would be dissolved.

Claudia clenched her teeth. So be it.

Slowly, dizzily, she swung herself out of bed, and picked up the phone.

'Hi.' Her voice was husky from lack of use. 'It's Claudia, Claudia Mayer. I'm back. At St Martin's Lane hotel. I'm sorry. Yes, yes I have. I can tell you everything, if you like. Ask for me at reception. But please – don't tell a soul. An hour and a half? OK. Bye-bye.'

She dry-heaved all the way to the sleek limestone shower. She washed her hair and every inch of her body. She tried not to look at herself. She dried her hair, applied lipstick – scarlet lipstick – and lashings of mascara. She put on a white lacy bra and matching knickers, little *white* knickers. She had a red dress from Stella McCartney that she'd bought for her and

Martin's anniversary of meeting – what a cursed day. It was a velvet clingy material, with a low-cut scoop neck, short sleeves and flared skirt. Since her recovery from the eating disorder, she'd put weight on her chest, and her cleavage swelled out of the top of the dress. She felt horribly exposed. She had also – stupid fool – bought a pair of red patent Jimmy Choo stilettos, more to look at than to wear; they were a tart's shoes, but so pretty. Well, she was certainly dressed for the occasion.

Now she had to make one last call.

Afterwards, she put her head in her hands. But she didn't cry.

She sat on the large white bed and waited. She moved once, to change the rainbow lighting over the headboard to a red glow. Then she jumped up to draw the blinds so that London would not witness her shame. And then she made an order on room service.

The phone rang beside the bed and she jumped. 'Yes. Yes. Send him up, please.' She swallowed. Her throat was dry.

There was a sharp knock on the door. 'Come in,' she called.

He was sexy – if you hated yourself, which she did. He was sexy – if you thought sex was a dirty, sleazy thing, which it was. All the same, she felt sick with fear and self-loathing. She watched him assess the situation. The cold, sneering expression on his face was replaced by a sly curl of the lip.

'Claudia,' he said, raking his hand through his hair. 'How nice of you to give me an exclusive. We've missed you.' He paused, lit a cigarette. '*I've* missed you.'

He'd do it. She'd known he would. It wasn't because he fancied her, it was about power, and rivalry. 'I've missed you too,' she said. 'Would you like to . . . sit down?' She patted the bed.

He sat down next to her and his leg brushed hers. She tried to focus on *now*. He was a man, a sexy, bad, unsuitable man, but no relation, and she was a woman who needed to get laid and they were going to do what all adults did – for fun. They did it for *fun*! She was not a girl of eight, lost on a desert island, with a bearded man pressing her face towards his lap.

Her inhaler was beside her, though. Surely, buried within the fear, she felt some excitement? She had always been such a good girl; turning bad should thrill her. It was still wrong, and she wanted to run; she could have smashed through the great glass window, she wanted to run so badly. She should focus on hating Martin, loving him but hating him, and getting them both out of a desperate situation with no more collateral damage than was necessary.

He offered her the cigarette. With a trembling hand, she took it. She inhaled, and started to cough.

He laughed and tweaked it from between her fingers. 'You're breaking all the rules today.'

She gazed at the floor. Roughly, he tilted her chin in his hand, forcing her to meet his gaze. His breath smelled of smoke and the red light above the bed reflected in his dark eyes.

'Yes,' she whispered. Oh God. His mouth was inches from hers. She didn't move. She felt his hand, snaking up her bare leg. *Trail of fire*, she thought, in a flashback to one of her books. She didn't want this, but she *did*. She couldn't help it. She shivered and tried to press her legs together, but he wedged his knee between hers.

'Oh, no, Claudia,' he murmured as his fingers reached her knicker elastic. 'Don't tease.' His knee pushed her legs wider, and his thick fingers probed deeper. She gasped and gripped his shoulder. 'You want it, bitch. You're as juicy as a peach.'

'Don't . . .' she whispered, 'stop,' and when words came out wrong she knew why. It was easier to fuck this man in cold blood than to make love to her 'fiancé' because her only experience of sex had been a hideous ordeal for which she'd blamed herself. The idea of sex with dribbling, moony love was revolting to her: she hated herself too much. Sex was supposed to reek of guilt and shame. It was perverse and this was the only way she would ever enjoy it. *This* was what she deserved.

She closed her eyes. *Breathe.*

There was a knock on the door. 'Fu—'

'It's our . . . room service,' she whispered. 'Wait.'

Seconds later, the door was on the latch and she was back, carrying the bottle of vintage champagne. The insides of her thighs were hot and throbbing. Carefully, she placed the bucket on the desk.

'How adorable,' he said. 'I'm being seduced.' She could see the great bulge in his jeans. He saw her looking, and laughed. 'It's all for you, baby. I've been saving myself.'

She thought she was going to pass out. He was so crude. She wanted to beg him to be gentle, but she knew he'd get off on her fear. She glanced at her watch. It was nearly time. She bit her lip to stop a whimper.

'I need . . . Let's have a drink,' she said.

He nodded at the bottle, and slowly, wobbling in her high shoes, she walked over to the desk. She poured two glasses of champagne. She took a great gulp of hers, turned and gasped. He was right behind her. He downed his, then shoved a hand down her front, harshly squeezing her breasts. His breath was hot in her ear, as he hissed, 'I'm going to give it to you good.'

He twisted her around and pushed her head down, so she was bent over the desk, and yanked up her dress. She heard the rip of his zip, and then he pulled her knickers aside, and rammed into her with a grunt. It was sharp white-hot pain and she bit her fist. The tears rolled down and plopped on to the glass desk. She was shaking. Don't panic. Relax, *relax*. She closed her eyes and tried not to resist. It felt a bit better then. His hands were on her hips, strangely gentle now. Could he tell she'd never . . . ? He was showing her how. She tried to move with him.

He leaned over her. 'You sexy bitch, Claudia,' he whispered, and she pressed against him. This . . . it . . . him . . . it was horrible, but it was *nice*. She was a disgusting, disgusting girl. 'Tell me how much you want it,' he said as he pumped into her. 'Say it.'

'I want it, Jim,' she said, and her voice was a moan of desire – because it was over; nothing would matter to her again. She was lost, and she might as well surrender.

'You *slut*,' said a quiet voice. 'You evil, lying slut.'

They both whirled around. Jim, smiling, unrepentant; Claudia, hastily pulling her dress down, her eyes glazed with a curious mix of lust and despair. Martin had walked in, as she'd known he would, and had obligingly witnessed the act that would part them for ever. She opened her mouth to speak but he held up a hand.

'Don't.' He paused. His face was pale. His eyes were narrowed and there was a single crease in the centre of his brow – just as when she narrowed *her* eyes. The expression was identical, stupid man. No, it was his fault, how could he not have known?

'I hope you get what you deserve, Claudia, and I think you will. And if I see you in hell it will be too soon.'

She stared at him, defiant, and he shot her a look, a look of such acute pain, it pierced her heart like a flight of arrows. *You think you're in agony? You have no idea*, Daddy. *I've saved you from insanity.*

He turned and left.

She sank to the floor. She put her hands over her face. Her breath came in wheezes, then not at all – she groped for the inhaler.

Jim tossed it to her, rolling his eyes. Then he lit a cigarette. 'I've been used,' he said. 'Haven't I?'

She waved away the smoke, smoothed the tears from her face, glanced in the mirror. They hadn't kissed and her scarlet lipstick remained pristine. 'What do you care,' she said. 'You enjoyed it.'

He grinned and traced his thumb across her lip. 'You have natural talent. So . . . where were we?'

She pushed his hand away. 'You were just going, boss. Take that as my resignation.'

He stared at her in surprise, and his nostrils flared. Slowly, he put on his clothes and picked up his notebook. 'You *are* a slut.'

She smiled wearily. 'Jim,' she said, 'aren't we all?'

She was a different person now. She had shed her meek, virginal skin like a snake. Life had wrung her out, done her wrong, toughened her up. It was true: the person who'd written that warning letter about Martin *was* a friend. But she had an enemy out there, she was sure of it. Someone had, painstakingly, led her to this, the lowest, most vile and desperate point of her existence. Why?

ITALY, JANUARY 1998

'Thank you,' said the woman as Isabella set the wild boar ravioli on the wooden table.

Isabella smiled. '*Prego.*'

The woman and the man, they looked so happy. It was good to see happy people. They were holding hands across the table. It made a nice change. These couples who sat, eating in silence, it pained her to see. It was not a good thing to see people eat without joy. Food and love: two of life's essentials. She thanked God daily for sending her Luca, her blessed Luca, busy in the kitchen, his dark curling hair falling over his handsome face. It was, she guessed, the second time around for these two – or perhaps the first? Many people, they waited longer now. The woman's wedding band shone in the candlelight. It was new, for sure. The man, he wore no ring, but Isabella knew love when she saw it, and the light of love was in his eyes.

'You marry, here?' You could ask. What harm in asking? Happy people liked to tell.

'*Sì*,' said the woman. 'Last Sunday. In the Church of La Madonna del Soccorso.'

Isabella's eyes widened. '*Molte congratulazioni!*' she said, smiling again to cover her surprise. 'I wish you great joy.'

Only villagers married in that church. These people, they must have influence. Movie stars, perhaps? They came here now, with their baseball caps and the sunglasses stuck on their faces, too thin, terrible, like starving children, even the men, picking at their delicious food like it was no good – the menu, change this, change that – and they looked at you, *Indeed, it is I, you know me, yes?* She had no time for movie stars. They came to her beautiful homeland not to admire, but to be admired, and they were not happy. She saw only need in their eyes, eyes that searched for something they would never find.

These people – *Americani? Inglesi?* – this bride and groom, they had good looks; the man, he was a fine-looking man, but not the movie star. Rich, she decided. The shoes, the smooth skin, the fingernails, the easy manner: ah yes, money beyond dream. But today, she saw, it wasn't the money that made him smile, it was the woman – as it should be.

'Thank you,' said the woman, and she smiled again.

'Thank you,' said the man, and she heard the tremble of great emotion in his voice. 'We feel that joy has come to us.' She tilted her head to hear. Perhaps his next words were not meant for her ears, but Isabella was skilled at lip reading – if she was not, what a waste of running a restaurant! She was sure he said, 'At last.'

LA, OCTOBER 1998

Emily

Emily wasn't good with money and, frankly, she'd always been proud of that. She'd never had to be. She was born into billions and she hadn't a clue how to live any other way. Anyone who was 'good' with money was in fact budgeting – talk about common. Housewives in, like, *Liverpool* budgeted. If you were rich enough, you didn't budget. You didn't have to think about money; it was just there, loads of it, like air.

She was missing Tim. He'd gone up to Cambridge early, leaving her alone in the apartment. She'd visited him once; it had been amazing to see him after two whole *weeks* – she'd even given him a chew in his room; he'd grabbed a cushion so her knees didn't get sore but they hadn't really *talked*. She didn't want to tell him about their ... her ... problems, because if you told your husband your problems, he thought *you* were the problem.

Horrible things had been happening – it had started a month before he left. Just awful. Stuff she didn't want to face or think about. Things she didn't want to have to deal with. After the first threatening letter, she'd told the housekeeper that *she'd* open the mail. She'd never opened anything but Valentine cards in her life. It was terrifying. The things they said. So cruel, so inhuman, when she was expecting a *baby* in a month!

The letters kept coming: she grew to recognize them on sight. They would have a vague return address, nothing suspicious, and then you'd open them to be confronted with that hateful red paper, and, in black, bold capitals across the top, '**CREDITOR'S NOTICE**'. She had no idea that people *lived* like this. How did they survive? How did they sleep, with the unbearable, suffocating stress of it all?

'**Take notice** unless you make **payment** of this debt within 7 days a **County Court Claim** may be issued against you ...

legal department . . . EvilCorp **Debt Recovery Limited** . . .'
Surely it was illegal to threaten people like this?

'We may issue a **County Court Order** against you and then put the case in the hands of the **bailiff** who will add their own costs to the **penalty charge** . . .'

'**Failure** to pay may result in **prosecution** . . . please pay immediately to avoid **further action** . . .'

And they *phoned* her – on her mobile, at home. She was stunned and furious. Not so much as a hello, they were brusque and rude. She had never been spoken to like that. She had never been spoken to like a *poor* person.

Tim had a bank account for home stuff, but for some reason, it was empty. She didn't have access to it, but the mortgage company – she hadn't even known he'd had a mortgage. What *was* a mortgage? – claimed there were 'insufficient funds' in the account and were threatening to 'repossess the property'.

'What?' she'd said, stupidly, on the phone. '*Take* it?'

She'd called Tim at Magdalene seven times, but he never called back. He was still rubbish at phoning. In a panic, she'd called the Earl, but he had refused to take her call. She'd written to him, but there had been no response and, eventually, her unopened letter was returned.

Her mother . . . she might have asked her mother to lend her some cash, but Innocence always got that closed look on her face, as if Emily had asked her for a pound of flesh. Innocence was weird with her money. *She* spent and spent, but she hated to give. Also, it was now a matter of pride. Innocence had been so mean about Tim being disinherited. If Emily asked for money, it would look like she'd failed *again*.

The only other possible source of cash was her father. She'd rather *starve*.

She had tried so hard. She had given *Hello!* seven exclusives in the space of three months – too many. She learned that she had 'cheapened' herself; she was 'over-exposed'. Also, there wasn't *that* much left to confide. Now the tabloids hated her, because she refused to be their 'friend'. She had briefly employed a PR. The stupid cow had advised her to 'smile' and 'be friendly', but the hacks were so rude, so enraging, why *shouldn't* she give them the finger?

Of course, the photo of her giving them the finger was reprinted in every crappy magazine, earning the slug who took it half a million quid. It had taken supreme self-sacrifice, but Emily had worn the same outfit, day in, day out, for a fortnight to spite them. That way, if she kept her hair the same, and a blank expression, there were no new pictures. But they were too powerful to fight. Now it was personal; they wanted to crush her. They were succeeding. The one time, since knowing she was pregnant, she had a glass of Baileys and a fag – *one fag*, because she was about to explode with worry and fear – there'd been a snapper hiding in a tree with his long lens.

She had been on the verge of signing a hundred-thousand-pound-a-year contract to represent a Bond Street jewellery store. Peanuts, but it would have helped. She guessed they were fooled by the marriage to the Earl's son, and the fact that her father was making a comeback, *and* she still had enough gorgeous clothes and shoes and bags and earrings to give the illusion of holding it together. The jewellery store was aiming itself at *young* people; Emily would add that 'dangerous', glamorous edge.

If only they knew.

When the photo of her looking like a washerwoman, with a fag, a bottle of Baileys and a big pregnant stomach, hit the front pages, there was a polite, regretful letter, explaining that, given her 'error of judgement' and the ensuing public condemnation, and their responsibility to choose a positive role model for the impressionable young women who were a growing percentage of their client base . . . our sincere apologies . . . good luck with future projects . . . and the sprog . . . now please fuck off.

There were other avenues to explore: an autobiography. But both her parents would sue. They'd said so.

Modelling? There had been offers, but Christ, she had a brain. Her father had grudgingly paid for a home tutor. Oh God, at school they'd predicted ten As, but this year had so shaken her, she couldn't concentrate: eight Ds and two Cs. Had it really come to *selling her body*? And now that she was desperate it was too late. She would have modelled knickers for BHS if they'd asked. But they hadn't. At eight months pregnant she was too enormous and the washerwoman shot had been reprinted too many times to count. The consensus was, she had *let herself go*.

She was sixteen, for heaven's sake!

She should have saved the interview fees, but seriously, *how*? It was amazing how fast you could get through a million quid. When you were lonely, bored, sad and poor, blowing cash was your only comfort. Just as when you were rich, in fact. She tortured herself with dreams of the old days when she and Mummy would breeze into Versace and they'd lock the store doors and bring out champagne on a tray. They'd spend a hundred thousand a pop and never give it a second thought.

Versace was no longer an option, so Emily had booked herself into the Priory for a fortnight, mainly to see what the fuss was about, and partly for company, but the press had dug out an old, old picture of her – in it, she was *plainly* fourteen! – falling out of a club, coked up to the eyeballs, and labelled her 'a drug addict'. She'd sued and won, but their printed apology had been so tiny, and hidden on page sixteen, that it felt like a hundred grand down the toilet. Also, the Priory had been shit. It was *nothing* like a spa.

It was the kind of experience that made you hate and resent the city – oh, and the fact that none of her so-called 'friends' spoke to her these days – so she'd fled to an exclusive *proper* spa on the Sussex coast. It had 'Gothic mullioned windows . . . rose-clad courtyard . . . log fires . . .

moats and streams ... an outdoor Californian-style hot tub ...' It was gorgeous and luxurious and *kind* of castle-like, but she realized she didn't want 'California-*style*', she wanted California.

So she had booked a flight to LA – commercial, but one had to be financially *prudent*! She was quite proud of herself! And, feeling the tension melt away, she'd checked into a bungalow at the Chateau Marmont. She was too ashamed to visit Quintin in the Hollywood Hills. She might see pity in his eyes and she would just *die*. Also, she was in a big huff with her mother. It would be hard to maintain the full huff if Innocence caught her pilfering from the fridge.

The Chateau was a gorgeous, sumptuous mix of old and new glamour, with a never-ending catwalk of A-list stars wandering by the pool and rarely swimming in it. None came over to say hello, so she ignored them, but it was a boost to soak up that privileged environment. Dad had once said that no matter how successful you were, LA would make you feel shit about yourself. No *way*. To Emily, LA was warm and welcoming, even if it was mainly welcoming her money. Well. Not exactly hers.

Just before leaving Britain, she had taken out five loans in her father's name, totalling three hundred thousand pounds. Well, what choice did she have? He owed her. Call it reparations. And when Ms Green found out and went ballistic – silly interfering tart – there would be thousands of miles between them. Ha!

The loans had taken care of the horrible, endless deluge of bills and final demands. She deserved a holiday at the Chateau after all her hard work solving her money situation. Sometimes she had dinner in the little courtyard, but she preferred to order room service. The food was yum and their fries were long and thin, like worms. It was a nice, cosy cocoon, and she was, in a fake bubble-life way, happy.

She was ready to smile at the teenage stars – *how* they thought they were cute, when they were bone-thin and bent over with osteoporosis like old women. She was even ready to be amused by how pleased the management were with their little faux-Gothic lounge. If something was ten years old here, it was considered antique! You couldn't help but be fond of LA. She remembered Quintin telling her the tale of being stopped by a cop on Ventura. He'd only had an old British driving licence, with no photo. 'It's an English licence,' he'd explained in his haughtiest voice. 'We all *know* each other.' The cop had nodded and let him go.

Emily had purposely put everything bad out of her mind.

The baby kicked, and she stroked its head (or maybe its arse) but she didn't think about it coming *out* in three weeks' time. She imagined Tim attending lectures, riding his bike around the city, punting along the river Cam, missing her. Of course he was missing her – she was his wife and, more importantly, no one fucked as good as she did. Like, they hadn't done it *so* much, but men were all for quality not quantity, right? He would never forget Vegas. The thought of Vegas and the poker table would keep his dick in his pants. She hadn't thought of the red letters: every bill had been paid off. And each loan company was being kindly repaid by the others. She hadn't read any of the tiny type on the back of the contracts: presumably if it wasn't in bold, it couldn't be important.

But, *God*, the Chateau wasn't cheap. And today, she had been gently but absolutely booted out of her cocoon.

It had been, like, *totally* embarrassing. She was lying on her white bed, staring at the white ceiling, thinking of snow. She wished, suddenly, she could build a snowman and slide down a hill on a sledge. The manager had knocked. He was discreet, gentle, charming, but she knew a this-is-IT-buster face when she saw it. Her latest cheque had bounced. She couldn't believe it. All that money gone so *quick*!

She'd blushed and asked the manager to bill Ms Green, her father's secretary. Just this once, Ms Green would take care of it. Not for *her* sake, but for her father's. Ms Green was like a king ordering the tides to stop: she battled and battled to maintain a squeaky-clean reputation for her boss even though that reputation had been torn to tatters long ago. Emily had wanted to say to the manager, 'And hint that you'll go to the papers if he doesn't cough up,' but he didn't look the type who would, so she hadn't.

But no worries. She had a plan. Well. She'd think of one.

She paid for a copy of *People*, to get change for the cab. And by the time she had reached page seven of the magazine, the plan was formed. According to *People*, her father's 'Easter Party' was taking place the following night. In October! Wow. Jack's god-sized ego had permitted him to re-schedule the Resurrection. Crazy. No doubt her invitation was lost in a sea of red letters.

Her mother's mansion in the Hollywood Hills was locked up. *Shit.* Quintin must be visiting his mother. Innocence was so selfish. Just because *she* wasn't using it, she hadn't thought that Emily might need a bolthole. Emily punched in the code that opened the gates. Innocence hadn't told her the code but she guessed it: 6969, what else? Then Emily broke in. No subtlety: she hacked through the mosquito screen with garden shears, then smashed a window. She headed straight for the second freezer, where she found a platinum credit card and forty thousand dollars in cash in a vacuum-sealed plastic bag. This bought her two plane tickets: one for her, one for Timmy.

She was going to fly straight to the Paris party and demand that her father bung her some cash. He wouldn't want to look mean in front of Tom Cruise.

PRIVATE JET, EN ROUTE TO PARIS, OCTOBER 1998

Innocence

Innocence wished that Jack was dead. He was getting on her nerves. He had a *lover* – some cheap tart who worked in the hotel and was the wrong side of thirty. It was disrespectful and he was so brazen about it. She knew it was his way of humiliating her in public. It was a cheap shot. She supposed that cheap was all he could afford these days ... He would never forgive her for appropriating his fortune – even though by doing so she had kept it in the family. *She* was responsible for his Second Coming; *she* had forced him to start afresh. And this was how he thanked her.

Innocence did not like to be made a fool of, especially by an idiot. Innocence lived by certain beliefs. She felt strongly that no one stupid should be rich. So the fact that her husband had managed to make a fool of her *and* millions in one year confounded and obsessed her. She lay awake at night wishing that something seriously nasty would happen to him, just to even the odds. His sudden, not necessarily violent death (she wasn't a monster) would make things right.

If Jack died, her life would be perfect. It *was*, almost, but not quite. The world was her bonfire and he was pissing on it. Today's paper carried a huge snap on page three of her husband kissing the tart across the silver bonnet of a Bugatti. Innocence squinted for signs of work or cellulite. She felt a tight pulsing in her chest and her hands trembled with fury. Her achievements in business were remarkable: her assets verged on a billion and she couldn't *list* the awards she had been too busy to collect. On the charity circuit she was regarded as a patron saint. She had spoken on behalf of the United Nations as a Goodwill Ambassador. She was a mother who remained a style icon and didn't have a fat arse.

And yet all her astonishing successes were reduced to a big

fat zero because that scumbag had cheated. *He* cheated and *she* looked bad, because if a man plays away, the world pretends horror but is breathless with spiteful speculation: *what* do you think is wrong with the *wife*?

She couldn't stand it. According to the paper, Jack had driven the car around the racetrack at 157 m.p.h. They should have crashed and burned. It annoyed her that Jack seemed invincible. It sickened her that his stupid Paris hotel had been a runaway success, *the* place to stay, with a three-year waiting list for rooms. She'd sent her hairstylist to check it out; Patrice reported that it appeared to be built 'from Liberace's dog-ends'.

How dare Jack throw a party to celebrate his resurrection? She couldn't believe that Tom Cruise would actually belittle himself to attend. Jack was a *criminal*. She'd skimmed through the famous names breathlessly listed by supposedly serious newspapers. Hollywood's new golden boy, Ethan Summers, an exceptional actor and easy on the eye; and the up-and-coming Mollie Tomkinson, gorgeous creature, enormous talent, lit up the screen – bitch. Why did these bright new stars want to associate themselves with *Jack*? She clenched her jaw – her smooth, tight (but not obviously tight) jaw. Innocence did not subscribe to the LA fad of signature surgery, where people could ogle your tits and exclaim, 'Oh, you went to Dr Octopus, I *adore* his work!'

She threw down the paper and tore off her white kidskin gloves.

She was aware that Jamie, her PA, had replaced the front page of the paper with *yesterday's* front page, because of today's *other* headline: 'LLOYD'S CHEAT AND WIFE SPLIT: *It's his-and-hers homes for disgraced tycoon Jack Kent and wife*'.

Wife! Wife! Was that all she was? How *dare* they?

Jamie removed her gloves and offered her a plate of skinned grapes. 'Sugar,' she snapped, and waved them away. Age would not thicken her.

How dare Jack not invite her to the bash of the millennium?

Innocence would attend regardless, the vengeful godmother, and she would curse the occasion and turn his celebrations to ash. If he were dead (the thought kept reoccurring), she stood to inherit everything. He might have a mistress, but she was the wife. There were now five Hôtels Belle Époque and Jack was raking in the profits. According to one gossip page, he and the tart had fucked on a bed strewn with thousands of fifty-pound notes. It enraged her that he was using her trick: that big pussy was a sap for rose petals!

How she would love to take on his quirky hotels and sell them to Travelodge.

Patrice fussed around her pink bouffant. Innocence found the minimalism of the nineties joyless and had stuck to her favourite decade, the eighties. For her, big pink hair would always be in. God knows what she'd do if anything happened to Patrice. She hadn't washed or dried her own hair for six years. If her husband or her hairdresser had to die – hell, there was no contest! It would be an honour killing. She wouldn't kill Jack for the money. The money would be a reassuring extra, but she didn't *need* the money.

If she killed Jack, she would do it for fun.

PARIS, 13 OCTOBER 1998

Jack

He was on a high. He was *winning*. He was back on top.

Innocence had been a big mistake, and she had made him pay. But maybe he would have paid anyway. Bad luck had attached itself to him like a cancer, until he felt as if it was part of him and he would never escape. For a while, he hadn't been able to shift the sense that there was a dark force out there, wishing him ill. Even now, he had four

101

bodyguards, ex-special forces. Maria teased him about it, but paranoia was part of his condition.

The threat felt real. And it wasn't as crass as someone trying to kill him. He was well protected. It was more of a malign presence, barely visible at the periphery of his life, which, just now and then, bared its teeth and triggered disaster. It was his imagination, of course. His conscience, even. Because he could only pinpoint *one* event that could have been brought about by an enemy, and that was Claudia falling in love with a stranger who turned out to be her birth father. Some sick bastard, he'd swear to it, had pushed those two together.

Thank God for Maria, watching over her daughter from afar. Disaster had been averted. Claudia had ended the relationship. He had no idea why, or if she knew the truth. The main thing was, she had done it. Now she could start over. These young girls: they bounced back. He couldn't think about her pain – it was easier to ignore it. The truth was, he couldn't stand the fact of a child of his in such desperate agony, so he blocked it out. Nor could he face the guilt of having betrayed his first wife Felicia by failing to protect her adored adopted daughter. As a parent, you always failed because whatever you did, your children's lives would never be perfect. Of course they wouldn't, but, as a parent, there was something crazy within you that couldn't accept this.

Meanwhile, Emily – beautiful, talented Emily – had messed up her own life without help. It was one of the greatest disappointments of his existence. As a child she had shown such amazing promise. He remembered reading *Cinderella* to her, aged four, and she had crossly corrected him when he skipped a few words. He'd omitted 'trimmed with gold braid' just to speed things up, and had discovered that his tiny girl could memorize a book after hearing it once. She was so clever. And she had thrown it all away. It was too painful to contemplate. Still, at least Emily had Innocence for a mother. She was genetically equipped to survive anything.

It was, he supposed, a good sign that she was already giving lavish interviews to *Hello!* in Tim's luxury apartment in Ecclestone Square and redecorating it. A Damien Hirst painting (if you could call it that) hung on the yellow-striped nursery wall between a charcoal of Tim's mother by his grandmother and a Suffolk landscape by his father. 'We don't know if it's a boy or a girl,' Emily had simpered to the hack. 'But we don't mind, as long as it's healthy.' They'd held a brash wedding party, paid for by the magazine, attended by a few bedraggled members of the smart set, a clutch of soap stars and various of Emily's drug buddies. Jack had declined the invitation – he was too hurt – anyway, it had clashed with a polo match.

He sighed. She was her mother's daughter. No doubt there would be a tenth interview after the baby was born. It was the only way he would get to see his grandchild. The rift was deep, bitter, permanent: the kind that could only be healed by cash. The boy, Tim, had plainly fallen apart after being disinherited. He was neat in a blazer for the photos, but his face had the look of a glazed doughnut. Prozac or Lithium? Jack wondered. According to *Hello!* Tim had taken his place at Magdalene, Cambridge, this month as planned.

Emily was to take 'time off' from nothing to be 'a mother'. She looked strained. Jack would wait until she was desperate, then sweep to her rescue like Richard Gere in that charming film about the prostitute: gratitude would make his daughter love him again. She would need money, if the husband wasn't working. It made Jack shiver, to think that Emily still craved social position – the same desire that had ruined him. She refused to accept that those ghastly people would always judge her unfit to be a Fortelyne, even if she'd kept her legs shut until the ring was on her finger; she was not and would never be one of *them*. That castle would never be hers: the Earl would commit murder before he allowed it.

Jack ran a hand through his hair and puffed on his cigar. He cared more than he wished about his children, but, Christ, they made it hard. Tough love was the best option – his opinion wouldn't change. What didn't kill you made you stronger . . . perhaps.

He wondered if the kids would show tonight. He prayed they would, even if Emily turned up for the goody bag and Claudia for a mope. He didn't care, he just wanted to see his girls. And he had promised Maria that tonight would be the night she would meet her blood daughter for the first time. He'd doubled his meds to crush the anxiety. What if Claudia freaked out? What if Maria couldn't cope? Every time the subject of Claudia came up, Maria turned into a twittering wreck. At least he had persuaded Maria – well, *begged* her – that the introduction should wait until much later. His excuse was Claudia would be more relaxed, but the simple reason was, he was scared and wanted to delay the reunion as long as possible.

Meanwhile, it was inevitable that Innocence would turn up and make a scene. Still, publicity was publicity. And a photo of her being escorted out by security – preferably with a flash of nipple or red knicker – would sell to every trashy magazine in the western world.

Innocence had used him as her own personal piggy bank. She had risen to glory on the back of his failure. If he didn't hate her so much, he'd have admired her cheek. The only thing that made the situation bearable was that he held the trump card and, one day, she would discover this and realize that he, Jack, had had the last laugh. They still fucked, occasionally. And when they did, he always thought, *This fuck was brought to you by the knowledge that you are the loser*. In other words, he was sticking it to her. To most people, sex was an indication of love, liking or, at least, appreciation. To Jack and Innocence, it was an expression of mutual loathing.

He adjusted his bow-tie and checked his watch. The swarms of paparazzi were crowding the pavement either side of the red carpet outside the hotel and the showbiz reporters were already doing their pieces to camera.

Helicopters buzzed overhead. There must be at least six hundred TV and press out there. His head of press had reserved prime spots on the pavement for the channels or programmes with most sway: AP, MTV, *Entertainment Tonight* and *Access Hollywood* got the front row, right up against the barricades. The police had blocked off the road, but it was *his* security maintaining order – the gendarmerie couldn't care less. He was going to greet his guests inside the front door: he was an egotist but he wasn't an idiot. They wanted the established names: Tom Cruise, Brad Pitt; they wanted the new kids on the block: Ethan Summers, Mollie Tomkinson; they wanted the superstars next door: Will Smith, Sandra Bullock, Matt Damon. Jack knew better now. He would be the perfect host and allow his guests to shine; he would let the glamour happen.

Prince was playing live: he was the one guarantee of a good party. Elton John was a pal – and he couldn't resist a decent piano. The food was fusion; it was incredible how much these celebrities *ate*. There were always bleats of 'Atkins' and 'the Zone' but you couldn't skimp on the food or the A-list left and next day at least one of them would turn up in *The Sun* inhaling a McDonald's.

The booze was courtesy of Krug, and Maria, ravishing in a turquoise silk Missoni dress and Givenchy scent, was draped in three million pounds' worth of De Beers yellow diamonds. They had also lent a bodyguard, which he'd teased *her* about; he didn't know whether to be pleased to be OKed by De Beers or pissed off she wasn't wearing the diamonds he'd bought her. On reflection, he was pissed off. He didn't need to be sponsored by a shop, but it was hardly meant as an insult so he supposed he'd let it go. His suit was Jermyn Street and his shoes were Hermès. He felt strong, powerful, and he looked even better. Rugged was the word. He was fitter than he'd ever been, with a personal trainer and a nutritionist, as well as a chef.

Jack intended to live for a long, long time, if not for ever.

'Darling, are you coming down?' Maria's gentle voice broke into his thoughts. 'There's a massive traffic jam of priceless cars full of famous people. You need to be downstairs to meet and greet. It's going to be amazing. The place looks just gorgeous, and there's a good feeling about it. The chocolate sculptures of Marilyn Monroe and Steve McQueen are *incredible*. And the cigarette girls are so sweet in their outfits. I wonder if everyone is going to end up in the pool, or if they'll be too precious about their hair. I should be used to them all by now, but I still get a little starstruck. Not with *new* Hollywood, but with, oh, Kirk Douglas, and Tony Curtis. Old Hollywood are the perfect party guests, they have such good manners and they'll never turn up to a black-tie event in jeans. Oh God, I'm a mess, can't you tell?'

He stroked her face. 'Angel, you're nervous, but not about the actors and singers and models and rock stars. You chat to them about their problems day in day out; you give them advice; you keep their secrets. *They* look up to *you*. You are half the reason they stay here, I'm certain. You, my darling, are nervous because later tonight I am going to introduce you to someone who I know will fall in love with you, just as I have, and will become a very special part of your life.' That was about right, wasn't it? The sort of thing women liked to hear?

Her eyes glistened with tears.

Wrong, wrong, totally wrong!

'You are the sweetest man. Thank you.'

Utter confusion.

She paused, wiped the corner of her eye. 'I can't wait. But I will. I think you're right. By midnight the guests will be taking care of themselves and I won't be so vital. No one will notice if you and I and Claudia slip out of the room.' She smiled up at him. 'Oh my *God*, look at me, I'm shaking all over!'

He smiled back and linked her arm in his. 'Shall we?' he said.

The ballroom was a mass of people, but it looked different to most parties and it took Jack a moment to establish what that difference was. Then he realized: universal beauty. Here was a gathering of human beings who enjoyed the greatest success and wealth that life had to offer, many of them touched with some talent, a few blessed with great talent, but almost without exception they were gorgeous: fair of face, tight of buttock and all the bits in between, and in honour of *his* celebration, they'd had their people plucking and buffing and primping and perfecting until they looked exquisite. Priceless. He was proud. He didn't care what the press wrote or said. He was *back*, he was *triumphant*. He was in with the in crowd.

Jack took a deep breath and launched into the throng. It was loud with laughter and the deep clink of Italian lead crystal. Business cards were already being exchanged, all the Who Knew Who, and What Do You Do. He squeezed Maria's hand as they parted – unless he took her prisoner in their suite, she was never off duty at the Belle Époque – and now she would be checking on the waiting staff, keeping an eye on the fussier guests (i.e. all of them), ensuring that no need went unsatisfied, tracking those who were sworn enemies (who had been fired by whom, whose wife had slept with whom): the evening was an assault course in diplomacy.

'Tom.' He smiled. 'How *are* you? So sorry Nicole couldn't . . . And the kids? Thank you so much for the . . . I haven't yet had a chance to . . . Looks very interesting . . .

'Madonna, sensational – white rhinestone? . . . I must get one for myself! I haven't seen you since . . . ? Congratulations, she must be . . . ? Lovely age! Well . . . how kind. I'm sure Emily would love to, once the baby is born.

'Mollie, congratulations on all your success, so thoroughly deserved . . . I admire your choices . . . and so courageous, lesser mortals would have worn a fat suit . . . And now, so tiny. Your metabolism, of course . . . But please, eat, *eat*!'

He was polished, suave, and not *too* pleased with himself –

at least, not that he let it show. He was as good an actor as any of them. Madonna especially. Ah, there was Emily, looking fit to burst, feeling Bruce Willis's bicep. Bruce didn't look too troubled. And right in front of her husband – *he* didn't look too troubled either. Ah, the wonder of meds. And Claudia, she looked rough as hell. Plainly, the revelations had shattered her. He swallowed and turned away. Maria was far across the other side of the ballroom, no doubt scanning the crowd every second for her long-lost daughter, but this wretched creature was hardly recognizable as a person. And yet, even with his feeble grasp of the workings of human emotion, Jack knew that when Maria's gaze did fall on her girl, she would see the most beautiful woman in the world.

He hoped the introduction to Maria would be a *happy* shock for Claudia. Jack wasn't the greatest father, but he could put the offer of a good mother on the table. It was the best he could do. He couldn't afford to grieve with her. Instead he would give Claudia the tools to cut short her pity party and move on.

There was a murmur, and he turned to see Innocence poised at the door. She was witchy in a bright red flamenco-style dress, which somehow complemented her pink hair. Rubies glittered at her throat and disappeared into her bulging cleavage. She was smoking, as usual, from a long black cigarette-holder – for a second he imagined it as a wand – and her heavily kohled eyes were slits. Her venomous gaze fell on Maria. Then, chin jutted in defiance, she turned towards him.

Anxiety rose in his chest. Her eyes widened, her eyebrows arched and he was treated to a provocative pout. She tossed her hair and strode fast across the dance floor towards him. He noticed – and another time it might have made him smile – De Niro step hastily out of her way. There was a hush. For a crazy second, he imagined she had a gun on her and, despising himself, glanced around for his detail.

They were on her in seconds. So discreet, and his guests

would have imagined, had they managed to wrench their attention from themselves, that this stunning creature was simply arm in arm with a couple of solicitous friends, keeping her warm as she swept outside to retrieve her mobile from the limousine, and, perhaps, list the origins of her shoes, dress and bag to *People* magazine. *Did* she have a gun? Had he forgotten his meds? Of course not and it didn't matter: the point was, while she still considered herself his wife, their relationship was long dead and he did not want her poison and spite to destroy his glorious evening.

He saw Maria place a friendly hand on Robert Downey, Jr's arm; she felt Jack's gaze and looked at him and smiled. And then her smile was frozen in time, as an ear-ripping bang filled the room with blinding fire and he felt himself hurled into the air with an almighty force. He gasped as a flying object hit him hard in the face – the bloody stump of an arm, a delicate diamond bracelet encircling the still-warm wrist. He stumbled on broken glass, smoke filled his nostrils and his mouth was dry with dust. The room fell into darkness; there was a deep rumble, a terrible crack and great chunks of cement rained down, a deadly hail. And then, in the crackling heat, he lost consciousness, and the screams of terror and pain of the great and the good and the beautiful subsided into black.

BOOK TWO

SUFFOLK, ENGLAND, 1969

Jack

'You posh git, Cannadine,' said Jack. 'This house is the size of Sweden.'

Harry laughed. God, his teeth were white. Jack decided he would only smile if the rooms were dimly lit. This place was built to make you feel small. Everything – the black and gold wrought-iron gates, the primly manicured gardens, the blue turrets and the yellow stone walls – boasted centuries of self-importance and snootiness.

An ancient bloke in a black suit was standing at the foot of the stone steps that led to the wide arched front door. The man nodded, humble, as the white Aston Martin screeched to a halt an inch from his polished shoes. Jack was embarrassed. An *old* man, bowing to him and Harry. He wanted to fetch the bloke his slippers and park him in front of the telly with a paper and a pipe.

'The old girl's a bit of a dragon,' said Harry in a loud, cheerful voice. He winked at Jack. 'You'll have to mind your p's and q's. But the totty will make up for it. You'll see.'

He glanced at Jack's suitcase. 'I'd leave that for the house steward, old chap,' he said.

Jack dropped it like a hot coal. He was sweating in his suit. His tie was too thin, too mod. Harry was wearing his tweed blazer the colour of puke. It had holes in one sleeve and the cuff was frayed – how come *that* wasn't a social blunder?

'Auntie!' boomed Harry as an elderly woman strode towards them. Christ, this must be Lady Templeton: the Ice Queen in a crazy hairdo, mad make-up and a knitted suit. The woman looked as if she was living in the *1860s*. He went briefly deaf with fright as Harry introduced them. She welcomed him graciously: all the right words, not one ounce of emotion. He admired it.

The old guy showed them to their rooms – the Bachelor Wing. Yeah, not for long!

Jack assumed his poker face. The huge painting of the general looked familiar. Fuck, that was a *Gainsborough*!

'Dinner is served at eight sharp, in the Red Dining Room. Drinks will be served in the Blue Room at seven fifteen. Please ring the bell if you need further assistance.'

Jack felt sick. He must *not* make a fool of himself. This was his big chance – his only chance. He wasn't going to screw up.

They'd been sitting in the meeting room at work. Jack was staring at a monstrous oil painting of a flotilla of ships, all grey, battling their way through a storm – the sky was also grey with a tinge of yellow. This was some pompous old fart's idea of optimism. He'd stick a Lichtenstein up there. *Wham!* That one with the fighter jet exploding: modern, dynamic, cool.

It's the end of the Season, Harry had said, interrupting his thoughts.

Jack had stopped himself from joking, 'What, autumn?'

Harry's aunt, Lady Templeton, was giving a dinner party for her younger daughter, and needed a few extra boys. It would be a hoot. 'Bit of a change for *you*, hanging round Carnaby Street with your dolly birds, then off to a Which concert.'

'The Who, you prat,' Jack had said, laughing. He'd been to a Who concert once, and Pete Townshend had smashed his guitar into an amp at the end of the show. He, Jack, was all for senseless violence, but it left him feeling *weird*. Maybe he just didn't like . . . waste. 'Go on,' he'd said to Harry.

This would be black tie. The daughter had a face like a gargoyle, but some of the other debs might be tasty.

'Sure she won't mind you showing up with a Yid?' asked Jack.

'Our family has many friends who are Jewish,' Harry had replied stiffly.

Jack shrugged, saying, 'Why not?' but actually, he was made up.

He didn't fancy any of the girls his mother introduced him to – all so boring, so familiar, like shagging your sister. Jack had plans. He only had a junior job at the broker's, but it was still the City. And considering that, unlike his colleagues, he'd gone to a grammar school, was terrified of rugger and didn't have a client list padded with ex-classmates, he'd done bloody well. Thank Christ for his key to society: the Hon. Harry Cannadine, that big friendly Labrador of a man on the next desk.

Harry was right, the cousin's face was not her fortune; her fortune was her fortune. She looked a state: white gloves; dress like a toilet-roll doll, shiny white material all gussied up with gold lace. She wore diamonds everywhere you could stick a diamond – there was one up her bum, if her posture was anything to go by. She spoke softly but clearly, sitting a chaste distance from him on the overstuffed sofa, kindly enquiring about bugger-all. But, of course, old Bat Features didn't want her daughter wasting time on a social zero like him, and whipped her away after eight minutes.

Two of the men strolled up and introduced themselves. They were both larger than him – superior stock, raised on hearty cooked meals and bracing exercise over hill and dale. They chatted smoothly around the confines of their patch: the markets, the racing, current mode of transport. Jack smiled to himself, because it wasn't any different, really, to his Uncle Ted from the East End, making small talk in the pub, asking the next bloke over his pint of bitter, 'What you driving?'

Jack had all but convinced himself that, posh as nuts or salt of the earth, they were all the same at heart, when one of the men – Charles, Tom, Dick, one of those jolly, dependable names – said, 'I walked from the station rather than pay for a cab, I'm such a Jew.'

Jack choked on his vodka. His face was red, as if it was *his* shame. As if, by being an actual Jew, *he'd* made the blunder!

The etiquette was probably to ignore it – not make the prick feel bad about being a prick. He would say nothing. He would rise above it.

'I'm Jewish,' he said.

'A turn of phrase, old chap,' replied one of the Titans, showing his back like a wall. 'Keep your hair on.'

They laughed, and he felt small, inferior, the sad little outsider turned away at the door. *You wait*, he thought. I'm as good as you. I'm *better*.

Then a great gong clanged, like at the start of a Carry On film, and he found himself walking into dinner next to a horse-faced girl in a shawl. He was still too hurt, too angry to speak, but he managed a tight smile. The room was vast and ornate. The table was crowded with silver cutlery, crystal glasses, pink roses and a porcelain sheikh holding a china seashell – for what? Fag butts?

The rest of the country was sitting in front of *The Avengers* with a plate of Birds Eye beef burgers on its lap.

Then he saw her and his anger melted.

She was a goddess. She had big dark eyes with long black lashes, a babyish roundness to her cheeks, and a red, pouty mouth – my God – and long blond hair, all wild corkscrew curls.

She was sitting next to him. He pulled out her chair. He couldn't stop staring.

She had on a fuck-off necklace and was wearing some

dress . . . *tits*. He couldn't stand the vogue for skinny birds; it was like getting it on with an ironing board. *Shit*. Not here! He sat down, grabbed his napkin and covered his lap.

'Thank you, sir,' said the goddess. 'You are too kind! I'm Miss Felicia Love. I'm delighted to make your acquaintance.'

An American! Of course. She had an open look. The English women were all so *covert*.

'Jack Kent. Pleased to meet you.'

'Mr Kent, I can tell.' She darted a glance at the napkin and sucked her lower lip. *She* knew what she was doing. He thought young ladies were different. He was shocked!

He couldn't swallow, which was a shame because it was the best food he'd never eaten: clear soup and crayfish, veal and beef. He'd planned to copy Cannadine's every move so as not to embarrass himself, but it was impossible to tear his gaze from her face.

'Are you . . . are you . . . ?' *God*, what was wrong with him? He couldn't speak!

'Am I somebody?' she said. She was teasing him. Everything she said, in that slow drawl, sounded suggestive.

'No! No – of course not. I mean, are you a friend of the family?'

She was from Minnesota. Her father worked in iron mines. She scrubbed up well for a miner's daughter. He had to laugh. He'd come here, hoping to land a posh bird, preferably titled, who would be a social asset, in life and in business, who would sneak him into the Establishment through the back door.

And, after three courses, he was in love – he was, flash of lightning, the whole deal – with a miner's daughter from Hicksville USA.

The butler (hatchet-face, never seen sunlight) stopped by Jack's seat with a tray. He supposed he had to take the plate – some pointless lace mat on it – the glass bowl, and the little knife and fork, to eat a bloody *apple*!

He took the lot and turned back to Felicia. She'd never

heard of the Rolling Stones! Suddenly aware of a tension, he glanced up and saw the whole table staring at him while pretending to sip their vintage booze. The Old Bat looked furious; as if she might flap across the table and bite his neck. He was cutting up his apple, so what? He glanced at Harry.

Harry was murmuring lies to a girl with knockers the size of barrage balloons. He was also cutting up his apple, but *Cannadine*, the big poof, had taken his lace mat off his plate and arranged it neatly under the glass bowl.

Jack was cutting up his apple *on* the lace mat!

He felt his face flush purple. He wanted to shrivel up.

Felicia Love locked eyes with the Old Bat. Deliberately, she grasped her apple and sliced it ferociously down the middle on the lace mat.

There was a pause. And then, slowly, the man on Felicia's left took *his* apple and, with a flourish, cut it open on the lace mat. And so it went on, around that stiffly starched table: a glorious ripple effect of rebellion, a sweet apple-slicing show of solidarity. Finally, as Jack suppressed a grin, Lady Templeton sliced *her* apple directly – if violently – on to the lace mat.

He didn't flatter himself. This surprising display of class was nothing to do with him: it was in honour of the gentle goddess from Minnesota. He resented the Titans no less. But he loved Felicia more.

'Felicia's a doll,' said Cannadine on the drive home the next day.

Harry was in a great mood because he'd fucked the girl with the massive knockers (daughter of some earl who owned half of Wales). But he knew how to eat an apple, so presumably, when the Old Bat found semen stains all over her seventeenth-century Persian textile bedcover in the Academic Room, the obvious culprit would be excused.

'But I wouldn't pursue it. Her old man's worth about fifty mill – inherited a bunch of iron mines from *his* old man.

Bloody Yanks. Never do things by halves. And they're Lutheran. I should imagine that, after yesterday evening's display, dear Papa will have received an urgent call from Auntie, and darling Felicia will have been booked home on the next flight. You blew it, Kent.' He grinned. 'You got to get in there fast – wham, bam, thank you!'

Jack lit a Stuyvesant. An *heiress*.

It couldn't hurt.

Actually it could. He didn't want her loot. He was well able to make his own. But her parents would think otherwise.

'I *will* pursue it,' he said, quietly.

Cannadine shook his head. 'She's from a different world,' he said. 'It'll never work.'

MINNESOTA, USA, 1969

Felicia

'Daddy, Mommy. This is my husband, Jack Kent.'

Her voice was a hoarse squeak. But there was pride, too. He was dreamy – and all hers. She adored everything about him: his accent, his laugh, his angular cheekbones, his beautiful body; even – oh, *especially* – she loved doing it with him, just thinking about it made her go all juicy.

She bit back a giggle. Terror always made her want to burst out laughing. Could you *imagine* if Mommy and Daddy had seen her just an hour before? They had been driving through a paradise of smooth lakes, pinewoods and prairie; everywhere was the blue open sky. Jack had swerved the hire car off the road, making her squeal. He'd pulled her into the meadow, and flung her down amid the yellow and purple wildflowers, and pushed his face into ... oh my! She'd squirmed, gasped, covered her eyes, protested, but he wouldn't stop! She didn't *want* him to . . . The sun's heat on her bare skin, the sweet scent of lush grasses, the delicious agony of his tongue, until she could hardly bear it . . . and then, another *world* of gorgeous sensation. She'd screamed with the intensity of the pleasure, her head flung back, her hands gripping his, and then, as the shudders subsided, she saw a fat bumblebee in a pink hollyhock, and she'd burst into tears of joy. Then, *then*, he'd kissed her mouth, and she could taste herself, and instead of feeling repulsed, she felt a growing squirl of desire in her belly, and she'd wrapped her long legs around him, and felt his . . . his *dick* (she still couldn't say that word aloud, she could barely think it!) grow big and hard, and, well, it was a good while before they'd gotten back on the road.

She couldn't look Mommy in the eye. She'd picked every speck of dirt out of her hair, brushed it, reapplied her pale pink lipstick, spritzed herself with Chanel No. 5, but she felt sex ooze brazen from her every pore.

Oh, she and Jack would be fine, she knew it. Sure, eloping with a Jew was a little more *challenging* than demanding a pink princess phone for her birthday *not* that stupid American flag brooch from Tiffany & Co., but once Daddy got to *know* Jack, he'd be sold. Ma and Pa distrusted what they didn't know, and they'd never met anyone of (as Daddy put it) '*his* persuasion'.

It didn't help that he was poor. Oh, but *everyone* was poor compared to them! Who else grew up in a dreary Gothic mansion surrounded by sculpted gardens, serene lakes and lily ponds, a golf course, a horse track, and acres of farmland? And she knew what her parents thought about Jews and money. But Daddy wouldn't say anything *too* offensive. If they could sit down and have one meal together – Jack would probably have to mouth grace – they'd see what a wonderful, kind, generous person he was.

Mommy sipped at her water with ice, and turned her face to the wall. But she was wearing her best dress, a blue Anne

Fogarty number, so there was hope. Poor Mommy. She'd lived such a buttoned-up life: she had all that money and no *fun*. All day, she patted her crisp hair and snapped at the housemaids and sip-sip-sipped at her glass of water. And she disapproved – oh, of *everything*.

She didn't cook, she didn't keep house, she wasn't involved in her own life, she just oversaw it. When she met Daddy she'd been a member of Ladies' Aid; she'd served him home-made cherry pie after his grandpa's funeral. She was a simple country girl then, in a hoop skirt. Being surrounded by priceless, pointless possessions had confused her; she could no longer see beauty in the sun rising in mist behind the mountains. Felicia couldn't give a damn that Jack wasn't rich – money was not a novelty for her, nor was it a goal. Daddy would see it her way. He was a cool dude, when off the leash – Mommy still didn't know that he let her gallop his horse and shoot his gun. She could hit a stag in the heart; she was an ace shot. Daddy called her his little tomboy. Oh, but she wasn't any more. Now she was *chic*.

She had a new monochrome wardrobe: a Courrèges short white coat and knee-length white vinyl boots, a silver mac from Fenwick's (ordered in from Paris), a white crochet dress from Biba, pale frosty lipstick, black suede Yves Saint Laurent thigh-high boots, fifteen Chanel suits, black Mr Freedom velvets with yellow stitching; all divine, all safely stashed at her *London address* – ooh, she couldn't wait to get back and shop! Mummy thought sixties fashion was for tarts. She thought showing your ankle was vulgar.

'Good morning, sir, madam, how do you do?' said Jack.

Felicia swallowed. He sounded so *British*, which was good, but . . . *alien*. He was a big man and even though the drawing room was vast, he looked as if he might suddenly crash sideways into the grand piano. She could tell his confidence set Daddy on edge. Daddy was going to shout. She'd suggested that Jack wear his wedding suit, it had looked so gorgeous in Scotland, but here, in the fierce heat, it looked silly. *She* was

121

wearing a Givenchy suit, like Elizabeth Taylor in *The VIPs*. She wanted to look respectable.

'How dare you,' said Daddy. 'How *dare* you stand here in my house and ask me that. How do you *think* I do?' He spoke in a quiet voice that made her wish he *would* shout. 'I am grieving the loss of my youngest daughter to you – a thief. You have no respect. You don't love Felicia or you would not have subjected her to such a public disgrace.'

'It's all this rock-and-roll music!' blurted Mommy. 'Elvis! It's disgusting, disgusting!' *Disgusting*, she muttered again, into her water. Her hand shook.

Felicia squirmed. Elvis was the *fifties*, Mommy. And she knew why he was 'disgusting' – because he reeked of *sex*. Mommy couldn't bear the idea of people doing it. But they had to vent their anger and disappointment. It was like turning on a rusty tap – you had to wait till the water ran clear. Her parents would have loved to have made a grand wedding as they had for her elder sisters, Camellia and Grace. *She* would have loved a grand wedding – she'd imagined the whole scene: a white velvet dress and a silk fan; sunlight filtering through a canopy in the apple orchard; her mother's jewels, the pink diamond and the tiara with emeralds the size of sparrow eggs – it had once belonged to a tsarina. Mommy kept it in a safe; she never looked at it.

'There is no disgrace, sir, in a woman being married to a man who loves her. I intend to look after Felicia for the rest of my life.' Jack stood with his chin jutted out. She loved his courage, but wished he would look a bit sorrier.

'More likely, sir, that you intend *Felicia* to look after *you* for the rest of *your* life.'

Oh my. 'Daddy, I—'

'Be quiet!' roared Daddy, making her jump. He glared around the room and his gaze fixed on Mommy. 'I think you've had enough water, Elaine.'

Mommy placed her glass on the side table a little too hard. *Crack!*

Daddy took a step towards Jack. 'I'm going to tell you something, young man, and you listen good. My girl was raised in a decent, God-fearing household. We've always been humble in the face of what God gave us. But *you*, sir, are bold and greedy. You lack courtesy. And courtesy is a superficial term for actions that have a crucial role in building the character of a decent human being.'

Felicia hardly dared look at Jack. Surely Daddy had let off enough steam. He'd start to calm down now. Should she suggest a tour around the estate? Daddy could show off his land, she and Mommy could sit in the drawing room and make conversation about . . . something. Perhaps a friend had died?

Daddy stubbed out his cigar in a silver ashtray. 'I am seeing my lawyer tomorrow, as I intend to disinherit Felicia. If I drop dead next week, my daughter will not receive a penny. What do you say to *that*?'

Jack smiled and lit one of his own cigarettes – without asking permission from Mommy. She couldn't believe it. He was so *cool*. But maybe a *little* deference would be wise, help smooth the path to reconciliation?

'I'm delighted, Mr Love,' replied Jack. 'This means there can be no rumours about me living off my wife. This way, everyone will know that I married for love, and love alone, if you'll excuse the pun. Goodbye. This will be the last time we meet. Let's go, Felicia. We need to make our flight.'

Mommy stared, taking a great slug of water – most unmannerly. Daddy blinked as if he'd misheard.

Felicia stood up, uncertain. She didn't care about the money, really she didn't, but it was so hurtful. She felt betrayed. She wanted to blurt: *What, will I never see you again?* She felt a crazy urge to run up to her room, fling herself on her soft pink bed and cry.

'Bye bye, Mommy. Bye bye, Daddy.' She didn't look back. She led her husband out of the room, and away.

EAST LONDON, 1969

Sharon

Fifteen-year-old Sharon Marshall walked into school and shut herself in the toilet. She felt sick with dread, and the stink of the toilets made her feel sicker. The cubicle door wouldn't close; she pulled her cardigan sleeve over her fist to slide the lock but it was broken. The pan was full of watery shit, and she retched. She kicked down the lid, tore off a sheet of shiny toilet paper, held it carefully so that her fingers did not make contact with the chain, and pulled.

Then she stood in the tiny cubicle, trying not to breathe the dense fetid air, or tread in any wet patches, reading the graffiti without wanting to: *Paul, I wanna suck your coke.* This was a top education establishment, so it was. What next? She had no choice. She was going to have to stay in the stall, with disgusting germs crawling over her, *all bloody day.* She hadn't thought about tomorrow. God, if only she hadn't spent *two months'* wages from the market on a haircut. Oh, but it was very black, very Mary, *very* worth it.

She carefully removed her make-up mirror from her knickers. It was a shard of glass she'd found in the street. Also out of the magic knickers came a small pot of rouge – nicely warm, ha ha! She used her fingertips to create a healthy blush because, Christ knew, it wasn't going to happen naturally.

There was a sudden barrage of noise.

'Marshall? Marrrrr-shall! We know you're *in* here!'

Bang! Bang! Bang! Sally was kicking open the door of each stall like a nutter.

Sharon slowly walked out of the cubicle, and stood, arms by her sides, as if she didn't give a toss. Standing with your arms crossed was more of a fuck-off, but not useful if you needed to deck someone.

'Yeah, I'm in here. I'm doing my fucking hair, so what?'

Sally's pale freckled face – she had a flat nose with flared nostrils like a farm animal – lit up with a leering triumph. She didn't even drop her gaze, she screeched, straight away, '*Love the shoes!*'

Her mates – Patsy Gapper, long, lank, orange hair, very sharp teeth; and Kerry Nelson, walked like a gorilla, *thunk, thunk,* mean left hook – cackled.

Sharon's body went *whoosh* in a rush of hatred. Not for Patsy, or Kerry, or even Sally. But for her parents: her mother, so pathetically meek; her disgusting father, always between jobs. An image of her mother, washing the jelly off a lump of canned ham, flashed in her mind. Sharon shuddered. That was her *life*. It was them she hated, for thinking that black ugly shapeless shoes with holes in them that had already been worn by a dead woman would do. She knew Patsy had seen her creeping out of the drab little store, its shameful sign pinned over the door: 'Homes Cleared'.

Her parents didn't care that there was punishment for being a pov, she thought as she went limp and held her breath while they forced her head deep into the toilet pan – 'Wait up, let's do a good thick piss in it first!' – roughly, so she hit the porcelain, gasped in pain, swallowed a load of toilet water and Sally's *urine*.

Sharon's mother knew her place and she'd raised her children to know theirs. Sharon's sister was doing time for attempted blackmail; her brother Gerry had hired a van to steal furniture from the Ideal Home Show. It didn't occur to them that they might *earn* money, because Mum had passed down her inferiority complex like a gypsy curse and her kids didn't know they were capable. *Other* people got rich.

Sharon disagreed.

She washed her hair in the tiny sink, using the grey soap as shampoo; she scraped the filth off it first. She styled it, carefully, calmly, in her broken mirror. Then she marched into the classroom, banging the door on its hinges, flung herself into a chair and swung her feet, encased in those vile second-hand shoes, on to the wooden desk. Miss Eliot went off like a firework, but Sharon was deaf to it.

She was going to get rich, and then she was going to buy a really expensive pair of top designer shoes for every fucking day of the year – *and* she wasn't risking prison to do it. She was a good-looking girl. She had other options.

LONDON, 1974

Felicia

'For your pleasure . . .' As Bryan Ferry sang the words, he seemed to look straight at her. Felicia giggled and pouted a little. God, he was gorgeous, even with silver eyeshadow and the tight spangled siren suit, and she was really in the mood. She smoothed her hands down her Yves Saint Laurent rainbow evening dress; it clung in all the right places; *one* advantage of her situation. She wasn't certain about the hair, the glitter was more her style than the afro, but she just wanted to scream with the fun of it all, and dance; she wanted to dance and dance until the rising sun kissed the stern London skyline a warm shade of orange.

Pity about old Grizzle Pants over there, perched stiffly on the red leather banquette like a cross parrot, the flirty pink cocktail she'd bought for him untouched. He did look so sweet though, in his terribly proper English suit – Douglas Hayward, crazy British name – and his black polished shoes. He was sulking, and it was so unfair. He could do with one of those cute little pills; *she* only took them for her figure. That would put some shake in his tail! She sipped her champagne, carefully, from the bowl, so as not to smudge her cherry-red lipstick, checked her cleavage (boobs were in again), looked up and saw Bryan Ferry checking it too. He tilted his head;

barely a movement. From nowhere, two burly men lifted her like a doll on to the stage.

She blushed pink as she looked into his dark eyes. Oh hell, he looked wasted, yet there was a raw sexiness about him, and he was holding her hand and singing for *her*, and she knew that every woman in the club – the slinky little actresses, the cool ice blondes, the diplomats' tarts – *all* of them loathed her to death and wanted to beat her to a pulp with their platform shoes!

She laughed and shimmied. There was a wolf-whistle from the back. Bryan Ferry pulled her hand into the air, teasing her close. Her chest bumped his, and he bent to murmur in her ear . . .

'Get *off* me!' roared a voice that cut above the music. 'That's my *wife* up there!'

Shouts of laughter and, once again, she was lifted through the air and plopped on to the ground. Jack – oh Lord, his face was like *flint* – grabbed her wrist and stalked up the basement stairs, yanking her behind him. A few people clapped and laughed. She glanced back at the stage. Bryan Ferry allowed himself a glimmer of a smile, the tiniest shrug, and carried on singing.

'Never humiliate me again, Felicia. You are out of control and I won't have it.'

He was like Daddy, she realized with a pang. He never shouted, but the fury in his voice chilled the life out of you. The buzz left her, like a ghost, and she shivered in the chill of the night air.

'Oh come on, honey, relax a little, why don't you? It was only a bit of fun.' She pulled her silver fox closer across her shoulders and snuggled her arms around his waist.

He shook her off. 'Jesus, Felicia, why don't you listen? You made a complete scene of yourself in that . . . disgusting *pit*. If you must go to a club let's go to a decent place, like Annabel's.'

'Annabel's!' Felicia felt rage rise in her throat. 'We

might as well go to fucking *church*! I want to enjoy myself!'

Jack grabbed her wrists and yanked her to him. 'Yes, darling, and you're enjoying yourself a little too fucking much.'

She tried to shake him off, but he was too strong. She stifled a giggle – if he wasn't so mad, this might be kinky. Then he scowled, and her mood dipped.

'Oh, what do you care,' she snapped, wanting the fight suddenly. 'You're never home, you're always at the office, and if you're not at the office, you're at Harry Cannadine's dumb *gentlemen's* club drinking G 'n' Ts and talking about . . . *horses*! Horses!' she screamed, assuming her iciest British accent. 'Why, pray, when we have not spoken of horses all year!'

'Let me tell you', he hissed, giving her wrists another shake, 'why I work so damn hard. I do it for *us*. Because you do nothing! Harry's wife took a bride's course, off Grosvenor Square. She learned how to cook and to turn a man's cuff! She has a role and she takes it seriously! She devotes every minute of her day to progressing his career. She hosts dinner parties; she is the consummate hostess; she puts him first, *always*!'

'Harry's wife is a stupid fat *sow* who never sees her own children. The Norlander is their mother, *she* just wafts in and wafts out. At tea that time, Alfie drew her a picture of a train and she didn't even *look*, and that little boy was crushed. I *hate* Harry's wife, dumb bitch, she makes me *sick*!' She was shaking.

'Felicia,' said Jack, more gently, and because his voice was kind, she burst into tears. 'Sweetheart, don't cry. It'll be OK.'

'No, it won't,' she howled, sinking on to the cold pavement. He picked her up and cradled her. 'I can't have a ba-aaaa-by! Never! All I want is a baby and I can't have one!'

'What are you *talking* about?'

She pulled away from him, laughing through her tears. 'Jack,' she said. 'Five years of screwing. No protection, no baby. You think that's normal?'

He bit his lip, shaking his head. 'I don't know,' he sighed. 'I wondered . . . I didn't want to upset you.'

'It's my fault,' she said. 'I didn't want to worry *you*. I know it's been crazy. I know it's been stressful, all this oil business, everyone losing money. I'm sorry I haven't taken more of an interest. But, I'm not . . . fertile. I saw Dr Isaacs. I should have said. I guess I was too ashamed. I still am. I feel like a failure. It's to do with this, this stupid heart condition – it runs in my family. It doesn't kill you – well, apart from Uncle Wallace and he wasn't married anyway – it just stops you from repeating the mistake.'

Very carefully, as if she were made of glass, he stood her on the pavement and stroked her hair. 'Oh God, Felicia. You are so precious to me. I'm so sorry, I love you so much. It's *my* fault that you didn't tell me. I've been a bastard, a typical City bore obsessed with work. The last thing you need to worry about is the bloody price of oil. You *will* have your baby. Whatever it takes, you – we – are going to have a baby.'

He kissed her, and she felt her entire body crackle and spark with love and hope.

LONDON, 1978

Claudia

'Tell me the story again, Mummy!' Claudia carefully removed the blackcurrants from her Ski yoghurt and lined them up in a row on the table, for later.

'OK,' said Mummy, smiling. Mummy always smiled. She was the most beautiful lady in the world. She looked like a princess. 'Well, once upon a time, about three and a half years ago, I was walking along the road—'

'Was Daddy at work?'

'Oh! No, Daddy wasn't at work. Daddy was walking along the road too.'

'He didn't have to stay late at the office?'

'No, darling. It was the weekend. Anyway. A nice lady came up to me, and she said, "I have a lovely little baby girl, but I can't look after her. Would *you* look after her instead and be her new mummy and daddy?" And we said, "Oh, yes please!" And then we took you home with us, and we gave you a nice drink of milk, because babies love milk, and we made you all cosy in your cot—'

'And you got Nigel the builder to paint my room pink.'

'Yes, because we love you so much. We love being your mummy and daddy.'

'When Daddy gets home from work, I'm allowed a sweet from the box.'

The Coca-Cola ones were yucky, but if you forgot and took one, Daddy didn't allow you a new sweet. Daddy was stricter than Mummy. He got grumpy because he was tired from work. He had to work to get money to buy sweets.

'Mummy, was the lady a poor lady?'

'What lady, darling?'

'The lady who gave you the baby. Me.'

Mummy's smile went away. 'Oh, I don't think she was poor but she didn't have a daddy for you. And I think she wanted you to live in a nice big house and have lots of toys.'

Bass was her favourite toy. He was a basset hound with big ears. 'We are rich, Mummy, aren't we?'

Mummy's smile came back for a tiny bit. 'We have enough, Claudia. It's more important to have a mummy and daddy who give you hugs than to have lots of money.'

'*Alfie* said we were rich. He said his daddy and my daddy got rich because of the shark.'

'Pardon, Claudia? What did Alfie say?'

'He said our daddies got rich because of the *oy-shark*!'

Alfie was a big boy. He called his mummy 'Nanny' and she wore a brown school uniform. It was cross-making when

130

Mummy didn't understand. It made Claudia want to throw her yoghurt pot across the room.

'The oil shock!' said Mummy, and started laughing. Claudia liked it when Mummy laughed. It made her feel happy. Then Mummy licked a tissue and wiped Claudia's mouth. It made it wet and nasty.

'Yuck, don't *spit* on me, it's disgusting!'

'Sorry, darling.'

'Mummy, why didn't the lady have a daddy for me?'

'Well . . . some ladies don't.'

'Did I grow in *her* tummy?'

'Yes, darling.'

'How did I get there?'

'Ooh, Claudia, guess what! Mummy and Daddy have got a surprise for you!'

'A present?'

'Yes, the best present there is.'

'Is it a Wendy house?'

'No, darling. It's much better than that. Now listen.' Mummy was pulling at her curls – she did that sometimes. She did it when Daddy was cross. 'We thought it would be lovely for you to have a baby brother.'

'I want a sister!'

Mummy got a worried look. 'Well, darling, we thought it would be nice to have a boy, because then he won't want to play with *your* toys.'

'I don't like boys.'

'Ah, but you like babies, don't you? And the Adoption Agency—'

'What's an agency?'

'Oh. I mean the lady who is giving us the boy baby says he is the nicest baby ever. There are no girl babies.'

'Are they sold out?'

'Oh! No, darling. You don't pay money to get a baby.' Mummy's face went pink. 'You can make a . . . donation.'

'What's that?'

'It's money you give to be nice.'

'Does it make sure you get a nice baby not a yucky baby?'

'No babies are yucky, Claudia. All babies are nice.'

'Will you be *his* mummy too?'

'Yes, darling.'

Claudia wanted a hug suddenly. She climbed on Mummy's lap and let Mummy kiss her hair. Mummy always smelled nice, of perfume. Mummy was her best friend in the whole world. She loved Mummy. She didn't love the new baby. Babies stank. Of pooh. There were nine blackcurrants in her yoghurt.

'I don't want the baby. I want him to go back to the lady.'

'Darling. He is *our* baby now. It's true that babies are a little bit boring at first. But when he gets a bit bigger, he will be your friend. And his name is Nathan. Baby Nathan.'

'That's a funny name.'

'Do you think so? It's an unusual name, but I think it's a very nice name.'

'Is Baby Nathan coming to live with us for all the time?'

'Yes, Claudia. He is coming tomorrow, and then we are all going to live happily ever after.'

ITALY, 1978

Jack

Jack squinted into the sunshine and smiled. The doe-eyed waitress bent low as she placed his Rossini cocktail next to his lounger, showing off her cleavage. He wasn't interested, but he appreciated the hospitality.

He sipped the iced blend of puréed strawberries and sparkling wine, and threw the *FT* to one side. The light glittered on the sapphire waters of the lake, and beyond it the snow-tipped mountains veered up to meet the cloudless sky. Some flash git had built a breathtaking holiday home at 40,000 feet. The building resembled a visor; it had a sweeping façade of tinted glass that haughtily surveyed the valley: I am above *all* of this.

It was definitely a man's dream, a place James Bond would be glad to retreat to with a bevy of blondes. Even now, Jack sometimes forgot that *he* could commission a pad like that. He'd been bloody lucky, going long on oil futures and other derivatives when the City was flapping like a goose about what OPEC would do next. But he was mediocre rich. He wanted to be ludicrous rich; private island rich.

He had a lot to achieve.

It was part of the reason they were here. He hadn't told Felicia; she didn't need to know yet. As far as she knew, they were having a glorious holiday in a sleek fashionable hotel to celebrate their anniversary, and other things. Jack had booked the penthouse suite. Every morning, they sat on their balcony in fluffy white dressing gowns, sipping espresso coffee and gazing at the golden sun as it burned through the morning haze. The orange juice, however, was *not* freshly squeezed. It was a detail, but Jack required perfection.

The grounds of the hotel were lush and extensive, maybe a little wild. The flowers that tumbled on to the neat pathways were red, pink, purple; he would have preferred a cleaner colour scheme. All white, perhaps? Red and pink clashed, Felicia would never wear the two shades together; why should they look any better fighting it out in a flowerbed? And the grass was coarse. He preferred fine English lawn grass. He wondered, was that possible over here?

The rooms were large, airy, and the teak four-poster had a delicious spring to it. A hard bed was supposed to be great for your back, but bugger that. Jack liked to sink into a mattress as soft as blancmange. He and Felicia had probably put the bed to its sternest test for a while. The antique mirrored headboard banged against the wall throughout; another time it might have annoyed him, but right now, nothing could annoy Felicia, and that she didn't care turned him on. She smelled of coconut sun oil and the heat of the day.

She'd worn a white floaty dress à la Marilyn, and as they'd taken the private lift upstairs after an exquisite dinner of venison and vintage Barolo, she'd taken his hand and slowly guided it down. He'd gasped – and started fumbling with his belt. She'd grown into her sexiness; her walk had changed, there was more of a knowing *curve* to it.

She'd pulled his hands away and sunk to her knees on the red velvet carpet. The sensation was so amazing his legs had almost given way. Then the lift had stopped – it wasn't private after all – to reveal a snoot-nosed Italian woman in sequinned black, with a blue feather in her hair and a dramatic beaded necklace of jet and diamonds. She'd screamed and smacked the lift button. Felicia had screamed also and smacked it from the inside – as a result, the lift doors opened, closed, opened, closed, the Italian woman letting out a piercing scream each time.

'Oh, go away then, why don't you?' Felicia had cried. 'It's only a dick!'

They'd both collapsed laughing.

God, he couldn't get enough of her. They'd barely shut the bedroom door before they were ripping at each other's clothes. Maybe tonight, after his meeting with the proprietor, they could order dinner in the room. He'd announce to his wife that just an hour before, he had bought *this* hotel: his first major investment. It would be one of the best days of his life. No shareholders, a small loan from the bank: he wanted the least amount of hassle.

He'd surveyed his prey for a long time. He'd discovered that the owner was in financial trouble and needed to shore up a larger interest in the south. He'd made a good offer, considering. The hotel was five-star, but a little worn. The recession had curtailed people's lust for travel, but

134

the economic climate was in recovery: it was a great time to buy.

He would take it to a new level. There was the possible issue of staff loyalty but he didn't foresee a problem. People loved to be employed by a grand hotel. It proved you were a good worker, it showed you could cope in a high pressure environment: no one would be rushing to give notice. They would be relieved that the business was once again in safe hands, that their jobs were assured. He had no intention of making drastic changes, just essential ones. The tradition of the hotel would continue, except better. A hotel like this should run off its reputation, and under his control, it would fly.

All he had to do was sign, and the place would be his. Tonight would herald the birth of his Roman empire.

He'd tell Felicia the news, and they'd have cocktails on the balcony, looking on to the lake as the sun set. Felicia was a country girl: she did like to fuck in the fresh air. He'd persuaded her to borrow Cannadine's nanny for the week; thank God she hadn't refused or they'd have spent the holiday living like monks. Not that Claudia was any bother, the child was an angel. He rolled over in his sun lounger to look at her.

'Hello, Daddy!' She waved to him from the diving board of the large freshwater pool. 'Watch me jump!'

She was so sweet in her little pink flowery swimsuit – and so fearless. No armbands and only just four.

'Are you ready, Mummy? Don't catch me though! I can do it!'

Felicia beamed. She was easily the most stunning woman there, in her red and white swirly bikini – probably he *should* have mentioned to her that the white bits went translucent in the water. 'Ready! Steady!'

'*GO!*' they shouted together. He laughed as Claudia disappeared into the blue then burst out of the water like a seal. She was divine.

It was Baby Nathan who was the problem.

Jack got a sick feeling in his gut when he thought about that child. The Adoption Agency's probation period of three months was complete and he was legally theirs, hence the 'celebration' holiday. But when Jack held Baby Nathan, he felt ... blank. There was no love there. Nothing. When he'd first held Claudia, it was a hallowed moment. He'd never forget what his wife had said as she cradled that warm bundle for the first time. Oddly formal words but so fitting: 'This child is my salvation.'

She'd written in her diary, and showed him: *I am so happy. My cracked heart is whole again. I am instantly a mother, I love that child with my whole being, I would crawl across deserts, I would swim across seas for that tiny girl.*

Nathan might have been a plastic doll for all the warmth Jack felt towards him. He hoped that a bond would establish itself in time but what if it didn't? Was it he, Jack, having some insane reaction to a male competing for Felicia's attention? Ludicrous! Or was it that you could take a dislike to a person, *any* person, instantly? Nathan had a face like a Halloween pumpkin, his mouth nearly always open in a grotesque howl. Jack felt dirty having such cold, unkind thoughts about an eight-month-old baby. But if he was honest, he hoped that a miracle would occur, and that Baby Nathan would vanish from his life.

Jack hadn't even held Nathan this holiday. Touching the child made his skin crawl. If Felicia had noticed ... he shuddered. Nanny was delighted to potter around with 'the tot' – he was impressed with the mettle of the woman, actually. He admired people who took their job seriously. He'd quite like Nanny to be *his* nanny, to organize his life. Felicia did her best – he recalled that dinner party where she'd served home-made lemon meringue pie with no base – but she wasn't super-efficient in that brisk, emotionless, British way that Nanny was.

He glanced at his watch, a white-gold Patek Philippe: nearly six o'clock! The meeting was at seven.

'Darling!'

Felicia looked up and smiled. Her blond hair was in a high ponytail, and he could see that sleek French woman under the large yellow sunhat hawk-eyeing her every move. Funny, how women watched women. The men could tromp around in green monster suits for all they cared.

Felicia hauled Claudia out of the pool and they both splish-splashed over.

'Sweetheart, I have some business with the hotel management. It shouldn't take long – an hour? I should be finished by eight. I might want you to join us for drinks in the executive lounge. Then again, I might just want to' – he lowered his voice to a husk – 'celebrate *privately* in our suite.'

Felicia arched an eyebrow. 'Well, aren't you just full of surprises and demands, my honey! I knew this was more than a holiday. So would you like me to be waiting in my little Italian maid outfit, or will a dull old Chanel evening dress and pink diamonds do the trick?'

He loved her. 'Surprise me,' he said.

They kissed.

'Be good for Nanny,' he told Claudia. 'Say . . . hello to Nathan for me. Night night, darling.'

He whistled in the shower – even though he was a terrible whistler; it was a small failing as a man. He whistled as he put on his ice-blue Ferragamo suit. (Its immaculate cut always met with knowing approval in London – God forbid that Ferragamo was the C&A of Italy! Still, at £850, he doubted it.) He whistled as he sauntered along the corridor to the Executive Meeting Room. Outside, a stunning young woman with shiny hair and blue eyes sat behind a desk. She stood up as he approached.

'Mr Kent, good evening. Mr and Mrs Maltese are expecting you. Your secretary has also arrived. Please follow me.'

If Maltese was going to drag along his wife, he should have brought Felicia. But this was a business meeting, not a dinner dance. It had been enough of a fuss to persuade his secretary that a weekend trip to Italy was not a punishment. He got the feeling that she didn't like to miss *Coronation Street*. She was definitely in line for the chop. He imagined getting Nanny dolled up in a business suit to take minutes – if only! But he suspected that stealing another man's nanny was worse than stealing his wife. It was out of the question. Once you'd stooped to nanny-stealing, your entire moral fibre was called into question. What next: goosing your mother-in-law?

He took a breath, trying to appear calm. Come on, Kent, it's business, forget what it means to you. It's only *business*.

He walked in, a relaxed smile on his face, his hand outstretched to greet Mrs Maltese first. Always the lady first – oh good *God*! His smile vanished, and so did hers. She wrenched away her hand and turned to her husband, babbling in hysterical Italian. Jesus, she was actually crying, the mad old witch! It was like watching a horror movie, except he was in it! Mr Maltese, an immaculate old-school gentleman – bugger, why couldn't he have been a louche old playboy – turned to Jack. The look on his face was utter disdain.

'I am so sorry, *sir*,' he said, 'but I cannot do business with a man who insults my wife. This hotel, it is a family business, and we have run it for many years. When I sell, it matters to whom. My reputation remains joined to this hotel, and my reputation is everything to me. I cannot in good faith hand over the lasso . . . pardon, the reins of this hotel to a person with such moral behaviour as . . . yourself. A deal is a deal, but it is not everything. I feel that my reputation is worth more.'

Even as Maltese issued a death sentence to a long-held dream, Jack marvelled at how beautiful the words sounded in that sing-song Italian accent. Even so, the man didn't know when to stop. Enough, already. You made your point. Jesus Christ though. He was furious with himself. He would *never*, *ever* make a mistake like this again.

'I understand, sir,' he replied. 'And I am extremely sorry. Thank you for your time.' He nodded – courteously, he hoped – to the old witch, and sauntered out of the room. Once he was in the lift, he stared at his shocked, sober face in the gilt mirror, and ... burst out laughing. You idiot, he muttered. You *berk*. Wait till Felicia heard this! He couldn't wait to tell her! She'd want to comfort him ...

'Darling! Darling! It's me!'

There was no answer. She was probably in the bath. He let himself in to the suite. He could hear the bath running.

'Sweetheart,' he shouted, ripping off his tie. 'I think you should know. As of today, a blow job from you is worth ten million quid! The old cow who saw us in the lift, she's only the hotel-owner's wife! Freaked out when she saw me, and that was it! No deal!' He was being so cool about it. It was, actually, a disaster. But there were other, better hotels. He'd learned a harsh lesson, that was all. He wondered why Felicia wasn't answering. She sometimes ignored him ('Jack, I will not be hollered at from another room!').

He shrugged off his jacket and peered in the mirror. And then, from the corner of his eye, he saw movement. He whirled around. Water was seeping out of the bathroom, a sly pool of it oozing on to the bedroom floor. He ran, skidding, and time seemed to stand still. She was lying, motionless, in the bath, like a beautiful sculpture. Her still soft red lips were slightly parted, and her thick blond hair tumbled gently over the sides of the marble tub. Her big brown eyes stared at nothing. He could see that she was dead.

That unspeakable moment seemed to yawn on for ever. He turned off the taps. He lifted her out of the bath and on to the bed. He heard himself sobbing loudly, out of control, like a child. 'Oh my darling, my darling, Felicia, don't leave me, oh God, please, no, oh God, I love you so much.' He dialled Nanny's room. Immediately, she took over, dialled reception, ordered an ambulance. And, out of nowhere, caught in a sudden hell, he had one shameful spark of a good thought. In the worst, most punishing way possible, his request for a miracle had been answered: the Adoption Agency could not surrender a child to a family with no mother. Baby Nathan was out of his life.

BEDFORDSHIRE, 1970–4

Sharon

Earl Grey tea was disgusting, like licking the inside of an old lady's handbag. In fact, *loads* of English upper-class habits were disgusting. They were a filthy lot, these royals. The Princess might wear earrings that dripped with pearls as big as gobstoppers but she didn't wash behind her ears. The old geezer was all right; bit of a twit, though. He'd asked where she was from. She said an estate in the East End.

'Marvellous,' he'd replied. 'Do you keep horses there?'

The toffs had no clue about ordinary life. It wasn't surprising. They lived in a beautiful fairy tale. Sharon had never travelled outside of London before. Her eyes nearly fell out of her head the first time she saw a sheep, *alive*, in a field – a whole bloody pack of them, just standing there. She'd only ever seen a dead one on a hook in the butcher's. And where were all the houses? The countryside was empty; there was nothing in it except trees!

She kept her eyes open and her mouth shut: it was a good rule to live by. If you didn't speak much, people told you more than they meant to. And you didn't reveal yourself as ignorant. Besides, she was curious to listen to the Princess talk. She'd expected her to sound like Queen Elizabeth, gargling plums, but she didn't. Her voice hypnotized you: it was gentle perfection, each word pronounced with the clarity of a silver fork striking crystal.

At night, she'd lie on her thin bed and mouth the words to herself. *Splendid. Vulgar show. A livery lunch.*

Life in a stately home she could get used to. Of course, she wasn't living it, although a lady's maid was a very important role. For now, it was enough to press her face against the window of splendour. Yes, she was a servant, but at home she'd been a servant also, only unpaid. It was a laugh to look after her mistress's wardrobe; the dresses were sumptuous, *spectacular* – in a Cinderella-goes-to-the-ball way. Sometimes she'd giggle to herself, imagining how the Princess would react if she laid out a pair of jeans. Her best mate from school, Cheryl, said it was luck – the hell it was. It had taken Sharon years to reach this point. She'd written to the Careers Expert on *Woman & Home* with her question. She'd put Cheryl's address on the SAE. She didn't trust her own family; they had no respect. The response was bloody depressing:

A lady's maid has usually worked as a dressmaker. She has to know how to iron and look after special materials. When her employer is to attend a function, the lady's maid must lay the correct clothes ready on the bed: gloves, handbag, hat. Often, they do their mistress's hair and make-up. Also they travel with their mistress; they must know the proper clothes to pack and unpack. They fold silk paper between the clothes, it is quite a talent . . .

She'd travelled to the King's Road on the bus and spent two months' wages on a white floral brocade mini-dress, a pair of white sheer Wolsey tights, and a pair of white patent shoes with kitten heels and ankle straps – *very* Twiggy, she thought as she surveyed herself in the mirror. And, thanks to her diet of poverty, she was very much the same shape. She accessorized with a cheap leather handbag; the outfit was so dear, she prayed that they'd assume the same of the bag.

She planned to march into Bazaar and ask for a job. But as she approached 138a King's Road that Saturday afternoon, she saw the two most chic young women in the window display tweaking an exquisitely attired mannequin, and her courage drained away. She walked home, hating herself.

'My uncle's a tailor,' said Cheryl doubtfully. 'He works in a factory in Farringdon. He might help you.'

The man's name was Mr Kroll; he was Polish and wore his hair slicked back, like a fifties matinee idol. He earned fifteen pounds a week making skirts, coats, jackets, by hand, for Harrods and Selfridges. He took pity on her. He made his own clothes at home; she could come and watch. It took him two days to make a coat; he didn't have the equipment. He pinched the patterns from the workshop. Every evening, she sat in his tiny basement flat. The room was hot and smelled of burnt fabric, because of the iron, but she liked the *peace*. He worked fast; his mouth full of needles, a tape measure round his neck and square bars of white wax in his pocket for marking the material. After a while, he let her cut; the cloth was soft to the touch.

She'd taken along samples of her work to the agency – she died when she thought about it. The woman (her platinum hair was blown back from her face as if she lived in a wind tunnel) said, 'How charming, but I'm afraid you're twenty years behind. Certainly, *once* a lady's maid would require the skills of a dressmaker. Now it's all so different, of course.'

Of *course*.

She couldn't just breeze into a top-level household as a lady's maid!

'There is a vacancy for a parlourmaid at the London residence of Lady Home,' said the old cow. 'You'll have to be vetted.'

Like a dog! She hadn't the foggiest who *Lady Home* might be, and was pleasantly surprised when she turned out to be the wife of the Foreign Secretary. It would make scrubbing shit pots worth her while.

The first time she'd stepped inside the elegant Nash house, with its curling stairway, gold embossed ceilings and glittering candelabra, she had to fight to keep her jaw shut. There were marble busts on pedestals in the State Dining Room, and beautiful portraits of ladies in flowing dresses on the panelled walls (no eyelashes, though, why did those olden-days artists never paint in eyelashes?). There were magnificent fireplaces, filled with logs – an arse to clean; she was relieved to see a two-bar electric fire standing primly before each one.

She didn't see as much of the toffs as she would have liked. They travelled, and she spent too much time in the kitchen, polishing brass. But it was a busy house, guests always dropping in, more work for her. She didn't care, as long as she could watch and listen. Once, she heard Lord Home shouting about 'the lights left blazing all night in every cupboard and room!' But it was the only time she heard him raise his voice. And the wife was jolly, laughing on the telephone: 'I never do know, when I go to bed, how many are actually sleeping in the house!'

That's because you don't have to skivvy after them, she thought, but the woman was kind to her. They had dogs, Labradors and a funny-looking thing, a cut 'n' shut called Muddle. The Mistress caught her petting it. She thought she was for it, but Lady Home (that dreadful blue tweed twin set did nothing for her round shoulders; she needed a lady's maid, someone who read *Honey*, at least) said, 'She's half corgi, half poodle. She's an odd-looking thing, but much loved.'

Lady Home was a *proper* lady, and he was a gent, and she noted exactly how. Lady Home was unflappable, she put people at their ease, never said the wrong thing. He was the same. There was a copper, supposed to 'tail' Lord Home the short walk to Parliament, but each day, she saw him invite the man to walk beside him; they always seemed to be deep in conversation. It was a fine education but she couldn't hang around. She did her time then returned to the agency with her golden ticket: a personal recommendation from Lady Home herself.

'As this is *royalty*,' said the old bat, greed shining in her eyes, 'you will be interviewed by the House Manager.'

This time, she took no chances. She saw the way he leered at her, and moistened her lips. Then she got down on her knees, unzipped his stiffly starched trousers – not quite as stiff as their contents – and gave him the Rolls-Royce of blow jobs. His cock was fresh at least; it smelt of Pears' soap.

She was enjoying herself when, to her annoyance, she found herself yanked upwards by her hair and bent roughly over the seventeenth-century mahogany and tulipwood desk (where a priceless blue and yellow porcelain parrot looked her dead in the eye). One hand forced her head down while what felt like a large cucumber prodded urgently round the back of her knickers. She stamped on his foot, and freed herself. Then, batting her eyelashes, she said, 'When I get the position, sir, I'll be at your beck and call, won't I?'

She waited as he called the agency, and watched him write the letter of engagement. Then she slowly leaned forwards over the mahogany desk, and gazed, for quite a while, at the porcelain parrot.

The Princess was a total bitch. She'd sit in the Morning Room, an extravaganza of marble and gold, resting her big feet on a gilt chair covered in antique tapestry, dropping cake crumbs on a carpet originally made for Louis XIV, and she'd *moan*. Once, she complained about 'the lower classes' taking part in a gymkhana in the field across the road from her front gates, mimicking their voices, not caring that *she*, the servant, was standing two yards away like a lemon! The woman had royal blood, money and privilege – and an inferiority complex!

The old guy was different. He'd come into the kitchen after a meal to tell Cook, 'That was wonderful.' It was more than her dad ever said to her mum! Mind you, everything had to be just so, or he couldn't cope. When his breakfast table was set, if something wasn't *exactly* as it should be – if a pot of jam was too far to the left – he'd call you in. He'd take half an hour to tell you how sorry he was, but it had to be put right. At first, she wondered if he was a bit slow, then it occurred to her that he'd never done anything – *anything* – for himself, *ever*.

The Queen was the nicest of the whole lousy bunch. She was lovely, like a very posh nan. Sharon worried about the Queen. She saw the people who worked for her and thought: God help you, not one of them gives a damn. *She* did the Queen's visits, and Her Majesty always asked after her family. Of course, Sharon only spoke when she was spoken to, she didn't like to chatter on – the Queen had a lot on her mind. Once, the Queen had come with her jewellery safe, and left the whole box with her for the night – that was how much she trusted her! Whereas day after day, she ran the Princess a bath, picked her stinky knickers off the floor, did up the clasp of her emerald and marquise-cut diamond necklace – 'That's two million, be careful with it!' – pinned the Vladimir sapphires on straight – 'That's an eight-million-pound tiara, please do mind!' – and there was sod-all intimacy, for the whole three years. She didn't care. She learned what was proper – and not. She sucked up etiquette like spaghetti.

She got to travel with the woman – when they stayed at the George V in Paris (*before* they sold off all the antiques) and the Princess left for the State Banquet at the Élysée Palace, she let herself go, for once, and danced on the balcony in the rain. She got to fuck the House Manager (it was a diversion) until he was sacked for sticking his hand down a parlourmaid's dress. The Princess was stalking down the pink marble staircase, saw them, and went mad; *she* wasn't getting any and didn't see why anyone else should.

He left, sour. 'They've got money,' he said. 'But they've got nothing else.'

She couldn't see the problem.

By the time Sharon Marshall met Jack Kent, she was quite the lady.

LONDON, 1978–82

Nathan

'Walk!' screamed Stockley. '*Walk!*'

The trouble was that Nathan was eleven months old, and try as he might, he couldn't walk.

Stockley ripped off his leather belt.

When Clare put Nathan in the bath that night, the water turned red.

Stockley was passed out cold on the bed. Clare glanced at her watch – ten past midnight – and sighed. She'd get a few hours' peace now and, God knew, she deserved it, after the evening she'd had. Stockley had been in an evil mood. She'd cringed at the noise, then she'd had to leave the room. No mother wants to see her kid suffer.

It was Nathan's fault. He always had such a face on him, bloody miserable child. Always cringed when Stockley came in the room – why did he *do* that? It made it worse. Stockley would get more and more tense – no one likes to be hated. You could hardly blame him. The snivelling would drive a saint insane.

All the same, she couldn't bear to see the kid hit. She *loved* kids, although boys, huh, boys were difficult, all that testosterone. She preferred girls. But she couldn't say no. Fostering was her only income – if you could call it that. The allowances were pitiful, barely enough for a pack of smokes.

She was a good foster mother all in all; it was the kids that were difficult. She was doing a good thing here, taking in these unwanted kids. She had to have something for herself. And Stockley made her feel good . . . *when* he made her feel good. He was a good man – all those muscles, from being a mechanic.

She'd treat herself. She deserved a treat. She nipped down-stairs – a nice can of McEwan's, pack of B&H, read of the *Sun* and, ooh, there were some Quality Street in her bag, she was sure of it. You got to spoil yourself! She crept back upstairs, holding her breath past Nathan's room. Sometimes she'd hear him grizzling but tonight he was as silent as the grave. She shut her bedroom door. Something felt different. No, she was jumpy, that was all. She wasn't sure when she dozed off, but she woke with a start. Her first instinct was to hide the empty can; Stockley didn't approve of women drinking. Bloody hell, how many fags had she smoked? It reeked worse than the boozer on a Friday night!

She must be coming down with something, she was sweltering. She coughed. Christ, some nutcase was having a bonfire. At this hour? There was a crackle, a loud bang and the light went off. She hated the dark! Shit, what was going on – it was like, fucking hell, the house was on fire – it was on fucking fire!

She screamed, 'Stockley, wake up!' but he was like a dead man. She staggered, whimpering, to the bedroom door, her hands stretched out against the blackness, stumbling over a sharp object on the floor. She was gasping, gibbering with fear. She turned the doorknob. *It was locked.*

'Stockley!' she shouted. 'Where'd you put the fucking key! The house is burning!' She dropped to her knees, shaking, feeling blindly around the floor – don't panic, don't panic – the key must have dropped out. Nothing. But it didn't make sense. She'd gone downstairs a few hours ago, the door had opened then. She was choking now, thick, acrid smoke was filling her lungs and burning her eyes, and the heat was terrible. She grabbed the doorknob again and screamed. It was as if she'd pressed her hands to the inside of a hot oven.

'Oh God,' she cried. The skin on her right hand felt wet and loose, and the pain shot up her arm; it felt as if a wild animal was eating her alive. Sobbing, retching, she crawled to the window. There was a hissing, crackling sound, and the edges of the bedroom door were lit up orange, as in *The Exorcist*. Hell was coming for her. She rattled the window, but it was stuck fast: Stockley, painting it over in the early days, slamming it shut before the paint had dried.

'Help me!' she tried to shout, but she could barely breathe. Only a thin whisper of sound escaped.

Her eyes stung, but she could make out a crowd of people standing on the pavement. Some had their hands over their mouths; a woman in a dressing gown was crying, pointing. A fire engine – oh for the love of heaven, hurry, hurry – and the pigs, and, and . . . Oh *why* didn't they get a fucking ladder up to her, and . . . 'Oh Christ, the flames,' she screamed as the bedroom door seemed to explode, and a great red ball of fire sucked into the room, or sucked the room into *it*. She felt the hair singe on the back of her neck—

Stockley was awake now, screaming. Penny for the Guy, she thought blankly, here is a man burning alive. He smelled like bacon. She was an animal now, she didn't care about him, his pain was white noise.

'*Help me!*' she screamed with her last breath, her raw fists leaving red streaks on the window pane, but even as the fire lapped, lunged, engulfed her, melting her skin in a sadistic blaze of agony, her terrified gaze fixed on a small figure, a blanket round his thin shoulders, standing alone, in the street.

Nathan.

He seemed to look right at her, and . . . *wave*? He was holding something in his little hand, something he wanted to show her . . . a key.

LONDON, SPRING 1980

Claudia

'There's Mummy,' said Claudia, pointing to the biggest, brightest star in the sky. Ruth's heart crumpled like paper. It was the same every night. At least tonight was clear. God help them if it was cloudy.

'Yes,' said Ruth. 'Now, darling, shall we go in and see JR and Daddy? You must tell Daddy all about the ballet. Oh, those dancing girls in their pink dresses! They were so pretty! And the man dancer threw you a flower!'

'They were fairies,' said Claudia, still gazing at the sky. 'I want to be a fairy too. When I die, can I be a fairy *and* a star?'

Ruth felt a rush of fury. Bloody Jack. He was her only son and she'd spoilt him. He was a stupid, spoilt man; he had no idea. It was all about *him*. Yes, yes, we have all lost husbands or wives, and of course, so tragic that Felicia had died so young, but Jack never considered *other* people.

For years, nothing – the odd visit, the rare phone call – and then the wife dies, and she, Ruth, is called upon like a . . . *grandmother* (she wasn't that old, especially after the surgery) to look after a motherless child because he is too damn selfish to do the work himself. He knew she didn't like children. They were not like dogs. If he hadn't agreed that JR, her beautiful collie, could come too there was no way – no *way* – she would have moved in. Jack seemed to think he could have his normal life while Ruth looked after the child. He was just like his grandfather, except in those days it was expected of men, the remote interest. At least Daddy had got things done. He had moved the family from Hamburg to Amsterdam, found a friend to hide them for three years, sent her to that God-awful finishing school in England – hah! How to turn from a cygnet into a swan on their dreadful food, all meat pies and sausages! Thanks to his grandfather, Jack had had it easy. And now, the first difficulty – and his answer? Get the secretary to book ballet tickets.

'You can be a fairy and a star right here, there is no need for dying. Tomorrow I ring my couturier at Harrods, and I order you a fairy costume, *and* a star costume, and Daddy pays. Now come inside, it is freezing out here.'

'Goodbye, Mummy, see you tomorrow,' said Claudia, and

walked slowly towards the grand front door. She looked such a young lady in her little fox-fur coat and matching Davy Crockett hat and the prized black patent shoes, but she was a baby, a *baby*. Ah, she could hear JR barking. She bet that Jack had forgotten to let him out, he must be bursting!

'Hello, darling, hello, Mother, how was the ballet? Did Baryshnikov throw Claudia the rose?'

'Yes, the short one in the tightest pants, he threw the rose. For that bit, I woke up. You have a very efficient secretary. JR! Darling!'

'Ruth, why is JR allowed to wear lipstick and I'm not?'

'Oh, just a little got on his snout when I kissed him! I will kiss you too if you like?'

'Mother, *please*. Would you mind putting Claudia to bed. I have paperwork. Goodnight, darling. Sleep tight.'

He was already retreating, up the stairs, backwards. He was scared of her, the bloody *mouse*.

'Daddy, please may I have a story?'

'Darling, it's late and you have school tomorrow.'

Claudia got that glazed look in her eyes that Ruth hated.

'Look what I have in my bag,' she whispered. 'Half for you, half for JR. Then we read a story, all together.'

'Not *Bambi*.'

A children's cartoon – how was she to know the deer mother would die? Claudia had screamed herself hoarse; they'd had to leave the cinema, everyone staring. And then her father gets the secretary to buy her the *book*.

Ruth helped the little girl brush her teeth, comb her hair and change into her nightdress. All this hefting you had to do with children, it was exhausting. Then she shared the KitKat – no way was she brushing the teeth again, one night wouldn't hurt – and read a book about a witch called *Meg's Eggs*. Bloody rubbish, but it was short.

Claudia hugged JR and gave him a kiss on his nose. She pouted, 'Am I wearing lipstick now?'

'Yes,' smiled Ruth. 'Here is an extra kiss from me to make sure.'

'Where's Bass? I need him to sleep with me. And Blankie. And I need all the cupboard doors shut so monsters don't come out of them. And please will you check under my bed.'

Ruth sighed, shut the cupboard doors, checked under the bed and looked around the vast pink bedroom. Ah. The housekeeper had folded the filthy rag of blanket on to a shelf, and placed the stinky furless toy basset hound on top. Ruth picked up both between long fingernails and Claudia snatched them, snuggled down into the wide feather bed, jammed a thumb into her mouth, curled a piece of blanket over her forefinger to sniff, and hooked Bass tightly under an arm.

Ruth tiptoed to the door, and when she looked back, the little girl's eyes were closed. Ruth marched across the landing to Jack's study and booted open the door – like a Nazi, it occurred to her, but she didn't care. JR trotted behind her. During the War, they had had a little schnauzer. They'd called him Tommy, after the British soldiers.

Oh, *mein Gott*, terrible to see a man cry. Also, the tiresome obligation for an appropriate reaction.

'Jack, darling, I'm so sorry.'

'Mother, I'm fine. You might try knocking next time. What is it?'

'It's Claudia.'

Jack smiled in that tense, terse, busy man way of his. To her he was always a little boy in shorts, swinging his skinny legs. 'She's doing well, isn't she? Little trouper.'

'No, Jack, she is *not* doing well. Her mother is dead, and the brother is gone.'

Jack sighed. 'Mother, she's too young to understand death. The most she can comprehend is absence. It's not the same for her as it is for . . . me. It's quite possible that it's no worse to her than if Mummy were asleep upstairs.'

The endless squeaking from the violins had given Ruth a

headache. 'That is bullshit!' she shouted. 'You bloody idiot! Mummy was her whole world! She's destroyed! Her little heart is shattered, in a thousand bits! She doesn't show it, that's all! She knows there's no point! You're not interested!' Ruth took a breath, and smoothed her fuchsia Karl Lagerfeld silk smoking jacket. There was a small chocolate fingerprint on the sleeve.

Jack rubbed his hands slowly over his face. 'Oh, God,' he said. Ruth tried not to hear the sadness in his voice. He looked at her. 'What do I do?'

Ruth shrugged. Just because you were a certain age, people expected wisdom. She had never been a clever girl, nor was she now. She'd relied on her beauty, and it had done well for her, once. During the War, her mother had dyed her dark hair a gorgeous copper red. The German soldiers had liked her: they weren't like the Gestapo or the SS. She was fourteen, she had no papers, and she wasn't frightened of them. She was probably a little bit stupid. But they were normal guys, mostly. She was chatting to one, and she'd said, 'What do you do in normal life?'

He'd replied, 'I'm a hairdresser. I can always tell when a woman has tinted her hair.'

She'd smiled, even while her heart beat fast. But the soldier had wanted nothing, only to chat and flirt with a beautiful girl. She'd wondered, after, what he might have done had she been less beautiful. If there was a lesson to be learned, it was this: whatever little you've got, use it. Her son had looks *and* brains, and he was wasting both.

Ruth sighed. It would help if JR would go and rest his nose on Jack's knee to help with the comforting. Lassie would have done. But JR was like any man; selfish to the bone. 'I don't know,' she said. 'But I see that in this house, no one talks of Felicia. It's as if she didn't exist. Claudia needs to know that when Mummy died, she couldn't help it, she didn't want to go. She needs to know that her mother loved her; that she will always have that love, that she will keep it inside, in her heart. She needs to hear it from *you*.'

Jack's eyes filled with tears. Ruth ignored this. She briskly patted his knee, then walked to the door. 'I know what you can do,' she said.

'Yes?'

'Find her a new mummy.'

Jack flinched.

'The child needs a mother,' said Ruth firmly, and closed the door. JR looked up at her. She raised her hands, pursed her lips and addressed the dog: 'They both do.'

AEGEAN SEA, LATE SUMMER 1980

Innocence

Sharon stood in the darkness and let the warm night air caress her face. The stars were a million diamonds spilt on black velvet. A great moon cast its silvery light on the water. She felt the quick movement of the boat rock her; she closed her eyes and listened to the gentle slap of the waves.

'Look,' said a deep voice, and there were dolphins, leaping out of the water, trailing sparkles of green glitter in their wake.

'What is it?' she said. She must have been transported to another world: that children's story, with the pirates, the crocodile, the boy who could fly.

'Phosphorescence,' said the man. '*I* prefer to call it fairy dust.'

'Oh,' she said. 'So do I!'

The man turned to her, and smiled. 'I'm Jack. Jack Kent.'

Thunk! went her heart. She would have liked a little more time to prepare. She hadn't expected him to be so tall. He was a stunning man. Often, when you saw people off the telly, they were uglier. He had just the right amount of sadness in his eyes.

But really, this was perfect. He'd caught her unawares. Men found that charming, did they not? The truth was, she had picked one private moment to indulge herself. You had to have the right amount of wealth to admire nature. Too poor, and nothing was beautiful, unless it was your chance to grab something. Too rich, and you were too spoilt to take pleasure in anything that didn't cost you a vast sum. Sharon Marshall had the perfect bank balance to appreciate the wonder of sea creatures dancing in the ocean on a summer night.

She had the Queen of England to thank.

She felt a *little* bad, but, well, the Queen had plenty, and what she didn't know couldn't hurt her.

Anyway, it was the Queen's fault. The Queen had all but encouraged her. And the Princess should have kept her mouth shut. She was forever going on about Her Majesty's diamond drop earrings. How in 1858, or was it 1885, Queen Vicky had had twenty-eight stones removed from a Garter badge and a ceremonial sword to make a 'collet diamond necklace and a pair of earrings'. She'd left them to the Crown when she died, and the Princess was convinced that *she* was due the ice as a Christmas present.

That night the Queen had entrusted Sharon with her jewellery safe, the Princess had opened it, in front of Sharon, 'just to have a tiny peek, give my favourite heirloom a whirl!' And she'd seen that it wasn't a state-of-the-art safe, it was one of those cheap crappy ones. She couldn't believe her eyes. It was a disgrace what they fobbed off Her Majesty with these days. Half the royal household must be on the take. Her brother Gerry could crack that kid's money box in two seconds.

She'd run to a phone box and called him. He started moaning about the hassle. His mate in Hatton Garden would want half the cut. Gerry, you spaz, these earrings belong to Queen

Liz, she wore them at her Coronation, this ain't H. Samuel we're talking about! His man would have to sell them abroad. That was if his mate could replicate them in – one *night*? You daft cow! Think about it, girl. You're doing a painting. It's not taking you twenty-four hours! More like a month.

But Sharon didn't give up that easily. Not when ten million quid was at stake. She had Gerry's mate work from photographs. So that when, an excruciating *seven months* later, she happened to be trusted with the jewels again, they were prepared. Gerry's mate got six hours with the real earrings, enough time to perfect the fakes, then the switch was made. In the end, it was a lot less than ten million. Two million each, the Hatton guy got three, but fair's fair, he'd done a cracking job: the fake earrings looked priceless. And the real ones made the favourite wife of an Iranian arms dealer very happy.

Sharon had remained in her post for another year: a lady can't have enough poise. Then she'd given her notice, returned to London, paid *cash* for a four-storey townhouse in Chester Row. That's SW1 to you. One's postcode was *so* important. She'd also taken the liberty of assuming a title. An English one was too risky since the peerage wasn't that big. Even *la noblesse* was a no-no. But, ah, to have it quietly spread about that hers was one of the nineteen families mentioned in the deed of armistice signed by King Matthias in 1487 as 'Magyarország természetes bárói', the 'natural barons of Hungary' . . . It was as simple as attending Ascot, providing *Tatler*'s photographer with the information, and saying 'cheese'. Of course, Ashford was an anglicized approximation of *Aczel* – there were variations on the ancient spelling. Hers was one of four dynasties styled 'count'. Yes, she *was* an 'honourable'. Tragically, her parents, her ancestral estate, and her documentation had been swept away in the Revolution. Prove that shit!

She couldn't resist one tiny flourish. She'd killed off

'Sharon' and rechristened herself 'Innocence'. It had the ring of purity and of new beginnings, and if it was good enough for the Pope, who was complaining?

Mind you, she did have a twinge.

Three years back she'd seen the Queen on telly for her Silver Jubilee, wearing the Hatton Garden fake diamond earrings. She owed it to Her Majesty to succeed *big time*. She had to be meticulous.

Toffs were a nosy lot. They couldn't rest until they'd placed you; it was all 'what school did you go to?' even if a person was in their fifties. She had invented herself a nice little CV. She was the widow of an industrialist: a long foreign-sounding name as people were too polite to say 'Sorry?' and it was hard to verify the existence of a man whose identity you didn't quite catch. They'd spent four years abroad: she decided on Australia. Her education: L'Institut Le Rosey, in Switzerland – same as the Duke of Kent and some bloke called Aga Khan IV – and in case any smart alec should try to check, she'd been expelled for smoking pot. You see, before Mummy and Daddy had perished in the fight for freedom in 1956, they had smuggled her to England, aged two, with a maid – now sadly dead – and a few valuables, enough to pay for a decent education. She had taken the precaution of paying one of Gerry's mates to forge an old birth certificate, allegedly her father's. Yes! One crucial piece of evidence had survived! The genius was, it was in Hungarian. She had left it, loosely hidden, behind an invitation on the mantelpiece, where Lady Helen was bound to see it and jump to the desirable conclusions.

That was the secret: to let her neighbours discover her, as she knew they'd prefer it that way. The estate agent couldn't wait to tell her the pedigree of each one, and she couldn't wait to hear. She knew it would be wall-to-wall toffs. The posh were like lemmings, they all swarmed to one area. There was no thought behind it, which suited her. She let it be known that she was interested in charity work – the NSPCC was always a good one – but she didn't push it. She thought of it as like catching rabbits in a trap. You let the rabbits come to *you*.

Lady Helen was the bunny she had her eye on. A big social busybody; always talking, not very bright. She looked as if she put a great deal of work into eating cake.

Sharon made sure to look dowdy but rich in her presence. The last thing she wanted was to be frozen out because of jealousy. She also emphasized to Helen that she, Innocence, was a traditional, *safe* sort of young widow. 'No one knows how to set a table / write a proper letter / address people correctly these days . . .' *Sigh.*

Miss Ashford received an endless number of excruciatingly dull luncheon invitations for her trouble, at which the food was disgusting, the company pompous, and the 'voluntary' donation a right bloody nerve. She met *no* eligible men, as Helen saw her as reliable entertainment for every purple old pisshead colonel who wanted to bore on about the War to a bosom for several hours. On a few occasions Miss Ashford was driven by tedium to consider hacking off her own head to test this theory.

And then, after fifteen months of suffering fools, she received one of those stiff white invitations, gilt-edged and embossed with curling black script that every aristocrat scurries to place on his mantelpiece:

The Hon. Harry Cannadine requests the pleasure of your company aboard his yacht My Fair Lady *to celebrate the occasion of his thirty-second birthday.*

Dress: Ancient Greece
Location: Aegean Sea, off the coast of the island of Eos
Transport: private aeroplane from Heathrow

Sharon Marshall hugged the invitation to her, and cried with delight. This was it. This was the little jaunt that was going to set her up for life.

Now she turned to Jack, so the gentle ocean breeze blew

her hair softly around her face, and smiled. 'Hello,' she said. 'Miss Innocence Ashford. But please do call me Innocence.'

LONDON, 1982

Nathan

The minute that Shanta saw that poor little mite, she wanted to give him the biggest hug of his life. But you couldn't go overboard on affection. The Powers That Were didn't like you to 'form attachments' to the kids – it wasn't fair on the kids, apparently.

Shanta sighed. Some people seemed to think that a heart of stone was a social worker's main qualification. The girl assigned to Nathan Williams had been useless. His case notes were sparse, and she'd not checked regularly on the level of care his foster parents had been providing. On the few occasions she *had* visited, she'd always written ahead. This might be standard practice, but use your noggin, girl. If there *was* abuse, the foster mum had time to cover.

The picture that Nathan had drawn of his foster parents in the fire made Shanta feel sick: two desperate scarecrow figures with gaping mouths and red hair of flames and blood. That poor child – he was *four* – should be singing songs about animals and making hedgehogs out of spaghetti and clay.

She had a good mind as to what he'd been exposed to instead. He flinched if a man came near him. And his eyes were empty; as if all hope had gone.

Shanta suspected it was more than the shock of losing his parents in the fire. Adults could commit the worst atrocities and the child would still love them. But Nathan was too young to understand the horror of the accident; he'd been more excited about the fire engines. He knew Clare and Stockley had 'got dead' but when asked how he felt, he'd shrugged as if he didn't understand the question.

'Nathan, this is going to be your new home, and I'm going to be your Auntie Shanta. So if there's anything you want to talk about, you come straight to me, and I'll sort it out for you, OK?'

Nathan looked at her. It was an empty look and she felt her insides curl. What had they done to him? She wished that Shakespeare House was a little more cheery. Goodness knows, they did their best, but there wasn't the budget to replace the stuff that got trashed and it was too sparse to be truly homely. She'd have to make sure Nathan wasn't bullied. 'It's always a bit worrying when you start somewhere new, isn't it, Nathan? I still remember my first day at school – I didn't want to go at all! But it was such fun in the end. I made lots of new friends. And I'm sure you will here. Are you hungry, my dear? There's shepherd's pie for supper, and a nice treat for dessert – apple pie and custard.'

It did cross her mind to ask if he was vegetarian, as a courtesy. After all, she was, not that the dinner ladies could get their heads around this concept. It was always: 'We've saved you some vegetables! And some gravy! Oh! It's got meat in it!' But who was she kidding? This child had never been given a choice about anything.

'I'm going to show you your bedroom. I wonder if you like Batman? I put a little poster of him by your bed. And we have some nice new toys waiting for you, because ... because your old ones ... Well. It's nice to have new toys, isn't it, Nathan?'

She smiled down at him. Oh, his wrists were skeletal. And he needed new clothes, proper clothes, not the cheap option. It couldn't be all about function. A cool pair of jeans would do wonders for his self-respect.

Nathan was looking everywhere but at her. Like a feral cat checking its surroundings for predators.

Shanta unlocked the door of Nathan's bedroom. Ah, it almost looked normal. Except for the reinforced window glass and the nailed-down table, it was very cosy. Shanta had snuck in a blue teddy bear from home – she'd been given a glut of soft toys when Karlwant was born. Council resources only stretched so far.

'There you go. Perhaps we could sit and read a book together, before supper. Look, we have *Green Eggs and Ham*. And *Fantastic Mr Fox*. These books are yours now, Nathan. I've written your name inside them. Why don't we read a few stories, and then I'll take you to meet some of the other chil—'

An almighty bang and a bloodcurdling scream. Oh *heavens*, what now? Just when poor little Nathan needed some peace and calm.

Freddie Walsh no doubt: a whirlwind of trouble and only ten. She tried to see good in every child, she really did, but Freddie Walsh, bless him, pushed the boundaries. Couldn't keep his hands off his tallywhacker – it wasn't *nice* at the dinner table. And there was the time he'd tattooed the new girl on the arm with a corkscrew. *How* Freddie Walsh happened to be in possession of a corkscrew in the first place . . .

'Wait there, Nathan. I'm sure it's just some bigger children having a bit of fun. I'll be back in a moment.'

Shanta hurried off in the direction of the fracas. A trot was all she could manage. It was those bunions. The doctor said they'd caused arthritis in her toes. You wouldn't imagine a toe could be so painful.

She caught sight of Kim Harris, pretty little thing, scurrying round a corner. 'Kim!' she called. 'Kim! Would you come here, please.'

The little so-and-so vanished. Shanta sighed. This was ridiculous. They were understaffed, only by one (still no replacement for Brian, that weirdo with the guitar; she'd had her suspicions) but it made a difference.

Well, whoever it was had simmered down. She'd best get back to Nathan.

She saw the closed door, and fear squeezed her heart. She tried to turn the handle. It wouldn't budge. 'Nathan! Nathan? Are you in there? Is . . . is someone with you?'

Stupid question. He hadn't barricaded the door by himself. 'Freddie? Freddie! Are you in there? Lucas? I'd like you to open this door for me please. Or I'm afraid we're going to have to take away your pocket money.'

She'd have to call for help. How could she have fallen for this? OK. Be calm.

'Freddie. Can you hear me? Nathan is only little, and we have to look after little ones.'

The little tinker. For all she knew he could have a *knife*. It was impossible, but Freddie had a knack for achieving the impossible and, though she shouldn't say it, always in a *bad* way. She put her ear to the door. A manic cackle, a whisper, 'Hold his arm, hold it *still*!'

A whine: 'I'm *trying*!'

Lucas.

'Nathan? Are you OK? Freddie, Lucas, I am going to call the Unit Head, and then, if I find that so much as a *hair* on Nathan's head has been displaced, I'm sorry to say that I am going to call the police. And DI Morgan really, *really* does not want to see you two gentlemen again this week. Now I'm sure that won't be necessary, as I know you are both good, kind boys but this behaviour is unacceptable. We don't want you to end up in Feltham!'

Shut *up*, Shanta. She was making it worse. And then – she'd never heard a sound like it – a long shrill scream of agony.

'Nathan!' she cried, and hurled her bulk against the door. With unexpected lightness it burst open, and she fell to the floor with a thud. Trembling, she scanned the room for Nathan, half expecting to see his dead body sprawled on the scratchy carpet. But oh! There he was, sitting calmly on a

161

chair. He looked . . . unscathed! *Green Eggs and Ham* was open on his lap.

A whimpering made her turn. Lucas had pinned himself into a corner. His face was chalk; he was hugging his knees to his chest. She followed his frozen gaze to where Freddie was hunched, just behind the door. His hands covered his eyes. Blood was squirting from between his fingers. A metal compass lay on the floor next to him, and – oh God – that small blob of pink and white jelly, it looked like . . . a piece of living thing . . . It couldn't be . . . please let it be . . . *vomit* . . . Oh but she knew what it was. Part of an *eyeball* . . .

As Shanta swallowed back the nausea and lunged towards the panic button, little Nathan looked up from Dr Seuss.

'He tried to stab me. He's a bad boy.' Nathan raised his voice to a shout and wagged a finger at Freddie. '*Bad* boy!'

AEGEAN SEA, LATE SUMMER 1980

Jack

If there was one thing Jack couldn't stand, it was a boat.

My Fair Lady was a *big* boat, and it was custom-made, interior-designed, handsome, obscenely luxurious, sleek, white and superior, with polished rosewood floors and red leather panelling. But it was still a boat.

He just preferred dry land. Sailing was too much like hard work. And he hated the idea of all that deep dark water beneath him; he couldn't bear the constant motion. Last time he'd spent a week on Harry's other yacht he'd congratulated himself on not being seasick, and then returned to London and spent the next seven days walking into doors.

He supposed the Aegean was beautiful. The tiny islands, with their little white buildings hunched in the middle of clusters of trees, had their charm. And the hot, dry sunshine stroked his face as if to say, 'There, there.' And Harry was doing his bit to be hospitable. Under his wife's nose, he had engaged two professional masseuses, both ex-Playmates. The night before, Jack had sprawled on pale silk sheets while Brandi and Candi had writhed, gasped and wriggled out of their little tight white uniforms, slathered each other in sweet almond oil, and tried their best to engage him in a threesome. He wasn't up for it. They'd left, and Jack found he was shaking.

He'd slung on his toga, picked at the fried whitebait, and wished that he hadn't been seated next to Lady Helen. Despite her charity work she was void of compassion.

It was two years since Felicia's death and it felt like two minutes. The horror of the funeral still made his gut twist. It had been as elaborate as Lutheran tradition would allow, in the prettiest church in Minnesota, with all of Felicia's favourite childhood hymns: 'Amazing Grace', 'O Master, Let Me Walk with Thee', and 'O Savior, Precious Savior Beautiful Savior'. He'd felt out of place, as if he were intruding on the memorial of someone he didn't know. Her parents had blanked him.

No one acknowledged that he was half dead with grief. Not then, not now.

Last night, one of the puddings (he knew now to say 'pudding' not 'dessert') was lemon cake, and he'd reminded Lady Helen of Felicia making lemon meringue and forgetting the pastry. The silly cow had tensed, as if mentioning his dead wife's name was a social gaffe. He'd necked a lot of expensive booze, and was about to tell her how bloody miserable he was. She'd put a warning claw on his arm and said, 'Jack, I do so admire you keeping a stiff upper lip on this matter. It helps you get over your upset far more efficiently. If one is weeping incessantly, one's emotion gets out of control.'

She was wearing a pearl and sapphire tiara. She'd got her maid to weave little olive branches and leaves around the

163

gemstones, presumably a nod to ancient Greece. She still looked the spit of a rhino in drag. He'd nodded, strangled his linen napkin under the table, and tried to swallow a bite of lemon cake. It stuck in his throat like a piece of bath sponge.

That night, he couldn't sleep.

Every night, he couldn't sleep. He didn't *want* to sleep because he never dreamed of her, despite wanting to, so much. At midnight, he'd wandered on to the deck, nearly tripped over a young, very beautiful woman, with ice-blue eyes, black hair and the sensuous curves of a Greek goddess.

Innocence.

He'd braced himself for one of those candyfloss conversations but to his surprise she'd been genuine. She was also widowed. She was obviously rich and posh, but reckless enough to commit to an emotion. She agreed that no one understood the loneliness, that on occasion you felt quite, quite mad, and how dare anyone compare you to a divorced person, they were so, so different from the bereaved: bitter, and yet with a strange glee about them.

'Everyone expects you to remarry in a snap,' she said, her husky voice catching ever so slightly.

She knew.

'Yes,' he said.

'I don't think I will ever marry again,' she said, sighing.

He suddenly wanted to run his tongue along the scoop of her collar bone. No. He didn't.

'I can't even look at a man,' she added. 'I see my ... husband, everywhere. Do you find that, Jack, that you're obsessed with the past?'

The way she said his name, in that scratchy voice of hers.

He lit her cigarette for her, and watched as she stared at a shooting star. 'Pretty,' she murmured as she sucked in the smoke, and he wanted to rip off her flimsy dress, and ... of course he didn't. Felicia was the only woman for him.

No sex in two years.

'Yes,' he said. 'I am. I . . . I won't ever marry again either.'

She smiled at him, softly touching her champagne glass to his chest. Now *why* was that *so* hot?

'To being alone,' she murmured, and walked away.

FRENCH POLYNESIA, NINE DAYS LATER

Innocence

She scrunched her toes into the white powdery sand and sighed as the warm tide of the lagoon lapped over her long brown legs. The sun sparkled on her smooth oiled skin, and the sea was a glaze of precious stones under the brilliant sky. She looked beyond the tiny desert island, lush with palm trees, to where the volcano rose over the gauzy horizon, and she knew that nothing in the world could better this.

Then again.

'Oh darling, *yes*,' she purred as the gorgeous man she was straddling pulled her white bikini aside. She slowly sank on to him, squeaking with pleasure, and he removed her top with one impatient tweak of its string.

He gasped, 'You gorgeous *bitch*.'

She wanted to make it last but she couldn't. She wanted it all, now, and so did he. That was OK – they'd do it again in twenty minutes. She bit, probably a little too hard, on his ear, then glanced at her Bvlgari-Bvlgari watch. It was 10.35 a.m. He kissed her – God, he knew how to kiss – and they rolled over in the sand laughing.

'Oops-a-daisy,' she giggled. '*Where* is my bikini top?'

Her voice was light but she was serious. It was limited edition Chanel. That was the problem with shagging on a beach. You got sand everywhere, and fine and sugary and white as it was, it was still sand and it *chafed*. And you ran the risk of having your pleasantly expensive designer bikini top float away on the tide like a leaf.

Sharon Marshall saw nothing good about wasting money. Two million quid hadn't turned out to be *masses*. The Hon. Innocence Ashford had hooked Jack Kent just in time. And one non-negotiable of married life was comfort. Never again would her shoes pinch. Comfort was the point of being rich. Screwing on the beach was fun, but actually she preferred doing it in the four-poster. It wasn't a huge problem. Men were like dogs, they could be trained.

'Excuse me! Sir! Madam!'

She covered her chest with her hands.

'Allow me,' said her new husband.

She tried not to smile and failed. She was just so thrilled to find him sexy. If he'd been a pot-bellied bore with a tiny cock, she would have soldiered on, but he was gorgeous. She'd struck gold.

'Mr and Mrs Kent, *je suis desolé*. I am excessively sorry to disturb you.'

She bit her lip. The manager looked as if he were about to cry. Even now, it was a novelty to be deferred to. She loved it.

'I apologize greatly, because I know you are on your honeymoon' – he attempted a smile – 'but how can I say? This is a small island, an intimate retreat, only twelve guests all in all, and I am frightened to say that *certain* of the other couples are objecting to your, ah, *frisking* on the beach. I am sorry again, but would it be possible to reserve your, ah, activity to your inside?'

Jack smiled, and the man smiled back, relieved. Although Innocence suspected he would have been happier had she been wearing a bikini top rather than her husband's hands.

'Monsieur Bertrand,' said Jack. (He knew the bloke's name: he was slick. She approved.) 'I apologize. The other guests will not be disturbed by our . . . activities again.'

The manager beamed. Now perhaps he'd scram and they

could continue *honeymooning*. She was prepared to compromise on the open-air mist-shower – it faced out to sea and wasn't overlooked. Though who would object to a free show? She bet it was a wife. That Raquel woman had definitely given her a look when they'd passed on the pontoon last night. Tough: her films were crap, she was knocking on forty, *and* the bloke she was with wasn't half as gorgeous as Jack.

The manager bowed. He was sweating. 'Thank you, Mr Kent. I am so grateful for your kind understanding—'

A faint roar from the ocean made her turn. The manager followed her gaze, squinting against the bright sunlight. She gasped and covered her mouth. She'd never seen such a glorious boat – it beat the shit out of Harry's. It was silver and sharp at the edges, like a shark.

She must act less impressed. No more gasping and covering her mouth like a ten-year-old. She knew why Jack had been attracted to her. He might think it was her face and figure, but it was so much more. This man wanted a woman born to the life he craved. She'd seen the light in his eyes when she'd introduced herself in her cut-glass voice. She was his way in, and up. She had to be that person, a woman of breeding, who would show only mild interest in yet another twenty-first-century superyacht racing over the bright blue sea towards her. She was Miss Innocence Ashford now: Sharon Marshall was *dead*.

Jack nodded towards the yacht. 'The other guests will not be disturbed by us again, Monsieur Bertrand, because all ten are being transferred to Hotel Bora Bora for two weeks at *my* expense. You will understand that I wanted to give my wife a very special wedding gift – and what could be more special than this little slice of paradise?'

What!

'You have bought the island?' said the manager.

This . . . this was *hers*? Innocence gasped and covered her mouth.

'Yes.' Jack grinned at both of them. 'I am the new owner of

167

Spyglass Island. *We* are the new owners of Spyglass Island.'

'Oh, darling!'

He kissed her neck. 'I've wanted to get into the hotel business since . . . for a while. Banishing all my guests isn't something I plan to make a habit of, but it's a unique occasion.'

'Absolutely, sir!'

'And of course, Monsieur Bertrand, with your many years of expertise in the industry, I will be relying on you to . . .'

She zoned out. This was better than she could have hoped. He was rich, but not as rich as *some*. He wasn't a billionaire, one of those men you couldn't see for the gold-diggers buzzing around them. But she'd done her research on Kent and knew that, one day, he *would* be a billionaire. She'd known, because she'd recognized herself in him. He was hungry for excess. The purchase of Spyglass Island was a fine start – and he wouldn't stop until the world was his.

Not if *she* had anything to do with it.

With many bows and smiles, Monsieur Bertrand retreated.

Innocence stretched out on the fine, white, powdery, chafing sand, and made eyes at her husband. He deserved it.

He sank to the ground, and she arched towards him.

'*God*, you feel so . . .' he muttered. She glanced over his shoulder. The guests were boarding the yacht at the end of the pontoon. Raquel was wearing a massive hat. Look over, look over – yes! She waved. Raquel turned away. Ha!

As the yacht departed, Innocence came.

'Thank you for my island, sweetie,' she purred.

Jack grinned. 'You deserve at least one wedding present that isn't crystal. And you did agree to get married in a shack on the beach . . .'

She laughed and stroked his hair. 'Why don't we host a little party in London?' She hoped he would interpret 'little' as 'big'. So many men did.

'Whatever you want, darling.'

168

She wouldn't book the Dorch – not yet. Maybe Claridge's. It was the place to have a wedding party, and always on a Thursday.

'You make me very happy,' she said. She meant it!

He kissed her nose. 'I was so lucky to meet you. You're . . . everything. We're going to be so happy together. You, me and Claudia.'

Claudia? What? Who? Who the hell was Claudia?

'She's an adorable child and I know that you two are going to dote on each other.'

The brat. She'd forgotten. Oh, Jesus. She was expecting to be the wife of a tycoon, with all the power and glory that that entailed. He was expecting her to be a . . . mother.

Innocence rested her head on his chest, so he couldn't see her face. As she stared balefully out to sea, the sun disappeared behind an enormous grey cloud. Oh, all right, it didn't – but it *fucking* should have done.

LONDON, AUTUMN 1980

Claudia

Claudia stepped into her wardrobe and riffled through it. She loved her wardrobe. It was big enough to hide in, but not too big. Daddy's new house was bigger than her *school*! She liked to take her torch, Bass, her Daisy dolls, and a blanket, and make a nest under the dresses. Nanny M. arranged all sixty-four dresses in the right order: the white brocade, the cream silk and chiffon, the pink beaded tulle, the fuchsia lace, the red voile embroidered with feathers and pearls . . . then, right at the end, in a plastic cover, the black organza, the say-goodbye-to-Mummy dress. Since Mummy had died she'd got a lot of stuff.

Claudia liked things to be neat. Mrs Print, the housekeeper, had given her a set of felt-tip pens for her birthday and she liked to arrange them in order more than she liked to draw with them. Daddy had given her another special present. It was a sparkly bracelet. It was too heavy for her wrist but if you sat in the sun, the bracelet made rainbows, lots of little rainbows. When Nanny M. saw it, she did that face. 'Is it inappropriate, Nanny?' she'd said, and made Nanny laugh.

But now Daddy had the best present: a new mummy. The New Mummy was being delivered today. Claudia picked her pink fairy dress – it was satin chintz with netting, sequins and wings. All her dresses were made especially for her by a man called Mr Kroll. She was a bit scared of him – his name reminded her of a troll. Then she put on her white silk tights. And her pink ballet shoes with the ribbons up the legs. The ribbons got a bit tangled up so she just did a knot. She'd wear her rainbow bracelet. Her tiara was lost. She tiptoed down the back staircase, dragged a chair into the main cloakroom, and got her white mink with the ivory buttons, and her Davy Crockett silver fox-fur hat. The hat was hot, and the coat squashed the wings. But she did want to show New Mummy *all* of her favourite clothes. She looked in the cloakroom mirror. It had a gold frame as in *Snow White*. 'I am naked without my lipstick!' she said aloud. 'Naked, I tell you!'

Claudia knew where Ruth kept her lipsticks – hidden all around the house, because if she needed a lipstick, it was an emergency, she didn't want to walk for miles, she wanted it to be right there! Claudia chose Corvette Red even though she hated to put her hand down the back of the conservatory sofa – there could be a spider and she hated spiders, even Charlotte. She wanted to make her eyelashes long but Nanny M. didn't wear make-up and Ruth kept her black paint in her handbag, so she did it with her black felt tip. It was harder to draw on your face, the mirror kept making you go in the wrong direction.

The New Mummy must have flowers. Claudia would pick

some. She wasn't allowed but if a grown-up said 'That's naughty' and you said 'They're for you' it stopped them being cross. She sneaked out of the staff entrance, crept past the guard, and started to pick the orange and pink snapdragons from one of the front gardens. No one noticed – she knew they wouldn't. Her house was full of people now: Mrs Print, a lady who cooked, other ladies who cleaned, a man who drove Daddy's car for him. And Ruth, and Nanny, but they were all busy, too busy to play – they always assumed someone *else* was looking after her. And today they were super-busy. There was a big grown-up party, because of Daddy coming home with the New Mummy. She couldn't wait.

Ruth was fun but she only pretended to listen and when she read stories at night she skipped bits. Nanny was nice but strict like a teacher – she made you walk everywhere till you got blisters *and* eat the skin on your custard. Daddy always bought her presents but he never asked her a question or took her to the park. Last time he'd said, 'But, darling, I've bought you—' and she'd said, 'I don't *care* what you've bought me, I want to play with my friends!'

He'd gone quiet, and she'd said, 'Did I hurt your feelings, Daddy?' And he'd said, 'A little.' It was horrible when grown-ups were sad, the worst ever, so she'd opened the present to make him happy. Earrings, again. They were beautiful but she didn't feel like making rainbows. She wanted to sit under the slide in the park with Imogen and Alicia and swap Walt Disney stickers.

And the only thing she wanted more than that was a mummy.

A mummy gave you almost *too many* hugs – exactly the right amount. She understood that you couldn't eat your cucumber if it had touched your macaroni cheese. She noticed if your toenails were poky inside your shoe. She knew that you might like to be read a baby story, even though you were a big girl. She knew that you liked to watch *Doctor*

Who but not if the baddies were winning. She knew that at night the bathroom light must never be switched off. She didn't shout if you were accidentally sick on the carpet and everywhere. She put your towel on the radiator for after the bath. Even if you hadn't said, a mummy knew when you had lost a toy and found it for you. No one else did.

Claudia sighed and tried not to cry. The last time she had cried about missing Mummy, *Daddy* had cried. She would hold a spider to stop Daddy crying. She'd eat avocado. She'd go to school not wearing knickers. She'd kiss Simon Larchkin who stank of wee. When Daddy cried it was more scary than a Dalek. She would do anything for Daddy not to cry ever again. But now . . . she sat up on the lawn. The huge black curly gates were slowly opening like magic. And there, still far away, like a toy, was the red car. It wasn't her favourite. She liked the big car with the silver fairy that she wasn't allowed to snap off. But the red car contained Daddy. Daddy was back!

Claudia jumped up and started to run towards the gates. The wind blew in her face and, after ages of running, her legs got tired. Then she felt shy, and hid behind a big pink flower bush. She'd wait and see what the new Mummy looked like. Her best friend, Alfie, whom she was going to marry, had met her new mummy. *He* said she was beautiful with long black witch's hair. Claudia said a princess could have black hair not just witches – even though she wasn't sure, actually – and thought that she would plait it. She looked down and let out a wail. Her tights were full of mud. For crying out loud! And now the stupid wind had blown off her Davy Crockett hat, right into the road!

As the car swept up the gravel path, Claudia dashed in front of it.

AN HOUR EARLIER, NEAR HEATHROW

Innocence

The novelty of owning a desert island wore off. Innocence compared it to buying a bag to match an outfit. For at least fifteen minutes after handing over the cheque, she'd be madly in love with the bag. By the next day, the bag was a bit less special. It wasn't quite so *new* – and, of course, even though she never threw anything away, she couldn't wear the same outfit more than twice. This made the bag redundant. By the end of the third day, the bag was stacked alongside all the other bags, just another yesterday's bag.

After three weeks of paradise, Innocence decided that Spyglass Island was flawed. Sod *bijou*, it was small. The staff were everywhere, like flies. She never bothered with the effort of acknowledgement, but she resented walking in the breeze of their air displacement.

She didn't like the tidemark on the beach in the mornings. It looked messy. Someone should tidy it.

She didn't like the brown palm leaves in the sea water.

It was too hot; they should find a way to air-condition outdoors.

Some of the cloud formations were an annoying shape.

Innocence gazed sadly at the tiny ice crystals that had formed on the window of the private jet. It was chartered – another word for hired. At this rate they'd never afford their own. She was wearing white calfskin gloves, partly for the look, but mainly to avoid all the germs from all the grubby down-at-heel millionaires who'd sat in this seat before her, sweating over its velvet cushions, farting into the soft fabric, exhaling halitosis into the recycled air. She shuddered. The vintage Dom served in antique crystal, the humidor because *she* liked a Cuban cigar, the charming steward (cute but not too cute): all the tailor-made luxury was invisible in her blur of fear. She saw a life of second-hand shoes all over again.

She barely knew Jack, not as a *person* – not that she cared. Knowing anyone as a person was overrated. Although with a husband she supposed it was inevitable, sooner or later. It was a shame, in the sense that sex was always hotter with a virtual stranger. If you stuck around, any lover got lazy. Superman would be revealed as Clark Kent.

Jack had seemed more impressive than most: smart without that pathetic urgency to talk about himself. Some people couldn't rest until they'd turned themselves inside out. It was just vulgar. She giggled to herself when she thought that, but then she'd always been a snob, long before the days of serving royalty. Even as a kid she'd curled her lip at the tart next door, hanging her *knickers and bras* on the washing line. Those were your *privates* – what a slag!

The only disadvantage to Jack's reserve was that she didn't yet know how to manipulate him. *She* could see that Spyglass Island was a diamond fast becoming a lump of coal. This hotel was their future, but it was stuck in the past. Every time she saw a waiter in a red waistcoat, she felt sick. To anyone younger than fifty, a red waistcoat was a flashing neon sign that spelled *NOT COOL*.

Jack needed to take action. And if he didn't know what to do, she would have to push him in the right direction. She'd fantasized about him sacking the entire management while she lay on the beach, smoking, sipping dirty martinis, perfecting her tan. Straight after they'd fuck like rabbits. She got off on ruthlessness, not red roses.

But he'd acted like a tourist, charmed by old crap because it was foreign. No, she didn't care to admire the sunset – it had no new tricks. Actually, she wanted to club the hotel pianist to death with a coconut. She wanted *real* food, not fucking new potatoes. M. Bertrand was an old-school twit stuck in the 1960s who'd be better suited managing a seaside hotel in Cornwall where they made banana milkshakes with Nesquik not fruit, and still sold golliwog postcards in the gift shop.

Jack didn't seem to have noticed *cause and effect*.

It was typical of the rich. They didn't see other people. Or maybe it was just typical of men.

But it was a problem. Even if they did manage to attract the ideal guests – cool, sexy young film stars, heiresses, rock stars, baby tycoons, awash with cash – *these* people would notice. And they wouldn't return. Jack didn't understand that to this superior breed, the turquoise lagoon would be contaminated by his nondescript staff. Ugly people were like an oil spill. The men only had eyes for the gorgeous girls, they filtered out ugly, but the gorgeous girls were hyper-allergic to the slightest imperfection. Ugly was old; it was death; it spat in the face of living for ever.

Her husband's first investment was a wreck, and yet he'd done nothing, said nothing, put *her* security at stake. She was so insulted.

There had been one charm-free tycoon she'd had her eye on but it hadn't worked out: he was twice married with five kids and a mistress; the will didn't bear thinking about. But she'd sat beside him at one of Harry's dinners and discussed his art collection. She'd swotted up on art history and was able to make the appropriate noises over the fact that he owned three Matisses, four Gauguins, two Pissarros and ten Courbets. He'd jammed a mound of salmon mousse into his mouth on a cracker, and said – spitting crumbs over her silk Dior – 'It's all numbers to me.'

All numbers! Oh! She'd *melted*!

But, alarmingly, Jack didn't seem to be a – there was a word for it, wasn't there? – a money-maniac. He was good company, but if she'd wanted a companion she'd have bought a dog. She still might. Had she made a mistake?

'Babe?'

'Yes . . .' She paused. 'Darling.'

She couldn't look at him. Men who didn't know how to stay rich were unattractive. They could look like Steve McQueen – irrelevant. If they couldn't make their money breed, they were weak, and the very idea of shagging a weak man made her skin crawl. He'd tricked her. He'd made a small fortune on the stock market. It must have been dumb luck. And a *small* fortune wasn't enough. God help her if Harry Cannadine had been the brain of the partnership – the brain cell of the partnership. That man was a shining example of why the aristocracy was on course to become extinct.

'Are you OK, babe?'

Even though she was actually trembling with anger, her instinct told her to conceal all hostility. He wasn't the type of man who welcomed criticism. What type did? Her mind buzzed with panic. What now? Divorce? After *one month*? She would be eating out of bins! She'd met his lawyer; you wanted to check his back for a dorsal fin. She'd put in close to a decade of work on this project. She'd gone public with Miss Innocence Ashford. She wasn't going to waste her. If her new husband was running with open arms towards failure, *she* would divert him towards success.

It was possible he was an idiot, but it wasn't a disaster. Her goals would merely take a little longer to achieve.

More than anything, she craved wealth and its blessed power. She understood the need of the supervillain to control billions of people – stupid little ants. She wanted that for herself, and the respect and fear that went with it. She craved a lifelong pot of fuck-you money. She would never have been happy as the Little Wife, just spending, bearing the snide looks of those who served her because they thought *whore*. No. She wanted to be the author of *her* infinite fortune; she wanted to be as omnipotent as Jack, and be recognized and admired for it.

A small problem: if Jack knew of her ambition, he would neither recognize nor admire it. To Jack, a woman with ambition was unfeminine, like a woman with facial hair.

But Innocence knew her own heart. She had stolen and she had earned, and the truth was she'd got the ultimate high from blowing what she'd *earned*. Incredible but true: a horrible irony. She compared it to having a cold and losing your sense of taste. You'd eat, oh, a scoop of albino ossetra caviar and you couldn't believe the *hit* wasn't there, so you'd wolf the whole pot, and still no satisfaction, just a vague, empty feeling. Well, that was frittering other people's money. For her, the spark was missing, and because she couldn't believe it, she'd spend faster, more and more – chasing that high – and in no time, nothing would be left.

Jack was fast looking like a little lamb lost in a financial wood, and if she didn't take charge, the money would be gone. He'd chosen a business that she had an instinct for. Her personal style was different but she knew what the right sort of people liked. This was her opportunity to create an empire which would truly be hers. You could only get so far on your knees.

It was a pity that Jack would be unwilling to share. She stifled a snort. No matter. The man would learn that sharing was good. She would teach him the value of the division of power. And there was only one way to make that happen: first, he would have to fail.

AN HOUR LATER

Jack

Jack allowed himself a smile. After two years of making money miserably, he was finally happy. It was strange to feel alive again. Innocence had done it. She'd saved him from a spiral of depression where every day had a serrated edge. He was bad at taking Valium. He preferred feeling suicidal to feeling mentally ill. He hated the idea of the pill taking control of his brain. It smeared Vaseline over reality; the whole world felt softer. All in all, he preferred the edge. But *happy* – that was new.

Spyglass Island had been a steal. The place was stunning: the light was different, so bright it made the world look hyper-real. But the hotel was a dump. It was advertised as 'authentic', another word for 'tatty'. Most of the staff were so old that the place felt haunted. He'd given them the opportunity to take voluntary redundancy – offering sums they'd be crazy to refuse – mainly to offset the guilt. He wanted them out of his head and finished with. Money was great like that: it solved problems.

He'd shielded Innocence from the worst of it. Their villa, on the water, was only acceptable because he'd ordered its renovation before their arrival. He wasn't sure that the gold tasselled furniture suited a desert island, but sod it. Anyhow, they'd spent so much of their time screwing that he suspected she hadn't noticed the décor – or the ghosts in waistcoats. He'd been lucky in this investment, not in the English sense, where they liked to insult you by declaring your success pure chance, but in the Chinese sense, of preparation meeting opportunity. After the Italian disaster, he'd been smarter. The events of that day in Italy had changed him. He had been pushed towards decisions that made him ruthless.

So he'd hunted for a weak company that was in trouble. Jack felt bad at first. He wanted to be nice. But he wanted to be rich more. He didn't know if what drove him was a desire to say 'sod you' to the world or simply to have a good life. He'd waited until the conditions in the stock market were perfect for the acquisition, and pounced. He would rescue the hotel – the banks were about to foreclose on its debts – but the price he paid was insulting. Still, if he hadn't exploited the situation, someone else would have.

It was the same with Innocence. He couldn't believe that such a woman was available. She suited him; she suited his situation. She was self-contained in everything but sex. They came together through sex – it was their main form of communication. He preferred it to talking. Talking got you into trouble. Women expected you to remember tiny things, and he never could. He wasn't good at detail. He didn't like to get too close to anything. Not any more.

Which was why along with the elation of owning his first hotel, he felt terror. A hotel was so *personal*. He'd close it for a year for renovations. He had a vision of its success, but the vision was blurred. It worried him. He knew what *he* wanted in a hotel, but what did other people want? He'd expected to feel desolate after his wife's death, but the shrivelling of confidence was a shock. He had less belief in his opinions. He was driven to bolder, showier moves to stop anyone from noticing.

He wasn't doing too badly. He'd made some good investments lately . . . He smiled at the memory of the private jet. He'd arranged for 'You To Me Are Everything' to be playing as they boarded. Chicks dug that stuff. But Innocence preferred 'Heart of Glass' – the only song they didn't have. So one minute she had the hump, the next she was groping him up and they'd done it in the bathroom.

He looked at her, sitting beside him in the pale red Bristol 401, hands folded in her lap; she had these genteel mannerisms and yet she was *filthy*. The upper classes, he supposed. They loved dirt, horses, sex; they barked 'What?' instead of 'Pardon?' They wore the ugliest clothes ever, and looked down on your hand-stitched Italian suit because it was made by *the wrong tailor*. He stroked her hair. She sat still, but it seemed an effort for her, as if there was this suppressed energy fizzing away inside. He loved that. She was young; she made *him* feel young, and he was so bloody relieved. He'd felt so old as a widower. Sometimes, he'd moved his head and felt his brain creak.

'You'll see your new home in' – he checked his Purdey watch – 'five minutes.'

She turned, slowly removed her shades. Her eyes were fiercely blue. 'Marvellous, darling.'

It made him laugh that when they were fucking, she spoke an entirely different language; frankly, it was like doing it with a brickie. 'Marvellous' didn't enter the equation.

'I probably shouldn't say this, and ruin the surprise but' – he waggled a hand towards her face. God, he was crap at all this – 'you might want some warning to, er, prepare. I've organized a wife-warming party.'

Innocence laughed. 'A *what*?'

She was pleased, he could tell. 'In your honour. A little get-together. Five hundred of my closest friends. Everyone wants to meet you. So I thought I'd make an occasion of it. A little wedding party party. The theme is *Moonraker*.' He shrugged. 'I thought it would be fun.'

He saw her look down at her white Chanel suit. Thank Christ for Martha Green, his secretary. Right, every time! He pulled a blanket off the back seat to reveal a pile of dresses. 'There's a few to choose from. The red one is Valentino. The crystal one is Ian Thomas. And the python print is Givenchy.'

He wasn't sure about the python print – Martha had gone a bit nuts. 'I hope you don't mind, but I *think* I know your taste.' He grinned. 'And dress size.' He paused. 'And there are some baubles back there.' Martha again: she'd suggested earrings and a necklace from Graff. 'You can't go wrong with diamonds,' she'd said. He relied on Martha. Martha knew best. He'd been right to employ Martha, despite the ... awkwardness. But, because of the circumstances, he was quickly forgiven. Martha – middle-aged, stiff hair, compulsive knitter, closet fashion queen – had seen him through the last couple of years. She would not be at the party tonight; her former employers were among the guests, and Jack did not want to rub salt in the wound.

Jack smiled at Innocence. He hoped she would choose the Ian Thomas to meet his friends. He kind of wanted her to save the python print for later.

She was thrilled. She always turned plummy when she was chuffed. 'The Valentino is *divine*,' she said. 'I'll look like a Bond girl!' She snuggled closer, leaning over the gear stick

180

to stroke his thigh. 'So terribly sweet of you, darling, *do* tell me more about tonight!'

It was hard to remember the details. Martha and the house-keeper had organized it. 'Well' – he must try not to sound vague – 'I want to keep some details a surprise, but Shirley Bassey is going to sing.' That had cost, but bugger it, you had to live, and he didn't think The Jam was Innocence's kind of thing. 'And Gualtiero Marchesi is cooking the food. Italian. He's also doing French.' He didn't know this Italian bloke to spit on, but two Michelin stars made him acceptable. He expected Innocence would know the name, but she gave no sign. He'd grown to like the upper-class habit of suffocating all emotion at its inception – it was dignified. Still, a *glimmer* of appreciation wouldn't hurt.

Never mind. It was nearly dusk, and the thousands of fairy lights in the grounds would be lit, it would be like magic. He'd ordered the gravel to be raked, and every stray leaf to be incinerated. Fucking nature. It was why he didn't own a country house. When he visited Harry's estate in Gloucestershire, the grey-looking sheep ruined the effect. 'Why don't you have the, er, shepherd wash them before you arrive?' he'd asked once, and Harry had laughed so hard that he'd shut up, embarrassed.

'We're nearly there,' he said. 'Guests arrive at eight, so you'll have an hour to get ready. And of course, you'll meet Claudia – she's so excited. But tonight is all about you, it's entirely in your honour.'

The trouble with women who were high maintenance – and Innocence was obviously used to the finest – you found yourself crawling up their arse just to raise a smile out of them.

'Pull over,' she purred.

'But ... we're on a main road.' He wasn't sure that he *wanted* to do it in the car – this was a Bristol, not a Ford Capri.

'Ooh,' she teased. 'We'll get in trouble!' She sighed, unzipped his trousers and straddled him. Oh *God*. She whispered in his ear. What! She was crazy. 'Do it,' she murmured. 'You might enjoy it.'

Driving while screwing: it wasn't *specifically* outlawed in the Highway Code. Wow. He was grateful that they were approaching the gates. Oh yes. He pressed the remote. Oh *Jesus*. He could barely see – it was fine when she ground down, but the ups created a bit of a blind spot. Oh, baby. He really hoped that the staff hadn't lined up to greet them. Well, this gave new meaning to the words coming up the drive. Oh *GOD!*

Oh God. He'd hit something.

LATER THAT EVENING

Innocence

Was there anything worse than someone else's misfortune spoiling *your* day? Nasty little brat. It wasn't even as if she was badly hurt. A broken leg and concussion and a snapped rib. And a crushed finger. Extensive bruising. Nothing, really. Still. The grandmother would take over, and Jack would be back from the hospital soon. She checked her Bedat watch. Half an hour till the guests arrived – plenty of time. She gazed closely at her face in the mirror. It was, she noted, an *ordinary* mirror. Jack would have to be taught how to blow cash – he didn't have a clue. That red car – what was it? A *Datsun*?

Innocence would have a mirror like the one in *Snow White*, a mirror fit for a queen, with a frame of solid gold. She batted her false eyelashes, half closing her eyes to admire the dazzling effect of her silver eye shadow. She really was the fairest of them all. She stood up, ran her hands over her svelte curves and glanced at the dresses on the bed. The fucking Ian Thomas was going straight in the bin. Jack wanted her to choose the couturier who dressed the royals so that all his braying friends would be reminded that he'd married class. The Ian Thomas was OK, she supposed, the crystal-beaded angel-wing sleeves were a glamorous touch. But it was hardly *Bond*. Maybe Oxfam could have it, or maybe she'd sell it on.

The python print was more her scene. It was gorgeous, overlaid with transparent sequins, and it clung like the snake itself. And the Valentino – if he was good enough for Jackie O, Valentino was all right by her. But the snakeskin dress was *made* for her.

Innocence sighed and zipped herself into the dress with the crystal-beaded angel wings.

There was a sharp knock on the door. The housekeeper. They were all the same, housekeepers. Like graduates from the SS.

'Madam. Would you like to inspect the house and the grounds before the guests arrive?'

Innocence waggled a delicate foot, encased in a silver sandal with a steel high heel. 'Thank you, but I'm hardly dressed for it. I'll leave that to my husband.' *He'll be back any minute, you silly cow, don't look at me like that.*

She'd already inspected the house and grounds. It was good to have space. A toff couldn't resist a tall thin house, where you were forever traipsing up and down stairs. Her townhouse had been no better than a council flat in some respects: the walls were as thin, and you could hear your neighbours shouting on the other side. It had made her feel watched, and uncomfortable – as if she hadn't progressed. Jack's house was vast and sprawling, with huge gardens. You couldn't *see* your neighbours, which was how Innocence liked it. There were too many people in the world. She liked the basement swimming pool with its dolphin mosaic. She liked the ballroom with its acres of oak floor that someone else had polished. She liked the curly staircases – the *something*-style staircases? Guggenheim-style! She hated the yawning gaps in her education.

Jack's pad was a little bit disco, which surprised her. He obviously liked modern art. Fuck: another cloud of ignorance. She cringed at the time she'd attended a gallery opening in South Ken and picked up a jacket lying on the floor. It had turned out to be the artist's signature piece, entitled *Absent Father*.

Talking of absent, Jack ought to be back by now. He'd need to shower and change before they greeted everyone as husband and wife. This was her moment of triumph, and she wondered if the diamonds were enough. She lit a Marlboro. She wasn't sure what to do. She opened the French doors and stood on the balcony. It was a cold, crisp, dry evening. She felt a curl of fear as a line of cars snaked up the drive – the Jaguar XJ-S, the Aston Martin DB5, the Triumph Spitfire, silver, black, bog green – the colours of combat. This was a disaster! Where the hell was he? He'd *promised*.

She tottered downstairs at dizzy, dangerous speed. The place looked spectacular. There were orchids, dyed black, every-where, their strong, dirty scent thick with sex. Rolling cameras shot moving images on to every wall against a soundtrack of Abba. *Very* proper. A tall man in a Ziggy metallic spacesuit was giving instructions to a gaggle of pretty waitresses with frizzy blond hair and silver hotpants – very retro, very cute. But *she* should be wearing hotpants. God, sometimes it was hard, act-ing toffee-nosed. Oh, sure the Ian Thomas was hot on *her* but, on second thoughts, a forty-year-old could wear it. This party was being held so that she could show off, and it was bloody unfair that she had to dress so primly.

The housekeeper sidled up, not quite meeting her eye.

'Call the hospital, find out where he is,' snapped Innocence. 'Please,' she added. 'Thank you *so* much.'

You didn't want to make an enemy of Himmler. Also, as hard as she tried to squash it, she felt rotten if she was rude to a servant.

The housekeeper smiled grimly and, without warning, a great noise of people flooded through the main doors – a fury of furs, cigarette smoke, jewels, laughter, glitter and alcohol. Innocence swallowed, forced herself to approach – someone, anyone – and introduce herself.

'Good evening,' she cried, a great, dazzling fake smile cracking her face. Her own wedding party and her new husband was too busy to attend. He and his wretched daughter were making a fool of her in front of all these people. Be charming, be lovely: the words ran through her head like tickertape. Imagine yourself a film star, you'll get through it, girl.

'Hello, gorgeous girlie, and who are you?' shouted a young man with slick hair and a bright orange shirt, taking her hand in his.

'I am Mrs Kent,' she replied, hoarse with repressed rage.

'What? Speak up!'

Her heart beat fast, and she ripped her hand away. 'I'm the hostess. The *host*. Excuse me,' she muttered. She felt close to tears, so she bit her lip hard. The housekeeper had vanished, to leave her to her doom. All these stunning, polished people: she already felt judged, and lacking. She must take control, but it was like trying to control a herd of rhinos in full charge. They were mostly young and gorgeous, born into wealth; she supposed that rich men had beautiful wives. Half of them were wasted. From their dress, more Bowie than Bond, they obviously thought they had something to rebel against. What – too much money?

She'd show them. There was a Giacometti statue of an anorexic – nasty – on a massive grey chunk of marble. She tossed the statue into a corner, hitched up her dress, scrambled on top of the plinth, stuck two fingers in her mouth, and whistled.

She felt a ripple of dying noise, as everyone gazed at her. Ziggy, sensing drama, fluttered a hand for Abba to be turned down.

'Welcome!' she cried. 'For those of you who don't yet know me, I am . . . Miss Innocence Ashford. *Mrs* Kent.' So stuff that up your arses. 'My husband, Jack, will be here very soon. A close relative of his has been taken ill' – no way was she going to allow Claudia even a dot of limelight – 'but even so, we want you all to enjoy yourselves and . . . *party*!'

She smiled and pouted a little, hoping that no one could see her shaking. There was a murmur; the faces looked friendly, or were they kindly . . . sympathetic . . . *pitying*?

'Bravo!' shouted a deep muted voice. Harry. Thank God. A cigarette dangled out of the side of his mouth as he scrambled to join her on the plinth. 'Three cheers for Innocence! She's a rock – an absolute diamond!' Through the haze of cigarette smoke, people started to clap and whoop. Harry winked at her. 'Come on, old lady,' he said. 'Let's get you a drink.'

She drank a little Bollinger, smoked a lot of Marlboro, blanked the sexy waitresses, ate duck, passed on the coke, ignored the orgies. (Ugh. The steam room would have to be scrubbed with Dettol *and* bleach *and* Vim.) At ten, Shirley Bassey swept in, wrapped in acres of white fox fur. It had been going OK, considering, but then Shirley had decided to compère, calling the host and hostess to the floor to dance to her greatest hit, 'Goldfinger'.

Shit. Innocence answered to no one. But this was *Shirley*. Innocence felt unable to disobey. She looked wildly around, as if Jack might appear by magic. It was as if he was dead. Harry was probably screwing a waitress in the pool. Why didn't any of the other men offer to join her? Maybe they didn't dare?

On rubber legs, she walked to the centre of the dance floor, nodded coolly at Shirley. Shirley raised a thin eyebrow, and began to sing. Innocence felt sick. Her body felt as if it was fossilizing. She forced herself to sway to the music. Her face was red as a poppy. Were people *laughing*? She decided to give them a show: she shimmied, writhed, flung herself around. And then, halfway through the song, she caught sight of a smirk on a pretty face, a colluding bark of laughter, and she couldn't bear it any longer. She stopped, shook her head at Shirley, and ran from the room.

Five breathless minutes later, she reached the main staircase, and looked up to see Jack ambling down it. 'Babe!' he cried. 'I'm here! You're gorgeous!' He was doing up his tie. His hair was damp. He had casually changed and showered, while she'd endured the most embarrassing episode of her entire life.

Innocence took a deep breath. But there were no words in the English language foul enough to yell at him. So she merely said, in a voice of ice, 'I have a headache, I am going to bed.'

'Darling, wait!' he said.

She held out a hand, stopping him. 'Please. Go.' She sniffed, wiped her nose on her crystal-encrusted sleeve, ran upstairs, threw herself on to the black-silk-sheeted bed of the master bedroom and burst into tears.

She stopped crying almost immediately. That idiot would pay for tonight. Shirley Bassey called herself a big spender – *hah*! Sharon Marshall would show Jack the meaning of *poor*.

As for Claudia: the competition must be eliminated. Innocence had plans for dear Claudia.

LONDON, 1985

Nathan

Nathan sucked in the night air like a drug. It was all right to be out of the secure unit. It was prison, whatever they called it. The same four grey walls and locked doors, and the staff were like prison guards. You were watched, always. If you were lucky, that was it. They beat you, some of them, but apart from that, they left you alone. He'd been fighting, every day, for the last two years. He liked a fight. It was something to do. It was good to make another person scream. But he was bored. His environment didn't bother him – like it made a difference if someone put up a fucking picture.

Charlie whistled at him, sharply, as if he was a dog. Charlie did all right by him. Charlie was the boss. It was OK. Nathan wanted to learn off him. The day that Charlie did *not* do all right by him, Nathan would open him up like a bag of crisps. But until that time, they were cool. Charlie was eleven, four years older than Nathan.

Nathan watched how Charlie did his work, with care. He'd asked to go to the British Library; of course, the staff wet their pants. Nathan went too. His world was so small, it was hard to believe that there were buildings this big, ceilings so high. His writing wasn't that good yet, but he could read – and remember. He had a good memory.

Charlie had been fostered briefly by a pair of white middle-class nobs who worked at some rag. Charlie knew how to ask for the right books and papers without looking wrong. The *Mail* was useful. *Tatler*. The *Standard*. The *Standard* told you when were the big events, who'd be there. The *Mail* said how rich, and where they lived.

Charlie would ask to take a piss, ring the *Standard* from a payphone – at 4 p.m., when the editors were rushed; whoever answered the phone would be the least important member of staff. Nothing fazed Charlie. 'Hello, love, I'm calling for Mr Bailey. His assistant here, Freddie Marks. Listen, features have commissioned a shoot with Lady Bracken early to-morrow at her West London gaff. The governor's scrawled the address on the back of a fag packet. I can't make it out – he'll string me up if it ain't sorted.'

They'd get the address, then Nathan would ask the librarian for the local history of the area. If it was an impor-tant house, the floor plan might be included. *Tatler* might even have done an article showing the inside of the house, and its tastiest valuables. It wasn't only the house you were researching, it was the people themselves. What they were like; who they knew. Rich people were stupid about protecting their stuff; they thought they were too important for anything bad to happen to them. Then Charlie and Nathan would go back to the home and merge into the general greyness of care existence.

The evening of the job, they'd go to their rooms and sit – same as the night before, and the night before that. No one would check on the third night – no time to waste on the kids who *weren't* causing grief. Nathan had been back in the care home for four months now, and it was his third job. The first had been a soft target to see if he was up to it – some mad rich old cow, lived alone; the hardest part was the bus route there. Every room in the monster house was crammed to the corniced ceiling with piles of newspapers, documents, books. It was as if she was slowly burying herself alive. They'd taken an old jewellery box, containing a man's wedding ring.

The second job had been trickier. The two-million-pound townhouse of an earl and countess, attending an all-night charity gala for underprivileged children in Africa – tables cost ten thousand pounds, Elton John was playing, and the flowers exploded into fireworks. It wasn't an evening you'd miss once you'd coughed up. They'd waited till two a.m.: whoever was there would be pissed or asleep. Charlie had stuck a bamboo pole with a hook on it through the letterbox, fished the spare keys off the fancy side table, opened the door and walked right in. It had been dark. Eerily quiet. Muted laughter from a back room: the kitchen. They'd calmly walked to the second floor, stuffed their pockets full of jewel-encrusted necklaces and rings from the woman's bedside table – she was helping underprivileged children in Britain more than she knew – and were trotting coolly back down the stairs when the bloody teenage son emerged from a bedroom, a big fat fucker, stark-bollock naked, with a sandwich in his mouth. He'd charged at them, bellowing like an animal; they'd dropped their haul and run. Nathan had retained a diamond ring, but he hadn't seen the need to mention this to Charlie.

Nathan frowned as his heart beat faster. In his head, he felt no fear. How dare his heart betray him? He swelled his chest inside his white shirt, defiant. You only saw the frayed collar up close. He looked like a poof. They both did. A fucking *plait* in his hair tied with a red *ribbon*. Charlie had it off one of the girls. The white stripe across his nose was wall paint: it itched and he'd have to scratch it off. They walked fast. Charlie was wearing lip gloss, and his expression said *Shut it*.

This house was surrounded by high red walls covered in ivy. There wasn't even barbed wire. Nathan carried a rope they'd nicked from a shed. For a tree house, if anyone asked. Charlie had a football under his arm.

It felt weird to Nathan that he could, to a random stranger, be a child for whom survival was a given, who had nothing more urgent to do than build a tree house.

The cars were queuing at the entrance to the drive, each car as sleek and curvy as a beautiful woman. Nathan allowed his gaze to skim over them and the gauzy silhouettes of their passengers; he noted the way they carried their heads, that upward tilt of the chin. He and Charlie didn't talk. The guards would be focused on the front gates. They found their position: a quarter of a mile along, where the one-way system kicked in. The lights would remain red for fifty-five seconds.

Go. Charlie gave Nathan a leg-up, slowly. He hauled himself to the top of the wall and looked over. Green stretched for miles; all this space, for *four* people, a proper lump of the planet. Then he jumped on to the lawn below. Charlie threw over the rope. Nathan hung on to it, his weight allowing Charlie to climb the wall from the other side. Charlie jumped down. Clear.

'What's the order of events?' said Charlie. He knew the

order of events. It was the same as Batman saying to Robin, 'Where's my cape?'

'There's a champagne conception in the Great Hall from eight thirty. Which is on the' – *never, eat, shredded, wheat* – 'west side of the property. The security is' – he paused again – 'a few of his hotel doormen working overtime.' He didn't sound like Nathan. He sounded like the man who had written about the party in the paper. The man had also written that, 'according to sources in the City', it would be Jack Kent's last party for a while. Nathan knew that the man was suggesting, in a sly sort of way, that something bad was going to happen to Jack Kent. Yeah. He was going to get robbed! But it interested Nathan the way the man said all that stuff. If you remembered how another person said their words, you could almost become that person. He liked that he could crawl into another human's skin: like a cannibal wearing the scalp of his victim.

Charlie snorted. 'Twat.' He dropped the ball, passed it to Nathan. 'And who are we?'

Nathan casually passed it back. 'We're Claudia's mates. Friends, I mean. She's ten. And there's another sister, Emily. She's three.'

'Fucking *names* of these people! We need to get away from this wall. Move. Look like you're having fun. What's she look like, this Claudia bird? Lush?'

Lush? All girls were disgusting! They made him feel sick. 'There weren't a photo.'

Charlie didn't stop walking and smiling and passing the ball, but his voice was cold. 'We're her mates, and we don't know her to spit on. You—' Charlie stopped. 'You should know.'

Nathan felt a swell of rage and satisfaction, intermingled. Charlie had been about to go off on one, but he'd checked himself. Even *Charlie* was a bit scared of him.

'We'll find out,' Charlie added. 'No sweat. This place is nuts.'

Beauty made no odds to Nathan. Everything was ugly underneath. The house was like a palace. White and long, with big low windows, and pillars. The garden was weird: full of hedges cut into the shape of birds. It was dark, but the flowerbeds were lit up. One flowerbed had been arranged so that red flowers spelt some words, and the white flowers were like the page: *Innocence is Divine.*

What? It was the tidiest garden; how did you get everything to grow so neat?

They were nearing the guests. He could see a few kids, round about Charlie's age. Good sign. There were a lot of poofy red jackets with the gold tassels, a lot of tight black drainpipe trousers. Adults in fancy dress. Weird.

Charlie bounced the ball, caught it, wandered up to an old lady in a tight gold dress. He tugged shyly at her skirt, not meeting her eye. 'Hi. Do you know where Claudia is, please?'

The woman beamed, her skin stretched tight. 'Well of course I do, I am her gr— her father's mother, after all! You are late, you bad boys, you have missed the swimming, I am afraid – the children are all changing for dinner. Go inside the house: ask someone to direct you, it is too big, too big to find yourself! You need the trail of breadcrumbs to find your way! Do tell Claudia how pretty she looks, even with her hair cut so short. Poor darling!' The lady frowned for a second.

'Thank you *so* much,' said Charlie, a real grin lighting his face.

They walked up the smooth stone steps, Charlie bouncing the ball. There was a man standing there in a police-type uniform. He had short hair and dark glasses. He watched the boys, though he pretended not to. Nathan ignored him – you would, if you were a rich kid living it up at a party like this. His eyes felt hot and sore with the bright fierce perfection of this place. His life was a million shades of grey. This house was like another country; it was insane with colour. There was so much light, so many things, and so big. It was like Wonderland, when Alice got shrunk.

Charlie's arm shot out as a big lady in a bikini and high heels waggled past carrying a tray of steak and chips. The steaks were small, with little sticks stuck in them, so you could take one. The smell was unbelievable: it made Nathan want to cry. All the food in the care home smelled like old oil. She bent low. Her body was painted silver. It looked weird. Charlie winked at her; he took three steaks and a load of chips. The security guy was looking over. All that work and Charlie would blow it for a bit of fried potato. She offered the tray to Nathan. His stomach growled. Nathan felt the guard's gaze hard on his back. He wanted to taste that food, so bad. He shook his head. 'No thank you,' he said.

He waited for Charlie to stop shoving food in his mouth. 'The guard is looking,' he whispered. 'We can't go upstairs.'

'The pool's got to be this way,' said Charlie. 'We'll get a look at the girl – she don't need to see *us* – then we'll head upstairs. There's got to be a back way. If anyone stops us, we're lost, right? This place must be crawling with servants.'

They jumped down some wide stone steps. The walls were white and there were seven big silver mirror balls hanging from the ceiling. Nathan imagined smashing them up with a hammer, the shards of glass like a thousand tiny daggers, and the mess of noise. At the bottom was another giant room, with doors off of it like you'd get in a castle, and the whole floor was covered in a fluffy purple carpet. These people were *nuts*.

'I think', said Nathan slowly, 'we should get what we came for and go. That guard was looking at us. We don't need to see the girl.'

Charlie went quiet. Then he shrugged.

Nathan said nothing. He sniffed. If *he* lived in this house, what would *he* want? A pole from his bedroom that he could slide down, like a fireman . . . into the *pool*? Not really. He didn't see the point of spending time in cold water, full of other people's piss. But these people, these pampered people with nothing to do but fuck around, they would want the pool to be right there, they wouldn't want to walk far . . . so, their bedrooms would be close by. He'd let Charlie check out the parents' room. He wanted to see the girl's room. The 'poor darling'. People interested him. He was interested in them the same way he was interested in flies: in the way they squirmed about after you'd pulled their wings off.

He was right. There was a curly dark wood back staircase, with white furry carpet your feet sank into like mud. They crept up it, and found themselves in an endless arched hall-way of white and gold. There was a huge stained glass window at the end, as you'd get in a church. Light streamed through it, even though it was night. There was a picture in the glass of a woman, or an angel. Could angels have black hair? It kind of looked as if people should worship her – she had a halo, and white wings. But in her hand she held . . . was that a *smoke*?

Charlie nudged him. A pink sign: 'Claudia's Room'. 'You check out the girl, see if she's got any stuff worth nicking. I'll do the main bedroom. See you back here in fifteen?'

Perfect. Charlie was a bit of a moron, it turned out. Nathan worked better alone. He knocked quietly, walked in. It was grey-dark, and you could hear the faint clash of music from downstairs. The room was a horrible colour, peach loo roll, and it wasn't as big as he'd expected. Like a medium-sized princess might have, but not the *main* princess. It smelled of flowers. There was a square jewellery box on a shelf with a ballerina on it. He padded towards it, opened it, and *shit* – it started tinkling out a tune, really loud, so he pressed it shut. But fucking hell, it was stuffed with diamonds and shit and just left there for anyone to make off with. Finders keepers. He'd take the whole box. He was walking towards the door, when . . . he froze.

A little gasp. Jesus Christ, there was someone in the bed.

He breathed slow and deep. His hand went to his pocket; his fingers curled smoothly around the knife. He padded

194

towards the noise. It was an irritating sound. He wanted to make it go away with the knife. The girl was huddled under the cover, curled up like a cat. The top of the pillow was poking out: she was crying into it. Sitting on a cabinet next to the bed was a little glazed china castle with lots of tiny holes in its roof. Inside the castle sat a tiny figure in a crown, and a spinning wheel. Nathan couldn't stop himself. He had the knife anyway. He switched on the light. Little bursts of light streamed from the holes in the castle roof, turning the room into a magic kingdom. He stared at the castle.

The girl was still sobbing quietly into her pillow (*shut up*), she had no clue he was standing right there, *poor darling*. He felt a rip of anger. What did *she* have to cry about? He should stick the knife through the bedclothes. But he'd want to look her in the eye as the knife went in. Where was the fun, otherwise? He glanced at the Sleeping Beauty night light. There was a glint of something inside. He reached his hand in, pulled out a small red velvet bag. With greedy fingers he forced it open. Inside was a fat little gold heart on a chain. He liked it. He'd have that. He dropped it into his shoe, then . paused. He dragged the knife very gently over the form of the girl, then, reluctantly, slid it back into his pocket. He didn't need the aggro.

He padded towards the door, holding the jewellery box, and crept into the corridor.

He felt the floor shake a split second before he saw the men. From nowhere, they appeared, a pair of angry gorillas: one burst into Claudia's room; the other grabbed him by the neck, hauling him two feet up the velvet wall. He flailed, struggling for air. The box flew out of his grasp, spilling jewels across the carpet.

'You made me look bad, you little prick, and I don't like that.'

There was a loud scream. The second gorilla emerged in a rush from the bedroom and punched Nathan in the face. It hurt like fuck. He'd had worse. The first guy dropped him, and he fell to the floor, choking on his own blood. It tasted metallic. 'He's fucking bleeding on the carpet. The bitch will flip. Get him out of my sight. Stick him with the other one, till the Bill show up.'

He felt sick. How had he been caught – *why*? It was Charlie's fault.

He was dragged downstairs by his hair, his nose swelling to twice its size, and flung on the floor in a kitchen, next to Charlie, who had a sour face, smeared lip gloss and the beginnings of a black eye.

Nathan sighed as a few thoughts occurred. One: he was going straight back to the secure unit, or worse. Two: *fucking* newspapers were careless with details, because, while they were perfect little Adam Ants, all the invited guests had come as Michael Jackson. Three: a tealeaf had been yanked out of Miss Claudia's bedroom and Mummy and Daddy were still partying. Grown-ups were cunts. A smirk lit his bloody face. He had her tiny heart in his shoe.

Poor darling.

ESSEX, 1989

Nathan

We've created a monster, thought Mark Stevens as he flicked through the case file. He chewed his lip (*stop chewing*), wishing that his hair wasn't thinning; it was a chink in his shrink armour. These bastards sized you up on sight; they had a cruel instinct for your weak points. He was dreading the meeting. The kid's life was a litany of disasters. Adopted. *Un*adopted. Abusive foster parents. In and out of care homes, secure units. And now, finally, at the grand age of eleven, *here*, at the juvenile detention centre.

They were too lenient. This small child had been described by his probation officer as 'the most dangerous person I've ever met'. He had probably burned his foster parents to death. He had, according to a witness, stabbed a boy in the eye. His violence was casual and extreme. Aged eight, he'd been briefly fostered by a wealthy couple. After one year, the couple had fostered a second child. Three days later, that child and the mother had been found dead in their swimming pool. The evidence was never 100 per cent *conclusive*. Bullshit.

Mark shook his head. A hair fell on to the page and he brushed it crossly away. Instead of being prosecuted, Nathan was moved to another home: oh, genius. His crimes weren't his fault: they were the fault of every adult who'd ever mistreated him. He'd got away with everything. Built up a sense of omnipotence and guiltlessness. It was an abuse *not* to discipline him. Yeah, OK, he was too young to be banged up, but why couldn't these people impose sanctions? They had the warmest, kindest hearts, but they were completely wrong.

It was a system of indulgence; it had spawned a psychopath.

Mark sipped his coffee: cheap, instant, from a polystyrene cup. He was the hired help, as far as this government was concerned. He got less respect than the inmates. The inmates with their drama classes, and their fabulous gyms, and their three nutritional meals a day, and their endless counselling. Mark was having his loft done and even the Geordie roofers turned their noses up at Nescafé. He'd been shamed into making them cappuccinos. God only knew what kind of a lousy job they'd have done otherwise.

There was sweat on his upper lip. Damn. He wiped it off with his sleeve. He could do this. He shut the folder, tucked it under his arm, nodded at the staffer. 'I'll see him, in his cell, but I'd like the door left open, please.'

Mark never made this walk without feeling like a very fat

model on a catwalk. It was a highly inappropriate piece of projection; he needed urgent work on his core image. Nathan was sprawled on his bed, one leg bent. He looked straight at Mark, a long, lingering look. Mark forced himself not to swallow. He was a singularly good-looking kid – *heart of the devil*. 'Hello, Nathan. I'm Mark. I'm here to have a chat with you today.'

The staffer dragged in a grey plastic chair. Mark wished there was a table. He wanted a barrier, however cosmetic. It was a small room and they were too close. There was a horrible intimacy. The heating was turned up full whack. They never got the temperature right. The room had the kid's scent. He felt like a gazelle invited to tea in a lion's den. This was a mistake. He should have insisted they met on neutral territory. My God, who was in charge here?

The kid had big, dark eyes with long eyelashes. He was beautiful, in fact. It was incongruous, even though he knew better. Shit, he'd dropped his pen. He bent to retrieve it but Nathan was quicker.

'Can I have my pen, please, Nathan?' Voice friendly but firm.

A slow grin. Ah *God*. Nathan was . . . rubbing the crotch of his jeans. Rubbing his dick with the pen. 'Come and get it.'

Fuck off, you pervert. 'Nathan, I'd like my pen back.' More rubbing. Mark sighed, standing up. 'Nathan, I am not going to talk to you unless you give me that pen.'

Nathan blinked, stopped rubbing, held out the pen with a contrite look on his face. 'Sorry, Mark. Do you want your pen back?'

See, *see*, he could do it! 'Thank you, Nathan.' He held out his hand to – *shit!* The little bastard had snatched it away again!

Nathan was actually writhing with pleasure at Mark's discomfort. Mark felt as if he might puke. Fine, all right, you know what, he'd fucking had it. Fucking builders, slave-wage employers, now this little arsepiece, treating him like

198

an idiot. His voice came out a hiss. 'Nathan, you can choose to be difficult, but let me lay this out for you. Your immediate future is not looking good. If your behaviour does not significantly improve, you are going to end up in an STC. You know what that is? A Secure Training Centre, run by Group 4. Prison guards. No clinical psychologists there, my friend. No cosy chats about how your head's wired today. Let me tell you, the baby arsonists and rapists and murderers in STC *beg* me to find them crazy so they can scurry back to the cotton wool of secure care.'

'A-hem.'

Mark jumped. The staffer was right there. Just his crappy luck. 'Mark, could I see you outside for a moment?'

He couldn't even look at Nathan. He didn't want to see him gloat. 'Yes, yes. Of course.'

He placed his folder on the chair, stepped outside, his heart hammering. His cheeks were on fire, and the sweat was trickling from his sideburns. Tomorrow he was going to roll deodorant all over his face. Your skin felt tight, as if you were wearing a mask, but anything was better than this humiliation.

'Mark. This won't do. Are you under some sort of stress at home? You're making it personal. You're letting him get the better of you. I think we need to leave it for today. Do you think you'll be able to cope with Nathan next week, or should I have a chat with your supervisor?'

Oh, terrific.

'I'll be fine. It's' – may God forgive him – 'my grandfather died. Last week.'

'I'm so sorry. My condolences. Perhaps you need a few days to yourself.'

'Yes. Yes. Absolutely.' *Shit.* 'Well. I'll just get my pen.'

He couldn't bring himself to say, like a five-year-old, *Nathan took my pen!* He'd fucking wrestle it off the little villain if he had to. His legs felt like rubber as he walked back into the cell. His face was carefully blank. He was frightened of an eleven-year-old. Nathan was lounging on the bed, whistling softly. His pen, he saw immediately, was lying on his folder on the chair.

The folder. He'd left the *folder* in the cell. The folder with all its classified details of Nathan's history: pathological and social. His skull filled with noise and he understood why people shot themselves in the head – anything to relieve that pressure. If anyone realized – if there were consequences – there were *names* in that folder. He'd be fired over this. Oh God, what was in there? Was it so bad? Yes. It was. *Everything* was in there. But then, Nathan didn't know that. He was, after all, eleven. He had no interest in a grey folder! It didn't look as though it had been touched. He glanced at Nathan's expression. It was blithe; nasty little sociopath. Well, Nathan didn't look as though he'd uncovered his secret past.

'Nathan,' he said, tasting the bile in his throat. See if there was any hint of a change, if Eve had bitten the apple. 'I hope to see you next week.'

Nathan stood up. Was that a smile? It seemed genuine. The boy opened his mouth and Mark wondered what vile obscenity would come out of it. Nathan cleared his throat. 'Mark,' he said – *warmly*? 'I hope to see you too.'

ESSEX, 1990

Nathan

Mark pushed his new glasses up his nose. They were Prada, very now, very Tom Cruise. And the number-one haircut at Toni & Guy was an excellent move, excellent! It disguised his receding hairline and rendered him cool in one fell swoop. Yeah. He was feeling good.

'Morning!' he sang to the staffer. It was great to be Mark

Stevens today. If he breathed through his nose, he could smell Christopher's aftershave lingering on his skin. The hilarious thing, all that guff about self-worth turned out to be true. He had done it. He was out and proud! And getting laid! But he deserved it. He was a good bloke.

Nothing could spoil his mood today. From a professional standpoint – and he was the ultimate professional, with a commendation to prove it, let us not forget! – it was of interest, the *primal* need a man had to be successful in his career.

He had Nathan Williams to thank.

The work he'd done with Nathan was remarkable. Let's spool through that satisfying memory again. 'The work you've done with Nathan is *remarkable*.' Those words, and the look of frank admiration on his supervisor's face, gave Mark a thrill that was close to erotic. He knew Professor Heaton had rated him unexceptional. But now his work spoke for itself and the Prof was forced to eat humble pie.

'The turnaround in Nathan's attitude and mental state are exceptional.'

Of course, he'd been modest, while toeing the party line, all, 'Oh, yes, well, nothing good that Nathan did had ever been noticed ... bad behaviours reinforced ... merely a question of reinforcing those good behaviours ... classic example of the subject needing discipline but also needing rewards ... most effective way of changing bad to good ... firm, consistent, warm ... blah ... blah ... blah.'

Cue fervent nodding, beaming smiles, pats on the back.

It amused Mark that chartered clinical psychologists, with all their genius insights into the human psyche, were undoubtedly the most gullible section of the population – and among those most likely to be taken for a ride by disreputable workmen. (He'd 'bonded' with the Prof, over a beer, on the subject of cowboy builders who managed to fall through your bedroom ceiling into your *bed*. Fortunately – oh my sides! – he hadn't been in it at the time!)

His heart performed a small flip as he approached Nathan's cell. It was so rewarding. Here was a kid labelled with a conduct disorder because of his aggression and lack of socialization. A kid with no friends; a kid who had always used violence to get what he wanted, who had therefore been excluded, his sense of empathy deadened, who had grown to be aloof and distant, and he, Mark, was the only person who had got through, the only person who had taken the trouble to teach him the skills he hadn't learned. ('What happened when you punched Jeremy? Everyone called you a wanker?') Mark had shown him how the roles and rules of friendship worked, the 'do you minds' and the 'how do you feels'.

Mark felt justifiably proud.

And now he had a little reward for Nathan. Well, a test first, and then, depending on the answer, a reward.

Nathan was reading a book. *Amazon Adventure*. Here was another thing. The kid was smart as a whip. No one, except yours truly, had given him the credit.

'Hello there. How are we today?'

Nathan grinned. 'Great, thanks. How are you, Mark?'

'Fine, thank you very much. Hungover, but fine! I could murder a coffee though, and not the dried granule sort. How about I nip to Gianni's and get us both a cappuccino? Or a hot chocolate, if you prefer?'

Nathan appeared to consider. 'I'd like a hot chocolate, please.'

Mark smiled. He carefully placed his copy of the *Mirror* (filthy rag), strategically left open at the relevant page, on the chair.

As he turned to leave, he had the sense of Nathan reaching for the paper. Like giving candy to a baby.

He was back in less than two minutes, having already purchased the drinks and left them in the office. 'No queue,' he said when Nathan looked up in surprise. Then, casually, 'What're you reading?' He took a sip of his drink to disguise his nerves.

Nathan flicked his fingers at the gossip page. 'This thing about Innocence taking Emily to the Romanian orphanage.'

Mark felt dizzy. 'Right,' he said. His worst fears, confirmed. 'Right.' Then, desperately hoping for an out, 'I imagine that, given your history, anything to do with adoption is fairly poignant for you.'

Nathan grimaced. 'Well, yeah. But it's not so much that. I *know* the Kent family.'

Mark's heart turned heavy and cold in his chest. So. There it was. One small error, a year ago, had enabled Nathan Williams to read his case notes and discover that an ex-member of the *Sunday Times* Rich List had, once upon a time, been his adoptive father. Mark's hand actually felt weak, as if he might spill his cappuccino. He quickly placed it on the floor, grateful to be able to hide the horror on his face. 'Oh, really? And . . . ?'

Nathan laughed. 'I probably shouldn't tell you.'

Mark laughed too. A feeble sound, more like a bleat. 'I'm sure I can take it.'

Nathan looked sorrowful. Oh God. Here it came. 'Well, ages ago, I broke into their house.'

Get lost! No *way*. Yes way! 'Nathan' – Mark tried to look stern, when in fact he wanted to shout 'hooray' – 'as you say, it was a long time ago, and I'm sure you regret your mistakes.'

'I totally do. That day, I made a *very* big mistake.' There did seem to be deep regret in his voice. Phew. Mission accomplished. Danger averted. He was in the clear. But well done you for checking – God, he was thorough. What a pro! Now it was time to move swiftly on. His insides tingled with anticipation.

'But, Nathan, you have made so many positive changes since. And in recognition of all that you've achieved, I have a surprise for you.' He hesitated, glancing over his shoulder. This wasn't exactly by the book, but there was no harm. It felt so satisfying to have Nathan's … he wasn't sure what … gratitude? Approval? He didn't want to analyse it. Frankly, you could overdo the introspection.

He paused. 'Nathan, we've spent many hours discussing your emotions around the issue of being given up for adoption.'

Nathan nodded.

'Your post-natal separation from your biological mother, we concluded, was an interruption of your natural evolution, and it had profound consequences on your state of mind.'

Nathan nodded again. There was a slight tremble of his lower lip. Mark pursed his own lips in sympathy. 'Clinically, being so abruptly robbed of the mental and physical bonding that began inside the womb left you with a bewildering, albeit unconscious sense of abandonment. Ever since your mother gave you up, you have felt incomplete, as if a part of your heart was missing, presumed dead.'

'Yes,' sighed Nathan, a sigh of the soul.

Drum roll *please*. 'Well. I've done a little bit of detective work, Nathan. I traced the agency you were placed with, shortly after your birth. It's now defunct, but all post was forwarded to the body that took over. They filed the lot. And, to cut a long story short' – he could feel himself blushing – 'I have something for you.'

He slid the envelope out of his pocket.

Nathan didn't move.

'Check it out.'

Slowly, Nathan reached for the envelope. Mark imagined the ceiling of the Sistine Chapel, the depiction of man touching the hand of God. It was *that* significant: a tiny miracle that meant so very much to one underprivileged boy.

I write this desperately hoping it will reach you and that you will find it in your heart to forgive me for what I did. I was too young to know what I was giving up and I pray that your life has been filled with love. Not a day goes by when I don't think of you and

ache to hold you in my arms. All I want to do is to come and get
you and never let you go but no one will tell me where you are – so
unfair, so unkind. Please, please, come and find me, my darling son
– I will be waiting for you.

Mark watched his face intently. He wanted to see Nathan's reaction. In porn they called it the money shot.

He wasn't disappointed. As Nathan's molten brown eyes scanned the letter, they slowly widened. His face drained of colour and his hands shook. He gazed at Mark unseeingly, as if he were in a trance. He swallowed, repeatedly, and for a horrible second, Mark thought he was going to vomit.

But then he said, 'Thank you,' in a hoarse voice, and managed a weak smile. He was in shock, of course. It was understandable.

Mark felt light and happy – he was a soppy old sod. But why shouldn't he feel good? He had achieved something that not many people achieved in their lives. He'd had the guts to break free of the rules to help a kid with promise, a kid who'd had a lousy run, who was misunderstood, and who deserved a break. Mark had given him that break – *he* had made a difference.

TWO HOURS LATER

Nathan

'I would like you to mould an image of how you see yourself,' trilled Miss Lawson, the art-therapy teacher.

Nathan's breath came smooth and deep as he concentrated on shaping the football-sized lump of clay. He hummed as he pressed and pummelled it. It felt so good to create, as if he were a god, but with one difference: he was creating his world *after* the betrayal. In his beginning, there was evil.

Nathan pressed his fingers tentatively into the sticky brown surface.

'See yourself,' said the teacher. 'SEE YOURSELF.'

He closed his eyes. Where would he begin? What was he? There were no mirrors in the room. Quietly, discreetly, he drew up a hand to touch his skin. He shook his head. When was the last time he had even looked in a mirror? He had to look in mirrors, didn't he? What about photos? The home outing to Southend: there was a picture of him there. Could he remember that? Grey sweater, grey shorts, scuffed shoes. A single scoop of ice cream running down his knuckles. That had been the day he'd seen the board. The big board with the painting on. The painting of the silly, drunk family. The kind anyone could walk up behind and stick their face in and get some cheeky memento of their holiday. A mother, a father and baby. All with their faces missing. Mr Davis said they weren't allowed to climb up and have their picture taken but some of them did. Nathan froze looking at it, staring at the baby with the missing face. The stupid parents: ignorant, drunk, cavorting. The fat faces filling up the holes, contorted, laughing, screeching; his ice cream melting.

His fingers tightened around the clay. He pushed them in, his thumbs gouging pits for eyes. Who was he kidding? He had no eyes. No face. No mother.

The liar's words ran through his head over and over like a chant. *My darling son my darling son.* Nathan stopped and curled over, gasping with laughter as the blood roared in his ears.

Miss Lawson was by his side in a second, her thin fingers grabbing at his wrist. 'Nathan, dear, would you like to start again? You seem to have made a mess.'

Nathan looked up at her. Slowly her face came into focus. She had a long grey plait and the sweet female stink of her made him feel sick.

'Shall we start again?'

He looked down. His fingers had carved long strips from the unmade eyes. His nails had dragged clots of dried clay, strewn them across the table. His mouth, punctured by two fingers, was nothing more than a puckered scream, as if he were gagging himself with his own hands.

'Take your hand away, Nathan. Let's start again.'

It was perfect.

'I've finished, Miss Lawson.'

'But, Nathan, are you sure? To me, it looks as if you have just begun.'

'That's right, Miss Lawson.' He smiled and made his eyes crinkle. 'You are exactly right. I have finished and I have *just begun*.'

BOOK THREE

FRENCH POLYNESIA, 1982

Claudia

Claudia scraped at the hot surface of the sand with a yellow spade and wished that Mummy would come back from the dead. She hated Innocence. And she hated Daddy. She hated school. She hated sleeping at the new school and only coming home in the holidays. She hated home. She wished she could live with Ruth and JR, but Daddy wouldn't allow it. Ruth lived at her own house now, and Claudia hardly saw her *ever*. Claudia had hoped that Ruth would be invited to the hotel party, and come on the private plane with them, but Ruth said she couldn't leave JR since JR bit his sitter.

Claudia sighed. It was a desert island and amazingly hot. Nanny had put sun cream on her and some of it had gone in her eyes and stung. Nanny was in bed with a migraine, an extremely terrible pain in her head that made her sick and shout at people to whisper. She'd told Claudia to read *James and the Giant Peach*, but it was dark in the room, and the door of the villa came open if you pushed, and there outside was the beach and the sea and it was all so beautiful and bright. Claudia wanted to swim to the clouds, but Nanny had said there were sharks in the water.

It wasn't dangerous though, because she was a fast swimmer. She and Alfie, whom she was (secretly) going to

211

marry, had lessons together, in her pool with that nice bald man, Duncan, who swam for his job.

She wished Alfie was with her but he was allergic to the heat. He was inside the hotel with his daddy, Harry, sitting by the fan in a hat and long sleeves. She liked Harry. He was fun. He threw her in the air and caught her, even though, at seven, she was much too big for that sort of thing. Her daddy wasn't fun. He was always away on work. And when he was away on work, Innocence was mean to her. She hated school, the food was disgusting, but she hated coming home too.

Innocence made you polish the floor on your hands and knees, like Cinderella. But at least Cinderella got to be beautiful. Innocence had cut Claudia's hair short; she looked like a boy.

Claudia put the spade to one side and scraped at the sand with her toes. It was hot, but if you scraped deep enough, it got cool again. It was good to be alone, but she was scared that Innocence would see her and get cross. Innocence always got cross if she saw Claudia. She wished that Mummy had tried harder to stay alive. If Innocence would like her, then Claudia would like her back. But she *hated* Daddy and she would always hate Daddy, because Daddy did nothing.

Stupid grown-ups. They were having a big party for Daddy's stupid new hotel, and there were people who wrote stories for the newspapers. There were people she had seen on the television, on *Top of the Pops*. Famous people. She wasn't allowed to watch *Top of the Pops*, but when Innocence was out, Nanny let her. It was a very important party, because Daddy wanted people to like his hotel. Claudia didn't like it. It was dark inside, like a haunted house.

Her head was burning hot in the sun: she felt as if she'd catch on fire in a minute. She really wanted to go in the water. It was very shallow, and you could see to the bottom, and some tiny fish. She jumped up – ouch, ouch, the sand was like stepping on an *oven* – quick, to the water! Oh, it was so warm, like a bath. It swirled around her knees, and her waist, and she splashed with her hands, and put her legs together and pretended to be a mermaid. Except she wouldn't go underwater, no way. It was horrible not being able to breathe until someone let you. It was quite hard to swim with your legs together, she needed a proper fish's tail. But, oh, the water was pushing her deeper, she tried to stop, but it was too strong, ugh, it was salty in her mouth – help – she couldn't – she was going under – choking – oh—

'Got you!'

A great big man like a bear, with a big black beard and curly hair, was smiling at her, lifting her up, up, up, out of the water. She was happy but she was crying and scared at the same time.

'It's all right,' he said as she spluttered and coughed. The water stung inside her nose. 'You're safe now.'

'Please don't tell my stepmother,' she said, 'or I'll get told off.'

The man looked serious. 'You shouldn't have been in the water by yourself, young lady. Anything could have happened. What's your name? And where is your stepmother? She should be looking after you.'

'Claudia. She's in the hotel, with Daddy and all the other people. I'm seven and I can look after myself. And what's *your* name?'

The man smiled but she didn't like him, even though he'd rescued her. He was too hairy.

'What's your favourite name for a boy, Claudia?'

'You're not a *boy*!'

'What's your favourite boy's name, Claudia?'

'It's . . . it's . . . Orinoco. You can put me down now.'

'Well, Claudia. My name is Orinoco, and I'm going to help you to get dry. If you're a good girl now and do as you're told, I won't tell your stepmother how bad you've been. It will be our secret.'

'I'm dry, Orinoco. The sun is drying me. Please don't tell her.'

'We'll see. Do as I say, and maybe I won't. We're nearly there.'

She could feel her heart going pit-pat pit-pat, but she didn't want Orinoco to get cross. She could tell that he was *almost* cross, and it was so, so terrifying when adults got cross. They turned into monsters.

Orinoco was looking about, and then he walked quickly to the beach hut, the one right at the end of the beach, away from the hotel. He put her in a chair. It was made of bamboo and scratchy. Orinoco locked the door.

'It's too dark,' said Claudia, but she said it in her head. She wanted her daddy. Orinoco was a baddie, and it wasn't her favourite boy's name any more. She could feel her eyes getting hot, which meant that she was going to cry.

'You're going to meet a friend of mine, and I want you to be very nice to him.'

She nodded. The seat of her chair was warm and wet suddenly, and she was shaking. Slowly, Orinoco unzipped his shorts. He put a finger to his lips, and she bit hers to try not to scream. It wasn't like Daddy's – it was much bigger, and upright, purple and disgusting.

Orinoco sat down on another chair and smiled at her, like a wolf. She wanted to run but Orinoco had locked the door. There was no glass in the window but it was too high to reach. It was hard to breathe, as if she was still in the water.

'Who saved your life?'

'You did, Orinoco,' she said, but her voice wouldn't work. It came out all croaky.

'That's right. And now you are going to say thank you.' He paused. 'Come and sit with me, Claudia.'

TEN MINUTES EARLIER

Alfie

It was the worst party in the world *ever*. Lots of adults shouting and falling over. The food was brill: a chocolate cake in the shape of the island, and trifle, and a chocolate fondue with marshmallows, and a fruit salad with cherries in it, and a massive barbecue with fat sausages, and prawns the size of bananas. There was a hog roast as in medieval times, but he couldn't get to any of it, because the adults were so greedy. They pushed, then told *you* off for bad manners! They were jumping in the enormous swimming pool that looked joined to the sea and some of them were *kissing*.

Alfie slid off the chair. His legs peeled off the seat like a sticker coming away from its backing. He had heat rash and insect bites that swelled and oozed yellow pus and his back felt hot and painful even though he'd only been allowed to go snorkelling for five minutes. He'd forgotten his sunblock in the speedboat.

It was misery. His daddy had said it would be fun, but it was only fun for the adults. The adults had behaved like children – his daddy and all the journalists had water-skied, and windsurfed, and gone spear-fishing. He'd stayed inside and drawn a picture of a Chieftain tank.

Daddy was still having a good time: he was sitting in the pool drinking champagne and laughing with a lady who had a red swimming costume and big boobs. Claudia's new mother.

He wasn't scared of Claudia's new mother. She was beautiful, but she smoked, like Cruella de Vil, from a long cigarette-holder. Claudia said she was a witch, and even though Alfie didn't believe in all that nonsense, he'd seen the wigs in the room where she kept all her dresses. They were like Indian scalps. He'd wanted to check them for skin and blood, but Claudia was too frightened that they'd be caught.

It was so unfair. He wanted to play with Claudia – she was all right for a girl – but Innocence had said she was resting, and *he* couldn't see her because her nanny wasn't well. He liked his room. The bottom of the bath was see-through, and the sea was underneath. It was cool. He'd seen a lion fish. The only thing was, if a diver saw your bum.

Alfie decided to go and find a tree to climb. There were hammocks all over the island, and brown rabbits and peacocks and squirrels. He wondered if Daddy had brought his ratter.

He trudged off through the trees, dodging the sunlight. Every time it hit his skin he itched. He saw a turtle, sleeping. And a pair of sandy flippers, and a diving mask, left outside a beach villa. He stared: a spear gun, propped against the wall. Alfie glanced left and right. *One* go. He'd have to find a fish – couldn't be too hard, the sea was full of them!

He lifted it and touched the tip of the arrow. He knew he shouldn't, but it was the same as seeing a notice that said 'wet paint'. It was bloody sharp. The gun was heavy and nearly as tall as he was, but he was very strong. The handle of it was just like a normal hunting rifle. Did you *have* to shoot fish with it? Unless there was some decent shade on the beach, he couldn't face getting to the water – every step across the sand the sun would sear into his flesh. He knew just how it felt to be a hog roast.

He'd creep among the trees and see if there was a way of reaching the ocean without being fried alive. Even the dappled sunlight filtering through the leaves of the palm trees irritated his skin. He could still hear the noise and music from the party. Keep walking. OK. Right at the far end of the beach, there was a tall stack of surfboards, next to a beach hut – ah, shelter – and further along, near the water, a couple of kayaks, left upside down on the sand. He could crawl along in the shadows, like a sniper, and from there the water was only a few feet away, and there were rocks. Perfect: fish *and* shade.

He hurried through the trees, gripping the spear gun in

sweaty hands, and darted in front of the surfboards. Then into the shadow of the beach hut – ah, this was *proper*, solid cool. He paused for a second, resting the spear gun on the sand and wiping his hands on his shorts. The enemy was in his sights! Then he heard it, and froze where he stood. It was the sound of primal fear and it chilled him to the bone. All the heat left his body in a shudder. The noise was coming from inside the beach hut: the cold hard tone of an adult with no mercy, and that terrible heart-stopping whimper of a child, a little girl.

Claudia?

Alfie held his breath and slowly, quietly, picked up the gun. Suddenly he was as calm as the glassy turquoise sea. He'd stalked deer with Daddy in the Highlands every year since he could walk. Daddy said he was a rotten shot. But he wasn't. No, it took a lot of skill to convincingly miss a beautiful enormous animal like a stag every time. He crept round to the window.

'Come and sit with me, Claudia.'

The man was on a chair with his eyes closed and a strained look on his face; he was sort of panting. Alfie could only see his head and shoulders. He heaved the gun on to his shoulder, took aim at the centre of that ugly forehead. It was only as he pressed the trigger that he started to tremble and shifted his aim to one side.

The man screamed. He seemed to fly backwards, in a bright red spray of blood. Alfie staggered with the force of the recoil and fell over in the sand. 'Claudia!' he yelled, scrambling up on jelly legs. His shoulder was a blaze of white-hot pain where the butt of the gun had kicked back. 'Claudia! Are you OK?' He jumped at the window, trying to see into the room. The man was lying on the floor, clutching the side of his head, moaning, gasping. His dick was out. The arrow was embedded in the bamboo behind him, neatly pinning a ripped-off ear to the wall. Alfie took a deep breath, and looked away.

Claudia had no clothes on and a sick dazed look. 'Claudia. It's Alfie. Move the chair to the window.'

She gazed at him, numb.

'*DO AS I SAY,*' he roared in his father's voice. It hurt his shoulder even to speak.

She started and pushed the chair.

'Quick.'

Gritting his teeth against the agony, he hauled himself up to the window. The man was staggering to his feet, and his face was grim like death. She climbed on to the chair. 'Come *on,*' he said. 'Jump.' He held out his thin arms. 'I'll catch you.'

She stared at him, hesitated for a second, and he was back in the Highlands, helpless, witnessing the gentle despair of a doe just before death. The man lunged, grabbed her, and she disappeared from sight.

THE POOL BAR, TWO MINUTES EARLIER

Harry

What a rack. Her nipples were clearly visible beneath the thin material. He was getting a stiffy. And she was looking at him *that way.* But she was the wife of his friend, and Harry did not shit on his own doorstep, despite the fact that Jack had done the dirty on him. His wife Helen had agreed there were mitigating circumstances, but the relationship would never be quite what it had been.

Ah well. A man could dream. You could drown in that cleavage. And when she uncrossed her legs, he could see the—

'Harry.'

'Jack, old chap! Splendid party. Your wife and I were discussing the stock mark—'

'Harry, where's Alfie?'

'The little chap? Sitting right over – ah, bugger.'

'Claudia's nanny woke up and she'd gone. I've had the staff check every villa, but there's no sign. Perhaps she's with him?' Jack paused. 'They wouldn't go in the *sea*, would they?'

Fuck. Helen would kill him if anything happened to Alfie. But she wouldn't have to – he'd kill himself. That little chap lit up his world. Why had he taken his eye off the ball just because they were on holiday? It was more dangerous than home. His heart shrank pea-sized with dread.

'We've got no time. This bunch of hacks – get them involved.'

Jack paused. Harry gave him a look. 'This is no time to be proud, Jack.'

'You're right, of course.'

'I'll get their attention,' said Innocence. She walked over to where the band was playing, and whispered in the ear of the lead singer – a Frog? Le Bon was his name, though he sounded English. Well, he sounded like a bloody racket. Not quite the thing, but Jack didn't take advice these days.

'I'm so sorry to interrupt your enjoyment,' she purred into the microphone, with a smile on her beauteous face – she was mint-julep cool in the face of disaster – 'but Jack's seven-year-old daughter, Claudia, and Lord Cannadine's ten-year-old, Alfie, have gone missing on the island. We *beg* you to join us in our search. They could be anywhere. They could be in danger.' She paused, lowered her eyelashes, seemed to swallow a sob. 'Thank you, so much.'

As Harry leaped out of the pool and ran towards the beach, he was aware of Jack glaring at his wife. What was his fucking problem? His *child* was missing, and he was worried about the bad press! But it was working. This bunch of alcoholics had trained themselves to function at 20 per cent proof, and off they all trotted after the prize, like sniffer dogs. At least the piles of coke they'd hoovered up would give

219

them energy for the search. For them, it wasn't about the lost children, it was about the story, but he didn't care. Just let Alfie and Claudia be safe.

He thundered across the sand, straining his eyes out to sea. 'Alfie,' he shouted. 'Alfieeee.'

And then, oh blessed day, a small figure staggering around in the distance, by a beach hut. 'Daddy, Daddy, *run*.'

'Alfie! Daddy's coming. Everyone, here!'

LAKE COMO, ITALY, A WEEK LATER

Innocence

'Darling, excuse me for just one second.'

Innocence hurried up the marble staircase to one of the Roman-sized bathrooms, closed and locked the burgundy-velvet and walnut-wood-panelled door, and sat her pert behind on the thick red marble edge of the tub. She stared at a white marble bust of a Greek god – some bald guy with a beard – and laughed and laughed.

After the horrors of last week, Jack would be begging her to take her place on the board. Which meant she would be able to call a halt to Plan B. Plan B would be so very harsh on poor Jack.

It was so kind of dear Gianni to lend them his charming lakeside pad for the *bambina* to recuperate. She'd always liked his frocks, and now she *loved* them!

She was half annoyed that Jack's refurbishment and renovations of the Spyglass Island Villa Retreat had turned out gorgeous. The wood was too dark, and he wasn't fabulous on detail, but he'd managed, without asking her opinion once, to create a desirable and exclusive destination – and all the new staff were young, beautiful, and didn't wear red waistcoats.

And, she'd realized – stupid only to realize *now* – that the hacks wouldn't have cared had he stuck a line of caravans along the beach. What mattered was that Jack had shown those dog-eat-dogs the time of their sordid lives. Booze, drugs, grub, all laid on. The grubby hordes had enjoyed frangipani massages, they'd sailed catamarans, they'd picked the pink curly shells off the white icing sugar sand and jammed them in their pockets: it was all about greed, grabbing as much as they could get. They were being bribed to make the love ooze off the page.

And it would have paid off. The rich and famous would have had their butlers ringing the phone off the hook to book the presidential suites, the ocean-view villas, the entire island all year round, and Jack would have thought he was invincible.

But, that mistress of disaster, Claudia, had managed to turn the jewel of her father's young empire into a piece of broken glass.

Now, he would see that he needed Innocence. For richer, he needed her.

The headlines were horrific. Innocence's particular favourite was the *News of the World*: 'PAEDO IN PARADISE – WE SAVE TYCOON'S KID'.

A story on pages 2, 3, 4, 5, 6, 7, 8 and 9 followed – 'As her millionaire dad drunkenly partied with a bevy of blondes . . .' – which managed to cover every grim detail, including the fact that Jack had once wet his bed aged eleven.

She'd covered *her* tracks well enough – had the wit to pay some dropouts from that posh school to sell a 'story' on her. She'd scanned the pages with shaking hands, but their main interest in her was her bust size. The photo of her was satisfactory – how *dare* Jack question her need for her hairstylist to travel with her! Once she was working *with* him she would also employ a full-time make-up artist. It was the 1980s. Image was everything.

And the image of Jack's fabulous island retreat was dirt. It would always be the island retreat where his seven-year-old had escaped being raped and killed by a nonce. Jack's own image was tarnished: he was a rotten father. He'd sacked the nanny but it was too little too late – why oh why wasn't he watching his kid? It was *his* island, that practically made it *his* nonce! The pictures on page two were of a rugged Harry Cannadine carrying a limp Claudia in his arms, and his handsome son and heir, Alfred Horatio Nelson Cannadine, hobbling by his side – having dislocated his shoulder while rescuing the fair maiden. Harry and Alfie were the heroes. 'Fucking Establishment,' Jack had muttered.

The only thing the *News of the World* had forgotten to mention was that the nonce in question was a journalist.

Innocence reapplied her crimson lipstick in the mirror while the goddesses etched into the glass gazed down with approval. She adored neoclassical. It was well OTT. Gianni had personally sourced every item from the world's auction houses, to recreate the palazzo as it was in the 1700s, when it had belonged to the aristocratic Cambiaghi family of Milan. The place wasn't complete, but so far he'd done a bang-up job. She adored the eighteenth-century Russian crystal chandelier. It had hung in the Imperial Palace in St Petersburg. And now she, Sharon Marshall of Hackney, was treading in the footsteps of lords, ladies, kings and queens – as an equal.

She'd better go and check on Claudia. She shuddered. They'd been unable to get her to speak. She was traumatized, said the doctor – a real brain surgeon. The doctor had given her an internal examination – probably adding to the trauma, but these men (idiots), what did they know?

Innocence had stood there on the beach last week, feeling shaky and sick. She couldn't stand the kid – every time Jack looked at his adopted daughter with love in his eyes, she felt her throat close in a fist of black hatred. And Claudia was so *stupid*. The girl deserved a good slap.

But *this*.

Innocence had pushed her way into the beach hut where some of the hacks were roughing up the kiddy-fiddler. 'Mind, please,' she'd said, and they'd shuffled back like naughty children. It amused her that they assumed she'd never witnessed violence – if a few feeble kicks to the groin were what you called *violence*. The perv had looked her up and down, an insolent grin, even though he was missing an ear, and rasped, '*Your* fault...' Miss Ashford had smiled sweetly, stamped on his face and broken his nose. Then she'd marched outside and smoked a cigarette.

It's *your fault. You* led him on. She'd been ten. Her mother was deluded, eaten up with twisted rage because she was such a hag that her bloke wasn't interested in her. Gerry had dealt with Dad, in the end. Sharon was nineteen then, far away and untouchable. Gerry had got him pissed, sliced him up, chucked him in the Thames. Dad was such an old cunt that when it came to suspects, the Bill were spoilt for choice. Gerry had always been fond of his big sis. He was a softie like that.

Innocence had lit another fag with trembling fingers.

Bad things happened and that was life. She didn't think about that shit – it was over, nothing good would come of having it in her head: the sour blast of beer breath on her face; his rough calloused fingers pressing purple bruises into her soft skin; the sick-making smell of his body, like microwaved chicken. People suffered worse, and she couldn't stand *whiners*. She'd got her revenge. He was dead and she was living, *very well*.

In a way, it was good that Dad had messed with her, not her kid sister, Susan. Sharon was tough. Nothing broke Sharon. But Susan would have been destroyed. Susan was a poppet, a little flower, *weak*.

Like Claudia.

Now, Innocence smoothed her hair, sashayed along the corridor to the guest bedroom where Claudia lay under a red and gold satin bedspread. 'Claudia?' she said.

The girl was asleep, her dark hair spread out on the pillow like that dead bird in Jack's painting. Ophelia. She didn't like that painting. It gave her the creeps. She'd have to persuade Jack to sell it to the Tate. He wouldn't care. He didn't like art – he couldn't see the beauty in anything – he could only see the pound signs. He was learning.

Innocence strode to the great window and opened the green and gold drapes. The sunlight was making rainbows in the fountain at the back of the palazzo. Innocence sat on a blue satin armchair, and lit up. A minute later, Claudia awoke, coughing.

'How are you feeling, love?' It felt strange to hear this unfamiliar softness in her voice. The word 'love' tasted odd on her tongue.

Claudia smiled. 'OK, Innocence,' she said. Her voice was barely there; she hadn't spoken for two days.

Oh, God. It was pathetic. This child was like a puppy, with her big imploring eyes, begging for love, so eager to please.

Innocence patted the bedclothes briskly. She couldn't actually touch Claudia. It was like approaching a house spider: you didn't get too close because of the fear that it might suddenly leap on you. But – Innocence breathed deeply through her nose – it seemed that the instant anger that always charged her veins at the mere sight of this interloper was ... diluted. For the first time ever, she felt ... a connection?

'Would you like something to eat?' She could do practical. 'The chef has made lunch.' She glanced at the elegantly hand-written menu on the side table.

Tortina di carciofi – Artichoke tart
Risotto Milanese e osso buco – Veal shank with saffron risotto

Her stomach heaved.
'I'm not hungry,' whispered Claudia.
Thank God. It was stirring up all those vile memories that

224

had done it. Innocence felt sick to her stomach, and if she caught so much as a whiff of that veal shank, Gianni would be sending her the dry-cleaning bill for his priceless seventeenth-century Ushak carpet. Jack would have to eat alone.

'OK, love, you rest. I'll be back in an hour or so.'

She hurried back to the bathroom and threw up into the red marble toilet. She was never ill. What *was* this?

She brushed her teeth ferociously – ugh, the toothpaste made her gag. And then she dropped the toothbrush into the basin, and sank on to the green and gold Empire-style divan with a bump.

She'd come off the pill the second she'd married him. You had to stake your claim. But the doctor had said . . . Oh, fuck the doctor, when was a doctor ever right? This was it. This was it! No wonder her clothes felt a little tight. She tilted her head back and smiled. She was pregnant. She was going to provide Jack with his own child – not like that barren bitch Felicia having to ship in some orphan brat.

Innocence smoothed her hair in the mirror, and turned sideways. Her stomach was still flat. She couldn't wait to tell Jack.

She skipped out of the bathroom, stopped still. Someone was calling her, in a hoarse, desperate scream. 'Innocence! Help! Help! Orinoco is coming to get me – please! I'm frightened!'

Oh, for God's sake. She stamped along the corridor and flung open the door. Claudia jumped. 'Shut up! Don't be such a baby! Shouting at me like that – how dare you. Stop making such a fuss about nothing! You just had a bad dream. Shut up and go to sleep.' She had a glimpse of Claudia's face crumpling before the door slammed. Yeah, well, get used to it. No one, certainly not some illegitimate brat that no one else wanted, was going to come between Jack Kent and his own flesh and blood. This child – *their* child – was her trump card, and the very fact that Claudia existed was a declaration of war.

As Innocence regally swept down the marble staircase to inform her husband that his line was to be continued, she sang a tune that must have been in her blood, a tune that the mothers of England had sung to their babies for hundreds of years:

Lavender's blue, dilly dilly, lavender's green,
When you are King, dilly dilly, I shall be Queen.

THE VERSACE VILLA, LAKE COMO, TEN MINUTES EARLIER

Jack

The Spyglass Island Retreat in French Polynesia was a sensation. For all the wrong reasons.

It was a disaster. But you couldn't legislate for evil. He didn't blame himself. No. Why should he? The hotel was his baby. Claudia was the charge of her nanny and Innocence. They were the guilty ones.

It worried him that Innocence didn't know her place, which was to further his prospects by moving in the right circles, to organize and attend the right social events, to provide him with a family to establish the Kent name as a bastion of all that was British and proper.

And here they were: guests of an Italian dressmaker. He had nothing against Versace himself – obviously a kind, decent man, ringing to offer 'friends' (he was tactful enough not to call Innocence a 'client') a haven to relax and recuperate in after a horrific experience.

But Versace wasn't high society.

Jack lit a cigar and flung himself on to an orange silk chaise longue. The whole thing was a nightmare. If he'd had a gun,

226

he'd have shot that pervert in the face. His PA – Ms Martha Green, or as he thought of her, Special Agent Green – had taken his arm and removed him from the beach hut. She wasn't going to have him do something he'd regret, certainly not in front of the tabloid press. She had guided him to Claudia, so that he could take her from Harry's arms.

It had been an awkward moment.

He was terrified. He could hardly look at his daughter. He couldn't see her pain because he knew if he saw it, it would become his. So he'd bleated trite words of comfort ('It's all right, sweetheart, you'll be OK') when Christ knew what that monster had actually done to her – or made her do. She wouldn't say, and although the internal examination proved negative for rape, the bastard had obviously done *something*. When Jack forced himself to meet her glassy gaze, he'd seen damage in her eyes. He'd looked away. He'd only ever wanted to protect his daughter and make her happy. No one likes to stare their failure in the face.

The hotel was fucked.

He fumbled in his pocket for a pill. He'd come round to Prozac in a big way. It amused him that he'd ever been so prim about prescription drugs. Vitamins for the brain, that's all they were. Helped it to function. Especially when washed down with a couple of Valium.

Sanity, he realized, was merely your commitment to holding on to it. He needed pharmaceutical aid to keep his grasp.

He couldn't stand the uncontrollable waves of panic caused by the smallest event, the way his mind zigzagged over every option. Marmalade with toast, or jam? Jam! No! Marmalade! It was that bad. Prozac gave him a superior detachment, it wiped his mind of that terrible, weak self-doubt, it crushed those ridiculous, girlish panic attacks, it made him the cool, calm master of the universe that he ought to be. And, let's face it, being on Prozac was a mark of your status. If you didn't need Prozac, well, you were nobody!

He'd have to open the season at a massive discount: it would barely cover costs. He had a lifestyle to maintain and with sister hotels opening in LA, New York and the Amalfi Coast his assets were stretched so thinly. He'd borrowed with the abandon of a man in a hurry for success and he was hostage to the goodwill of the banks – 'the banks'!, as if they were grey, faceless entities, when they were in fact run by a most particular breed of people, as ruthless as they were charming, rich, important *posh* people who loathed upstarts.

They wouldn't foreclose on one of their own, which was why he so desperately needed to be accepted as one of them. It was all right for Innocence, she was born to it. She could afford to be eccentric – he hadn't initially realized how eccentric. Had he known he might have . . . well. He was all right. He was no fool.

Harry could only do so much. Innocence had given the strong impression that she was fabulously connected, but she seemed unwilling to exercise those connections. Once, at a benefit in Chelsea for old soldiers, the Duchess of Kent had waved at Innocence with a puzzled look, as if she couldn't quite place her. Jack had strode towards the duchess for an introduction; Innocence had purred, '*Manners*, Jack!' and led him in the other direction.

He shook his head, watching the blue smoke rings waft towards the ceiling.

A knock.

'Enter!'

The butler: small, ancient, Italian, suspiciously black hair. 'The phone is calling for you, sir.' He paused. 'It is *not* the newspaper. I have word.'

'Thank you.' Jack nodded and lifted the receiver. It was very . . . *gold*.

Ten minutes later, he put down the phone and punched the air. 'Yes!' he shouted. 'Yes, yes, and fucking *yes*!'

He summoned the butler and ordered a bottle of Dom Pérignon 1966. He knew bugger all about booze (except how to drink it) but he'd paid a sommelier to put together a cellar. The guy had worked for Sol Kerzner so Jack supposed he knew what he was talking about. He travelled the world, bidding for bottles at auction. He cost, but you had to look as if you knew about these things. They probably taught History of Alcohol at Eton. Two great crystal bowls of bubbly were fizzing away when Innocence appeared at the door.

She looked especially beautiful – ah, *mine*, all mine! She also looked stunned at his grinning face. Fair enough. For the last week his mood had been as black as tar. 'Darling,' she said. 'Is everything . . . OK?'

He kissed her, whirling her round the gigantic room. 'It's fantastic.' He grinned. 'I've been proposed for a membership of Lloyd's. I'm about to become elected as a *Name*. A Lloyd's Name!'

Innocence seemed to tense.

'Darling, that's nice. But . . . *why*?'

His head jerked in surprise. She knew *why*. It meant that he was finally recognized by the English landed gentry as one of *them*. Did she doubt that he was worthy? It enraged him that she believed they must have an ulterior motive – her suspicion reflected badly on *him*.

He thought about his own, long-abandoned community. Ruth didn't give a toss about religion, but the other women were deadly. One man's wife had converted from C of E; she was probably more knowledgeable about Judaism than the whole synagogue put together, but she would always be 'the convert'. Even though this stranger was allowed into the fold, she would never be quite as equal as those who were born to it.

Was that how the Establishment regarded *him*? No. He was a self-made man, he was married to nobility. He deserved to be a Name.

'Because I have a huge cock. They must have heard the rumours.'

She didn't laugh. 'Why ask you *now*, the week after your

business has been hit by this ghastly publicity and its future is so . . . uncertain?'

She knew how to wind him up. 'Look, love, it's sweet of you to be cautious on my behalf and, to put your mind at rest, I still have to undergo a ball-breaking interview. But, *entre nous*' – hm, breaking into French: classy or common? Best get Agent Green on that one – 'it's a done deal.'

'Who proposed you?'

'Altringham. The banker. A friend of a friend of Harry's. You've met him.' It briefly occurred to him that Innocence might have wielded influence, but he dismissed the possibility. 'His agent will be *my* agent, although I'll be in a different syndicate.'

'Is Harry a Name?'

'Is that relevant?' He could almost feel the Prozac clash swords with the roar of adrenalin.

'Darling, Harry has excellent financial advisers. Whereas your advisers are scared to go ag—'

'Nonsense. As I recall, you are not involved in any official aspect of my business and—' He stopped. She looked as if she were about to speak, but had reconsidered. 'What?' he snapped.

'How much are they asking from you?'

'It's not your concern.'

'Please, Jack. Just tell me. I'm your wife.' Innocence did not usually sound humble.

He sighed. 'They'll ask me to deposit a bank letter of credit for two hundred thousand pounds. And I have to give evidence of an additional three hundred thousand of net worth. The more money I put up, the higher the premium income I'm permitted to receive,' he added quickly. 'They're practically giving you something for nothing.' He grinned. 'I can scrape that lot together in no time. Maybe sell a painting. I've seen the way you look at the Millais.'

Innocence sat down hard on a sumptuous chair. She didn't look happy. 'What's the risk?'

He snorted. 'There *is* no risk! We're looking at an institution with three hundred years of straight profit!'

'But say the impossible happened?'

She was really winding him up. His fingers itched to pop another pill, take the edge off. He gritted his teeth. 'I deposit enough stocks and bonds to cover any losses that Lloyd's might have to pay out. But that's not going to happen. Now, darling, can we stop with the inquisition, and celebrate?' He snatched up a champagne bowl and drained it. 'Here.'

She took a small sip from the other champagne bowl.

'What? Nineteen sixty-six Dom not good enough for you?' His nerves were jangling like church bells. Trust a bird to hack through 25 mg of anti-hassle medication.

She stroked his face. He wanted to jerk away, but . . . ah, the touch of her. 'Sweetheart,' she murmured. 'It tastes disgusting but . . . for a good reason. I also have some news. We're going to be *parents*.'

He stared at her, starting to laugh. His *own* – No, he mustn't think like that! A new baby! His heart pumped through the fog. 'That's fantastic!'

She looked coy. 'I suppose I'm thinking like a mother. I want to safeguard our future . . . our *baby's* future. I don't mean to upset you, darling.'

'Sweetheart, don't be silly! You're right to be cautious, absolutely right!'

She gave him a shy smile. 'I . . . I worry that if the impossible *did* happen, and Lloyd's, as an insurance company, sustained huge losses – I know it's terribly unlikely – but it's still a gamble, and I worry that you could lose every single possession you've worked so hard for, including your hotels, including our *homes*, and Baby might be homeless – and I couldn't bear it, to think of our poor little baba, *suffering*! And I just wonder if it might be prudent to place some of the possible – oh, what's that word?' She blinked prettily. 'Yes, assets, in someone else's name.' She paused. 'Claudia? Or your mother?'

He frowned. The woman had a point. 'Claudia is too young. It's not possible. And my mother – I couldn't trust her not to do something nuts. She'd sign everything over to the RSPCA.'

Innocence nodded. 'I love you, Jack. I suppose I shouldn't, but I want to . . . protect you . . . us.' She patted her stomach.

He felt a rush of love. She was a mass of hard edges, but she had a heart as sweet and as soft as pink marshmallow. 'Innocence, I think you're going to make a wonderful mummy. Clever you.'

She giggled. 'You had a *big* part in it.'

He gently placed the champagne bowl on the side and pulled her to him in a fierce kiss. She sighed, moulding her sumptuous curves to him. He groaned, and pulled her to the floor. She wriggled out of her little black lace knickers and sat astride him. Oh, God, she felt so *good*. She wrapped her long legs around him. Oh, fuck, oh, yeah, oh—

'Babe.' Her lips nuzzled his ear, her voice was husky, and he had to fight to keep control. 'I think you need my help.'

'You're – helping – me, baby. You're – helping – me.'

She slid off him, down, down, and – oh Christ. His eyes were practically rolling in his head.

'What I mean is—'

'Stop talking! I mean – don't stop! *Ooh, yes!*'

'I'd like to take a more . . .'

Uah!

'. . . active role in your . . .'

Wo-oh!

'. . . affairs.'

He pushed her off him, zipped up. 'What', he said, 'do you mean?'

'Hey,' she said, and she was a tiger, purring. 'I want to make sure that a week like the last never happens again. Remember last week?'

He shuddered.

'It will have repercussions.'

'A few.'

She stroked his firm stomach with a touch that made him shiver. 'Darling. I can be so much more than *this*. If I were your director of marketing, I would have hand-picked those journalists. Your choice – I believe he only joined the company three months ago – invited along a child molester.'

'That prick is fired and will never work again. I intend to sue the shirt off his back.'

'And you're looking for a replacement?'

He smiled at her. 'But that would be nepotism.'

'Oh,' she murmured. 'But keep it in the *family*.'

He cupped her heart-shaped chin and softly turned her face towards his. 'You really want this, don't you?'

There was something in her eyes.

He stroked the hair out of her face. Why *should* she want this? She had everything: status, money, and now a baby. Unless she had plans he didn't know about. He was paranoid, even on 25 mg.

'Angel. You have the most important job in the world: the job of bringing up our child . . . children.' He felt himself blush. 'You can spend, spend, spend, but leave the earning to me. I'm afraid I'm old-fashioned like that. I don't want my wife working. I don't want her to be seen to be working. Perhaps some token charity fluff: kids, MS, breast cancer is hot, but nothing more serious. I don't want you to encounter any stress during your pregnancy.'

To be honest, he expected a tantrum, even tears. But she merely nodded and said, 'As you wish, darling. I only wanted to help. I understand. And forgive me for being so silly about Lloyd's. You have far more experience in these areas – and it's a wonderful opportunity for you.' Then she gave him a light kiss on the cheek, smiled sweetly and parted her legs a little. 'Are you sure you don't want to finish what we started?'

As Jack pumped away, Innocence longed for a good-quality feather duster to brush the cobwebs from the chandelier. You just couldn't get the help these days. 'Mm,' she sighed. 'Oh yes, oh, *Jack*.'

Sharon Marshall had a thousand ways of being persuasive. It was just a pity for Jack that he was so unwilling to be persuaded. A simple yes would have made life so much easier for him. But, he was stubborn, and Plan B was already in action.

Poor Jack. It was like taking candy from a baby. Not that she'd actually *do* something so wicked – although, of course, it would depend on the baby . . .

LONDON, 1990

Nathan

'She's expecting you,' said Mark, grinning like a monkey from the orange Citroën 2CV's driving seat. 'No pressure! Do you want me to wait here? Or should I pick you up later?' His laugh sounded forced. 'Now, remember, I could get into deep doo-doo for this, mister! We're supposed to be at the zoo.'

Nathan smiled. 'Chill, Markie,' he said. Mark loved it when Nathan called him Markie. 'I'll give you a shout. But I may be a while.'

Mark nodded. 'I know. It's a pretty big deal, this. You take your time. Just give me a bell when you're ready.'

Nathan waved. 'Cheers,' he said, and stood there until Mark took the hint and drove off. Her house was big – a *whole* house, not a half-house or a joined-up house. Those were crap. It had three lots of windows at the front, and the roof came right down. It made the house look half asleep. There were red roses growing up the wall in a neat, confined way, and a black garage. The front was a perfect square of grass. There were flowers all around it. Tall white funeral ones, lemon-yellow ones, bright pink ones, massive daisy ones. He didn't know the names of any of the flowers. It was a nice house. It was a very *smart* house.

He glanced down at himself. His jeans were from Topshop; he looked the business! Mark had insisted. It was, after all, a special occasion. The flowers were his idea too. 'Women go nuts for flowers,' he'd said – like *he* knew! They were pink; Nathan didn't know what sort. It looked like she would, though.

He walked up the path and rang the doorbell. Suddenly his heart sped up. What if she had a family – a bloke, children? He didn't think so, though. The house looked too tidy. There were no plastic toys dumped in the drive. He was glad of that. When he saw a plastic toy, it made him feel ill.

Footsteps. *Click-clack, click-clack.* High heels. Wooden floor. The door swung open and the woman said, 'Hell— Oh my God!'

He stared at her. For *real*, he stared at her. His stomach turned to hot liquid, and he breathed hard to stay upright.

She stared back. She was pretty old – like, thirty. She had his eyes.

She saw it too. He smiled, shyly. She put her hand over her heart, hiding it. 'Simon?' she said. 'My God. Is it you? Simon!' She took a step back. 'Would you . . .' She swallowed. 'Would you like to come in?'

Very polite. Polite, grown-up talk. Had he come far? Had he walked? At least it wasn't raining! But when she made them each a cup of tea, he noticed she reached for the prettiest china, in the top cupboard, and that her hands shook. She kept looking at his face, looking away. At his face, away, then back again. He was saying that she had a very smart garden, oh, and these flowers were for her, and—

Suddenly, she sat down quickly on the chair, gasping, as if she couldn't breathe. 'How?' she panted. She was crying, a lot. There were *double* tears rolling down her cheeks. He felt himself being grabbed and squashed to her. Now *he* could hardly breathe. She smelled of perfume fit to choke you. He didn't want to, but he put his arms around her neck and squeezed. He had to steel himself not to jump away to the other side of the room, shuddering. It was the same feeling he'd got after he licked a toad for a bet.

'Oh, Simon.' Her voice was a deep groan. It was like how women sounded on 15 films before they had sex. He felt like he might puke.

And Simon was a crap name. It was the name on the birth certificate, the one *she* had chosen. He couldn't say how wrong and bad it made him feel, to be called by the wrong name.

'It's Nathan.'

'Nathan! Of course. Your friend Mark said, on the phone. Oh, Nathan!' Now she was stroking his face, gazing into his eyes, all over him like a rash. It was too much, *way* too intense, like having a gun pointed directly at your head. He could smell her breath.

She pulled him to her again, her arms heavy around his neck, and talking, non-stop talking until he felt like his head might explode. How had he found her, she knew he would come, she had written so many times, but no one would tell her where he was, thank God, it was a miracle, she had prayed for this day, she had never dared believe it would come, she had to pinch herself – and him! – to make sure he was real, he was beautiful, what a beautiful boy, and so grown up, she was so sorry, but she was so young when she'd had him ('when *I* had *you*': *how dare she, the cheek, like sticking her tongue down his throat*), her parents had hit the roof, called her a tart (*yes*), forced her to give up her baby, she'd had no choice, done as she was told, made to feel ashamed, you thought times had changed but, bloody hell, they hadn't changed one bit, but she'd hoped, she'd always hoped, he'd had a better life because of her – their – decision . . . dumb, hopeful, weak face, big watery eyes gazing at him, *his* eyes, please don't tell me anything *bad*, don't let *me* suffer, just make it OK for *me* . . .

He was fine. He had been fostered once or twice, but it had never worked out, and now he lived in a children's home.

'A children's home!'

The horrified look on her face assumed that unwanted kids were all sent to live in pink fairy-tale palaces, little princes and princesses, running around making daisy chains and riding Raleigh bikes and eating fondant fancies all day long, *stupid, stupid bitch.*

'And' – shy, hesitating – 'do you have children?' Pause. '*Other* children?'

She looked sad and happy at once – what a dumb look. 'No . . . No. I never did. It just never . . . happened for me.' She stopped. 'I was married, not to your . . . father. With him . . . It was on holiday, I never saw him again.' (*Slag.*) 'I married, quite young.' She laughed quietly. 'Probably to escape from my parents. It wasn't a happy time. I'm divorced now.'

'I'm so sorry. Poor you.'

'Oh no,' she said, but he could tell she was pleased that he'd said it. 'In many ways I'm fortunate, I suppose. After the divorce . . . very generous . . . and sadly, my parents died three years ago . . . a car accident . . . I don't have to work.'

She was a proper Girl Guide.

'I suppose,' he said carefully – it was always good when you copied how *they* spoke, and she spoke like a jug made of bone china – 'it's great not to work. But it's sad to have no parents.' Your gift to *me*.

'Yes.' She sighed. She sounded as if she was twelve and he was the grown-up! 'It is a little . . . lonely sometimes.' A timid smile. 'You are my only family, Nathan. Thank you for coming back to me.' She leaned in for another hug, greedy to take the love that she didn't deserve.

He suffered her insolent touch. 'I'm really happy I found

you. But . . . I've got to go back to the care home now. My . . . social worker is coming to get me. Please can I use your phone?'

When Mark finally showed up in his tin can, Nathan burst out of the front door and gulped the fresh air. It was as if he'd been trapped underwater.

Time for one more assault. She let go, after what seemed like years, but didn't step away, and he wanted to gag. He smiled. 'It's been incredible to meet you.' *Get out of my space.* He paused. Should he? Too much? Fuck, nothing was too much for this nutjob. '*Mummy.*'

She practically came. 'Oh! Thank you . . . *darling.*' To Mark: 'Does he *have* to go?' Tears.

He made a point of looking sad and blowing kisses as they drove off.

'How do you feel?' said Mark. Mark loved that question. Mark must have asked him that question fifty thousand times. But go easy on Mark. Mark had taught him a lot.

'I feel *great,*' said Nathan. 'She is everything I wanted her to be.' Cross my heart, hope to die, stick a needle in my eye.

LONDON, 1991

Paula

Sometimes, at night, she'd creep in to his room and watch him sleeping. Then, he looked so young and pure that she could almost believe no time had passed at all, and that he was still a baby. He would always be a baby; he *was* a baby. She wanted to bite his bottom! She'd confessed this desire to him, jokily – although she was half serious – and they'd laughed about it together. It was amazing how similar they were. They found the same things funny. And they had the same eyes. But it wasn't just the physical side. She noticed that his mannerisms were like hers, the way he used his hands to emphasize a point.

She noticed everything.

He was used to having nothing: she could see that. She couldn't bear to think about it. She was so happy to be able to *give* to him, when, that is, she'd finally gained custody of *her own child* – bloody ridiculous, the red tape. That it had taken a whole year was an absolute disgrace. Those awful, awful left-wing people at that ... well, it was a *prison*. 'Home' indeed! She'd shuddered to think of her baby trapped inside with all those nasty little criminals. How *dared* they make him out to be all those terrible things. Of course he'd gone a little off the rails! She'd had everything, and even she'd stolen an apple from her friend's lunchbox when she was, what, seven? She still felt bad about that.

God bless Mark. He knew that Nathan had reformed. He was the only one of that bunch even qualified to provide a character reference; he'd known Nathan for years. It pained her that she hadn't, that there were great yawning gaps in his precious history that she knew nothing about.

She'd blocked out the agony for so long, over a decade, that now it was all rushing back and, despite the unparalleled joy of holding him in her arms, of breathing in the heavenly scent of her own child, the immensity of all that she'd missed hit her – it was like being smacked in the face with a cricket bat.

She couldn't give him enough, do enough for him. She had to always be touching him – it was like an addiction. She thought she'd want to tell all her friends – huh, *what* friends? After the divorce they'd all taken his side, followed the money. People were shallow. Anyway, she found she wanted to keep this miracle to herself, keep *him* to herself. She felt like a dog with a bone. She wanted to drag Nathan behind the sofa and growl at anyone who came near him. He was her property. She couldn't share him, not for a minute.

She'd given him the largest bedroom. She'd had it painted specially, with the ceiling a galaxy of stars and planets. She supposed he was too old for a train mobile, or even a helicopter lamp, but she didn't think he'd mind that she'd bought him a box of toy soldiers just to *have*. She'd got him a computer (Apple of course), and a stereo, and a plasma TV. And roller skates. And a bike. And a tennis racquet. And a selection of designer clothes, and Nike trainers. And a mobile phone – so he could call her, if he went out, and she could call him. She needed to hear his voice. She *feasted* on the beautiful sound of that voice.

He also had his own bathroom. He was very hygiene-conscious for a teenager – he took at least two showers a day. So what if she was spoiling him. Her only child had been deprived and the thought made her sick to her stomach. When social services had finally agreed that she could foster Nathan, she'd asked if she should hire a van to move in his things. He'd replied, 'What things?'

She couldn't bear to think that he had gone without. She asked if he would ever forgive her, and he'd replied, 'There is nothing to forgive.' He didn't eat as much as she would have wished; he was a little too thin. Just listen to her! So maternal! But oh, he was beautiful, quite stunning to look at, and it wasn't just because she was his mummy. She was so proud to call him her son.

Whatever he told her he liked, she remembered. In fact, he was only discovering now what he liked. He hadn't had access to any significant choice before – he'd never eaten an avocado, or an olive! He'd never been abroad; she'd got him his first passport. It was amazing to have ... *purpose*. The garden was beautiful, and so was the house, but there was a limit to the satisfaction you could derive from a house, a limit to the number of times you could re-do the lounge, or rip out the kitchen. With Nathan, there was no limit. There was always something she could be doing for him.

She was a good cook, but it had been no fun cooking for

one. After her divorce she'd lost a stone. Whereas, during their eight-year marriage, her ex-husband had gained three. Now she rediscovered her skills. Nathan loved Italian food: spaghetti alla puttanesca, lasagne. He was a little nervous of trying Thai, but her green chicken curry put paid to that! And he was so appreciative, so grateful: it broke her heart, because she guessed that no one had ever cooked a special meal for him before. He'd eaten junk, or stodge; basically, whatever was cheap.

It was disgusting, how he'd been treated.

Now he was going to have the best of the best. He'd already started at that secondary school – *school*, what a joke! It was more like a juvenile detention centre, full of foul-mouthed thugs who, if you walked past them, made a point of including the word 'fucking' in every sentence. A police officer was stationed outside as they swarmed out, to protect the public. She couldn't wait to get him out of there.

She'd enrolled him at the best private school in the area. It was heavily over-subscribed but it helped that there were 'exceptional circumstances'. That said, his 'background' (grr) required an assessment by an educational psychologist. She was nervous – she didn't trust shrinks – but Nathan had per-formed beautifully. He was an *easy* child; you could see that he found the other children fascinating. He talked less than he listened. The shrink had said that he was skilled at 'reflect-ing'; she guessed that was good. Oh, and he was independent, which they loved.

He was thriving. He embraced every experience, and it gave her deep satisfaction to know that she had improved her son's life, given him the chance to ski in Austria, camp in the New Forest, sail in the south of France, act in front of a real theatre audience, learn to play the guitar, and form friend-ships with the *right* children. He was popular, said his teachers, always ready to hear other kids' problems, yet never complaining himself. Mentally, he was impressively . . . *adult*, they'd said. His head ruled his heart. He was highly controlled; they had never seen him express a negative emotion. This was fine, as long as he wasn't repressing his feelings. Perhaps he needed encouragement – acknowledgement from a trusted adult that sometimes it was permissible to let go? But this was a minor detail! He was funny, even-tempered, charming, superb at sport. He needed extra tuition in maths and English, but he'd soon catch up. The head teacher had called him an asset to the school! He was perfect. The perfect child; the perfect son.

'Darling!' she called. Nathan was holed up in his bedroom, as usual, listening to Metallica. At this age, it was normal. She couldn't bear it for too long though; she craved his company. Now she'd lure him downstairs. She'd bought a video of *The Breakfast Club*, and she thought they could snuggle up on the sofa and watch it together. She'd made a nice dinner. She'd bought Angus mince and made her own beef burgers, with home-made chips, and a token lettuce leaf.

'Coming, Mum!' He was so obliging. He had his quiet moods, but he was, for someone approaching puberty, a very cool customer! She wouldn't say he was cold, or detached – she didn't like those words at all – he was his own person. Yes. But he was also her treat, her pleasure, her only delight.

'There we go, darling. I've put the ketchup and the English mustard on the side, I know you like to add it yourself. And the pickled cucumber, thinly sliced, yes? And one slice of tomato. And here's your Coke. Ice, no lemon.'

She did like to show him how closely she'd studied his likes and dislikes. She needed him to know that she was a Nathan scholar, an expert in Nathan studies. She knew she was maybe a *little* needy, but she lived for his love. She wanted to engulf him in her love, but she wanted him to love her *back*.

He did, he did.

'Thanks, Mum. It smells great.'

'My pleasure, darling.'

She leaned in for her kiss. They kissed on the lips, a tradition she'd established and jealously maintained. Once or twice, when she'd puckered up, he'd turned his cheek, but she preferred to kiss him on the lips. It was more intimate, more special, it was what *she* wanted, and even though the child always comes first, the mother has the right to have a few of her needs met!

She sighed, and as she watched him eat, couldn't resist stroking his hair. He flinched and she pulled away her hand, hurt, her eyes fast oozing tears.

He laughed. 'No, I had a mouthful of mustard!'

'Oh, poor baby!' she crooned, giddy with relief. She was so silly where Nathan was concerned, so sensitive. But she worried over nothing. Their adoration was mutual. She picked a chip off his plate and fed it to him, then licked her own fingers. It was as if they were one person. She couldn't believe that she'd lived for so long without him. She cursed her stupidity for not understanding this incredible gift: the love between a mother and child. It was an everlasting honeymoon, and she would gladly die for him.

LONDON, 1986

Innocence

'Don't think I care if *you* catch anything, but if you give anything to Emily, I'll kill you for it.'

That girl had no idea, stroking dogs in the street. They could have any number of diseases, and Emily was only four. 'Hurry up, stop dawdling, you're so *slow*.' Innocence grabbed Claudia's wrist, digging her nails in, and dragged her across the road to where the driver waited in the Bentley.

She was a plain child – now. Misery and pre-pubescence

243

had been harsh – the girl was at least two stone overweight.

Innocence slid carefully into the front seat, while Day Nanny strapped Emily into her car seat.

'Mummy, I want a new tutu, a Sugar Plum Fairy tutu, because I've only got the White Swan tutu, and Sylvia has got the Sugar Plum tutu, and she's *taunting* me, because it's pink and mine is only white, so can I get the Sugar Plum Fairy tutu, *please*, Mummy? I'll be good for the rest of my life!'

'Darling, of course you can get the Sugar Plum Fairy tutu. Why didn't you say when we were inside Harrods?'

'I was eating my chocolate cake, remember.'

'Of course you were, sweetie. Don't worry. Day Nanny, will you ring when we get home and order it? Order three. The dressmaker has her measurements.'

'Harris, can you drive at high speed, because Mummy bought me a new rabbit, and I want to get home to feed him. His name is Petronella. He's a boy rabbit but he doesn't have a willy. Do you have a willy, Claudia?'

'No, Emily. I'm a girl. Girls don't have willies.'

'I think you got one. I think you got one under your fur.'

'Emily, sweetheart! Oh, Day Nanny, isn't she precious! I must remember to tell everyone at Harry's tonight! The things she comes out with! Of course, the fat ones do start puberty earlier. *Under your fur!* Do remind me, Day Nanny, to tell everyone! Harris, you too!'

'Mummy, can Claudia have a tutu? Then we can be twins.'

'No, darling. Claudia's too fat for a tutu. A tutu is only for pretty girls, like you. Claudia, for fuck's sake' – God, the child was a moron. Innocence turned in her seat and jabbed Claudia hard in the fleshy thigh – 'your big fat elephant knees are digging into the back of my chair.'

'I'm sorry, Innocence.'

'Shut up. Emily? Emily, darling! Why are you crying?'

'*Stop* being mean to Claudia! Claudia is my *friend*!'

Oh! Innocence felt her cheeks burn. For a second she was lost for words. That devious, spiteful little brat had bewitched Emily. Innocence could barely believe it. She'd turned darling Emily against her own *mother*. She felt sick. How had it happened? Those bloody nannies – Day Nanny, Night Nanny, Weekend Nanny – were all the same. Slack. They let Claudia entertain Emily, while they chewed gum and called their boyfriends. She knew that Claudia played dolls with Emily, and told her stories – Claudia was not allowed leisure time of her own – but she had no idea that the situation was so critical.

Innocence clenched her teeth and lit a cigarette. So, Claudia was Emily's friend. Well. She'd put paid to *that*.

SCOTLAND, 1986

Emily

Emily loved having a sleepover at Timmy's house. Timmy lived in a castle with turrets and battlements, like a prince. He wasn't a prince though, but his mummy and daddy were an earl and a countess. But Emily was allowed to call them Pat and Fred, because they were Daddy's friends. Before she was born, it had been Daddy's job to look after their money. He'd put it in vests.

Timmy had a baby brother and sister, but he was the biggest boy, and Mummy said he was the most important. He was the most fun. He had a stinky dog, who was a greyhound, and carpets with holes in them. And it was very cold in the castle, but there were blankets. Timmy's garden went on for ever. Mummy said it was a hundred thousand acres, which is the biggest number you can get. There was a wood full of bluebells and Timmy and she rode ponies through it. She got Pippin, who ate carrots off her hand, although you had to make your hand flat or he thought your fingers were carrots. There was a pond, with ducks, and a moat that went all around. Timmy said his daddy sometimes swam in the moat, but Timmy didn't because it was too cold, and he thought it might have duck wee in it. Emily liked playing on the drawbridge, and the tower that used to be a dungeon. She was the princess, and Timmy was the prince, and he rescued her. And then the prince got in trouble, and the princess rescued *him*, to make it fair, because it wasn't so nice, sitting in the dungeon. It was dark and smelled mouldy.

Emily was scared of Timmy's daddy – he shouted and wore a skirt. But sometimes Timmy wore a skirt too, when it was a special occasion. It was OK for children, because it was dressing up, but not for grown-ups. She liked Timmy's mummy. She wore green Wellington boots, even at the dinner table. She let Emily pick strawberries from her vegetable garden. When Emily stayed, if Timmy's daddy was in a good mood, they ate dinner together in the big hall, which had lots of big old sewings on the wall. They had candles, and a massive fire in the fireplace instead of electricity, so it was like camping. If Timmy's daddy was in a bad mood, Timmy and Emily ate fish fingers in the nursery by themselves. Timmy's daddy was almost always in a bad mood when Emily stayed. Emily liked eating in the nursery so she didn't mind. Afterwards, if they went to the kitchen, Cook would give them each a glass of Coca-Cola with a slice of melon in it. Emily stayed in the guest bedroom, in a four-poster bed. You needed a stool to climb into it because it was so high. A black cat called Bertie slept at the bottom of the bed, and there was a special stone to clean your hands with in the bathroom.

'Let's get our Coca-Cola now, Timmy. I've had enough fish fingers, I'm full up.'

'OK. But it's not a race.'

Emily led the way to the kitchen. She liked to be first. First the worst, second the best – but not really! 'I'm going to have melon in mine, Timmy.'

'*Lemon*, Emily. Lemon, not melon.'

'Hello, Cook. If you smoke you'll die. We've eaten up all our fish fingers and mash. We'd like our Coca-Cola now— AAAAAAAAAAAAAHHH!'

'Gracious, love, what's the matter? Oh Lord! The cat's got a rabbit. Well, that's nature for you.'

It was disgusting and sick-making. The poor rabbit's grey fur was all torn up and ripped and inside it was all red and blood everywhere and it was properly dead, and the pretty black cat that she sometimes kissed on the nose was *eating* it with its face right inside all the red stuff. Emily felt sick, and then she *was* sick, and it tasted of fish which made her sick again, all down the front of her velvet dress with the white lace ruffles.

'We've a townie here, my Lord, and no mistake!'

Cook was trying to take off her dress but Emily couldn't be near anyone because she couldn't breathe properly because she was crying so much. 'I want to go home now, Cook, please can I go home.'

'Come along, come along. What a fuss! She's just a cat doing cat things. You can't go home now, love, it's ever so late and it's such a long journey—'

'I want to go HOME, I want to go HOME, I want to go HOME, I want to go HOME, I want to go HOME, HOME, HOME! HOME! HOME! HOME! HOME! HOME! HOME, I want to go HOOOOOOOOOOOOOOOOOOOOME! I want to go home, I want to go h-h-h-h-h-h-o-o-o-o-m-m-m-me!'

'I understand, Miss Emily. You want to go home. Calm down or you'll choke on your tongue. I'll call her ladyship. If she's agreed of it, Vincent'll warm up the Land-Rover.'

'Don't cry, Emily. You can come and play another time. But the cat is always hunting rabbits.'

'Timmy, I need to get home. It's an emergency. *I've* got my own pet rabbit, called Petronella, and my big sister Claudia is looking after him while I am here. He is a special rabbit with soft peach-coloured fur and ears that go back like aeroplane wings. He isn't a field rabbit, he is a Harrods rabbit. He sits in my lap and lets me stroke him. He is very tame, and he likes apple, and I love him and I want to make sure that he's OK. I am very worried about him, he is my favourite thing, even more favourite than my Sugar Plum Fairy tutu. I don't want to see *that* broken rabbit that is died again, it makes me feel sick. Cook, I don't feel very well. I think I'm going to—'

Cook was a liar, liar, pants on fire. It wasn't a long journey from Scotland to London at all; it was a very short journey. Pat helped her wash and put on a new dress, and then she waved goodbye to Timmy, Vincent took her suitcase and helped her get into the car, and after five minutes it was morning and she was home!

'Hello, Mummy, I'm back!'

'Hello, my precious. Pat told me you had a fright. I'm so sorry you were upset by the dead rabbit. Shall we go and stroke Petronella to cheer you up? Claudia says she's been looking after him for you, so I'm sure he's fine. Shall we take some carrots for him to eat?'

'Yes. Where is Claudia? I missed her.'

'Claudia's busy now. She said she'll see you later.'

'Oh. OK.'

Emily skipped into the kitchen garden where Petronella had his hutch. 'Petronella!' She looked but she couldn't see him. Usually he made a scratchy noise when she called his name.

'Open the door, darling.'

'It smells! Claudia promised she would clean his hutch every day, because Petronella does so many poohs.'

'Perhaps she forgot, darling.'

'But she promised!'

Emily got on her knees and pulled back the lock, and opened the wooden door. At first, she wasn't sure what she was seeing, and then a fly flew right in her face and she started to scream, and gag. And she looked harder, and screamed and screamed, and gagged and gagged, until Mummy pulled her away.

'What's wrong? What's happened! Emily!'

Emily looked at her sister's stupid worried face as she hurried towards them on her big fat legs and felt so angry it was as if the whole world might explode. She shook off Mummy and ran at her sister, screeching, clawing and punching.

'I hate you, I hate you, stupid old Claudia! You *promised* me you'd look after Petronella and now she's dead and bloody and worms are crawling on her and there are flies eating her and one flew in my face and nearly in my mouth, I hate you, I hate you, and I'll always hate you, you killed her because I had a rabbit and you don't and if you get a rabbit I'll kill it and I'll kill you!'

'Emily! Please, stop it! It ... it *can't* be ... oh my God ... Innocence ... tell her. I don't understand. Petronella was fine! I cleaned out her hutch last night, you saw me. This – ugh, it stinks – it can't be ... This rabbit has been dead for days. Are you sure that some—'

'Shut it, Claudia. Don't lie. You didn't feed Petronella because you were jealous and spiteful and you hoped she'd die, because you don't want Emily to have anything nice. You're a nasty piece of work and you should be ashamed of yourself. Apologize to Emily.'

Emily felt too sad to stand up so she fell on the ground and cried and cried. She was the saddest ever about Petronella, even more sad than about the field rabbit. But she was the most saddest about her sister Claudia, because she thought Claudia was her friend when Claudia was only pretending. Claudia had hurt her feelings – the worst thing.

'I'm sorry, Emily,' said stupid old Claudia.

'Sorry doesn't *count*!' screamed Emily. 'Shut up, you idiot! Make her go away, Mummy, I hate her and I hate her!'

'Please leave us, Claudia,' said Mummy, and Emily saw that she didn't have a cross face any more. 'Emily is no longer your friend.'

THE LLOYD'S BUILDING, LONDON, 1989

Jack

Jack noted the eighteenth-century nautical paintings that adorned the walls of the grand boardroom, and smiled grimly. Time was when he would have replaced them with an Andy Warhol fighter jet. He'd come a long way. Then, he was a wannabe. Now, he was one of them, and he recognized the beauty and value of these sombre paintings. They still weren't his thing, but he understood.

He was sentimental about this room because he'd had his interview here. Interview! There had been a jovial, schoolboyish atmosphere, and Sir Peter, the chairman, had said, 'Give me a blank cheque with your signature. That's the risk you are undertaking as a Name at Lloyd's.'

It had shaken him, to hear it put like that, but he'd popped a few diazepam in the grand marble hall and the anxiety churning up his stomach had dissolved along with those little yellow pills. Of course there were risks – this was insurance, after all – but he would be on the right side, because when did insurance *ever* pay out when you really needed it? That's what the small print was for.

Fact was, he felt safe with business. It was so much easier to do business than to do . . . family. He didn't enjoy family life and that was the cold truth of it. Claudia, once the light of his life, had turned into a dumpy, sullen child. He had nothing to say to her. If ever they were in the same room, he struggled to find a topic of conversation that would interest them both, and ended up silent.

It was plain that she and Innocence disliked each other, which annoyed him. It was so *inconvenient*. The rare mealtimes they suffered as a 'family' were torture. If Claudia was present, Innocence would have a face like an Easter Island stone statue. A few months ago, her face rigid with fear, looking about for Innocence as she spoke, Claudia had asked Jack to let her attend a local day school so that she could visit Ruth more often. He'd told her, 'We'll see.'

But the atmosphere was so much lighter when she was out of the house. So when Innocence suggested packing Claudia off to a new boarding school, Jack had agreed. He'd tried to write letters to her, after she'd talked about another girl whose pigeon-hole had an envelope *every* morning from either Mummy or Daddy – a rota, apparently. Other parents: how they loved to make everyone else feel like shit with their smug little arrangements. Eventually he'd sent her a postcard of a London bus with a punk on it: 'Hope you are well and behaving! Love Dad'. Ms Green had chosen the postcard.

Claudia had come home in the spring. They were all off to New York, a working holiday, as the Apple Core Hotel was being tarted up and he wanted to finesse some details. He had been shocked to see her. In two months she'd gone from blimp to shrimp. She was bone thin – she had the ragged ill look of a scarecrow. He'd never liked thin. Even in the Twiggy days he'd loathed the fact that tits were out of fashion. He'd always felt that women looked best when they weren't half starved.

He, Innocence, Claudia and Emily had eaten breakfast along with two or three assorted nannies in the hotel restaurant. What a fiasco. The room was gorgeous: sleek, white, modern, but not too severe. He'd paid top whack for an interior designer who understood mood lighting, and there were crammed bookshelves to add a bit of colour and large canvases by a young English artist called Tom Hammick, whose *Norfolk – Sea and Sky* drew you in and calmed you, as surely as if you were being rocked to sleep on the waves. Jack liked to think that Hammick created the twentieth-century equivalent of those ancient nautical scenes, minus the ships; just the dark blue of the sea and the light fresh sky – you felt free, looking at those paintings.

The breakfast menu was sumptuous. The Apple Core served a proper fried English breakfast, beautifully done. He couldn't believe the current disrespect for food. Ms Green had taken her son (he hadn't known she had a son) to a café in Marylebone for lunch and his cheese on toast had been microwaved! But here the orange juice was freshly squeezed, not from a carton. The croissants were warm and baked that morning, so the butter melted as it spread, and the coffee was superior-quality knock-your-head-off stuff. The pièce de résistance: it served PG Tips, a proper cup of tea in the USA. Fuck that Liptons shit!

His chief accountant had pursed his lips, but there was still a fine margin, and Jack knew that the pleasure of a perfect breakfast was worth its weight in rebookings. No one was a tourist these days, and they resented being treated as such. Delicious food served in pleasant surroundings by charming staff: it was more than a recipe for success, it was a guarantee.

The Kents must have been the first people who had sat in those soft silver-backed chairs in that sun-streaked dining room staring at a chic glass vase of white lilac and been bloody miserable. Claudia had nibbled at a piece of dry toast, sighed, sipped water, patted her concave stomach, and murmured, 'I'm *so* full up.'

Innocence had a scowl so fierce that it was creasing her forehead; a feat as she had recently had . . . it was a new treatment that did away with laughter lines, he hadn't been listening when she told him, just watching her mouth move. What was it called? 'Buttocks'? Innocence had shuddered at the sight of food, drunk four cups of tea containing three sugars, and was waggling her foot in a nervous tic under the table – caffeine? Nicotine? Irritation? The woman was a poised whip of barely contained aggression. Claudia cringed beside her like a dog expecting a kick.

Innocence rarely looked happy. He didn't know what she'd expected: to rule his empire *with* him? He'd made it pretty plain at the start. He needed a woman who would lift him up where he belonged, and she would be handsomely paid for her trouble, but not in that way. He had a select team of highly intelligent (and highly paid) motivated specialists who ran his interests. Innocence had good instincts but she was inexperienced in business. She was born into privilege, she'd never even worked!

So, Innocence had done her bit, but reluctantly, which pissed him off. It had been an acquaintance of *hers* – one of the many men schmoozed during her charity-lunch years, as she called them – who had sponsored his membership at Lloyd's. He'd assumed it was Harry's influence, since the guy mixed with that set, but it turned out Harry knew nothing of it. Innocence had done her duty, and yet . . . She hadn't wanted it to happen – there was an underlying sense of competition, a resentment of him treading on *her* aristocratic toes. She wasn't sharp enough to understand the collateral benefits that came from being a Name. The investments he was able to make subsequent to his inauguration, the investors he was able to attract – he believed that snobbery and class had added thirty million to his worth in three years.

Why *couldn't* money buy happiness? It bought everything else. And yet the thought of the four of them, designer-clad and sour-faced around his exclusive New York hotel breakfast table, plunged him into gloom.

Emily, at least, had enjoyed the food. She was seven years old and had the social decorum of a wolf. She had gobbled up, with her mouth open, a plate of pork and apple sausages with bacon, tomatoes, mushrooms and scrambled egg. She'd then crammed a Danish pastry into her mouth while drinking a chocolate milkshake from a straw. As a finale, she'd spilled the half-pint milkshake all over her pink dress, the chair and the floor. The rest had spread across the table and dripped on to Jack's cashmere pinstripe trousers.

Emily had then had what appeared to be an epileptic fit – wailing and howling and jumping up and kicking over her chair. This had provoked a bout of coughing so dramatic it had made her violently sick. He'd felt as if he was in *The*

Exorcist. Jack had resisted the impulse to call security and hauled her out of the dining room himself. It was like trying to wrestle with a prize salmon, and he feared that several of his guests had been splattered with chocolate milkshake and vomit as she flipped and arched on her way into the lobby.

It had been so *astonishingly* unrelaxing. He blamed Innocence for spoiling Emily. She was like an out-of-control three-year-old. His chief concierge had organized a private helicopter tour of Manhattan, but Jack was overjoyed when the inscrutable Ms Green murmured about the video conference with LA having to take place at nine rather than twelve because of five other pressing appointments at ten, ten thirty, eleven, eleven fifteen, and a quarter to midday. He'd escaped to the boardroom, flanked by Ms Green, the Head of Management, and the CFO of Élite Retreat Enterprises, and discussed budgets with relief.

This was where he excelled, and he found that he disliked Innocence for her presumption in thinking that *she* deserved a place around this grand oak table. He also disliked her for disliking him for withholding it. She had a nerve. She was living the high life because of him. Her paltry two million wouldn't have lasted a few months with her spending habits! She might have opened a few doors, but it was his shrewd nature and business savvy that had built an empire. She couldn't even raise two kids effectively. Claudia was a fuck-up and Emily was a brat.

He hadn't even allowed her to dabble in the Science Lab: his nickname for the Spyglass Island retreat in French Polynesia, the place where he tested ideas and made his mistakes. There, she couldn't do much damage – the damage to Spyglass Island had already been done. It was the only hotel still operating at a loss. After the paedophile fiasco, they'd made the mistake of going *too* cheap, which had discredited the hotel further and attracted a bunch of Eurotrash. They'd pulled back sharply from the error, revamped, bumped up the prices – and three months later the place had been reduced to a pile of firewood by a typhoon.

He'd considered awarding Innocence a token directorship with a big salary and zero power, but she was too pushy – it had put him off. She was forever presenting him with her cute ideas: going-home presents for every guest; a personal horoscope prepared for those who liked that kind of horse-shit. It had put him off *her*. The sex had dwindled, and Jack was a man who liked his sex. It had also occurred to him that Innocence liked *hers* – so what was *she* doing? She wasn't a big fan of sex for one. As she said, she didn't like to get her hands dirty.

She wasn't joking. One evening, he'd walked in while Innocence was having a bath, and she was wearing *yellow rubber gloves*.

She'd seen the look on his face and said, 'Water ages your skin.'

It was true, he'd thought, staring at her, that she had beautiful, soft, youthful hands, but . . . 'This doesn't happen by itself!' she'd said, indicating her gorgeous form with a huge yellow glove.

'No,' he'd said, backing out of the room.

Jack wanted to shift in his seat, but fidgeting was a sign of nerves, and his lawyers, his PA and his advisers were flank-ing him in a severe grey line of suits and briefcases along one side of the table, so he sat still, a study in self-possession. Truth was, he was bricking it, and he could feel the sweat cooling damply on his Jermyn Street collar. He tended to chuck away his shirts after a few wears – he wanted to rip this one off now.

There had been ugly rumours – well, more than *rumours* – surrounding Lloyd's for a while now. He'd known about Sasse 762, the syndicate of 110 Names forced to cough up forty million dollars until the Committee had stepped in and relieved them of most of the liability. One hundred and twenty thousand dollars each, in the end – not so bad.

Anyway, he'd been told it was an isolated case. But the panic hadn't gone away. There were murmurs of fraud among underwriters. In the previous year, there had been ridiculous claims, enormous cash calls, refusals to pay, suspended Names – it was a series of events as unlikely as the existence of the Tooth Fairy and Jack had shut his ears, ignoring the sense of dread in the pit of his stomach. At first he'd been relieved when his agent and sponsor refused to confirm that anything was wrong. The most they'd said about Sasse and the others was 'wrong syndicate – bad luck'.

But as the stories persisted, his relief had evaporated.

Jack hated to speak ill of the aristocracy but he was beginning to distrust his sponsor — where the fuck had Innocence met this slimeball? Now that Jack was less willing to be impressed, he saw the man with new eyes. He was so smooth, so slippery you expected to look behind him and see a snail trail. His heart beat fast, fighting its way through the medication. What exactly was at stake here?

Everything?

He wouldn't believe it. He couldn't. Lloyd's *had* to be OK. Only three years ago, the company had moved into a glittering new space-age building, twelve storeys high, gunmetal grey, with gorgeous views over the City and the Thames. He fingered his gold membership card. It would be the same as being betrayed by your own mother.

These people *had* to take care of him. He had trusted them, as much as he trusted anyone: they were in charge of the country because they knew what they were doing. He was half ashamed of this reflex respect for authority as it reminded him that he was, at heart, a commoner, that he believed, in some way, these people were better than he was. It was pathetic, but it was a conviction that he was powerless to control. And he *wanted* to believe in them. It was like believing aged five that your father was a benevolent god: if, or when, that belief was shattered, you were shattered with it.

He stood as the Chairman stepped into the room, followed by what Miss Green termed 'an Embarrassment of Pinstripes'. He didn't *want* to stand – he felt that his status no longer required him to stand. His status was why he had ordered his driver to park in the Chairman's reserved parking space. But he stood, because he wanted to be perceived as a gentleman – not a man who had earned his status, but one who had been born to it.

'Jack, old chap,' said the Chairman, swooping down with a crushing handshake and a tight smile. 'Always a pleasure. I hear you want to love us and leave us.'

Jack nodded. 'Correct.'

The Chairman pursed his lips. 'My dear fellow,' he said. 'I'm afraid it's not quite that simple.'

MIDDLESEX, ENGLAND, 1991

Claudia

When she got married, she'd have sex once, to have a baby, then never again. Claudia just *knew* that this would cause a stink with her husband, whoever he might be – some perfect man, around twenty, living his life in alarming ignorance of the fact he was destined to be with her. But her hero would have a strong sex drive; he wouldn't be masculine otherwise: she'd read enough Harlequin romances to know the score. It was frustrating and confusing. She was resigned to becoming a spinster and buying a load of cats.

Claudia sighed, kept walking up the hill to Ruth's house and tried not to cry on the street. She wasn't like other sixteen-year-olds. Her life was a total disaster, and it had been a disaster from day one. She had the worst luck of anyone, ever. It always went wrong for her. She despised her blood mother for giving her away, she was angry at Felicia for dying, she hated that witch, Innocence, who had tricked Daddy into marrying her, obviously for money: *unlucky*. They weren't happy. There was no hugging, ever, just crisp exchanges of information.

They'd fallen out of love. God, her marriage would never be like that. They'd be kissing all the time. Just no . . . shit . . . why was sex such a big thing? She liked the seduction bit. Every night she dreamed of a handsome stranger, dark, tall, with strong arms (she hadn't yet assigned him a face), pulling her to him in a passionate embrace, possibly in the desert . . . well, somewhere hot anyway, with bougainvillea and her in a white floaty dress. She'd been running from him, hair flowing in the breeze; a gentle protest, then he crushed her lips to his.

And then . . . what? He drove her home and they folded the washing? She liked the idea of the chase. Just not what happened when you got caught. She couldn't stand the idea of a man she fancied seeing her *exposed*. She didn't feel sexy, or – gross word ahoy – *sexual*. She felt disgusting. The idea of doing *it* . . . fluids . . . smells . . . it made her feel dirty and ashamed. She knew she should be over the 'incident' on Spyglass, but she wasn't and she never would be. The second a boy tried to kiss her – Alfie, once, for a joke, on her fifteenth birthday – she'd sweat and tremble and feel that man forcing her head down – and then she'd retch and gasp for air that she couldn't get as her throat constricted like a drawstring bag, and she'd fumble for her inhaler.

Not attractive.

In her mind, she was still a fat, awkward fourteen-year-old, even though she'd lost the weight. She'd done it by puking. She wanted to be thin enough to snap. But she was a pig – she'd be good for days, eight raisins and three peanuts for breakfast, lettuce for lunch, crispbread with a scrape of butter for dinner – but then a sly little idea about gorging herself on chocolate would creep into her head . . . a wicked roll-call of

KitKats, Mars bars, Toblerones flashing before her eyes ... and the desire would swell and balloon, consuming her, *harassing* her, taking hold – torturing her with pernicious spite, urging her on, until she stuffed her face.

She'd feel sated, for a brief moment. Then the self-loathing would swarm over her, and she'd sneak to the bathroom and jam a finger down her throat. Afterwards, she'd feel high and desperate, weak and triumphant. She hated herself. Why not – everyone else did. When the first cash call came from Lloyd's, this year, darling Emily remained at her precious public school, but stupid Claudia was removed from hers and stuck in the local comp. The girls there were savage.

She had no reference point for a stranger who came up and spat in your face for no reason. It was like being dumped in a foreign country where you broke every rule without realizing and were brutally punished. Once, after she found that someone had used her shoulder bag as a ... toilet, she'd made the error of reporting it. The following day, a girl strode up and head-butted her, breaking her nose. Innocence had taken her to a private hospital without comment. Claudia had said, 'I tripped.' Her stepmother had replied, 'I didn't ask.'

She was vile. And Daddy had pretended he couldn't see it, the coward. Emily was supremely selfish – out only for herself and what she could get. But most people were fooled. At nine, Emily was bright, beautiful, charming and talented. A fabulous horsewoman. An excellent skier. She could ice skate, ballet dance, sing – of course she could, she was tutored by experts. She excelled in English and maths. She was crap at chemistry but who cared about chemistry? She was funny, charming and people loved her. They didn't see her dark side: her jealous nature, insane ambition, crazy rages, the fact that not only did she need to win, she needed everyone else to lose.

It was so sad. They'd been friends, once.

Daddy had built one of the most successful businesses in

the world. But he'd failed to build a family. As a unit, the four of them were a pitiful failure. And it was getting worse.

Daddy had been in a foul mood for three years now. Ever since it had dawned that he hadn't been proposed as a Lloyd's Name because he was a good old boy, but because he was a gullible, social climbing *nouvie*. What was the phrase in the newspapers? *Recruit to dilute*.

He was financial cannon fodder; he and his new money had been used by those who had inherited theirs: to sponge up a fraction of the blue chip insurance firm's monstrous losses. Daddy was already paying out but the worst – the ultimate financial death blow that would reduce them to poverty – was imminent. The fear – *his* fear – was palpable, and catching. Like waiting for a monster to hunt you down and eat you.

She worried *for* him, despite herself. No one else did. Innocence and Emily seemed oddly unbothered. Maybe they didn't realize the seriousness of the situation. Maybe they thought that some miracle would occur, and it would be all right in the end, that Lloyd's would make an exception for them. No, no, we won't take *your* money, and your furniture and your house. You're too important – you're *you*! People were curious like that. They believed that nothing bad could happen to them, only everyone else. Claudia believed the opposite. Everything bad could happen to her, and it did. It already had.

She had three real friends in the world, and that was it. Her grandmother, Ruth, her childhood pal, Alfie, and her pen friend, Lucy. If it weren't for them, she'd struggle to keep sane. She didn't see Ruth or Alfie as often as she wanted to, and as for Lucy, they had met only once, and she was so stupid she couldn't actually remember – but Daddy held such huge parties how could you remember all the people who'd come over and said hello? Well, she and Lucy would meet again – one day.

Innocence disapproved of Claudia seeing Ruth, because Claudia was Ruth's favourite. Ruth, unlike everyone else, had no time for Emily, and this made Innocence as mad as a rabid dog.

Alfie was still a good friend, but he had his own life mapped out. He was probably the only good thing ever to come out of Eton. He was reading economics at Oxford. He'd train as an officer at Sandhurst, and would end up in the City. He would marry a solid, sexy girl with a raucous laugh and strong hips whose father was a judge. She'd be disgustingly fertile and they'd have four beautiful blond children. They'd live in a fabulous country house, own chickens and an Aga. Claudia couldn't think of a worse animal than a chicken, and she had zero interest in cooking, but she still hated Alfie's fantasy bride and imagined many a Sloane-inspired fatality: teeing off at Wentworth, golf club strike to the head; terrible weather at Ascot, slipping on to racecourse, trampled by runaway horse; Queen Charlotte ball, hastily accepted dance invitation, choking to death on olive . . .

Thank God for Lucy.

Lucy understood. Lucy understood because she was in a similar situation. There was so much bile and rage in Claudia's head that if she didn't let some of it out she felt as if she would explode. So it came out in her letters to Lucy. Lucy knew more about her than anyone else on this earth, and Lucy didn't judge. Their friendship had begun two years ago when Lucy had plucked up the courage to initiate contact. She'd met Claudia at one of her father's parties. She was the daughter of a friend of a cousin and she didn't know anyone; they'd chatted briefly. Claudia probably wouldn't recall (she didn't) but now Lucy was writing to thank her for being so sweet. To be honest, she needed a friend, someone kind: her home life was . . . less than ideal.

Boom!

Claudia had recognized a soulmate and written back, eagerly. Poor Lucy. It was her stepfather who was the problem. He was an alcoholic who beat her. Her mother was in love and preferred not to see it; she had once offered Lucy a cover-up stick for a black eye, claiming 'this heals bruises'.

Claudia's life story poured out into those letters to Lucy. *God*, if Innocence only knew! There was no way they could meet now; Lucy's stepfather was a control freak and Lucy wasn't allowed out of the house without an 'adult', even though she was sixteen, for Christ's sake! But Lucy was planning her escape. She was going to get a job at a newspaper, doing something, anything, even if she started off on work experience; it would be so glamorous! They should *both* do it, then they could chat all day – well, apart from the work. Look, it would be easy, they could both write, couldn't they?!

Lucy made Claudia laugh. And her idea about working on a newspaper wasn't so bad. It wasn't as if Daddy was going to offer her a job anytime soon. Not that she'd want one – she was looking to escape her parents, not spend more time with them.

Claudia smiled to herself as she approached Ruth's front gate. Ruth lived in a house that was 'far too big' for her. She hated it, 'but Jack insisted'. That was Daddy, thought Claudia, imposing his will on others. He did a really crappy impression of love, like an alien reading instructions from a book. She hurried up the stone steps and pressed the buzzer. JR was already barking, which was normal. He really was an annoying dog. If he were human, he'd be gay: an elderly actor, waspish, swishing around his townhouse in a red velvet housecoat, smoking a cheroot.

Ruth was usually waiting at the window. Claudia knew she was lonely and Ruth hated that she knew. Claudia peered in, cupping her hands to the glass. Oh, *God*. Oh, no. It couldn't be. On the floor, by the lounge door, she could see – an *arm*. The hand was moving, stretching towards – anything? Claudia felt her knees turn liquid. She hammered on the glass, shouting through the letterbox, 'Ruth! I'm here. It's all right, you'll be OK. I'll call an ambulance. They'll be here – wait . . .' You *idiot*. 'Wait!' She'd had a heart attack or a

262

stroke, she was lying on the floor close to death, and Claudia said, 'Wait!'

Even as she fumbled for her mobile and dialled 999, even as the ambulance screeched to a halt, the fire engine with it, the fire-fighters breaking down the door, even as Ruth was lifted on to a stretcher, an oxygen mask placed over her mouth and nose, even as she sat in the ambulance as the medics tried to revive her grandmother, and even as the doctor, his sombre look lending a sad finite authority, said the words, 'I'm so sorry,' her head was lousy with thoughts of her own stupidity.

But then, as she splashed cold water over her face, trying to erase the image of JR's furry bulk being lifted into a white RSPCA van, she said, aloud, 'No.' And then, 'I am *not* to blame.'

It was not her fault. She had done all she could to look after her grandmother, but she was, effectively, a child, and powerless. Those with the real power – Jack and Innocence – had done nothing. She could discount Innocence; Innocence was a wicked witch, what did you expect? But Jack. Daddy. He was Ruth's son. Her only child. And, as in every other area of his personal life, he'd chucked money at the problem, because to him, people were problems.

He'd stuck Ruth in a big house, miles from anywhere, so if some business associate asked, he could say he'd 'taken care' of his mother. Yeah. He'd taken care of her the way the Mafia took care of people. And now, thanks to him, Claudia only had two friends in the world.

Her mouth set in a thin hard line.

'I tell you something,' she said to the pale ghost in the dirty mirror – and it was as if the ghost was making a vow to her, not her to it – 'that bastard has it coming. And *I* will bring it.'

Innocence

'That. And that. *Both*. No. The Prada. And the Chanel. The black and gold! Do they have it in pink? Tell them to get it. Have it all delivered to my suite at the Core with the shoes. So hire a truck.'

Innocence snapped shut her mobile and brushed some imaginary speck off her shoulder pads. The new hair looked *fab*. Big – Bonnie Tyler didn't know the *meaning* of back-combed – and a fierce fuchsia pink. Fekkai had been reluctant, murmuring that the eighties were no more, but she'd pressed.

The pink hair was more Essex than Eton, and Jack would faint when he saw it, but tough shit. She owed nothing to that fool. Not *now*. All her life she'd wanted to have fun and you know what? She was fucking having it. Her new dog, a tiny little thing, was dyed pink to match.

The spending frenzy had started after lunch, when she'd caught a newsflash before the LCD was hastily switched off. Jack hadn't bothered to ring.

She'd swept into Tiffany & Co. en route to her hair appoint-ment, and bought a three-row diamond and platinum necklace for $52,000. It felt a little bargain basement, so she'd sat in the salon, flicked through *Tatler*, and asked her assistant Jamie to ring Bvlgari in Bond Street and pay cash for the unique 87-carat diamond necklace that was – according to an advertisement in the mag – available exclusively for private viewing. There was a photo. She didn't need a private view-ing. Who cared about cost? Just box the thing and send it over! It was an 87-carat diamond necklace: what's not to like?

There was also a page entitled *'Priceless is More'*, a senti-ment with which she agreed, so she'd ordered a pair of cabochon sapphire earrings with briolette diamond drops at £500,000 from David Morris, and a 44-carat cushion-cut sapphire necklace with 182-carat diamonds (POA) by Harry Winston. *POA* my arse! POA was like a red rag to a bull. She wasn't going to make an *application*. Students made applications. There was also a POA platinum ruby and diamond necklace by Moussaieff, so she told Jamie to buy that too. Afterwards, she felt better. In fact, the new jewellery plus the pink hair and the dog were a real lift.

Fekkai was a sweetie. He'd told her, 'It's important that your hair says a lot about your personality, and gives a sense of your lifestyle and the mood you're in.' Quite. And for a long time, her hair – in that stupid Alice-in-Wonderland style that Jack so adored – had proclaimed the exact *opposite* of her personality.

As from today, Innocence and her new pink hair were all about *her*.

The salon was a nice cocoon and she was going to emerge from it as a butterfly. Not a whisper about today's events. Her people made sure that she didn't set eyes on a British newspaper. She sipped her coffee, relaxed as her feet were massaged and admired her perfect skin in the mirror. The light flattered, but with her face, *every* light flattered. She tried not to think about the nightmare of the last six months, but today – the day that their beautiful house in Hampstead was emptied of every last stick of furniture and possessed by Jack's creditors – it was impossible. Yes, they had other homes: the brownstone apartment on the Upper East Side and the place in Bermuda. But the Hampstead house was the flagship property. It was mortifying. It shouldn't have happened. She knew it was 'only a house' but it was her dream house, and she'd imagined that it would be his – hers, for ever. She hated that Emily had to go through this, losing her *home*. It was traumatic. She was traumatized.

A disaster such as this revealed who your friends were. Innocence believed that most people were as shallow as puddles. People liked you but your money was an intrinsic part of their like, because in their cold little hearts they felt that having money said something desirable about your personality, just as losing money (or worse, being poor) suggested something unappealing. Perhaps you were stupid, or uneducated, different. Perhaps you might try and drag them down with you: your poverty and bad luck might be in some way catching.

So when, six months before, Jack had turned up on the doorstep at 2 a.m., pissed as a newt and a dishevelled mess, his Thomas Pink shirt ripped on one sleeve, his black Lobb shoes muddy and scuffed, reeking of whisky and cheap cigarettes, his eyes wild as he slurred out a list of crazy numbers and rambled about unlimited liability and asbestos claims totalling two billion pounds before finally collapsing face-down on the recovered antique oak wood floor at her Christian-Louboutin-encased feet, and croaking, 'I'm ruined,' Innocence felt her indifference turn to hate.

She had expected this. She had *planned* for this. His loss would be her gain. So she was aghast at the overwhelming waves of seasick terror that chopped around her insides at the news of the inevitable. *She* was the architect of this torment. Jack's belief in his own ruin was essential to achieve her goals. And yet the situation – brought about by her own free will – still scared the hell out of her.

But this was because his stupidity affected *her*.

In the weeks that followed, she saw that Jack was shocked at the so-called friends who snubbed them at parties. She was astonished at his naivety: what did he expect? Yes of course she was angry at those people who had attended their parties, eaten their food, snorted their coke, drunk their champagne, fucked their guests, who now treated them as if they were invisible; yes of course if an opportunity to wreak revenge on these morons arose then she would grab it with the greatest pleasure. But the huge storm of cold everlasting fury and hate brewing inside her small frame was reserved for Jack.

She'd let him stew in his misery for a month while the list

of assets that Lloyd's would grab grew longer and longer. All their properties, their cars, their paintings, the business – they had six gorgeous, exclusive Élite Retreats dotted around the most beautiful and awe-inspiring places the planet had to offer. All of this belonged to Jack and so all of it would be seized. Emily would have to quit her exclusive private school and attend the local comp, where the drugs were altogether inferior and the pupils smoked Superkings rather than Silk Cut. Their household staff would be 'let go', and there would no longer be a wardrobe budget.

Jack took to stumbling home drunk and not shaving.

'Get up,' she'd said, after four weeks of enduring his impression of a tramp. 'Meet me in the drawing room when you're sober.'

The order was made with a confidence she didn't *quite* feel, because how do you explain to your husband fraud and theft on a grand scale, and how do you persuade him that each crime was committed for, ahem, *his* benefit? She must choose her words carefully. After all, her methods of preserving empires and fortunes were a *little* quirky ... She smiled as she remembered her business meeting with Mr Jones, all those many moons ago ...

LONDON, FEBRUARY 1983

Innocence

Lancelot Jones, QC, sat behind his enormous oak desk and looked sternly over his steel-rimmed half-moon spectacles at his client, who was perched meekly on a small hard chair in the middle of his huge velvet-curtained office.

'I'll reiterate,' he said. Ladies were always impressed by legal jargon and long words. 'If your husband has no liabilities, he can do with his assets what he wants. He can give them to the man in the moon. But if he has people with possible claims on him, and he gives them to the man in the moon, then he is transferring his assets with a view to defrauding his creditors. If he does this, the transfer he makes is *voidable* rather than void. A court will say it shall be set aside.'

Lance paused to check that his client was looking suitably awed. She reminded him of Sophia Loren in that silver mink coat that swept almost to her elegant ankles. She wore a diamond necklace, and a silver mink box hat, and black lace-up boots with high heels. What a saucy little minx. A warm feeling of pleasurable anticipation stirred inside him. 'However,' he continued. 'If your man doesn't expect to be in trouble – and he doesn't, for the poor fellow has not been given notice by his syndicate of a bad year, and we are certain of that – *then*, if he puts some of his assets in his wife's name: grand! Absolutely fine and dandy! Of course, the judge would have to know what information the individual had at the time he made the transfer.' Lance removed his spectacles, and smiled. 'I should say, at the time he *allegedly* made the transfer.'

He paused, licking his lips. She was hot totty but he was none too shabby. Since the cholesterol test he was off fatty meat, and had scaled back the booze: his belt was tighter by three notches, and all the walking he did over the Downs – he was in good shape. His hair was all his own; silvery-grey, very distinguished.

A *small* show of gratitude wouldn't go amiss.

His client smiled demurely and fanned the air in front of her face. 'The winter sun turns this office into a greenhouse, Mr Jones. Would you mind terribly if I drew the curtains?'

'Be my guest.' Suddenly his throat was dry.

His client rose with smooth feline grace, sashayed over to the window and pulled the curtains shut. Then she returned to her seat and sat, smiling, her hands folded neatly in her lap, the voluminous mink pulled close around her. Damn, she was good. He had a tent pole in his trousers.

'I'm sorry,' she purred. 'I interrupted. I believe' – a flutter of those incredible eyelashes – 'you have something for me.'

He coughed. 'I do indeed. The Land Registry has been most obliging. Very relaxed. As agreed, I lodged the Land Certificates – or the Title Deeds – on your behalf, with a . . . hmm, I do dislike the word "forged" – let us say "inspired" . . . an inspired request for transfer. Naturally, the Land Registry requires an indemnity from the owner. I must say your impression of your husband's signature is excellent, I doubt a graphologist could tell the difference. On your instruction, an expedition fee was paid, and the new documents, for all six of the hotels plus the homes in Bermuda and Manhattan, were returned to my office by registered post this morning. I backdated every transfer as per your request – thus, to all intents and purposes, Jack signed everything over on the day you became his bride. Congratulations, Miss Ashford. You are now blessed with a rather splendid property portfolio.' He looked up.

Innocence arched an immaculately plucked eyebrow. 'It seems almost too simple. Are you sure the Land Registry has actually *transferred* ownership? Don't they carry out checks?'

Lance smiled. 'My dear, why should the Land Registry suspect a thing? Not many wives do what you have just done. Which is fortunate. It makes it easier for you to be a naughty girl.'

Innocence showed her teeth. 'Mr Jones,' she breathed. 'You have *no* idea.' She smiled again. 'But you will.' She carefully removed her hat and the coat. Underneath, she was wearing a black Yves Saint Laurent bustier and corset. Her stockings were fishnet, and her black lace panties were barely there. Her breasts were pushed up and together, serving-wench style. He froze where he sat as she slid from the chair on to all fours and crawled towards his desk. He almost lost control then and there. He gripped the sides of his chair as she deftly unzipped his trousers.

'By the way, Miss Ashford,' he choked, gasping at the sensation. 'Thank you most heartily for your swift settlement of my fee note. It's a rare treat, in these boom and bust days, to receive a cheque by return of post. Your husband, if I may say, is not quite . . . so . . . fastidious.'

'Not so *fast*,' murmured Innocence, and she pushed his chair back, wriggled herself up and over the desk, so that her peachy behind was inches from his face. 'Help yourself,' she said.

God. She was worth everything. Not that anything was at risk: they were both as safe as, ahem, houses. When his wife's duplicity was discovered – or revealed – Kent would be forced to keep his cakehole shut and cooperate, or *he'd* be left with nothing. It was the E-type Jaguar of plans: elegant, classic.

He was panting like a dog as she led him by the pale blue Turnbull & Asser tie to where the silver mink lay on the floor. She ordered him to lie down on it, and straddled him, her gorgeous pussy in his face, and gave him the beginnings of another explosive blow job. He couldn't restrain himself a second longer. He pulled away, leaned over her and thrust into her from behind, rutting fiercely. My God, she was a beauty. When, finally, he couldn't hold back any longer, the waves of ecstasy were so intense they made him feel faint.

She wiped his prick on the silver mink, zipped him up and straightened his tie.

'Can I fetch you a glass of water, Miss Ashford?' he said.

She smiled. 'Thank you, Mr Jones, but no. You *could* fuck me again if you like, though.' She glanced at the mini-fridge in the corner of the office. 'Is there butter in that fridge?'

Afterwards, dizzily, he helped her into her coat. She re-applied her shimmery pink lipstick, brushed her hair, and powdered her nose. He watched in awe. What a woman. He handed her the hat with reverence.

She pulled the mink closely around her, and reluctantly he

sprang to the door and held it open. 'Let me walk you to your car.'

She pressed a restraining finger to his chest. He wondered if she could feel its wild effect on his heart. 'You've done more than enough, Mr Jones,' she replied, and winked.

He gazed after her, wishing that there were more papers to sign – anything to keep this visiting angel in his grasp. 'A pleasure doing business with you,' he called after her, and listened, until the sharp click-clack of her stiletto heels on the stone steps was swallowed into the hum of yet one more busy day in the big city.

LONDON, 1992

Emily

When Emily was five she'd snogged her own father. He was kissing her goodnight and she tried that twisty-mouth kissing she'd seen on TV. Daddy had pulled away and laughed, but she didn't see what was funny. Now, when she remembered, she giggled with embarrassment. *So* naive!

Not any more. She was pretty sussed. She was ten, after all, nearly a *woman*. She smoked (into the Hoover, if Daddy was in the house), she drank (Kir Royales – everyone did in Verbier – or Jack Daniel's and Coke) and she had perfected the art of the blow job – using a cucumber. ('I like eating vegetables,' she told Cook. And she did. The cucumber doubled up as a vibrator. It was important to know *your* pleasure, not only his.)

Of course, the *ultimate* test of her skills – on a real penis – was yet to be achieved. She was working on that. The last time she'd stayed at Fortelyne Castle, she'd asked Timmy if he'd ever kissed a girl. 'No *way!*' he'd replied. 'Girls are disgusting.' He'd paused, and added gallantly, 'Present company excepted.'

She realized she'd had a narrow escape. Timmy wouldn't get *his* blow job until she was a pro. There would be brothers of friends to practise on, although maybe . . . not *just* yet. She should probably wait until she was at least eleven. And it was important to let Tim experiment first, with that stupid clutch of interchangeable Sloanes who trotted around after him with their tongues hanging out. A few orthodontic braces caught in his foreskin and he'd appreciate a girl with *finesse*.

Emily was going to marry Tim and be queen of the castle, even if he didn't know it yet. She'd have to be quick, or he'd be matched with some buck-toothed heiress whose father owned Wales. The trouble with Timmy was he was so shy and quiet, he'd obey Pat and Fred even if he loathed the girl. Well, *she'd* prevent this tragic romance from ever taking place, by getting in there first. You had to make your own luck. Daddy had always said it; his reason, Mummy said, for refusing to offer Claudia a job. (And quite right, lazy cow!)

Emily was smart as well as hot. She was probably the only girl her age who didn't give a toss about Wet Wet Wet. What could Wet Wet Wet and all the other old men who made a pile out of giving teenagers wet dreams do for *her*? Nothing! Her *father* liked Wet Wet Wet – need she say more? Who had time to waste lusting over nobodies? If she listened to pop, it was the classics: Tears for Fears and Soft Cell and Simple Minds – those men were baboon ugly, but their music was beautiful. Her favourite song: 'Don't You Forget About Me'. She played it to Tim. He'd been force-fed Wagner since the age of two, so he was blown away.

Timmy was her destiny; he was a sweet boy, and the heir to a wonderful, privileged life. Her life had been shit-hot so far, and she was terrified of losing that. She didn't think she could cope if she wasn't *somebody*. The great relief of being born rich was, you didn't have to try. You could piss on their coffee table and people still found you charming. She *was* charming, however, because she always got her own way. She had her own Wardrobe Maid, a woman employed to colour scheme her closet, dry clean her clothes and maintain her shoes and bags.

In the holidays, she travelled. NY was always fab, and Positano was so chic, but her favourite was Spyglass in French Polynesia. She loved surfing and reef-diving, and her instructor didn't know it but that winter she was going to show him just how well she could breathe through her nose. The place itself was a little shabby – Daddy had lost interest – but it was always deserted, and the staff treated her as a goddess. It was Emily's secret. She loved to be around people – she *needed* to have people around her – but Spyglass was her annual retreat from civilization.

She had three vast pink bedroom suites with adjoining bathrooms; she had three homes, all in gorgeous, luxurious postcodes in the hippest cities in the world. She attended a fucking bore of a school – it was, after all, *school* – but you paid a fortune for them to make it as bearable as school could be. Her problem was, she was too clever. Some of the girls in her class couldn't read Shakespeare – they couldn't read *Smash Hits* without their mouths moving.

Mummy indulged her. Whatever Emily wanted, Emily got. Claudia was the solid, stupid, black sheep. No one cared about *her*. Very occasionally, Emily felt a twinge of pity, but then, Claudia shouldn't be so *feeble*. If she stood up for herself, instead of cowering, Emily would have more respect for her. She was eighteen, trying to be a 'journalist' – like, maybe she couldn't be an air stewardess – and she was a total party pooper, with a face as long as a horse. She didn't even know how to apply eyeshadow. I mean *hello*! Yeah, Emily had had it good.

Which was why she'd had the shock of her pampered life when she'd realized all that she had, all that she *was*, could vanish – *poof!* – tomorrow.

It was a few weeks ago. She'd hoped to see her parents bouncing on the bed together. They were shagging, she knew that. It fascinated her. It was quite *icky*, but it gave her a warm feeling. Her friends at school shrieked and shuddered at the very idea of s-e-x, but Emily had seen it and it looked wild.

But instead of trotting upstairs, her mother marched into the blue lounge, in sharp jerky moves. Daddy, who looked untidy, followed her slowly, his hands in his pockets. She knew there wasn't going to be any s-e-x. She pressed her ear to the door. Their voices started off low, but fast got loud and shouty.

'I knew this would happen!'

'Oh shut up! The Chairman of Lloyd's and all the other financial geniuses who've worked in the business for forty years couldn't foresee this happening, but *you* – the woman who didn't even finish *school* – you foresaw it. You just knew that all those miners dying of asbestos poisoning decades ago, you knew that one day their grandchildren would claim reparations and *break* the most famous, most reliable, most failsafe bank—'

'It's not a fucking bank, it's an insurance firm, and you calling it a bank says it all! I *knew*, because unlike you, I wasn't blinded by a desire to be a nob! When you became a Name, the rumours were just beginning, and because I made discreet enquiries of the right people, *I* discovered what most people had no clue about – that in the very near future there was the possibility of huge, unimaginable loss, and I tried to warn you, but you didn't want to know, you didn't want to hear – you were too vain, too eager, too determined to—'

'Shut up. So you told me. And I didn't listen. And now we are about to be raped of everything I own. I may lose the business – the liabilities currently stand at seventy-eight million. However, you win the moral victory. Congratulations. Is that it?'

'Of course it's not it, you stupid *fool*.'

It was horrible to hear Mummy and Daddy arguing like this. She knew it was about money. Then Mummy's voice went quiet – Emily could hear her murmuring, on and on. Then silence. Then a great roar from Daddy that made her almost jump out of her skin.

'YOU THIEVING COW – YOU – IMPOSSIBLE! HOW? *EVERYTHING!* I CAN'T BLOODY BELIEVE WHAT I'M HEARING!'

Emily tried not to bite her nails. It was her only fault. Nanny would have to buy some more of that anti-bite stuff.

Mummy screamed back, 'It was my only option! Better me than them!' And then, 'I can't believe you're reacting like this! You're so fucking ungrateful! I've saved your stupid skin! I've saved your future! I had to do it! For you – for us – for Emily!'

Mummy was *such* a user.

More murmuring. She pushed her hair out of the way impatiently. And then, Daddy: 'They'll take everything back from you.'

'They can't. Because *you* made the transfers, as far as they know, before you became a Name. In other words, you made the transfers thinking that everything was lovely and profitable at Lloyd's – because if you *didn't* think that Lloyd's was a failsafe, then of course you wouldn't have become a member shortly after. So that proves you didn't make the transfers to avoid liabilities. You didn't think you would *have* any. Yeah? They were a wedding gift, as far as anyone needs to know. Darling, I had to do something to cap your losses. This way, you sacrifice a little rather than the lot. Let them hate you – you'll be crying all the way to the bank.'

'You think you've got me by the balls, don't you ... *Sharon*?'

Sharon? Who was Sharon?!

Mummy laughed, a scary cackle of a laugh that made Emily's spine tingle.

'You think you're clever, Sharon. And you are, you are. Because yes, you have everything now. And I see that there's nothing I can do but go along. If I report you to the authorities, we're *both* left with nothing. I can only maintain my lifestyle by *your* grace. If I want to have any part in running *my* empire, it can only be as an unpaid figurehead. I'm forced to toe the line. Hat off to you, Marshall. You got what you wanted. You had me fooled. I really bought the lie wholesale.'

Bugger it, Daddy! Speak *up*! Emily's heart was pounding wildly. It was serious. It was, like, Daddy had lost all their money, and maybe Mummy had got it back, but no one seemed sure or happy about it. Would she still be going skiing in Verbier this winter?

'I say again, because you appear to be deaf: without me, you would have lost everything, don't you *get* that?' And then, calm, amused: 'Darling Jack. Think of me as your guardian angel. A-ha-ha-ha!'

Emily felt sick, and her head was pounding.

Then something smashed, and Daddy hissed, 'Laugh now, sweetheart, but I swear to you, you won't be laughing for long.' And *he* laughed, a nasty, bitter laugh that made her want to cry with fear. What could he mean? There was silence from Mummy – rare – which meant that *she* didn't know either. Maybe he was just pretending because he was cross.

Angry footsteps approached the door, and she leaped up and ran. As she hurled herself into her bedroom and slammed the door, there was one thought in her pounding head: *Snow White married the prince, and they lived happily ever after.*

However, she knew now that you had to choose your prince with care. Boys were more stupid than girls, so they needed *you* to marry *them*. Emily would choose a prince who could take over where Daddy left off. She would help the prince stay rich, just as Mummy was helping poor Daddy now. Except she wouldn't let her prince lose so much as a penny. She would choose a sensible, obedient prince, who wouldn't argue or be difficult like Daddy.

Aged ten, Emily chose Timmy.

NEW YORK, 1993

Innocence

Jamie scurried over, nearly tripping over the pedicurist in his haste. 'It's Mr K., madam.'

She wrinkled her nose. He wrinkled his nose. She sighed and put out her hand for the phone. 'Darling.'

'What the *fuck* are you doing? Bermuda just called to say two point six million has been debited from the account – two point six million on *baubles*. Are you *nuts*? And today! When we're under media *and* government surveillance. And from the offshore account – the *offshore* account – that's money that shouldn't exist, and you've blown it out of the water, you stupid cow. You don't even have *access* to that account – at least, you shouldn't, so tell me, whose cock have you sucked, who do I have to fire?'

'Oh, simmer down, Jack, keep your knickers on. You know I can't bear' – Innocence twisted her head to get a better side view of her pink bouffant – 'vulgarity. Of course I wanted to blow a little cash before I can't afford to!'

'You can't afford to now! They're repossessing our house! They've taken the Aston Martin, all the Porsches, the Bentley, and the Range Rovers. They've taken the Picasso, the Pissarro, the Monets, and my favourite Giacometti – today I have lost forty-two million quid. Gone, goodbye. No – thanks to you, I've lost forty-*four* point six million quid, and the assets that my accountants have worked so carefully to secure are now in jeopardy. I wonder, is this because you are such a thoughtless, selfish *brat* of a woman, or is it more sinister?'

'How *dare* you.'

Since her confession, their relationship had gone sharply downhill. It hadn't been fabulous before – it hadn't been fabulous since Jack had realized the extent of her ambition – but after she'd told him about her own secret brand of financial planning, his attitude towards her had changed entirely. He wasn't only questioning how well he knew his wife, he seemed to be questioning whether he knew her at *all*. She didn't let this bother her. He'd already put a private investigator on her and discovered that Miss Innocence Ashford and her aristocratic heritage was a crock of shit, that in fact he'd married plain old Sharon Marshall off a Hackney estate. So what? There was nothing he could do! He was stuck with her.

'I dare, because I have little left to lose.'

Innocence considered the truth of this. She giggled. 'You have *some*.'

There was a sharp intake of breath at the end of the line. 'You'll pay for this. You wait.'

'Like you're paying now?' she said sweetly. Her voice turned harsh. 'Listen, Jack. I did what I had to do to save us *both*. And to save Emily.' She didn't bother to include Claudia. She was tired of pretence.

She was tired of being the only clever one in the marriage. She was tired of being the caretaker and getting no credit for it. Around the world, *he* hit the headlines. His six Élite Retreats were booked solid by the rich and famous for the next eight years. Each time she'd made a suggestion – about the service, the design, the food – he would get a sniffy look on his handsome face, as if she was an idiot, babbling nonsense. On her next visit, she'd discover that her idea had been implemented – always with great success. He was profiled in *Vanity Fair*: they asked her along for the shoot but only because her cleavage would shift copies. She knew they saw her as the Yoko to his Lennon. The more serious publications ignored her, as if she were a bad smell. He was never going to grant her any power voluntarily, so she'd been forced to snatch it.

'I'd like each toenail painted with the Stars and Stripes. Yes.'

'*What?*' snapped Jack. 'Where are you? You better not be somewhere *frivolous*. The fucking *Mail* would love to splash you over the front page sticking two diamond-encrusted fingers up to your supposed impoverishment.'

'I wasn't talking to you. I am now. You should be *grateful* that forty-two million is all you've lost, and you know it. The house had to go, in a big blaze of publicity and woe, to show that you, like all the other Names, have lost *everything*. The truth is, you've only lost a fraction of your wealth. Those off-shore accounts are untouchable – well, *Lloyd's* can't touch them. And our – sorry, your business is still intact. People might hate you, but they can't *touch* you.'

'Forgive me if I don't *entirely* agree. Forgive me if I'm not quite as chipper about the business as you are.'

'Darling, you know that what's mine is yours. Whereas what's yours is Lloyd's.'

Thousands of miles away as he was, she was sure she could hear him grit his teeth. Innocence sighed, and cut him off without a goodbye. 'Could those stripes be *pink* instead of red, sweetie?'

LONDON, 1994

Nathan

She'd wanted to take him to the football; after all, wasn't that what all sixteen-year-olds wanted to do, apart from shag and

279

drink and smoke and piss around with their mates? He'd agreed, because he did like to tick all the right boxes. People, especially *her*, couldn't cope with anything different. Different was weird. They couldn't handle it. So he smoked, and drank, and shagged, and pissed around with other boys his age – the perfect image of a teenager – and he went to the football. He enjoyed it, but not for *their* reasons.

But for the special day itself, a Saturday, he asked if she'd take him to see a show. Of course, she was delighted.

She'd been so proud when he'd played the title role in the school's performance of *King Lear* in front of all the parents, teachers, casting agents, talent scouts. He found her pride offensive. After all, his talents had sod all to do with her! Her only role was as facilitator. She had enrolled him in a famously arts-orientated school; if a pupil did a particularly splendid fart important people applauded. All she had done was to put him in a place where his genius would be dis-covered. His jacket pocket was solid with business cards. Everything was going to plan. After today, he'd make some calls, and his future would be assured.

After *today*.

His mother's delight had vanished when he told her the name of the show he wanted to see: *Annie*.

Her emotions were curious to him. They were so loose . . . like diarrhoea. She was a person with no self-control; she had no idea how to rein herself in. Everything she felt, you saw. Nothing was private. It was like watching a car crash. She thought she was sensitive to his needs and feelings, but like everyone in the world, it was really all about her. *Her* needs. Everything he said to her had to be relayed through her Me Filter before it bounced back to him.

So when he asked his birth mother – the woman who'd abandoned him when he was a day old – to take him to see a West End musical about an orphan, her face had flattened in dismay. Perhaps he wanted to see it for the same reasons that millions of other people had gone to see it – it was a thoroughly entertaining, harmless bit of fun. Perhaps he wanted to see it because when he was a kid, one of the girls in the home had been given a tape of it, and they'd all belted out the songs together – oh, the irony!

But no, all *that* wouldn't occur to her. *His* needs, *his* desires were the afterthought. Her immediate reaction was: how does this request relate to *me*? It must be about how I dumped him when he was a newborn and made him an orphan who suffered untold pain at the hands of evil adults even though I, his mother, was alive and well. This request is therefore hurtful to *me*, and my face is going to sag with self-pity, and I'm going to reply in a small wavering voice, 'Oh. Oh, yes. I'll take you to see *Annie*. If that's what you want.'

As it happened, this time her Me Filter was right.

He felt a rush of excitement. He'd waited so long for this. He allowed her to stroke his hand, even though it made him want to batter her. But it was good for him, all of it: an exercise, a dress rehearsal for the rest of his life. He sat beside her in the theatre, savouring her discomfort throughout the matinee performance. At one point he could tell that she was wiping away tears – *not*, you could be sure, tears for his pain and misery. He was sick of her tears. Other people had blood running through their veins; she had salt water.

'Mum, that was *top*, thanks so much,' he said as she hailed a taxi, grey-faced. It had been torture for her – or so she'd be telling herself in her self-obsessed drama queen head. Torture! She had no idea. He loved it when she was like this, the silent, suffering martyr. He made a point of being super-cheerful, ignoring her agony as if it were invisible, feeding off her despair, grinding it deeper like a screwdriver through her heart, chattering away blithely, pressing her to buy the cassette so they could listen to it when they got home – oh, just his little joke!

'Can't wait for dinner, Mum,' he said. 'I'm starving.'

She managed a weak smile. 'It won't take me long, I

prepared most of it this morning. You could have a shower while I get it ready.'

'Sure.'

He turned his face to the window, watching London speed by in a blur. She'd taken off her best shoes, as she always did the second they stopped walking, and was rubbing her feet together. *Skritch, skritch.* The nylon of her stockings made a sound that set his teeth on edge. Not long now.

'Thank you.'

She paid the taxi fare and he unlocked the door. She managed to prise a kiss off him before he escaped upstairs. He washed his face with Dettol and spat into the sink. Then he showered, washed his hair, shaved and changed. It was an occasion and he wanted to look his best. The huge bouquet was standing in water, by the window. He'd managed to sneak it in after school without her seeing – a fucking miracle as she was always watching, *always*. It was a tradition he'd established a couple of years ago: every Friday night he'd bring her flowers from one of a few flower shops in Hampstead. Preparation was everything.

Tonight, it was a glorious extravaganza of yellow flowers: roses, foxgloves, freesias, snapdragons, dahlias and calla lilies. He opened his wardrobe and fetched a single stem from the back. It was pleasingly withered, and was shedding, as expected after a week without water. He took one of its fallen leaves, folded it into a tissue and stuck it in his pocket. Then he placed the withered stem in among the fresh blooms, so that it was barely visible.

'Dinner's ready, darling!' she called. So was he. He galloped downstairs.

'These are for you, Mum.'

'Oh darling!' More welling up. 'They're absolutely stunning! Darling, it's *your* birthday! You shouldn't have!' He loathed how her mood was totally dependent on how he treated her. Now she'd been given a little pat on the head, she'd cheer up. It was pathetic.

'Why don't you put them in water,' he said. 'We can have them on the table as we eat. The freesias have an amazing scent.' He'd be fucking glad when this was over. He was sick of sounding like a poof.

'I'll do it now!'

Of course you will. He didn't want to touch the vase.

She arranged the flowers, placing them carefully in the centre of the table, and they sat down.

'It looks delicious.'

She beamed. 'You made a good choice. Bitterleaf salad is *so* yummy – for a salad!'

Yummy. Fuck's sake. How old was she? Four?

'So have you varied the recipe, or just stuck to the usual?'

'Stuck to the usual! I know how you like what you like! There's rocket, baby spinach, lamb's lettuce, curly endive, chicory, radicchio and watercress in there, nothing more, nothing less. And I made double the usual amount of passion-fruit sauce.'

Blahblahblah.

'And the fish pie smells great. Tomato juice would go well with this, Mum. Is there any?'

'I'll have a look. I think there is, somewhere in the larder.'

'Can I have ice and lemon, please?' He paused. 'And a splash of vodka?'

She laughed. 'Oh, why not! I think I'll join you!'

As she rattled around the kitchen, he took the tissue out of his pocket and delicately placed the wilted leaf in her salad. Then he poured a slosh of passion-fruit dressing on top. He was pouring his own when she came back into the room with his drink.

'Your health.' He smiled as they clinked glasses. She groped for his hand. She *always, always* had to be touching. It was vile.

He grinned. 'Let's eat!'

'Let's! I've already had a nibble of the fish pie – it's delicious, if I say so myself!'

Subtext: I'm a good mother. I'm a good mother, aren't I? *See?*

Stupid dumb bitch; didn't think it was strange that a sixteen-year-old would want to spend his birthday evening with an old hag who called herself his *mother*.

He shovelled the bitter salad leaves into his mouth. She ate daintily, but finished the lot. He couldn't stop grinning. According to his research, it wouldn't take long. It didn't.

'I don't feel so good,' she gasped. She looked greenish. She clutched her stomach. 'Oh my *God*.' She staggered to her feet, but collapsed. 'Nathan,' she breathed, 'help me.' She was panting now, writhing on the floor, moaning in pain. 'I can't . . . breathe . . . going to be . . .' She vomited on to her precious African rug. 'My head' – she was sobbing now – 'hurts. Oh God, what's happening to me . . . help me, please, I . . . I'm going to die . . .'

He crouched beside her and tenderly stroked the sweaty tendrils of hair from her agonized face. 'Mummy,' he said. 'It's OK. You *are* going to die.' He watched her struggle to lift her head. She couldn't do it and sank face first into her vomit. 'I've been planning it . . .' He paused and laughed. '. . . since before I met you!' Her entire body was shaking. He watched with interest. 'Digitalis poisoning. Pretty cool.' Her eyes were rolling in her head and she was white with pain. 'Fucking listen to me, you bitch!' She met his gaze, her eyes dull with agony and disbelief, and he smiled. 'Thank you. A little courtesy is all we ask! So, where was I? Ah yes. So, year in, year out, the fucking flowers. Those idiot florists think I'm such a *doll*. So I save a foxglove stem from last week, I don't nurture it, in fact I leave it to rot without food or water and it *withers*. Same as a child, do you *copy*, Mother?'

Her eyes were glazed. He bent, shouted in her face, 'I said, DO YOU COPY, BITCH?'

'Nathan,' she rasped. 'I . . . love you. So much.'

'Love,' he said. 'What *is* that? You don't love me, Mummy.

284

You *think* you do, but it's referred love. Like referred pain. You only love yourself. Your love is only in one place, it just *seems* to be in another. There *is* no love for me, it's a fallacy.' He paused. 'You don't get it, do you? OK, try this. Your love for me is moonlight, yeah? Oh *God*! Do I have to explain everything? There's no such thing as moonlight, dummy! It's the *sun's* light, reflecting off the moon's surface. You think you love me but your love for me is moonlight.'

She looked at him, bleak, blank.

'Oh, what's the point? Like trying to educate a squirrel.' He patted her leg. 'You do deserve this, you know, Mummy. Apart from all the shit I've suffered because of you. I suffered before I hunted you down, and after. I mean, I've been *abused* by you. This fucking touch, touch, touch, kiss, kiss, kiss: it's harassment. I've had to disinfect myself every night. So . . .' He watched as she tried to lift her head, but sank again into the vomit. 'Here's the scenario. You suffer the worst pain you've ever imagined, while I go out for a birthday pint – pre-arranged – with my friends, and when I get back in a few hours' – he glanced at his watch – 'or I might get lucky and stay out all night, your stupid weak heart will have stopped. I'll call the ambulance, but it will be too late. When they cut you open for the autopsy, they'll find that you accidentally ingested a leaf from the pretty but lethal foxglove. What a tragedy! But kind of plausible, don't you think? Its unfortunate placement on the table . . . one dying stem that shed just *one* leaf . . . into your salad. Enough to kill. The top leaves are the most potent, you see. I did my homework! No one, however hard they try, will be able to prove it was murder! Once again I'll be the poor orphan – well, not *so* poor, thanks to you. I shall be able to start my life again, on *my* terms.' He rocked back on his heels. 'Aren't you proud?'

The sweat was pouring off her, and she was doubled up, convulsing. And she stank of vomit and diarrhoea. Death was gross!

He bounced up, wandered to the hall and got his favourite

black leather jacket. All the phones were safely out of reach. There was nothing she could do.

'Don't worry about me,' he called. 'I'll be fine. Thanks for the leg-up. The world will be mine!'

'Please,' she croaked. 'Please.'

'Please, *what*?' he snapped.

She was struggling to speak. 'Never ... meant ... hurt you ...'

These people! Honestly. You needed the patience of a saint! He stumped back into the room. 'Yes,' he said. 'But so what?' And then, 'Sweetie, don't flatter yourself. It's not about you. It's about *me*. You aren't number one on my shit list, you're the fucking hedgehog I ran over on my way to battle.' He clenched his teeth to stop himself from pounding her brain out of her head right there. 'You know,' he hissed. 'People like you are so *fucking* tactless! I didn't *want* to think about Jack Kent – the prick who took over ruining my life where you left off – and now you've made me and I'm SO UPSET!'

The sound of himself screaming brought him to his senses. He glared at her, breathed deeply, and tried to calm down. Eventually, he nodded, rolling his shoulders back to loosen the tension. 'Jack,' he said thoughtfully. 'My argument is mainly with Jack. You were my Six Day War. Jack is my Vietnam.' Then he smacked the side of his head lightly. 'Duh! I almost forgot. There's one more thing!' He removed a flick knife from his pocket, and waved it in front of her nose. 'Hey, there's nothing to be scared of, Mummy! You won't feel a thing.'

She was retching, whimpering with fear. Her nervous system had gone to pieces. And her bladder control.

'Mummy! Honestly. What a baby! I'd love to cut you up alive so you could experience a teeny weeny bit of the torture and misery that *I've* been through. But the bore of it is, a mutilated corpse would look suspect. So I'm forced to forgo the pleasure of your screams. Here's the plan. As the grieving son, I'll insist on having the last look at you in your coffin before the lid is shut for ever and you're lowered into the ground. Oh, and by the way, I'm going to ask for you to be dressed in that peach trouser suit – the one that makes you look fat? I'll ask not to be disturbed, and no one will disturb me, because you have to honour the bereaved. It will only take a few moments – I've rehearsed with that whiney little cat of yours. I'll pop them out like peas from a pod and one slash of the knife – oh, bless you, you don't know what I'm talking about! Your *eyes*, Mummy! As you've always said, you have my eyes.'

She started to convulse. He grinned, sliding the knife back into his pocket. 'They're *mine*, Mummy,' he whispered softly. 'You have my eyes. I want them back.'

BOOK FOUR

PARIS, 13 OCTOBER 1998

Tim

Tim stumbled to his feet, coughing. He ran a trembling hand through his hair; it was full of dirt and rubble. His legs gave way and he sat down on the ground. His trousers were torn and his knee was wet with blood. An explosion – a *bomb*, a bomb had gone off. He had nearly been blown to shreds by a *bomb*, and there was devastation all around, like a scene out of the Middle East. He crawled over broken glass on his hands and knees, willing himself: *Get up, get up, run*; he was climbing over – oh good Christ, a body, a woman. Half of her face was blown off. He turned aside to retch.

The air was filled with smoke and dust, and there was a huge hole in the ceiling. People were sobbing and crying; *he* was sobbing and crying, and the groans of the injured and dying curdled his blood. He could hear the wail of sirens. He was frozen with shock and his head ached as though it would split in two, but he was alive, he'd survived. He needed to get out, there could be another blast, but his legs wouldn't obey orders. If he got out of here intact, he was going to make the most of his existence – yes he was. No more lying. He would be true to himself, and when he graduated from Cambridge he would *not* attend Sandhurst. He wanted nothing to do with the military. He would deal in art – yes he would. Today he had seen death and felt a fear like no other. But it wasn't fear of death itself – it was the cold crawling fear of having wasted his life.

'Here, let me help you.' The voice was rich, deep, kind and calm – the voice of a hero – and Tim, in a daze of wonder, allowed the young man to lift him to his feet. The young man was strong and tall with an angel's face and Tim let out a squeak of fear. Maybe he *was* actually dead and in heaven? The angel, breathing hard, hauled Tim's right arm around his shoulder and hefted him towards the exit. 'You're going to be fine. What's your name, friend?'

'Tim Fortelyne,' he croaked, and the angel – no, he was real, alive and earthly, his own age – smiled. His face was dirty with ash but he was unusually beautiful with white, even teeth, and Tim knew he was *someone* of note. Normal people did not look this perfect.

'I'm Ethan,' said the young man. 'You stick with me, you'll be cool.'

The *actor* – the guy was an international superstar at twenty – he had saved the world at least twice on screen, and now he was saving Tim. 'So very kind you are,' he whispered, and then dizziness overtook him and he blacked out.

LONDON, OCTOBER 1998

Emily

She had been thrilled to realize that she was being airlifted back to Britain. The thrill hadn't lasted. The NHS hospital had been like something out of 1950s Calcutta. She had been put on a *ward*. Beyond disgusting. Two along, the patient was handcuffed to the bed, with a couple of policemen with sub-machine guns standing guard. She was terrified, horrified – had demanded to be moved to a private hospital, only to be told by a disapproving nurse, who called her 'girl', that no private hospital had their 'excellent' resources.

Resources? Two hellish weeks, during which she barely slept. In the dead of night, the woman in the next bed prayed to Jesus, half sobbing, half hysterical; to Emily it sounded like voodoo. The food was, like, totally poisonous, and McDonald's didn't deliver, so she ordered a hamper, daily, from Fortnum's, not knowing how else to survive. If she had to use the communal bathroom, she had to hold her breath so that she wasn't sick.

Finally, *finally*, she'd been moved to the Portland. It was almost as bad. She *hated* this hospital. It masqueraded as a hotel, but they had no idea. The food was a fucking joke, so this time she'd ordered an organic, no-gluten meal-delivery service from Selfridges on credit, and she'd spent three hours on the phone ordering silk cushions from Liberty and sheepskin rugs from Toast, Diptyque scented candles, porcelain dinner plates, a red La Chapelle side table, and a white leather Versace chair for the tiny room. She had it repainted in organic paint (best for baby). As for the bathroom, she would have had it ripped out and redone by Philippe Starck for her stay but they wouldn't allow it – *ridiculous*, when it would be at *her* expense! The bathroom was like something out of a Bombay slum. She imagined.

The room was now bearable, but she was so mind-numbingly bored of lying here. The bleeding had reoccurred. They didn't like bleeding when you were seven months pregnant. Still, the baby's heartbeat was fine and, according to the v. cute doctor, her cervix looked 'gorgeous'. She'd smiled then, for the first time in a long while. Smiling made an interesting change from crying. Weird but true. It had sounded like bullshit when they said it in biology, but now she had discovered it for herself: people actually *were* 90 per cent water.

There was a quiet knock. Her heart leaped. But it was probably the doctor, or the nurse, or the cleaner, or the million other people who kept barging in every other minute to jab a

293

needle in her arm or stick a funny paper thermometer in her mouth. Private hospital, my arse! There was *no* privacy!

'Yes?'

'Emily! Oh my God, is the baby OK? I'm sorry for not ringing first. I came the second I heard.'

She flopped back on the five duckdown pillows. 'Hi, Claudia. At fucking last.' The sight of Claudia, hollow-eyed and wretched with a broken arm, was not exactly cheering in the *abstract*, but Emily felt a lurch of triumph.

'So are they monitoring him? Or her? What is the . . . can they save it?'

'The baby's fine.'

'Oh! Thank *God*! They can work miracles these days, they really—'

'Claudia, I lied. The baby's heartbeat did *not* stop. I just had to' – she could feel her voice rising to a shout – '*GET YOU HERE SOMEHOW*!'

Claudia sat down on an Eames chair with a thump. 'Don't . . . you . . . so . . . *wrong*.' She sighed. 'But I understand. I'm sorry for not . . . coming before. I . . .' She paused. 'This room is rather gorgeous, for a hospital. I brought Alfie with me.'

'*Alfie?*'

Claudia blushed. 'Yes. You know. Alfie Cannadine. He was so upset to hear about the . . . *thing* . . .'

'The bomb?'

'He and Harry flew to Paris that night. Harry organized for everyone – us to be transferred by private air ambulance to – to English hospitals, although I, obviously, didn't need to stay for long. Alfie has been *so* sweet. He made dinner for me every night of the first week: chilli con carne, Bolognese, home-made burgers, and brought it in. I don't think he realizes I'm vegetarian. He doesn't know about . . . Well, he knows I broke off my engagement . . .' She blushed.

'You fancy him,' said Emily.

'No!' hissed Claudia. 'He's been seeing that Polly girl for three years. They're *very* serious, so don't say a word.'

Emily rolled her eyes. Claudia was obviously rolling from one heartbreak to the next. Presumably it distracted her from obsessing about Martin. 'So where *is* Alfie?'

'Outside. He's happy to wait. He doesn't feel sure about the etiquette of visiting you when you're—'

'Oh, Jesus. The paparazzi lie on the floor when I get out of cars! The whole world's seen my ass. Bring him in.'

Claudia beamed and hurried to the door. Alfie entered, carrying a stylish bouquet. He looked slightly surprised to see forty-nine other stylish bouquets. She hadn't seen him for at least four years. She remembered him as a posh geek, but, oh *shit*, he was gorgeous. A rugby player's physique, and he'd grown into his generous features. She was *meticulous* about putting her 'face' on – a few weeks of not giving a toss and disaster!

'Emily,' he said with convincing concern. 'So good to see you again. How are you feeling?'

'Like crap,' she said. She'd meant it as a joke, but her eyes filled with tears. She roughly wiped them away. 'I'm scared, OK? I'm scared. I'm scared about having a baby, I'm scared of the bomb, I'm scared if a leaf falls off a tree.' She saw the glance between them. 'So now you're here, tell me,' she said. 'I order you to tell me *now*.'

They were silent.

She could feel her voice rising in hysteria. 'No one will *talk to me*. They've removed the plasma and even the Tunisian cleaner can't be bribed to bring me a paper. I ordered *Hello!* to be biked over and they confiscated it at reception. It is driving me *round the fucking twist*.' She grabbed Claudia's broken arm and squeezed. Her sister gasped in pain. Good. Alfie, like the gentleman he was – God, she was tired of gentlemen, her next husband would be a brickie – stepped quickly between them.

'Please don't upset yourself, Emily, though Christ knows, I understand. It's only that you're in a delicate state, and Claw doesn't want to raise your blood pressure by talking about a traumatic event.'

Claw?

'Listen, Alfie. This is all very cute: flowers, hushed tone, furrowed brow. But if you or she don't tell me why not one member of my family has visited me in hospital the whole time I've been here, and why there are two armed guards standing outside my room twenty-four hours a day, I am going to ... I am very powerful ... I know people ...' She stopped. 'Please,' she said. 'It's worse not knowing. So tell me the truth. Daddy. Mummy. Tim. Are they *all* dead?'

BARBUDA, A TINY ISLAND IN THE CARIBBEAN SEA, NOVEMBER 1998

Tim

Cheating abroad didn't count. Cheating didn't count if she'd never find out. And cheating didn't count if you didn't love the person you were cheating with. This was not love. He wouldn't kid himself. He might persuade himself it was love, but truly he knew it was lust. He stretched out on the luxurious white four-poster, and his body felt like jelly in a thoroughly satisfying way, as if, after years of deprivation, it had at last been employed for its correct purpose.

He lit a cigarette, tipped back his head and watched the smoke curl to the white ceiling. The sunlight streamed into the room and he wriggled his toes in the warmth. The walls of his room were white slatted shutters that rose up until there was nothing between you and the deck and the beach and the sea. And to his left, there was the aquamarine pool, and the baby palm trees, and the azure sky. The sand on the beach was a pale shade of pink, and they'd laughed about it. The previous night, they'd eaten goat stew at the Palm Tree restaurant, and they'd laughed about that. He would have laughed about his granny dying, he was so blissfully happy with his new lover. Nothing could pollute the dream. It *was* a dream.

It barely felt real. At least, it felt as if he was briefly living another man's life – another man's *charmed* life. No one could harm him here. He was 100 per cent safe. He had been rescued from a nightmare, a nightmare that had begun way before an unknown suspect had blown up the Hôtel Belle Époque and quite a few of its guests. He wasn't sure how many had died. He preferred not to know. He had a vivid memory of being swept from danger by a ministering angel – *Ethan Summers* – and then the tape ran out. He'd had concussion. It was strange to be told that, but it had to be true. He supposed that concussion wasn't necessarily instant. But Andy, his gorgeous private nurse, had gently filled in the blanks in his memory. He was still a little befuddled, and it was easier not to ask too many questions. Andy discouraged it as bad for his mental health, and he was happy to agree. His condition required rest, sunshine, a change of scene – Barbuda certainly provided all *that*.

He should really call to thank his father for picking up the bill, but the telephone network on the island was dreadfully unreliable and he wasn't up to a tricky conversation. He didn't really want to speak to anyone from the outside world. He needed to cocoon, and recover. Andy had been a darling – speaking to Daddy on his behalf so that his father wouldn't feel snubbed. Tim had told Andy it was *imperative* that his father's olive branch was grasped with both hands: a great deal, everything in fact, rode on their reunion.

'I know something else that should be grasped with both hands,' Andy had murmured, pulling off his towel to reveal an eye-watering erection.

Tim had felt himself harden in response. What perfect symmetry! He had crawled across the bed to oblige.

It had crossed his mind – but no, he refused to feel guilty – that if the unnamed enemy had not bombed his father-in-law's grand party, he would not have been injured, he would not have suffered post-traumatic stress disorder (tosh, but the private doctor seemed convinced of it), he would not have been ordered to recuperate in exotic seclusion, and he would not have met Andrew, the man who had changed the course of his life for ever.

And he refused to feel bad about his wife. Emily was recovering slowly – Andrew was in touch with her doctors – but it was for the best that they didn't speak. She was in a delicate state and the least emotional upset could have an adverse effect on the baby. It was curious to think that she had once attracted him, but lust was like running water, it had to go somewhere. He couldn't feel sorry for her: she had trapped him into marriage, whatever she claimed. And of course she had planned the baby; it was her bad luck that she had planned so *wrong*.

He didn't like being married to Emily. It was drab. She'd tried to cook for him, on Cook's day off! She was a terrible cook, truly terrible. And she tried to change things. He liked his loo rolls kept in a wicker basket adjacent to the loo, not on a holder. He liked the black and white photo of his mother as a young girl wearing an Alice band right next to his bed, not a cluster of empty Coke cans. And every Christmas Eve, he liked to go back to Fortelyne, where he and his mother would decorate the tree with trinkets handed down from generations. He hoped his parents would have forgiven him by Christmas – after all, it was the season of peace and good-will. They'd wrap presents, eat mince pies and drink mulled wine, and Mummy would put an orange in his Christmas stocking, and the dogs would lie at his feet.

When he'd told this to Emily she'd looked aghast. 'Ohmigod,' she'd said. 'Like, can't we get a sitter and go to a club?'

Even if she suspected that there had been a . . . hiccup in his fidelity, he was certain that Emily would remain his wife – not because she loved him, although he thought she did, but because she would never entirely relinquish hope of becoming queen of Fortelyne Castle. Alas, she wasn't to know that the true queen of Fortelyne Castle was *himself*...

'Turn over, my little pony,' whispered Andrew, and Tim shivered with delicious anticipation. Without question, this was the best afternoon of his life. Screwing this god of a man, sipping cocktails in a hammock strung between two palm trees, feeding each other fresh lobster, going for a dip in the warm Caribbean Sea, wandering along the private beach, finding a romantic spot that wasn't overlooked ... although that teenage bird-spotter with his long lens camera had given them a fright, or perhaps, they'd given *him* an education...

As his head grew light with the beginnings of his fourth orgasm of the day, Tim decided that his recovery would take another two months at least.

LONDON, OCTOBER 1998

Innocence

It was vile and disgusting and she would have suffered a panic attack – had she been the weak, spineless, pathetic sort of person who *suffered* panic attacks. As it was, she hadn't removed her white gloves since stepping inside the building – the vast, ugly, soulless building, full of the sort of mentally unstable pond life she'd run from long ago. She held a silk leopard-print Hermès scarf over her mouth and nose. There was a high risk of catching a fatal bug in this place – Ebola wouldn't surprise her.

At least, if Jack *did* emerge from his coma, there was a fighting chance that a germ would see him off. Innocence sighed and carefully rested her Gucci shades on her pink hair. Today it was in a low, demure ponytail: 'We're thinking humble,

299

we're thinking chaste, we're thinking *stricken*,' Patrice had declared, nodding approvingly as Samson gently patted talcum powder to whiten the healthy flush of her cheeks. 'Oh, *bravo*, Samson, *bravo* – the instant pallor of grief!'

She had paused dutifully on the steps of the Whittington hospital – *NHS!* – so the assembled press could take her picture. The paparazzi had shouted dirty jokes to try and make her laugh; fortunately Patrice had taken the precaution of insisting that she wear a pair of cheap nylon knickers from Woolworths to ensure that she maintained an expression of deep and genuine sorrow. She was carrying a gift bowl of exotic fruit (which she intended to eat herself), a teddy bear from Harrods (adults who owned soft toys should be *shot*) and a duck-egg-blue cashmere dressing gown from Paul Smith. The 'gifts' had been assembled in a rush: the man was in a coma, what did he care? Her outfit, however, had required detailed planning. Long ago, in the shit-filled bog of an inner-city sink school, Innocence had promised herself a pair of shoes for every day of the year, and she had more than kept her word.

W wrote editorials on her closet. Or rather, they should have. Now that she was a fashion icon (*Rainbow* magazine adored her style and Hurley could go fuck herself) her wardrobe required its own staff. Jasper Jones and his company Closet Fairy had taken charge. Now Jasper colour-coordinated every item, and each outfit was separated into A and B wardrobes from current and past seasons. Innocence kept a wardrobe for trousers, a wardrobe for dresses, a wardrobe for shirts, and another for coats. Each item was kept in a garment bag with a photograph attached. A computer tracked which outfit was worn when, and a 360-degree 'catscan' camera generated an all-angles image of every look as Innocence stepped out of the door. At the end of each season, Jasper archived key pieces, *possibly* for Emily, but that depended on her mood – right now it was a fair bet the V&A would inherit.

According to Patrice, UK *Vogue*'s tips for winter included

diamonds, epaulettes, feathers, gold, lacy legs, purple, see-through, velvet and zips. Frustratingly, he had forbidden Innocence from wearing all of these things at once. So, for today's mercy mission, she was meekly attired in a black cashmere polo-neck body by Ralph, a stiff flared skirt with netting by Calvin, black leather ankle boots by Prada, and lacy – she had insisted – black stockings. Her bag was Louis, but a *small*, pious Louis. It was, cried Patrice, a sexy, witty take on Julie Andrews in *The Sound of Music*.

As she ascended in the disgusting shabby lift, she held her breath – it reeked of disinfectant and death – and wondered how long she would need to hang around. Surely visiting hours should be cut short if a patient was on the brink? But less than two hours, and the media would accuse her of a 'brief, token' visit.

The gossip and speculation had been *horrible*. Under-standable, however: it was no secret that she and Jack were united only in mutual loathing, and, of course, some sluglike hack, wanting to make a quick dollar, had dug up last year's interview with Oprah. Quote: 'Yes I do hate him, and I do wish he were dead. Of course he knows it, why else has he surrounded himself with former Mossad agents? He's *wetting* himself with fear of what I might do – and rightly so!'

Entirely tongue in cheek, Oprah roaring with faux-outraged laughter – oh what adorable British dark humour, with the vulgar audience whooping away in support – and now, suddenly, her words had been turned against her, taken out of context and, while Scotland Yard had no intention of taking such garbage seriously, it was upsetting, personally hurtful and bad for business.

She might *feel* murderous, but in fact, she had no wish to kill Rumpelstiltskin. Let him spin straw into gold for years and years. There would be all the more for her, as his wife, to inherit when he *did* go. This attitude seemed perfectly sane and obvious, so it was annoying that other people couldn't see it.

301

They were so busy focusing on the Wife He Never Loved Like the First, they were blind to a truth that was plain to Innocence and had been for a while. Jack had an enemy – a deadly, vengeance-seeking enemy – and he or she was creeping closer all the time. Talking of which, watching the Belle Époque being blasted to bits had been a Kodak moment. God, it served him right! In her wildest dreams, she could not have imagined a more fitting end to his arrogant 'Easter Party'. *Easter!* Comparing himself to Jesus *Christ!* Innocence was not a Christian, but in this instance she was certainly a defender of the faith. How ironic that when he'd ordered his heavies to turf her out, he had probably saved her life. One didn't wish to speak ill of the dead, but she wasn't sorry that his bit on the side, Maria, was pushing up daisies. That would teach her to steal another woman's husband.

Today, she would (as she did every day) whisper in her husband's ear, 'Poor Maria is dead, I'm so sorry for your loss,' in the hope that receipt of this fact would prompt a turn for the worse.

But he remained stubbornly immune, in his dream world. She also read to him the *LA Times*'s eulogy to Mollie Tomkinson: 'Comparable to the untimely death of River Phoenix, a tragic and shocking tale of a precious, God-given talent cruelly struck down before its prime.'

But Innocence couldn't feel bad for pretty young dead girls.

She had cheerfully read aloud the editorial, which bluntly suggested that Jack's immoral business practices had ruined many lives, thus he was responsible for the creation of a raft of enemies. Perhaps in these desperate times it was sadly inevitable that one of these had resorted to terrorism? And while in no way did they condone cold-blooded murder, it could be argued that the blame for Mollie's death on the ill-fated night of the Easter Party ultimately lay with her host.

Furthermore, it was said that her bereaved family were

considering suing his arse for a hundred million dollars in lost earnings.

Innocence allowed herself to be patted down by Jack's security. The agent was dour and non-smiling in a black bomber jacket and he didn't meet her eye. 'The thrill's all mine,' she muttered as he finally nodded towards the door.

To her surprise, he followed her in.

'I don't think so,' she said.

'But I do,' he replied. 'And I've got the gun.'

'Oh, for God's sake,' she muttered. But in a way, she was glad for the company. She hated being with Jack. It felt as if death was in the room and she didn't want to be contaminated. She would have preferred for her entourage to soothe her – Patrice, Jamie, Samson – but, PR-wise, it was better to be alone. The security guard was better than nothing. In fact, he *was* nothing. People like him did not get noticed by people like her.

She inched around the bed. It was hard to look at her husband in this helpless state. Weakness of any kind repulsed her. He looked so grey and shrunken, and she could barely suppress a shudder at the spaghetti of tubes attached to him. And the *smell*. It was sickly sweet, as if something, or someone, was slowly rotting. She sprayed her Chanel No. 5 around the room as if it were mace.

'This is the ugliest place I have been in for fifteen years,' she said aloud, and sighed. The neurosurgeon who'd operated on Jack's head injuries had said that it was 'hard to see into the future'. No doubt he'd be along shortly, in his self-important white coat, to bore her with further platitudes. The truth: Jack might recover fully, or die in the night. And if he didn't come out of the coma within the next two weeks, she was going to suggest – or perhaps it would be wiser to prompt the doctors to suggest – that his life-support machine was turned off.

Innocence jammed two teddy bears on Jack's pillow, one alongside each ear. Then she pulled her chair close and rested her hard leather boots on the soft mattress of his metal bed, slowly but firmly pushing his motionless legs to one side until she was fully comfortable.

Then she ripped off the fruit bowl's cellophane wrapping and ate a cherry. There were a few doubles, and she hooked a pair over her ear. As a child, she'd never seen a cherry; as an adult she'd watched Alfie's podgy little sister dance around the Cannadines' vast and ornate sitting room wearing 'cherry earrings' and wanted to slap her face. She flipped open her gold Chanel vanity mirror and admired the cherries. The million-pound Graff diamonds set them off nicely.

I am, she thought to herself, lighting a cigarette under the impassive gaze of the guard, finally living my life as I wanted to live it from the start.

'Not in here,' said the guard, nodding towards the ceiling.

Shit. If the sprinkler system came on, legionnaires' disease was a given. She stubbed out the fag on the side of her chair.

'I may seem untroubled', she said, coolly, 'over Mr Jelly Head here, but I am *crazed* with grief. Only I prefer to keep my pain and desperation to myself. It is the height of vulgarity, selfishness and bad manners to inflict one's extreme emotions upon a third party. Also, in case you were unaware, I am a very private person.'

The guard blinked, and appeared to check his watch.

'I'm *sorry*,' she said, irritated. 'Am I boring you?' *You great ape.*

He didn't respond and she turned away in disgust. She had more pressing matters to attend to. Her husband's solicitor should have got back to her by now. She needed to speak to him urgently about the will.

She *deserved* to inherit everything. If it weren't for her, Jack would have lost everything, instead of most things. Not only that, she was the mother of his daughter – his *blood* daughter. During the past year, their relationship had been curt. He had the mistress. Husband and *wife* had probably slept in the same bed – well, not exactly *slept* – only three times in the last twelve months.

But that was a hazard of extreme wealth and un-trammelled success. You shared stunning palatial homes around the world, but you were rarely in the same mansion at the same time. *You* had to attend to your interests in New York, LA, Bermuda, Positano, while *he* maintained his in Paris, Rome, Madrid. *He* had a charity benefit in London, while *she* must attend a fashion show in Milan. Being a Power Couple was impossible: you either had power, or you were a couple. She and Jack vastly preferred power to each other. It had got to the point where they were strangers who occasionally met in the night. After one such meeting, during which they'd screwed in the shower, she sliding slowly to her knees (something she hadn't done with Jack for years), she had curled up next to him like a viper in the great ornate bed with its antique mirrored headboard, and smiled.

'What?' he'd said, eyes narrowed.

At this point he'd always be struggling with guilt about Maria. About the *mistress*! About having *betrayed* her! He'd feel guilty for having fucked his wife! She always enjoyed watching his face at this point.

'Don't feel bad,' she'd said, stroking his chest. 'It's good for the children to know that we still . . . *love* each other.'

He'd made a noise like a pig. 'Oh yes,' he'd replied. 'And how will they know? Are you going to send them a tape?'

She'd giggled. 'Actually I'm being interviewed by *Harper's* next week. I'll find a way to drop it in.'

'Don't,' he'd said.

She'd tilted her head, as if considering. 'Very well, darling. As you wish. I shall claim that the marriage bed is cold,' *so as not to upset your little tart.*

He'd seemed gratified, and she'd coiled a strand of his hair around her finger and wriggled closer. 'Darling,' she'd said. 'Of course I won't upset you by being . . . indiscreet about us. But I *am* serious about Emily. And, er, Claudia. I hope you aren't planning to do anything . . . *silly* with your inheritance. You know, darling, that I am going to leave everything I have to *you'* – an easy promise, she had *years* on him! And a second, amended will cutting him out like a cancer – 'because ultimately, I want to leave everything to the girls.' A lie, but a *white* lie. 'And I know of no better guardian of their fortune than their father.'

She'd taken a sip of Barolo to disguise her anxiety.

He'd twisted the Hermès crystal goblet out of her hand and yanked her towards him by her favourite necklace: a lizard made of hundreds of emeralds, with ruby eyes and claws of white gold, scampering on a criss-cross grate of black diamonds. It had cost over a quarter of a million pounds, and it was her little friend.

He had crushed his lips to hers, and she'd felt a pleasant stab of desire and repulsion. Then, roughly, he'd pushed her back, and stared into her dark eyes.

'As I've always said,' he'd declared, 'I will leave everything to my wife.'

She'd closed her eyes in a shiver of delight and writhed her body joyfully over his. 'Let me', she'd whispered, 'take you on another guilt trip.'

I will leave everything to my wife. You couldn't speak plainer than that. If he had actually said it, then it was true. Jack was a man who lied by omission. It was not his style to tell a blatant fib. That had been three months ago, and nothing had changed, so why did she have this niggling doubt? Perhaps it was just in her nature to distrust. All the same, she wanted to see the will with her own eyes. Only then would she be satisfied. She checked her watch, shoved a stick of gum in her mouth, yawned widely. Hang around in this Victorian slum for another . . . *Christ*, hour and three-quarters . . . and then leave, delicately wiping away a single tear for the front pages. Her handkerchief would be pink – better not to look too like a mournful widow, that would be construed in the gossip pages as jumping the gun.

There was a bang, the door burst open and the room swarmed with uniformed police and the blinding light of television cameras.

'Oh my God,' she shrieked. 'What are you doing? There's a man trying to die in here! Get out!'

'Miss Innocence Ashford?' said a senior-looking pig with acne scars and grey hair. 'I am arresting you on suspicion of the murders of Mollie Tomkinson and Maria Radcliffe, and the attempted murder of Jack Kent. You do not have to say anything . . .'

LONDON, NOVEMBER 1998

Innocence

It had been the proudest day of Caroline Cartright's life, joining the Met. She'd wanted to join the Force since she was five years old. She'd been crap at ballet. What was it the teacher had said? 'Like a horse stamping round a paddock.'

She was cut out for this job; yes, she was. She was tough, but fair; always had been. There were enough bent coppers, but she wasn't one of them. She liked helping people, and she could break up a fight in a pub. She had a nice easy manner; she didn't rub people up the wrong way. She was five foot nothing: when she said, 'Come on, lads,' the biggest, scariest geezers stopped beating seven shades of shit out of each other, mainly out of surprise.

The women were meaner and more vicious. But even then, most of them had a weak spot for kindness. She was calm, she was patient. She never called them 'ladies' – patronizing, like a red rag to a bull – and she preferred to give them an option, not an ultimatum or a threat. She gave them the choice of keeping their dignity: 'Let's try and sort this out another way. Here, are you all right, love?' There was something deeply calming about being called 'love', like your nan might say. People's anger tended to melt, and it made her think that most of them hadn't had enough kindness in their lives.

Caroline prided herself, in a quiet way, on being able to handle any human being, no matter how drunk, violent, or psychotic.

Miss Innocence Ashford was her first failure.

They'd brought her in to the station in handcuffs, and it had still taken six male officers to restrain her. Caroline had never seen anything like the pandemonium of jostling, screaming reporters that chased her to the door – she'd felt sorry for the woman at first – they were like a skulk of foxes after a chicken. But Caroline's compassion soon drained away. She was one of the interviewing officers, and the entire time the woman had stared at her with such coiled venom, it had taken every ounce of will not to flinch. She was mortified, and just a bit resentful. No one likes their balloon popped. Even though Ashford was handcuffed to her chair, and that chair was nailed to the floor, *and* they were under observation, Caroline couldn't shake the feeling that she might lunge through the air, chair attached, like one of the no-good vampires in *Blade*, and bite through her neck.

The aura of evil intent was potent.

'I want my call,' the woman had said, and Caroline had jerked in her seat. There was a sudden guttural edge to the woman's voice, and the words she'd used ... *Scum*, she thought, before she could stop herself. This woman might have all the trappings of wealth and class but at her core she was the underclass, and, as such, she had nothing to lose. She had the desire, the desperation, the capability of committing any crime, no matter how brutal, to drag herself upward.

Miss Innocence Ashford had rung her solicitor. Caroline had hoped it would calm her.

Not exactly.

The conversation had been short, but explosive.

The woman had dropped the receiver and started screaming. Caroline and another officer had run into the room in alarm, thinking she was fitting. It was like watching someone morph into a demon before your eyes. Whatever the bloke had said, it had caused her to go stark, raving mad. She was thrashing about like a soul possessed, spitting with rage, and screeching uncontrollably, to the point where, if she didn't watch it, she was going to get a whack.

The woman was babbling and shrill, but the gist of what she said was clear enough: 'I'll *kill* him, I'll *kill* him, I'll slit him open and cut out his heart, I'll pull out his entrails like fucking spaghetti and ram them down his throat. How dare he do this to me, how *dare* he – oh my God, from the *day* he met me – how dare he *treat me like this*, how dare he *do* this to me!'

'Language,' Caroline had murmured mildly. 'I've heard what you're saying, we all have, and you're doing your case no good at all – it could all be admissible. Sit down, lip up, and I'll make you a cup of tea.'

Well, the woman had just *flown* at her. She was swarmed just in time, but even the combined weight of DC Barton and PC Kruger, *and* DI Russell – all pastry fans – could barely contain her. As she was bundled into her cell in plastic handcuffs, the woman had spat a response. Caroline felt like wiping her memory clean with a bar of soap! As her nan would have said, pursing her lips more in sorrow than in anger, 'And that's all the news that's fit to print!'

LONDON, NOVEMBER 1998

Emily

Emily sat by her father's bedside and tapped her foot. 'You bastard,' she said.

There was no response. He lay there, supine, his mouth open, dried spit at the corners, his breath quiet and rasping. Puffing hard, she leaned across the bed and hissed in his ear, 'I hate you. I just hate you. You're the worst dad *ever*. You don't care about me. Everything I'm going through is, like, *your* fault.'

She clenched her jaw. You couldn't even *sulk* when your dad was in a coma. It was, like, the ultimate 'whatever'. She didn't care if he died. OK, she cared a *bit* – if he died then she would be even more alone than she already was. He'd already abandoned her, because he didn't approve of her lifestyle (ironic, considering his own) and he'd abandoned her because he was a selfish, spiteful, lying bastard, and it would be so typical if he decided to bloody die and abandon her for ever.

She couldn't believe, she *literally* couldn't believe what he'd done. His latest betrayal was cruel and absolute. If it got out – oh my God – when Innocence was already under suspicion, about to be tried for attempted murder . . .

Emily could barely take it in. She'd discharged herself from hospital the minute she'd heard of her mother's arrest (paying the outrageous bill on credit), caught a cab to the police station, and demanded to see her mother. Being a waddling nine months pregnant opened doors, and she'd been allowed a short visit.

Four harassed-looking men in suits were on their way out. Innocence had screeched after them, 'Six hundred quid an hour, you bastards, and I'm still sitting here. What am I paying you for? Thirty quid a piss?'

'Nice,' Emily had murmured. 'Well, I see you're fitting right in.'

Her mother had waited until the solicitors were out of earshot. Then she leaped up from her chair and snarled in a hoarse whisper, 'Jack and I were *never married.*' Bizarrely, she was prettier without lashings of make-up and fake tan. She must have lost her voice from screaming so much. She'd shaken Emily by the shoulders and hissed in her face: 'Your pig of a father *never* married me!'

'Don't be insane,' Emily had said, breathing hard. The baby had just about halved her lung capacity. 'Is this because you got married abroad? It still counts.' Emily knew about marriage law; she'd researched it before marrying Tim in Vegas. She hadn't wanted to take any chances.

'*No,*' husked her mother. 'It's invalid.'

'Mother, it doesn't matter if a local farmer cracks a coconut over both your heads. If that's a legal marriage ceremony according to the *local* laws and customs, then it is legally binding in Britain as well. As long as you aren't cousins.'

Innocence had shaken her head wildly. Her hair needed a wash. 'It wasn't the ceremony. The ceremony was fine. And the bloke was kosher, accredited, licensed, all that shit.' She'd swallowed. 'But the ceremony took place in this little place on the beach – *he* owned it – he never said – and *it* wasn't licensed for marriage ceremonies. *He* owned it, *he* knew it wasn't licensed, *and* he stored the documentation with that shit of a lawyer of his, to prove it. *I was never his wife!*'

Emily had gulped. 'So . . . what does this mean? Surely you have rights? You lived together . . .'

'Are you eating any vegetables or fruit?'

'*What?*'

'Try and eat a mango,' Innocence had muttered, before shouting, 'We were rarely under the same roof! We probably spent a total of two years in the same house – it's not enough for me to have a claim.'

'So . . .'

'He married his MISTRESS!' Her mother glanced nervously at the door, as if they might be overheard. 'He left her everything! He tricked me. I *knew* he was up to something. I confronted him, and with his hand on his heart, he said, "Innocence darling, I am leaving everything to my wife." Only it was Maria! Fucking Maria Radcliffe! They married in secret, in bloody Tuscany, this year!'

'But, Mummy, Maria is dead.'

'Yes!' Innocence had rasped. 'And dear dead moulderingaway Maria has left everything to her *daughter*.'

'Oh my God. A stranger! A stranger gets all our money!'

'No,' Innocence had hissed. 'No. *Claudia* gets it! He was only shagging that little cow's real mother! Claudia gets it all!'

Emily had reeled back in shock. Her mother had shaken her head, and hissed. 'And that's the *best-case scenario*.'

Stammering, Emily had asked, 'What's the worst?'

Innocence had pulled Emily close and whispered in her ear: 'The worst is that this fact is made public, and some greedy fucker who Jack stiffed in the Lloyd's disaster puts two and two together.'

Emily had shaken her head, not understanding.

Her mother had let out a shrill squeak of fury. 'If I was never his wife, then when he – *I* – transferred all his assets into my name, they could claim that it wasn't legal.'

'That's crap, Mother. I'm sure it is. He could transfer his assets to whomever he liked, so long as he didn't do it with the intent of avoiding his liabilities. If you were the person named in the document, then it doesn't matter if you were his wife, his aunt or the boy who shines his shoes.'

Innocence had swallowed. 'Jesus, Emily. I hope you're right. Because this is not about money – not any more. It's about motive. Christ, I need a cigarette.' She'd paused. 'This is going to get out before the trial. I know it. And then, Lloyd's or no Lloyd's, I'll be looking at life.'

Emily gritted her teeth to stop a squeak of rage, and glared at her father's unconscious form.

Bad luck had a way of finding this family.

It would have been far easier for her to accept that a stranger was to inherit her father's kingdom than it was for her to accept that her sister was getting it all. It wasn't as if Emily was mean, just that, like, when you're rock bottom, it's hard to be happy for your sister's glorious success. In fact, it's impossible. You can hardly stand to be conscious for the evil green thoughts that eat at your heart; you cannot help but compare *her* bloody astonishing good luck to *your* crap, shitty luck, and even if you don't totally hate her, her blithe happiness in the face of her frankly undeserved good fortune – when it should have been *you* – turns you sour against her, and you can't help but wish her ill.

Look. She would have been fine about a stranger getting it all. Someone she didn't know. It's OK if someone is rich and successful and happy whom you *don't know*. Then it's harder to compare your crappy shit life to their fabulous luxury one.

Her life was crappy, and it was shit, and the baby wasn't even born yet. She was surviving off a pathetic allowance courtesy of her Scrooge of a mother. It felt so wrong. *OK!* magazine were offering for a Baby Interview – that would pay the Lindo Wing fees – but after that, if she wanted to keep this kid in Ralph, she'd be required to think out of the box. Jesus! Money, money, money! Because she didn't have any, it was all she thought about. It was like a disease: financial anorexia.

And her husband, who might have helped out by, say, selling that enormous shag pad of his in New York, had literally disappeared in a puff of smoke. The bomb had gone off – boom! He was *gone*: in*fucking*communicado.

He'd written, of course. It was undoubtedly the correct thing to do: to correspond with your spouse after her head had nearly been blown off by a large incendiary device.

Tim wrote a good letter, full of concern, assuring her that he was being kept informed of her day-to-day health, that he'd be back to look after her as soon as he could, but he was abroad (she noted he was vague about where, and she didn't recognize the stamp). His father, he said, had organized it, had insisted that he recover from his 'emotional trauma' in a hot place, with private medical facilities.

It was just a lie, she was certain of it, to separate them. There was no way the Earl even knew the phrase 'emotional trauma'. Emily imagined he would have gagged, trying to say it. Emotional trauma was for whoopsies. An Englishman would fall on his sword before admitting 'emotional trauma'.

But here he was, wheeling it out, as an excuse to keep Timmy away from her. It just showed how deeply the Earl disapproved – no, *hated* their union.

It made her sad and depressed. Was Tim not even going to bother to be there for the birth of his baby? Tim was kind of weak, but when he was on form, he made her laugh. He was good company. He was stunning. He was good in bed. She was *chuffed* to be married to him. If only he could be strong, and have faith in her, she was sure that they would be a great couple. And if they were a great couple, a fine *family*, then maybe, eventually, the Earl might relent – and he would get his inheritance, and she would get her castle, and it would all end perfectly after all.

There were a lot of 'ifs'.

And right now, it seemed that *Claudia* was hogging all the money, all the luck. Claudia was officially heiress to a billion-pound fortune and not a penny for Emily! It was just the worst thing, *ever*. Claudia would be getting Jack's money, whether Maria was alive or dead. It had nothing to do with Maria. It was Jack's wish that Claudia got the money. She wasn't even his blood daughter. She was no relation! At least Claudia didn't know about the inheritance: the lawyer had only told Innocence because it was 'pertinent to her defence'. *Claudia* got the money!

Emily looked at her father. There really was no hope of him suddenly waking and being persuaded to change the will.

Of course, Emily would get her mother's fortune in the

end. But Innocence was the kind of mother who'd hang on until she was 105, and Emily saw little cheer in inheriting great wealth when you were older than forty and decrepit. Claudia would get her inheritance in, like, a year. Emily would have to wait for hers for ever!

'You bastard,' she said. 'You BASTARD!' she screamed in his ear, with all her might. Then she felt a warm sensation. She looked down. 'Fuck,' she said. Her waters had broken – all over her last pair of Jimmy Choos.

LONDON, NOVEMBER 1998

Claudia

'DFK? Billy from AP. How you doing?'

Claudia smiled, despite herself. She'd met Billy on a press trip and he'd dubbed her 'Dorothy from Kansas'. She didn't quite know why, but her instinct told her it was a fond nickname; vaguely insulting, but fond.

'Billy! I'm . . . OK, considering. Freelancing. How are you?'

'Doll, I'm fine, but something's come up you need to know about. Mate of mine, Italian geezer, owns a picture agency – they're paps, yeah? There's a shot come in – you'll want to have a look. This is a head's up, doll. I don't think you can stop it.'

'Oh my, what is it?'

'I've put it on a bike. I'm sorry, girl.'

What on *earth* could it be? Her father was in a coma. Her mother was in a police cell. What else was there to go wrong?

Great. Now she couldn't relax. Thank heaven. Here he was. She signed her name and snatched the package. There was a blue folder inside. She opened it, pulled out the photo, and sat down with a thump. Oh *no*. Poor, poor Emily. How disgusting. How *could* he? She was having a baby! He was supposed to be ill – how *dare* he? Poor Emily.

'Billy? Claudia. Oh *God*. What can I do?'

'Not much, doll. The snapper stands to make a million. So unless you have a bit of spare change knocking around . . .'

'Has it gone out yet? Has he talked to anyone?'

'Yours truly. That's it.'

'Can he give me . . . a few hours?'

'I'll put in a call.'

Oh Christ. She grabbed her coat and took a cab to the station where Innocence was being held.

'I'm sorry, love,' said the officer at the front desk. She was kind but firm. 'She isn't allowed visitors.'

'But I'm her *daughter*.'

'No visitors, I'm afraid.'

'Then, could you . . . give her a message? Could I speak to her on the phone?'

The woman hesitated. 'Wait there. What did you say your name was?'

Claudia stood, drumming her fingers.

The woman returned after a minute. 'I'm sorry,' she said. 'But your mother doesn't want to speak to . . . anyone.'

Me.

Claudia sighed. Now what? Ms Green? Ms Green wouldn't understand. Claudia knew exactly what she'd say. *One million pounds? What nonsense! This is extortion! I shall call the police!*

Her parents could afford to buy Bolivia, and yet not one penny of their billions was available to her.

She caught her breath. There was one more option. Now, Claudia, are you sure this isn't just an excuse? *No*. What could be more important? She needed his advice. She glanced at her watch. It was ten to one. She might just catch him as he headed out to lunch.

The taxi to the City was agonizingly slow. The traffic was just appalling. When she reached Threadneedle Street, she

316

jumped out and ran the last hundred yards. If he didn't have a work lunch, he always grabbed a sandwich from the Italian deli – tuna, beans, mayonnaise, on toast. There was his building, a tall, grand, shiny, we-make-money building. And, oh, she'd recognize those rugby-player's shoulders anywhere.

'Alfie, wait!'

He whirled around. 'Claudia!'

A short, barrelly blonde appeared from behind him. *Yick*, the fiancée! It occurred to Claudia that she had reacted to seeing the woman as a vampire reacts to garlic. She prayed it wasn't too obvious. From the look on the girl's face, it was.

'Claudia, let me introduce my fiancée, Polly. Polly, Claudia is a good friend from childhood.'

'Hi,' said Polly. Claudia found it interesting that Polly managed to smile and shake hands while keeping all the relative muscles slack.

'Poll and I were meeting for lunch. Join us! It'll be fun!'

Oh God.

'Alfie,' she said, gazing up at him. He looked back, his green eyes piercing hers. There was a bemused smile on his face. When she looked at him, she always saw two people: the adult and the child. His blond hair stuck up the same way it had in childhood, and he had the same dimple in his cheek when he laughed. He was so kind. It made her heart ache because she might – had things gone well, instead of terribly – have fallen in love with Alfie. He had saved her once and, in a way, he would always be her hero.

'Alfie, I need to speak to you urgently. In private.'

He looked startled; *she* looked as if she'd been slapped.

'Darling,' Alfie said. 'Claudia and I will go and talk in the lobby. Why don't you go on ahead? I've reserved a table.'

'Thank you,' said Claudia. 'Sorry that sounded so cryptic.'

Alfie grinned. 'There is no doubt that Poll is now convinced you are about to inform me that you're expecting our child. I imagine it will cost me at least three very dull evenings at the opera to put right. So, Claudia' – he smiled

317

again as he opened the door for her – 'what event could be so terrible that it prevents you from joining me for lunch?'

She told him, and the smile vanished.

'I don't know what to do,' she said. 'Emily is about to have a baby. She's already had bleeding. This could really damage her health. I'm sure – almost – that my parents would want to stop it, at any cost. But neither one is . . . available. I've just thought – I could call the Earl!'

Alfie shook his head. 'Claudia, there is no possibility of you being able to stop this photograph from emerging. It's all done digitally, isn't it? It's not as if you can buy the negative. If they want to print it, they will, and one million, two million is not going to stop them. Even if you could get your parents to pay, there's no guarantee. Someone, somewhere, will have a copy on file and, one day, they are going to sell it. And then your parents will be accused of bribery. It's a lose-lose situation. Don't get involved.'

She was quiet. She wanted to curl up on the silver-flecked black marble floor and go to sleep for a thousand years. She gazed at the huge modern paintings. She liked the one with the bright red splodge in the middle. The place reminded her of one of her father's homes . . . Bilbao? She couldn't remember which. She hadn't visited for a long time. He mustn't die. She hated him but . . . he mustn't die. And she couldn't even speak to Innocence. It was crazy to think she had been arrested. She didn't like Innocence but she cared about her. In a warped, weird way, she needed her.

'You're right,' she said, slowly. 'You're right, Alfie. There is nothing I can do.'

He squeezed her hand. 'Claudia, don't worry about the baby. People have healthy babies in the most terrible circumstances. She'll be OK.'

'Look,' she said, not wanting to let go of his hand, 'you should go. I'm sorry about getting you in trouble.'

He winked. 'Ah, if only.'

They both stood, and he kissed her on the cheek.

Ah, if only. It meant nothing. Anyway, she reminded herself, you couldn't sleep with Alfie. You can't sleep with a nice guy. You can only sleep with men who confirm your self-loathing.

She caught the bus back to the office. She had never gone on public transport as a child, and as an adult, it was her treat to ride on the bus. She sat at the front at the top, and let herself be lost in the beauty of London. The dirt, the litter, the spitting in the street: it made no difference. When you loved a person or a place, no matter how plain, they got better looking every time you saw them. The bus route was long and winding and extremely slow. But there seemed no point in rushing.

She should call Emily and warn her. It could even be too late. The *Standard*'s early evening edition would soon be out. Claudia stepped off the bus. It hadn't yet reached her office but she didn't want to go back. Tomorrow, they'd see the papers and she wouldn't need an excuse.

She sat on the first bench she saw, shoved on her sunglasses and gazed at the people hurrying past, wishing she had their families instead of hers.

At five, she bought a *Standard*. She stood still and frantically leafed through it. But there was nothing. Maybe it was too . . . *wrong* for the *Standard*. The *Standard* aligned itself with all of that type. Perhaps it wouldn't want to alienate the Earl. It was a shame she couldn't say the same for *The Sun*, the *Mirror*, the *Express*, and . . . the *Mail* would come up with some sly excuse to run it: 'How dare this photographer take this picture – is privacy no longer sacred?!'

There was no point going home. She sat in a café, staring at the walls, until the first editions hit the pavement by Charing Cross Station. She scanned the front pages, looking, looking . . .

It was midnight. She rang Billy on his mobile. 'Billy, Billy, *what* is going on—'

'Easy, Tiger!' He paused. 'You at the hospital?'

319

'What! No! Is it my father? Oh—'

'It's your sister. She's gone into labour. It came through on the wire at three.' He paused. 'Close, then, are you?'

'I should be with her – there's no one else.' She had nearly cut him off before she realized. 'Wait! Billy, what's happening with the shot? Who's bought it?'

'No one,' he replied. 'They won't touch it.'

'They won't? *Why?*'

'Ah, DFK. Are you a hack or a girl in gingham with a smelly little dog? Emily is *having a baby*. She's a *new mother*. She's untouchable. If they run the picture, it makes them look bad. Today, they want baby pics. So you can relax. Today, Emily is safe.'

'And tomorrow?'

'For as long as she stays useful. Chin up, Dorothy. Go see your sister.'

THE LINDO WING, MIDNIGHT

Emily

'I have a *son*,' Emily whispered to the pillow. 'I have a son.'

THE OLD BAILEY, LONDON,
A YEAR LATER, 1999

Innocence

She'd known all along that she would not be convicted. She had the best, the most expensive briefs in the country. And

320

her barristers weren't bad either! Oh, woman, you're hysterical. Innocence tossed her hair and stuck her nose high, before recalling that Mr Humphrey Slater, QC, head of her legal team, had forbidden her to make what he called 'provocative gestures'.

She was a whisker away from telling them all to go to hell. The case was ludicrous and, perversely, it infuriated her that they took it so seriously. Of course they had to mount a 'spirited' defence, but their grave faces and their silly wigs and their endless ringed binders gave credence to the ridiculous and bizarre accusations. Of course the sordid truth had been leaked, giving her a motive to want to kill Jack. Hell, yes, he'd lied to her since the day they'd met and diddled her out of everything. But she *hadn't known it*. The jury would believe her.

Even if they didn't want to, they would believe her because women didn't bomb people. She might have the wealth to organize a hit, but this was hardly her style. It was a bloke's idea of murder: *I'm gonna blow you up!* Duh! Surely every female sitting on that jury would understand that had Innocence discovered the truth – her husband was not her husband, he had married his lover in secret – she would have dealt with it the honourable way: she would have looked him in the eye and stabbed him in the heart with a kitchen knife.

Naturally, she'd kept this line of reasoning to herself.

She had done pretty much everything she'd been told to do. She'd tried not to let it show in her face that she thought the jury was a bunch of knuckle-dragging morons. Could they even understand English? She resented having to 'tone herself down' so as not to alienate them. Slater had put it tactfully, but what he meant was, 'They hate you because you're rich and beautiful and successful, so try and make yourself plain and drab and sorry, so they hate you a little less.'

She had taken enormous care with her wardrobe. She had called in Jones, who had been marvellous, sourcing forty-nine variations on a sober black Amanda Wakeley trouser

321

suit, and flat black heels. 'Oh my God, I couldn't,' she'd cried on seeing the flats. 'I'll look like plod!' And, cursing the day that Jack was born, she had allowed Patrice to colour her pink hair *brown*. It would rinse out, but it was miserable.

The briefs had advised no jewellery, not even her 'wedding' ring, because that might imply she was delusional, wanting to maintain the fraud of being 'married' to him. She had argued that not to wear it might imply she was bitter. Better delusional and bejewelled than bitter and boring.

So she'd worn her wedding ring, her enormous rock of an engagement ring and a white gold and diamond Royal Oak watch, £82,850 by Audemars Piguet at Marcus. Slater had done a double take and said, 'I'm afraid it's too showy.'

She had replied coldly, '*I'm* not afraid.'

Those plebs on the jury wouldn't know the difference between Piguet at Marcus and the Next Directory. To the untrained eye, she could have been dressed head to foot in Marks & Spencer. For a split second and the first time in years, Innocence thought of her mother. How proud she would have been to have a daughter who could afford to dress head to foot in Marks & Spencer.

Her mother was dead now. Sad.

And really, she *would* go to prison before she dressed in high street clothes in front of a worldwide audience. The media frenzy was pleasing. They'd come from as far as Japan. And *all* of them wanted to stay in her hotels. *Ching!* She couldn't look too drab – that would reek of guilt. The police had been forced to block off the streets, just as at Diana's wedding (she refused to think of Diana's *funeral*), and her armoured van had an escort: *five* motorcycles. Nice to know they cared. Of course, the attention was also (she was forced to grudgingly admit) to do with the fact that a *celebrity* was dead, oh boohoo. She'd seen one of Mollie Tomkinson's films and snapped off the DVD after ten minutes. There was a limit to the number of times you could watch a scrawny teenager suck in her nostrils and make a face like a camel to force her thin lips into a pout. It had surprised her quite how many people were upset about Mollie. Those awful spotty American kids, shouting insults at her, in the street, on the first day. The eulogies in the papers. Even the police hadn't anticipated such crowds. The second day, she'd been smuggled in through another entrance.

The case had dragged on. A number of Hollywood stars – did they *ever* tire of the sound of their own voices? – had given evidence by video-link.

It wasn't even *evidence*. But apparently there were a million different ways to say, with great dramatic edge, trembling emotion, and a troubled, sincere yet courageous expression: '*I* saw her escorted out, *I* saw she was pissed, and then *I* was blown off my feet, sustaining a chipped toenail, as everything went *boom*!' To them, it was no more than an audition. To be honest, she wasn't listening to them speak, she was trying to figure out who'd had work. At least one A-lister's receding hairline had suddenly grown back.

She was grabbing at straws to keep sane. She felt sick with the stress of it. Every day, some embarrassing detail about her life was pulled to pieces in front of everyone. And Slater was stunningly slow to say, 'I fail to see the relevance of this.' It was also the first time she'd heard the details of Jack's love affair with this Maria woman. It was horrible. It seemed, from what his staff and associates were saying – she hoped the jury would note the absence of any *friends* – that Jack and Maria had actually fallen in *love*. How? The woman wasn't young, she wasn't gorgeous, she wasn't rich, she had *nothing*! She was off the street!

Slater had encouraged her to cry in front of the whole room. Or at least he'd said, 'If you do sense the pricking of womanly emotion, do not feel obliged to hold back.' Slater was quite the twat.

Anyway, she couldn't cry. She was too stunned. When she thought back to that brief paradise on Spyglass Island, she was genuinely hurt.

Jack hated her, but she knew he would not want her to go to prison. She was linked to him – apparently not for better or for worse – but they were still linked and he would not wish to be linked to a felon. Also, she was still the mother of his daughter. She believed the worst of him, she *knew* the worst of him as fact, but she knew he hadn't planned this. He'd nearly died himself, for fuck's sake! No. There was a third person. Someone else had organized the planting of that bomb, not to kill, but to maim. The truth was, whoever it was knew what they wanted, and had achieved their goal precisely.

The room was hot and stuffy – all these disgusting people breathing their germs into *her* air – but Innocence shivered.

Someone hated Jack, and someone hated his family, and that someone had awesome unchecked power, because no one got to Jack; none of his many enemies, forged through the misery and betrayal of his miraculous escape from the Lloyd's disaster, had ever reached him, though many had tried. His wealth, his influence, his legions of *people*, his ever-present security – ex-Mossad, the best – all of these impressive, impenetrable layers surrounded him, ensuring that he was inaccessible to the common man. He only travelled by armoured car, he only ate in his own restaurants, he only slept in his hotels, he only flew in his own planes. If he attended a public event, his security swept the area. He was protected. These days, anyone who wasn't someone never, ever came within spitting distance of Jack Kent.

And yet.

Someone had the wit and power and rage to overcome all of this.

They had *got* to him.

The love of his life was dead. The mother of his child was on trial for murder. Even the girls had suffered. There was Claudia's engagement to her *blood father* – she'd had some kind of breakdown after finding out. And now, in the context of everything else, could she be sure it was pure coincidence? It had all gone so wrong for Emily. Poor Emily with her dreams of castles, and now, oh *God*, a mother. Innocence had insisted on paying for a nanny, and a maternity nurse. Alone, Emily would be a dreadful mother; she hadn't a clue, she was a little girl. There was no way she should have sole charge of a baby, that little angel: *one today!* Surely, this media circus would soon end – it had been hours – and Innocence would be free to go straight to the apartment in Ecclestone Square to hold her grandson on his first birthday.

'It's George's special day,' she'd told Emily. 'Don't attend court. Once I'm acquitted, Charlie will drive me over.'

She couldn't *wait*.

It made her smile every time she thought of Baby George. Unfortunately, she thought of her grandson, one year old today, wondering what he would make of his first taste of birthday cake, so often that she had smiled happily throughout the prosecution's gruesome description of Jack's many injuries and the grim photographs of a burnt, half-headless Maria. There had been murmurs and gasps of disgust from the idiot jurors and the dumb public bench and Slater had jolted her sharply with his elbow. She had quickly assumed a sombre expression, but it was hard to maintain. Baby George, one, already! It was the most peculiar thing that had ever happened to her. She loathed kids, and here she was, smitten.

'La-La,' he called her, the little precious. So adorable. He had found the perfect word to replace 'grandma'.

She bit back a grin and tried to pay attention. The chief counsel for the prosecution was wittering on about the Forensic Science Center in San Francisco. Blah blah, evidence and analysis on the Unabomber case, most highly respected in the world, able to maximize the information that could be obtained from extremely small samples of explosive residue, dust particles, hair, radioactive isotopes . . . yawn . . . and we call on expert witness Professor Blah de Blah. Jesus, she had to keep pinching herself. The Professor was forty-five, but apparently still cut his own hair with kitchen scissors. *He* started droning on, something about the most minuscule amounts of oils remaining on a fingerprint enabling them to tell the general age of the suspect, his diet, and whether he smoked. 'Everyone leaves a chemical or biological signature that we can investigate.'

Yeah, yeah, big clap, so *what*?

A new *suspect*.

Oh my God, she was off the hook!

Everyone craned their necks as a man, surly and unshaven, was led to the dock in handcuffs. Innocence nearly fell off her chair in shock.

Gerry. Her *brother*! That common criminal! That fucking loser! She stared at him – she must be hallucinating. She hadn't seen or heard of him in fifteen years. Well, no. He'd managed to contact her once, to blackmail her – threatening to reveal her thieving past – and she'd laughed at him. Her exact words: 'It's too late, sweetie. I'm untouchable. Back to your hole! *Ciao!*' Whatever he was doing here, it was bad news. Her eyes burned into his back, and slowly he turned and looked at her. His ratlike face oozed loathing but there was triumph in those sly eyes and she knew immediately: she was going down.

He 'admitted' everything. And the forensic evidence confirmed it. *He* had planted the bomb – a crude device made at home – on his sister's orders. She had paid him three million in cash.

'He's lying,' she stammered to Slater. 'It's all lies. Someone paid him – but not me. I'm being set up.'

She wanted to scream and shout, but she was numb with shock. *Who* was setting her up? *Who?*

Slater regarded her with regret.

And now . . . hours . . . minutes . . . seconds later, the head juror was standing, clearing his throat. She glanced at her bank of lawyers. Each one sat stiff and stern, apprehension on their self-important faces. Surely they could *do* something?

326

She noticed a trickle of sweat run from Slater's ear to his neck.

'And in the case of Tomkinson v Ashford . . .' Yes, yes, come *on*, '. . . we find the defendant guilty on all charges.'

The word 'guilty' rang in her ears, and she smiled stupidly because she couldn't believe it.

There were screams of delight, and sobs, from the public gallery, where Mollie's mother sat fat and ridiculous in a tacky black veil. She caught a glimpse of Claudia, still and silent amid the chaos, shaking her head, and that evening the *Standard* would carry the screamer: '*NOT INNOCENT!*'

Twenty-four hours later, heading towards Greygates prison, without having seen her grandson eat cake on his first birthday, she still couldn't believe it. But it was true. Sharon Marshall, aka Miss Innocence Ashford, had been convicted of the murders of Mollie Tomkinson and Maria Radcliffe, and the attempted murder of Jack Kent, and was sentenced to twenty-five years in prison without parole.

FIVE YEARS LATER, 2004

SUNDAY TIMES MAGAZINE: EXCLUSIVE
THE HON. INNOCENCE ASHFORD, CLEARED OF ALL CHARGES, SPEAKS: 'MY TIME BEHIND BARS'

The bubblegum-pink hair is back, and so is the attitude. 'Thank God I'm free!' says Miss Innocence Ashford, sparking up a Marlboro and watching the smoke curl to the vaulted ceiling of her opulent Hampstead mansion. She shudders, although her smooth forehead seems incapable of a frown. 'You have no idea what it was like to walk out of that place. I would compare the happiness of it to my wedding day – although that itself would be a lie!'

'That place' is HMP Greygates, a sprawling Victorian Category

B prison housing five hundred inmates, where Innocence spent a traumatic five years in a cell six feet wide – 'any narrower, sweetie, and you go mad' – wrongly convicted of planting the bomb that seriously injured disgraced tycoon Jack Kent and tragically killed the eighteen-year-old film star Mollie Tomkinson. And the 'wedding day' that Innocence can now refer to with a wry smile, is the day, twenty-four years ago, that Kent went through the motions of marrying her.

'Sweetie, I had *no* idea!' she cries. 'I was in love with the man.' She only discovered that her alleged husband had tricked her, later marrying his lover, Maria Radcliffe – also killed in the explosion – and cutting her out of his will, when she was accused of plotting their murder in the Old Bailey, five years ago. Bitterness, apparently, was the motive.

Sprawled the length of a Pascal Mourgue amethyst wool sofa and snacking on edamame beans, she laughs aloud, although her blue eyes are stern. 'I don't need his money, I have my own! Élite Retreats is the most successful association of hotels on the planet. I am so lucky with my people. The business was run so perfectly while I was . . . residing.' There is a delicate pause, while the butler serves PG Tips in Wedgwood Jade. Miss Ashford dunks a Rich Tea biscuit, and rolls her eyes in bliss. 'The case was patently ludicrous from the start,' she declares, her voice sharp, 'and I thank my legal team from the bottom of my heart, and also the talented forensic team at the FSC in San Francisco for uncovering the new evidence that released me from that hellhole.

'I do feel so sad that Gerry' – her voice trembles – 'felt he had no choice but to end his life.' She jumps up, and sadly strokes a large Swarovski crystal stallion, rearing up on a solid walnut side table. 'But I suppose he had done a terrible thing, accepting a bribe in order to implicate *me* . . . his suicide note made such heart-rending reading. Did he kill himself because *he'd* been set up? Oh, darling, you mean because he never received the money he was promised?'

Miss Ashford is quiet, in sober contemplation. She walks back to the sofa, takes a sip of tea with shaking hands, then puts her tea to one side, and rests her hands in her lap. It is apparent, although she struggles to hide it, that she is devastated by her brother's death. 'Oh, *no*,' she says, eventually, 'I am quite sure not. He was, despite it all, such a decent man. It must have broken his heart to have betrayed me. And I only wish he had named the evil person who tricked him – it's frightening to have no idea, but I suppose he was too terrified. Darling, would you like a satsuma? Pascal! The satsumas. What it is to be deprived of fruit. Other prisoners incurred tobacco debt, I incurred tomato debt! My *God*.'

She is surprisingly small in the flesh, with delicate cheek-bones, tiny feet and a raucous laugh. She says she never ate lunch inside as she felt she didn't require the energy. It is 11 a.m., on a Thursday, and she is resplendent in purple vintage Armani and silver Miu Miu heels. A diamond-encrusted emerald the size of a sparrow's egg sparkles at her throat.

'I've always appreciated fashion,' she purrs, nibbling at a satsuma segment which Pascal has peeled and relieved of its pith. 'And now I appreciate it a hell of a lot more – pardon my French!'

She gazes around her lounge – it is the size of a gymnasium (she has one of those also, *and* staff quarters, *and* a 'gift-wrapping room') and the décor is faux flashy, in a tongue-in-cheek way. Great crystal chandeliers hang from the ceiling, the white carpets are thick and lush, and a life-size pair of porcelain jaguars guard the door. There is a Louis XVI-style three-panel floor screen with gilding and garden scenes, perhaps to cut down on draughts.

Knick-knacks cover every surface: a gorgeous Italian painted bombé chest with green floral and foliate painting and parcel gilding supports a diamond-encrusted model of the Eiffel Tower, a china bowl of china fruit and china vegetables, a bunch of lidded crystal urns and various hand-painted enamel keepsake boxes adorned with gems and tiny statues of bluebirds kissing.

In the centre of the room, there is a large Renaissance-style throne, of purple and gold velvet – only *one*, mind.

The coffee tables are carved of Madagascan ebony, and at the far end of the room, below an ornate Georgian-style carved gilt-wood mirror, is the hugest Italian marble fireplace I have ever seen. A fire burns in its grate, despite it being late August.

The outer wall is entirely glass. We are afforded a view of her extensive lawns, X-rated topiary – 'Darling, I simply tell my grandson that the hedge lady is giving her friend a piggy back' – rose gardens, pagoda and heated Olympic-size pool.

How did she manage the contrast of daily life? 'It was tough. The régime at Greygates is harsh, and some of the screws were worse than the prisoners. I didn't appreciate my cell mate, Sarina, being called a "Paki". Apart from the obvious, she is Chinese! It was disgusting. But if you answer back, which I did – no one speaks to my friends that way – you get put in the seg. A lot of the time we were treated like animals. The exercise area – the size of my lavatory – was surrounded by granite walls and barbed wire and the screws called it "the pen".' Her expression is serious. 'As if we were *pigs*. The discipline problems are not to do with the inmates. Apart from the breakfast porridge, which was actually superb, the food was horrible – stodgy, and lots of cheap meat. Association – when you're allowed out of your cell on some evenings to go to the TV room – was often cancelled with no explanation. Can you imagine: two days of twenty-three-hour lock-up! And for some inmates, it was impossible to make a phone call.

'Me? Oh, I had no problem. The girls were supportive. I had a little trouble, early on, but I dealt with it. I do abhor violence but one has to self-defend. Also, I worked hard – I was a wing cleaner. I've never been afraid of hard work – and I loathe dirt. When I first got to C-Wing, they still slopped out. Vile. Thank goodness, there was some kind of inspection and they put a stop to it. Now it has proper sanitation. And there was rubbish strewn in the communal area. I enjoyed organizing the clean-up. It gives you a sense of control.'

Miss Ashford stubs out her cigarette, and sighs. 'It makes you grateful,' she declares, rubbing her newly manicured hand along the peach-skin soft sofa. 'I am grateful for a comfortable bed, a pillow at night, I am grateful to be able to walk in my garden and breathe in the scent of a rose. When you have been stripped of your privacy and your freedom, you see the world in a different light.'

On average, the prisoners in Greygates earn £5 a week. Miss Ashford's business is said to earn her £45 million a year. Has the stay at Her Majesty's pleasure changed her perception of money?

'The shop was so expensive! I look at Harrods' prices with kinder eyes! Of course, you could order the bare necessities from the canteen – not the best products, I have to say. How did I cope? I read the Bible. I prayed. I imagined I was lying on the beach in Malibu. One has to strengthen oneself spiritually if one is to have resilience. It was pointless to hope for an improvement in the actual facilities; only if you were strong in your heart could you find peace in that place. Some inmates filled in Request and Complaint forms, but I didn't bother, not after I'd seen one ripped up in front of my eyes.'

Is she resentful? 'Prison takes so much away from you: your trusting nature, for one. I'm as jumpy as a cat. I've had to forbid my staff from standing behind me. You may have noticed, they are all wearing little bells: a temporary measure until I regain my calm. But one mustn't brood. I concentrate on the future, and I hope to use the wisdom I have gained to help others. I have to accentuate the positive, or I would go mad. The truth is, I have missed the formative years of my grandson's life. I have missed the birth of his little sister – my darling granddaughter, Molly. They don't know me, and that is very painful. I would have liked to have helped my daughter begin her journey as a mother.

'I have been unable to support my stepdaughter, Claudia, who has bi-polar . . . Oh, what is it, when you swing madly from lunatic depression to a weird high? Well, *some* mental disorder, poor angel. *Entre nous*, not the greatest luck with – whisper it! – *men*. A childhood friend of hers recently married; there was a secret crush. I do know she was dreadfully jealous – I mean, upset about it. But she's ever so brave. She plods on, chipping away, writing her little articles about cabbage soup diets and so forth – so noble. But family is important, it's what grounds you, and without me as her anchor, I fear she was quite lost.'

There is a tiny growl at my feet, and a bright pink shih-tzu relieves itself on my ankle. 'Baby! Bad girl! But how fortunate your ankle boots are plastic not leather! Oh dear, she missed me. I hired a private zookeeper to look after her while I was gone but plainly, it wasn't the same. She's like a daughter and now she's playing up dreadfully. I think she was traumatized by my absence.'

Was Miss Innocence traumatized? She smiles. 'As you know, I visited church on Sunday. It was important to me, to pray. Giving to God gives me a lot back. And I am more sensitive than people give me credit for. Early on, I had panic attacks. The space is so confined. The metal bunk is so basic, and the blanket is so . . . *cheap*. And the toilet had no privacy – entirely degrading. I was freezing cold at night. And I don't like mice and fleas. And it was hard to sleep at first, because of all the noise. Banging on walls, and shouting. The guards are always opening and shutting these great metal doors – I'm convinced they do it on purpose – and often, I heard fellow inmates screaming.'

She seems to hesitate, and her mouth trembles. 'Initially – they assumed I was guilty of murder – they put me in a cell with a killer. That shook me up. She actually confessed in a way. I don't know if she was trying to scare me, but it certainly worked. She'd stabbed a love rival. She said to me, "I'd do it again, just to hear her scream." I don't think I was ever so frightened in my life.'

Miss Innocence dabs at her huge blue eyes with the back of her hand, and sips at an ice-cold crystal glass of Badoit. 'Fortunately, for me at least, this person was moved to another jail.' She pauses, shaking her head. 'I drew a great deal of strength from my family and the letters they sent. My son-in-law, Viscount Chateston, in particular, was in constant touch. And of course' –

she claps her hands – 'it was such a lift to keep track of Jack's amazing recovery.

'When I was convicted, he had recovered consciousness but they didn't know if he would ever walk again. And now, well, to see him you would never know that anything was ever amiss. Of course he'll never be quite right in the head in the emotional sense – that's the part of his brain that was affected, the doctors say – but then, *I* say, they didn't know him before!

'What? Oh! It's all nonsense, fabricated by the press! It's forgiven, forgotten! We're *huge* friends, enormously fond! This is why it's all been so ridiculous! After my stylist, he was the first person I saw – well, I was practically blinded by all the flash-bulbs. I don't seek the attention – I am a very private person – but I do have respect for the public. If you are in the public eye, and they've supported you, and they have – they adore my hotels and (I'm not talking about the business side now) that means so much to me on a *personal* level. You *owe* it to them, to share a little of the wonder of your life, the bad as well as the good.

'But yes, I visited Jack. Sorry? Oh, *no*. I forbade him to visit me in jail. I forbade all members of my family from going to that place. Claudia did visit once. It was too painful to have her there, smelling of the outdoors. Also, I certainly didn't want my grandson to hold that experience in his memory. A prison is not a place for children. I feel so strongly about that.'

Miss Innocence Ashford smiles in the direction of the gold side table which – alongside a cobalt frosted glass bottle with an etched portrait of Innocence on its side – is covered with silver framed photographs of her grandson George, and little Molly, and their beaming parents – for Tim and Emily Fortelyne are the happiest family. 'I know, isn't it wonderful? Everyone was critical because they were so young, but Emily always knew her own mind. She is such an intelligent girl. Even the Earl has come round.

'Now.' She leans forward. 'I have an appointment with a prison charity. They do such good work and of course if I can be of any use in an advisory or fundraising role . . . Is there anything else I can help you with? Would you like something hot to eat before you go?'

I assure Miss Innocence that I am fine, and she kisses me warmly on each cheek. 'It was such a pleasure to meet you,' she says, gripping me remarkably hard by both shoulders. 'I so enjoyed it. I'm afraid I talked for hours! Do call my assistant Jamie – he'll put you straight through – if you have any further questions.'

She sees me out herself, waving away the butler, and I am left standing on her marble front steps, gazing into the impassive face of a stone lion, breathless and not a little star-struck by our encounter. Her charm is hypnotic, her lack of self-pity astonishing. Reader, he should have married her!

© *Sunday Times Ltd*

CENTRAL PARK, NEW YORK, 2004

Innocence

Innocence hummed to herself as she skated gracefully around the rink, *swish, swish,* her white skates cutting along the ice with a satisfying speed. The freezing air bit at her skin and made her eyes water, and she skated faster, relishing the wind in her pink hair, smiling for the cameras, smiling at the crisp blue sky, smiling at the city. From here its buildings seemed compacted, tall, powerful but not too close: a friendly giant guarding her from a distance.

That moron from the newspaper had lapped it all up. Her interview with Oprah had been equally successful. She had presented herself as humble, forgiving, a little fearful, but optimistic. She had shown photos of her grandchildren, she had shed a tear; she had shown courage. She had explained why she had chosen New York for her Coming-out Party: it was a city that understood suffering, it showed spirit in the most dire of circumstances, and it flew the flag for freedom. She was still a little sore at the British 'justice' system.

The party was to be held at the Apple Core that evening, but first, she and the Family were having a Private Moment for the press, on the outdoor rink. While too much was never enough, the Coming-out Party, to which guests were invited to dress ultra-glam, was a small affair: only one thousand people. Tickets were three thousand dollars – except for Jack's ticket which was thirty thousand – with proceeds going to the families of the victims of 9/11, of *course*.

It was select, it was exclusive, and the electronic scanners at the door were state of the art. She wanted a 'big do', yet the idea of crowds made her shudder: she had a fear of being shanked. Foolish – it hadn't happened inside, why would it happen now? But she couldn't rationalize her fear; the dread that it might happen was just as bad as it happening. It astonished her that she felt less secure on the outside than in.

She pulled the Siberian white tiger fur coat – 'Of course it's fake,' she'd told the tramp from the *Post*. 'It's just a very *good* fake' – closer around her, and went into a spin. There was applause. She smiled, dug her heel into the ice, and clapped a hand over her mouth as if stifling mirth. What she had missed in prison was the loss of status, the fact that she was not appreciated or fawned over. It was wonderful to feel important again, to be made a fuss of.

It was a basic human need, being made a fuss of. The Americans understood this to a degree that the English didn't. The English were too hung up on dignity and not being labelled a show-off. The Americans knew how to celebrate achievement; here there was no shame in success. She was going to spend more time stateside; more time in the gorgeous Hollywood Hills residence. Now that she was out, she craved the outdoor lifestyle, the space to roam, the sun and the sea, the mountains and the big fuck-off cars.

Claudia was skating miserably around the ice. Today she

335

looked particularly miserable, and on edge. She kept looking over her shoulder. She was the worst person to invite to a photocall *ever*. Now that Alfie was married to his horse-faced girlfriend, she mooned around like a lost dog. She had never recovered from falling in love with her own father – what an *idiot*!

She smiled as Emily and Timmy skated past her, holding hands with George. The nanny and little Molly waved from the side. She was proud of Emily. She was a smart girl. She'd made herself the darling of the British press; she'd cut down the number of interviews, but when Molly was born, she'd made a point of sending a gorgeous selection of photos *free* to the picture desk of every paper and magazine. Now that Timmy had graduated with a 2.1 in History of Art, and was working at a Chelsea gallery, now that she had a fighting chance again of living in a castle, she had got herself back on track.

Emily had launched her own perfume, designed her own fashion line (for a high-street store but then, beggars couldn't be choosers), she had even modelled it. She had also put her name to a fashion page in one of the posh monthly magazines. There was talk of a salad dressing, but it was early days.

Innocence was reluctantly impressed at her daughter's survival skills. Emily had repaid her every penny of the allowance that Innocence had given her before she was put away. Emily was probably holding out for the big bucks, but it was still a nice touch. She suspected that Emily was still furious with the family – Jack for favouring Claudia, and Claudia for being favoured – but now that she was no longer destitute, she was able to keep a lid on the rage.

Secretly, Innocence thought that a bout of poverty had done Emily the world of good. She no longer expected other people to pour her drinks.

And where *was* Jack? 'Fear of Bad PR' was a wonderful thing. It had forced him to hop on a plane (well, maybe not *hop*) and to go through the charade of playing happy families. Ah, there he was, in a black leather jacket. Oh *dear*, visions of George Bush trying to look 'hip'.

'Jack, sweetie, join me on the ice!' she hollered, and grinned as ten camera lenses whirred in his direction.

He laughed, with difficulty, and his minders shuffled close. 'I would, darling,' he roared back. 'But I prefer manly sports. I don't like twiddling around. I'd be gripping your wrist as tight as handcuffs – you'll think you're back in the joint!'

She tried to sound amused, and failed. 'Oh come on, sweetie! Don't be such an old man! You've only got *mild* arthritis. Come on, one whirl around the ice. It's not as if I'm asking you to *marry* me!'

He gave her the finger. There was a frenzy of whirrs and clicks. *Damn.* That was the thing about damage to the frontal lobe. He was a liability. He was no longer able to judge what was socially acceptable. Emily had been hugely upset, she had confided to the *Mail on Sunday*, when he had sent his granddaughter a card on her first birthday that read, 'Happy Birthday, dear Molly, love from Jack'. Even the Earl's secretary had signed off as 'Grandpa'.

Innocence raised an eyebrow and stepped daintily off the ice. Patrice was on hand with a hot chocolate and a cigarette.

'Thanks, sweetie.'

She sashayed over to Jack and sat beside him. 'You've aged in dog years,' she murmured in his ear with a loving smile.

'You look fat in white,' he replied, ruffling her hair. He knew she couldn't stand for her hair to be touched.

'I pity you, being a widower *and* a cripple,' she sighed, stroking his brow. 'When you haven't had a lay in six years – I mean, without paying for it – you're bound to be cranky.'

He roared with laughter, but she was pleased to note that the heartiness was forced. 'Speak for yourself, Fat Ass,' he whispered, slapping her knee with quite painful affection. 'Or did you find yourself a couple of crack hoes to play with while you were banged up?'

She laughed uproariously, delicate hands cradling her throat, although she would have rather liked, at that second, to cradle *his* throat. ' "Crack hoes", Jack? Oh darling, have you been listening to Aswad again?' She tossed her hair (it didn't move). 'And, sweetie, you know I swing both ways.' She smiled. 'It would be foolish of me to rely utterly on men, for anything. Why limit your options?' Pause. 'Oh, I forget. You don't have any.' She winked. 'Play nice for the press, and maybe later I'll let you watch.'

She stood up and nodded to Jamie, who clapped his hands. 'Those guests requiring transport to the Apple Core, please come this way,' he announced. New York had some duff traditions and those stinky horse-drawn carriages that hung around Central Park were the worst. Innocence couldn't think of anything more ghastly than being towed along under a germ-riddled flea-infested blanket by a farting pony, with its arse inches from your face. So she had hired *all* of them to ferry assorted family and skating guests to the party, but *she* was travelling in a pink glass pumpkin coach, drawn by four white stallions. God bless America!

Unlike Jack, Innocence knew what made a good party. Karaoke. Oh, sure, there was other music. All the kings and queens of pop had fallen over themselves to offer their services because of the charity element – God, these people were so transparent. So she'd agreed that a few of them could come along to sing their little songs. Justin seemed like a sweet boy, and it couldn't hurt, although none of their music was her thing. And of course, it was quite a compliment that Abba had offered to reconvene for the occasion. But would Abba make her look old? If only the Spice Girls hadn't broken up.

She also liked a good dress up. Fuck Audrey Hepburn – *her* style icon was P. Diddy, a man unafraid of a good fur and a nice diamond. One of the most hateful elements of jail was being forced to wear cheap, itchy, ugly clothes, *the same as everyone else*. Now that she was out, she could use haute couture as a barometer of her wealth and status again; she could rise above the flotsam because when Karl Lagerfeld designed a one-off pink mohair body stocking in *your* honour, it put every other pretender in their place.

Today she was wearing a clinging pink Dior satin off the shoulder gown with forty thousand pounds' worth of sequins, crystals and jewels sewn into the fabric (Galliano was another designer who embraced extravagance, she couldn't *abide* a tightwad), a diamond tiara and red suede Mary Jane pumps by YSL. She relished the sensual feel of expensive tailoring against her skin. In fact, now that she was out, pretty much *everything* made her feel horny.

She'd told Jack the truth – she *had* had a few bitches inside. Girl power and all that. But you couldn't beat a nice prick! As ever, she found Jack's animosity attractive, although the animosity would have meant shit had he not regained his muscle tone. As it was, his physiotherapist needed a medal for services to womankind. One of the few times she'd laughed in prison was on receiving a scrawled letter from Emily, who was a most lazy communicator, that had expressed her horror on catching sight of her father's legs under his hospital gown. 'His left leg definitely looked *withered*. Eeek!'

Now, after a strict regime of Pilates and physiotherapy and lean protein, every firm and manly bulge was where it should be. Who needed brains? Innocence tried not to cackle. She might lure him up to the penthouse suite. Possibly, if she was in the mood, she might invite that dumb blonde East Coast heiress to join them. She was twenty-eight, fair of hair and dark of eyebrow, jaw-droppingly stupid, not *too* thin, and her name was Muffy . . . Buffy . . . Fluffy? Innocence couldn't recall. She was the kind of person you ached to bully in bed.

Innocence was in a punchy sort of mood.

She stood on the balcony to give her welcoming speech, and surveyed the room. Everything was perfect. The caviar had been flown in from Petrossian Paris on Robertson

Boulevard, LA. It was a long way but you want what you want. The strawberry margaritas were sublime. The new Baccarat glass chandeliers lent an enchanted quality to the atmosphere. Every guest was exquisitely attired. Yet she was restless. There was a tension in the air that was making her brain itch, and she knew its source. She whirled around.

Claudia, sitting glumly on a chair. That stupid child, she had a face that would spoil milk.

It occurred to her that the room had gone silent, and people were looking up expectantly, slight confusion blurring their smiles.

She hastily slapped a saintly look on her face. 'Welcome,' she purred as Patrice handed her a mike. 'Welcome, and thank you. Thank you for being here. Your generosity and support means so much – to me, and to the brave people of New York.'

If she could shoe in 'courageous' and 'spiritful' – was that a word? – she might even win over that slut from the *Post*.

'I think that very few of us live a life untouched by grief or tragedy. Whatever our status, whatever our bank balance, whatever clothes we wear, cars we drive, house – or houses – we live in, the loss of those we love – temporary or permanent – must come to us all. But let us not be bitter! Let us count our blessings. And let us remember that loss is the price of loving, and the fact that we have love, and courage in our hearts, must give us hope. Let us not lose our spirit! Let us remain . . . spiritful. With this in mind, I urge you all this evening to dance and eat and drink and celebrate life. Relish the good and wondrous gifts that it offers us, while remaining mindful of the bad. Speaking of which, I raise my glass to Jack, and indeed, to my whole beloved family.' Jesus. Patrice had gone all poetic on her – he was going to have to watch himself. 'Thank you – and enjoy!'

There was a storm of applause and a riot of flashbulbs. She posed, briefly, turning elegantly to one side, chin down, one shoulder forward – one didn't want to look *wide* – and swept gracefully down the curling staircase. If she didn't get laid in the next thirty minutes she was going to go *mad*. That said, she had prior business. There she was, the little madam.

'Claudia,' she barked. 'We need to talk.'

Claudia jumped. She looked frumpy in a yellow satiny strapless dress that sagged around the chest. 'What's wrong with you? You look like you've been taking style tips from Gwyneth Paltrow.'

Claudia's only response was to shrug.

Innocence gripped her by the upper arm and hauled her into a side room. Only then did she notice the girl was carrying a brown briefcase.

'And what the fuck is *that*?'

'It's nothing.'

'Bullshit. This is a party, not a conference. It looks out of place and weird. What is it, and why have you got a face like a dead halibut? You turn that frown upside down, dear, or my public will think you aren't happy for me.'

It really pissed her off. Claudia wrote for a few decent magazines and yet she'd never asked Innocence for an exclusive.

Claudia gazed at the floor, and a great rage filled Innocence, and she stamped her foot. 'Look at me when I'm talking to you!' she screamed.

Slowly, Claudia lifted her head, and looked Innocence straight in the eye. 'It's to do with Emily,' she muttered.

Innocence felt a lurch of irritation. 'What are you talking about? Emily is *fine*.'

'What's to do with me?' said a clear, indignant voice.

Innocence whirled around. 'Don't creep *up* on me! Jesus!'

'Emily.' Claudia looked white as milk. 'I need to talk to you about something.'

Emily nodded dismissively. 'Fine, but later. Timmy adores Abba, and I am not going to miss "Dancing Queen".'

Now Claudia looked green. Innocence hadn't actually realized it was possible for skin to acquire a greenish tinge.

341

Remarkable. It matched her eyes, but did nothing for the dress.

'Are the children still up? I do want to show them off. The *New York Times* is so hard to win over.'

Emily shook her head. 'Nanny is putting them to bed, Mother. She has a very strict regime. I don't interfere. Anyway, I gave the *Post* an exclusive: they love the idea that the children are getting a traditional English upbringing. The poor baby was yanked out of her Dior tracksuit and forced into these, like, totally hideous velvet pantaloons, and we had to promise George a motorized off-roader for making him wear a kilt. They used some of our clothes for the shoot – it was David LaChapelle? He's such fun to work with, a real artist. It was like shooting a music video. My stylist had worked with J-Lo, and Beyoncé, and my make-up artist had worked with Jennifer Garner and Uma Thurman, and they really knew what they were doing. There was *such* a great vibe! Timmy had the writer enthralled. He was telling them about the ancient curse of Fortelynes: you know, the belief that if the redcurrant bush that grows by the moat withers, then so will the male line. The truth is, it withers, like, every year, because it's so fucking cold, and the Countess just plants another one in its place so the Earl doesn't find out and go mental. And Timmy was telling her about the ghost in the Blue Room. There have been five sightings in the last twenty years. He wears an Elizabethan ruff, and is always reading a book; he appears to be concentrating very hard on the page, despite not having a head. *I've* not seen him, but the Countess has, *and* Cook. Oh, and he was also telling her about how he was a "hands-on" dad, how he reads *Wind in the Willows* to George every night – although he didn't mention that George hates it, and would totally prefer his *Spiderman* comic. Anyway, she *lapped* it all up; she must have spent four hours with us. She said she wanted to see how we operate as a family, and she was just entranced. She was impressed that I only use Nanny six days a week, and that I get Cook to make the children organic food, and that I've achieved this perfect balance between my home life and my work life, *and* I'm only twenty-two. She was quite cheeky, asking about our love life, but I don't care. We have a great sex life. I said we were very adventurous, if that wasn't, like, *way* too much information, but I said the thing about being so young is that you feel you can do anything and never get tired. I don't *get* these mothers who are *tired*, I suppose they're the ones who have children when they're really old, like, thirty, and anyway, I think it's so important that you make time for yourselves as a couple, so it's not, like, just about the kids. Timmy and I go out every Saturday. We might go to a charity ball, or a musical, or fly to Bermuda for a spa break, because, as Timmy says, we fell in love on a Saturday, and conceived George on a Saturday, and Timmy writes me a little love note every Saturday to mark the occasion – he's so thoughtful like that. And she was just drooling, like, "Oh my God, don't talk to me, why can't I find a guy like that, sensitive and at ease with his emotions, let alone one with a frickin' *castle*!" I think she was actually jealous of me, but I can't blame her. I am so lucky with Tim. He's even interested in, like, my *clothes*. He gave me an amazing idea for the spring line, to underlay the satin flare skirts with organza voile, *and* he suggested adding a squeeze of lemon to the salad dressing. He said, you know, if I'm, like, going to endorse it, I have to, like, not completely barf when I taste it, otherwise it's selling out. He's just totally a reconstructed male. Anyway, I think she went home to write it for tomorrow's paper so, like, you'll read all about us tomorrow! Yay!'

'So . . . they didn't want to speak to *me* . . . as La-La?'

'Grandmother, Mummy. Just say it. No.'

'Fair enough. Although I do find it slightly odd. After all, I am the story, one would think, having just been freed after five years of wrongful imprisonment, whereas you give an exclusive insight into your "private" life almost every week.'

'I think I might know why—'

'Hello, hello, evening all! What's this, a mothers' meeting! Angel, I've been looking for you all over. They're going to kick off with "Money, Money, Money".'

Timmy looked dashing in his dinner jacket; the slick floppy hair was so stylish and rat pack. These rich toffs and their model wives made fine-looking stock. Emily didn't deserve him, spoilt little cow. 'Oh well, darling, they're playing your tune, you should go, don't mind us.' It was too much. What a brat, stealing the limelight. Any other night, she wouldn't have minded, but it was *her* party, *her* turn to shine.

'Actually, maybe you should wait, Emily, just a minute until I—'

'JESUS, Claudia, what the fuck is it? You're like a mosquito, fucking whining in my ear. Just *say*, already, and put us out of our misery!' Innocence glared at Claudia. Emily also paused, eyebrow raised, hand on slender hip. She looked stunning in a pale pink Vera Wang top, white Prada micro-shorts and gold Christian Louboutin sandals with platinum heels. Timmy looked down his aquiline nose at his sister-in-law.

Claudia ducked her head, and slowly opened her briefcase.

'What the fuck have you got in there, a bomb?'

'Not exactly, but it's . . . nearly as bad— No, Innocence, relax . . . Well, don't *relax*, but . . . Timmy, I think you must know what this is about. The *News of the World* are going to run with it tomorrow, and I think they've tipped off the *Post*. In fact I'm surprised that you haven't been called by reporters.'

Innocence looked at her son-in-law. He seemed about to puke.

'As you know, Claudia, it is a family rule' – he smiled at his wife, his expression strained, and grabbed her hand – 'it is a family rule that we turn off our mobiles at five p.m. on a Saturday. Nothing is so important that it can't wait till Monday morning, and if it's to do with the children, then

344

Nanny can send Jonny, the under-butler, in a car. If it's work, however, she knows not to disturb us. As a matter of fact, I *have* received a number of ... curious messages from reporters but I don't speak to any member of the fourth estate unless the conversation has been officially sanctioned by Emily's PR.'

Something was definitely up. His voice had a strange half-hysterical lilt. He was terrified, panicking.

'Well, Timmy, I . . . I know people—'

'If you *know* people, Claudia, why don't you shut them up? Why don't you make them fucking *go away*? This is outrageous. I have instructed my lawyers and they are going to *sue*—'

'Timmy, you can't sue a paper for printing the truth. They have photos. They have a *lot* of photos. Photos from six years ago, on that island; photos from last week, on Hampstead Heath. And if you don't mind me saying, Tim, I find it all pretty low – pretty disgusting when you have a wife and a family. You know, the papers even have a code name for you. They call you "Duke of York".'

'Hello! Hello? Am I, like, invisible here? What the *hell* is going on? Can someone please, like, put me in the loop?'

'"Duke of York"? I'm not a Duke, I'm an Earl! Or I will be. What the dickens is that supposed to mean?'

Innocence was starting to feel odd. She was getting that oh-my-God-no feeling. It began with a cold, leaden lump in your stomach, crawled its icy fingers up the length of your spine, and settled with a clammy, choking I-can't-breathe sensation around your neck. She cleared her throat. 'Viscount,' she said, and she heard the high, panicked note in her own voice. 'Whatever is going on? Have you been less than saintly? Have you done something ghastly? Put your name to an anti-hunting bill, voted for the Liberal Democrats? What is it, exactly, my dear, that you are keeping from us?'

Slowly, Claudia opened the briefcase. Her hands were

trembling, and a sheaf of grainy black and white photographs slipped on to the floor.

They all looked. They all saw.

Emily gasped.

No one spoke.

And then, swiftly, Emily snatched up a photograph. It showed her husband, gripping a tree, an ecstasy on his face, being *ridden* by some bloke in a woolly hat.

' "Oh, the Grand Old Duke of York,"' said Emily in a voice as clear as a church bell. ' "He had ten thousand men . . ."' She dropped the photograph. 'I'm going now. I'm going . . . away. If the papers want a comment, my comment is . . . I am filing for divorce.'

Innocence felt a tingle. It started in her left arm and travelled all the way down to the tips of her fingers. She balled her hand into a fist. 'Timmy?'

'Yes?'

Now the itch was gone, replaced by an ache. Tim was clutching his nose in both hands. Blood dripped from between his fingers.

'Thank you, Mother,' whispered Emily. 'I couldn't have put it better myself.'

'I'm so sorry,' said Claudia. 'I just . . . wanted to warn you.'

'Great . . . sure . . . thanks a lot.' Emily paused. 'Claudia, can I ask, are you, like, *autistic*, or just retarded?' She turned to Innocence. 'Mummy. Tell Nanny that I'll . . . send for her and the children . . . in, like, a week. I don't want them to be around me if I'm . . . not going to be myself.'

She turned to her husband. 'Know this. I loved you. The castle was a bonus. Maybe, one day, I will be able to forgive that you betrayed me, in the worst, the grossest way. I'm not talking about gay sex, I am talking about all the bullshit, all the lies, the deceit. Your whole life with me was a cowardly pretence. One day, perhaps, I will be able to forgive you for all of that. But as long as I live and breathe, I will never, ever forgive you for betraying our children.

I hate you. You have ruined my life, and I hope you rot.'

'Emily!' cried Tim. 'Wait!'

Emily half turned.

'Please. Please don't go. I can still offer you . . . what you want. I can provide security.'

Emily's look could have melted paint off a wall. '*Security?*' she said. 'You moron. I could get security in a fucking prison. I'm not some doll from the fifties, you prat. You're not rescuing me from a humdrum life of filing and fetching coffee. I'm *now*, honey, I'm today, I'm tomorrow, and girls like me don't settle for a shit life with an arsehole in return for not having to do paperwork. We want more for ourselves than a shitty pair of earrings at Christmas along with a new Dyson from a man who doesn't care. We don't shut up and smile while you fuck around because we can't pay the phone bill ourselves! We'll work in a shop and like it better. We want to be *honest*, look our kids in the eye. You can't buy our silence; you can't *pay* us to sign up to your crap idea of what we deserve. Women like me are wise to that, you fucking fuck, we want money, and *love*; we want the whole fucking Happy Package, and we'll get it ourselves because we are smart and *hot* and some loser with a few quid is not our only hope, you . . . *fool.*' Emily gave a strangled sob, and fled the room.

Innocence lit a cigarette. 'Get.'

Timmy and Claudia bolted.

Abruptly, Innocence sat on the floor. Never, in a million years, would she have done this in ordinary circumstances, in a Dior gown.

She stared unseeing at the smouldering fag. A blob of ash fell on the shimmery pink skirt. When she brushed it, it left a grey smear. Innocence sighed and shook her head. Jack and the East Coast heiress were off the hook – her libido was *nil*. 'Jesus,' she muttered. 'Life sucks.'

7,000 FEET ABOVE PHOENIX, ARIZONA, MARCH 2005

Mark, Personal Assistant to Mr Ethan Summers

'Pull harder, Mark! They've almost got the control zone!'

He struggled to breathe – G-force was crushing his chest, his ribs were powder in there – and pulled back on the joystick in a tight turn. The fighter jet wheeled at a 90-degree angle and he felt the blood sucked from his head. Don't black out, don't black out, tense your legs, tense your stomach – *resist*, goddammit!

'Now go. Go up to get him!'

The plane juddered against the fierce blue sky, and as his heart hammered out of control, he caught sight of the enemy arcing to his right. 'We have visual contact.' He gritted his teeth and squeezed the trigger. The cockpit rang loud with the clatter of machine-gun fire and smoke flared from the other plane. 'He's hit! You got him, soldier! We *won*!'

Mark's entire body pulsed with triumph, or perhaps he was trembling all over. The high was electrifying. It was the coolest, most terrifying thing he'd ever done. That knife-edge manoeuvre his instructor had put him in – he *was* Maverick. It was totally awesome. *He*, Mark, had won a dogfight. It was incredible, even the bit when he'd flown upside down at 250 m.p.h. and his head had become a cannonball, its great weight threatening to snap his spine in two like a breadstick. He had won, he had *won*, he had – oh, *shit*.

'Can we go again, Skip?' said Mark. 'And this time we need to lose.'

'Nice try, friend,' said Ethan, taking off his Ray-Ban Aviators with a grin and punching Mark on the shoulder. 'But don't mess with the best!'

Mark beamed as Ethan's co-pilot shook his hand and said, stuttering slightly, 'I'd fly with you any time, Mr Summers.'

He watched, unsurprised, as the real life Top Gun – a man who had shot four enemy aircraft from the skies over Iraq – blushed and added, 'I'm sure you hear this all the time, but we're big, big fans of your work, Mr Summers. Would you . . . would you be so kind as to sign a hello to my wife?'

Ethan was happy, so Mark was happy. Job done. In the last month, they had taken an Advanced Air Combat class, hunted anaconda in a Brazilian swamp, gone bull-riding in Montana and fired the gun of a Chieftain tank. Not to say that Ethan wasn't content riding the crystal waves in Malibu alongside Cameron and Matthew, but most of the time he wanted his adrenalin supersized. He thrived on *real* danger, and it was Mark's role, therefore, to provide it.

Mark liked to think that so far he had done a pretty good job.

He also spent a good half of his life scared out of his wits. As they flew back to Burbank in the private helicopter, his legs still felt shaky and the sweat poured off him. The heat of the desert was insane; it was like trying to breathe in an oven but somehow Ethan remained suave and cool while Mark boiled up like a potato. But, man, despite the terror, what a thrill! He didn't *love* the helicopter – seat-of-your-pants way to fly – but after the fighter jet, it was a sedate old lady.

He *loved* telling the little people what he did for a living: Chief Personal Assistant to Mr Ethan Summers. You watched their eyes bulge and their mouths drop open with awe. And quite right. He, Mark, was the gatekeeper; he was the one who woke one of the biggest stars in Hollywood with a triple espresso in a Versace mug each morning; he was the one who ranked each call – consequently, he was the one who got his ass kissed and a fucking load of 'swag' (*gifts*, baby, *gifts*) because he was the key, he had the power. He had the ear of the King, and if anyone wanted anything from Mr Ethan Summers, they had to go through Mark and they knew it.

All the little people were jealous of the Hollywood celebrity lifestyle, and with good cause. If they only *knew*!

They had left the Malibu beachfront villa at three a.m. Ethan had had a quick thrash in the pool, eaten a couple of egg-white and steamed vegetable burritos, and they'd jumped in the 1963 Ferrari 250 GT Berlinetta Lusso to get to the airport. It was a second-hand motor with 56,000 miles on the clock, but you'd forgive a car anything when its previous owner was Steve McQueen.

Marky didn't swim, but when he had a moment, he loved to sit in the hot tub or on the balcony and gaze at the pool boy's butt, or, indeed, the calm blue of the Pacific, which glittered in the sunshine beyond the pristine lawns.

It was a while, however, since he'd had a moment. There was a lot of admin and he didn't trust anyone else. Of course, Ethan had his people – the agent, the publicists, the lawyers, the manager – but Marky was his buddy, his *fixer*, his closest friend.

Mark knew the real Ethan, a rare privilege that made him proud. He admired Ethan for retaining a degree of mystique, as in the old days. Could you imagine Cary Grant revealing to a tabloid what he ate for breakfast? None of your damn business! Mark was a fan of the old-fashioned form of showbiz: when I play a role, it's better that you *don't* know who I am.

It was a shame that there were certain journalists who disagreed with this sentiment, but Ethan's crack legal team were slick, omniscient and unforgiving. Those who attempted to make a buck by spreading false and defamatory slurs were crushed like ants. Ethan valued his privacy. And it was an attitude that obviously worked: the Oscar win had worked its magic. The requests for meetings, the forests of scripts, the salutations were still pouring in, weeks later. Mark had arranged for most of the bouquets to be sent to Cedars-Sinai, along with the chocolate cupcakes and the exotic fruit baskets. The silver Mercedes, the Breitling watch, the Luxuriator diamond frames, the 1982 Cheval Blanc, the platinum jewellery, the Marc Jacobs and Paul Smith suits, the LCD screens: all the free shit would be auctioned off and proceeds sent to St Jude Children's Research Hospital.

Ethan wasn't like other, inferior stars. Mark's lip curled as he recalled the sight of the anal one from *Mates* pawing through a goody bag at Sundance. Ethan did not accept freebies. He had integrity and he liked what he liked: he didn't 'need the free shit'. Oscars night itself was always a scream. Mark loved to hear the juice they didn't report: John's face, tight as a drum; Vince, get some fucking lipo, show some respect; that kid from the Hobbit malarkey, *how* gay?; Jessica, popular girl, *ick*; and of course he had marvelled at Ethan's superb acceptance speech for best actor. Wait, he could remember it, word for word:

'When I was a kid the only time I saw movies was when I waited for the bus in front of the store window. It wasn't in my realm of reality to imagine that I could one day *act* in a movie, and to receive this honour tonight humbles me, reminds me of where I came from – basically, nowhere – and tells me that any kid, no matter how poor or disadvantaged, can make his or her dream come true.'

Mark secretly thought it a shame that Ethan was at a career stage where he could skip red-carpet events unrelated to his own work – Mark adored red-carpet events – but as Ethan had confided to *Vanity Fair* in a rare interview, 'You always feel like you're having your ass kissed or you're having to kiss ass.' Cute, that last bit, as if Ethan objected to having his ass kissed!

But he was honourable. He did not take anyone's free shit. He didn't like to owe people. He was about the only star who shunned the 'hospitality suites' that sprang up in LA in every fabulous hotel or salon in the pre-Oscars week. He loathed the devil's pact of grabbing products and treatments for free – from getting your arse sandpapered to your new porcelain fucking teeth – then being forced to pose, shamefully exhibiting your greed, for the vampires at *InStyle* or *People* magazine. He liked everything to be square. He found it more satisfactory to pay for things himself. Oh, and he could. You knew a man was fuck-off rich when he lived on the scraped-off top of a mountain. The 23,000-square-foot, Hollywood Hills mansion was beyond cool. It had taken nine years of hard graft to reach this point, but Ethan had made good choices.

Mark appreciated it. He busied around that place like a mother duck around its nest – he couldn't have been more proud had he laid every brick himself!

The vast three-million-dollar trophy pool was finally complete. It had taken two years. The pool had a waterfall, and a garage-door-sized water screen dense enough for a movie to be projected on to it. At the end of the pool stood a four-million-dollar sculpture – Ethan was such a culture vulture, unlike some of these vapid Americans. It was . . . Oh, what was it? A stunning work by Arno Breker, *The Wounded*, of a man clutching his head in pain. It was, as a Californian might say, like *totally* deep.

Ethan's first pool party last Saturday, a week after the Oscars, had blown people away. It was easily better than one of Elton's bashes, always banging on about AIDS. Couldn't people enjoy themselves for five minutes without being forced to feel guilty? And it totally outclassed the *Vanity Fair* do – all they did was chuck out free cigarettes! Even the studio's Oscar party: goldfish tanks overhead that leaked and short-circuited the lights? Please! A step away from painted silver girls in cages pretending to be tigers! Ethan's party was old-school class. The food was gorgeous, delicious, simple: caviar, roasted veal, Maine lobster. The dessert: Pinkberry. Mark liked the green-tea flavour; Ethan preferred vanilla: the stuff was addictive. People had to eat something, *eventually*, so it helped if there were no fat or carbs (choose your poison) within spitting distance – or they'd be spat.

Mark found it disgusting. Plainly, at least ten of the world's biggest box-office stars had raging bulimia. Hurl your guts up all you like, but not in *my* boss's six-thousand-dollar

Japanese toilet. Plainly, Elitist Portable Restrooms didn't meet their outlandish expectations. But it did not occur to these people to clean up after themselves and it was vastly unpleasant to see *spatter*, or worse, to smell it, sour and drab. It was a detail that belonged in another sadder, sorrier life, Mark felt. Here, amid the splendour and wealth and exclusivity, it was strange and incongruous. Wrong.

The staff had served Cristal and cocktails: LA specials, like the Sunset Sour from Bar Marmont and the Burning Mandarin from Katsuya – Ethan's personal favourite. He was such a gourmet, he loved the surprise kick of the chilli after the sweet sugar and the citrus tang. Then guests had kicked back on floats and watched horror movies – *The Omen* and *Psycho* – under a full moon.

Ethan was way too cool to show his own movies, although, if you insisted (it would be rude to disappoint die-hard fans) there were screenings of *Parajumper*, *Hit Point* and *Sick Day* in the indoor theatre. As with every room in the house, it was exquisitely furnished with signature pieces, painstakingly sourced by the interior designers from every corner of, well, mainly Italy.

Soft, sinkable-into Galante chairs from Armani Casa, upholstered in lustrous metallic silver, added to your viewing pleasure – or perhaps you favoured the white leather Unique chairs from Versace, butter soft and delicately stitched. The mood lighting was remote adjustable, and there were candles everywhere. Ethan liked the romance of a naked flame – softie! In fact *Mark* had discovered the Little Joseph candleholders by Maxim Velcovsky for Qubus: a porcelain child's head, gloriously gothic, bald until the dripping wax christened him with hair. He, Mark, knew what Ethan liked, better than some woman with zero per cent body fat, huge white teeth and a degree in bullshit.

The fireworks display, a big deal because of the regulations, was the final touch. The Yanks didn't do fireworks like the English, and these were specially imported from the

UK (*beautiful, stunning, money to burn*). At least one A-list star had left early with a bad case of the Not Got Enoughs. Actually Mark suspected mental disorientation triggered by the sight of a room of books: Shakespeare, Freud, Dickens, Tolstoy, Nigella. 'Like, you *read* all these?'

And the head of the studio had, biting his fist, sent over a minion to suggest that Mark should call his PA with the designer's details.

But mostly, guests had enjoyed themselves: their egos were flattered, their particular needs anticipated and met (allergy to soy, aversion to the colour yellow, phobia of clocks, fear of bald people, etc.). The music was loud and retro, and there were private corners to retire to if you were a squeaky-clean blonde starlet, daughter of Hollywood royalty, who craved a threesome with your drug-dealer boyfriend, your best girl and a vial of crystal meth. That was the sweet thing about Ethan: he wasn't into that sort of filth, but he didn't judge. He liked people to indulge their pleasures – at his expense, maybe, but not his reputation. Talking of which . . .

Mark had cringed watching this month's eye candy attempt to pull rank with a desperate, flamboyant show of intimacy. Ethan was too much of a gentleman to humiliate her in public, but the whole party witnessed the one-way flow of affection. Her days were numbered.

First, she'd failed to come close to an Emmy for her excruciating sitcom *Curb Your Extremism*, in which she played the angst-ridden teenage daughter of a reformed terrorist dad. Second, she got jumpy if she found herself in a room without a reflective surface.

Ethan did not do drugs, he preferred a good honest walk up Runyon Canyon, whereas this crazy bitch thought cocaine the nutritional equivalent of a celery stick. Then she'd pig out on Tootsie rolls and scoop peanut butter out of jars with a spoon, after which she'd cry and puke and spend the next four hours running in the gym, bingeing on yoga, and sobbing on the phone to her therapist: LA had chewed her up, she couldn't take the heat. The other day she'd arrived sobbing on a *bike* – not a motorbike, a *cycle*. Duh! She was hysterical because someone in a Hummer had, quite rightly, thrown a bottle at her and shouted, 'Get a fucking car!'

Ethan would go back to dating French waitresses: cute girls with high self-esteem, no expectations and dignity. Ethan was twenty-seven, no longer young, and he was deadly serious about his career. You had to work at staying hot. The most hilarious thing anyone ever said about LA was that it was 'laid back'. Ethan had plotted each move and he wasn't ashamed of that, unlike every other megastar who lied to the papers, 'Oh, I just fell into it!' It took years to establish and maintain the correct image. You didn't get to be A-list by being flimsy. Amid the endless bullshit of Hollywood, focus was everything. Ethan was busy on set filming *Transmission*, otherwise he would have dumped this liability by now. But Mark had prepared a stack of cuttings in a clear folder for Ethan to read back at the house, then she'd be out. Of course, Ethan would want to break up with her the old-fashioned way, but Ethan was too soft-hearted. Once he was given the green light, Mark would see her off with a text and, to soften the blow, a silver Hermès Kelly bag.

Ethan was busy: he had no time to waste with losers. Other stars had business interests; restaurants, racehorses. Ethan's interest was people. He did charity work, but he didn't go on about it (unlike Angelina Jolie. Would she ever shut up?). He'd saved lives when the bomb had gone off at the Parisian hotel. He'd quietly paid for the rehabilitation of certain of the injured, but it wasn't common knowledge and Ethan didn't want it to be.

Mark felt warm when he considered how thoughtful Ethan was. He put *intelligence* into every action and he understood people. That would be the secret of his worldwide superstardom and his global success. Ethan was hugely powerful; he could accomplish anything, but his star was still rising, which Mark felt was the most thrilling part of all. *Now* he was hot, the buzz was about *Ethan*.

When you were bank, when you were a household name, when you were Tom Hanks, Diet Coke, KFC, that's when it all slowed down and got boring, that's when you stopped doing good work and started doing rubbish, because you had arrived. Once you had arrived there was nowhere to go.

Mark liked to think that Ethan's success was in some small, yet significant way partly down to him.

N. CRESCENT DRIVE, BEVERLY HILLS, JUNE 2005

Emily

Ah, the Platinum Triangle. But you could forgive people for having tons of money when they had no taste. She'd managed a peek in the vast kitchen and it was full of brown units and the floor was linoleum: what were they *thinking*? Still, the location was great, near to the Pink Palace, and not so far from the Polo Lounge if you'd had a few. The house itself was a great, gaudy mansion, a Tuscan villa Californian style; it was a pity that the interior reflected the owner's personality. It was giddy with cream marble and paintings of trees, and the carpet on the stairs was covered in durable plastic. Not cool. She couldn't help thinking what she could have done with a house like this, had she had twenty-eight million dollars.

The outside, at least, was gorgeous. As you ascended the wide stone steps to the giant front door, you passed a great pond full of koi carp. When Emily touched her finger to the water, one came to the surface to be stroked, like a cat.

The swimming pool was blue and serene and surrounded

by palms and the view swept on for ever. Beyond, tables and chairs had been set out on the gently sloping lawn. It was cooler up here, in the heavens of LA, and she was glad she'd bought a wrap. You did feel charmed, sitting high above the rest of the world, with billions of dollars' worth of movie stars and industry hotshots squeezed into such a small area – a couple of acres, but a tight fit for all those egos – and it was nice to feel entitled, if only briefly. To everyone here, she was one of *them*, or near enough.

She put up a good front. In LA, at least, they had no clue that she was hanging on to her sanity by a thread. Her cash situation was precarious, and every time she thought about it, which was by the minute, her heart lurched. Since the divorce, she hadn't made good on her promises – or threats – to Tim. She hadn't found love, and she hadn't made money. The perfume hadn't sold; no woman wanted to stink of failure. She'd given an interview to the highest bidder – a right-wing tabloid – and the female hack had portrayed her as hysterical and bitter.

Suddenly, she had the Plague.

The worst of it was, she had two kids. She didn't mean it like *that*. She had two wonderful kids and she wanted so much for them. It was fine, failing, when it was just you. When you failed with kids, it was hard to look at yourself in the mirror each day. She was terrified that George was already screwed up from the divorce. However you spun it, kids wanted Mummy and Daddy to live together, love each other: nothing else could make it right. She thought with dread how, as soon as he was able, all the sordid details would be available to him. He'd just Google *Fortelyne Emily Tim gay affair* and a hundred thousand words of pain would appear.

Little Molly she was less worried about. She was sixteen months old, and for now, Mummy and Nanny were enough. But it wore you down, not being able to afford your lifestyle. She couldn't bear to think that the children might lack *anything*. She couldn't quite believe that her parents, either one of whom could have bought this opulent hilltop estate from the interest accumulating in one of their many offshore accounts, had refused to bail her out. She was too proud to ask, and all hints were ignored.

Her mother was happy to lavish the children with designer clothes, expensive toys and pay for George's school fees. Despite having served at Her Majesty's pleasure, Innocence had no idea what it was to live in reduced circumstances. Her last gift to the children had been a nineteen-thousand-dollar Victorian playhouse from Posh Tots: wraparound porch, stained-glass windows, faux-wood floors, *window boxes* – Emily was a breath away from getting the thing assembled and moving in herself. Actually, she wasn't. There was no *space* for the stupid Victorian playhouse as Emily had no *garden*. Emily (under Nanny's instruction) had sold it on eBay, and spent the proceeds on a tan at the Portofino Sun Spa in Beverly Hills, a BlackBerry, a bunch of clothes from Kitson, a Hello Kitty babygro from Kitson Kids, and a Spiderman Web Blaster.

Beyond dumb, frivolous, useless crap, the wallet was shut tight as a clam. Innocence felt (Emily knew it) that her daughter should make it 'on her own', as she had. It *so* pissed her off because, as anyone with half a brain knew, Innocence had got to be fabulously rich by cheating, stealing, fucking, lying and treading on people's heads. It wasn't a legacy you should want to pass on to your daughter.

Emily had no savings. *Savings*: the word reeked of poverty.

She was renting a three-bedroom apartment in Park La Brea for $4,200 a month. It had a private patio, hardwood floors, plantation-style shutters, granite counters, and there was a concierge service, security and a gym. But she didn't like to *rent*, and she didn't like to live in an *apartment*.

The worst moment had been when she had taken little George to the apartment building for the first time. He had walked into the lobby and dropped his jacket on the floor.

'No,' she'd said, snatching up the jacket, quailing with embarrassment. 'We don't own the whole place, just a . . . bit of it.'

An apartment was basically a *flat*, and she couldn't stand being squashed into a space, with strangers above you, below you, and either side of you. It was awful living in such cramped conditions – 1,800 square feet. She needed acres of land. It was what she was used to. She was slumming it and to wake up in that place every day was a slap in the face. Also, it was across the road from the Grove: all those gorgeous shops with all those gorgeous things. God, the irony!

Emily snatched a glass of champagne off a passing tray, and tried not to down it in one. If you were seen to drink more than one unit of booze here, you had a problem and, before you knew it, there'd be an intervention and you'd be whipped off to AA. She'd seen a 'dry' actor casually sip a glass of red at Pane e Vino and three people on surrounding tables pick up their cells. The only plus side was that your sponsor was probably a household name.

So she did most of her drinking at home, after the kids were in bed. Some days, it was hard to be with them. Her state of mind was not good and you couldn't always fob them off. George was old enough to see through her frozen smile and it disturbed him. When he put a small chubby hand on hers and said, lip wobbling, 'Mummy, is it my fault?' she felt sick with shame and self-disgust.

Anyway, it was her father's fault. Jack – the coma had done nothing for his personality, which was a waste – had given her a job. She was vice president of press relations at the Bel Air Belle Époque. *Vice*.

What a bastard. He was a master of fucking up his kids. No one knew how to screw with your head better than Daddy. He paid her just enough to keep Nanny on, and Isabella, although Isabella might have to go. The other day, Emily had waltzed past Isabella's shoes (taken off at the front door) and done a double take. A pair of boat-sized Manolos! The bloody cleaner was wearing *Manolos*. Of course: she also cleaned for Rod Stewart and his wife had spring cleaned. All the same, it didn't make Emily feel good. Or rather it didn't make Emily feel *better*.

Emily urgently needed to feel better.

She fingered the company credit card. She'd only had it in her possession for three days; before then, if she'd wanted to take a client to lunch, she'd had to pay for it herself and claim back the expenses. She would have probably been better off taking a job as a sales assistant in Wal-Mart. It would have been less crippling to her self-esteem.

Her boss, Agatha, a woman with a too-long neck and a British accent straight out of *Mary Poppins* (*twat*), had never married, nor had children, or indeed any kind of inter-personal relationship that might have interfered with her work, and Emily was certain of being despised by this creature on every level. Emily was young, she was sexy, she had kids but no money, and she was here through nepotism. It made Emily spit because she knew her father had only given her a job because he knew she'd be brilliant at it.

On handing her the credit card, Agatha had said, in her clipped, icy tones, 'In case you thought otherwise, we no longer lunch big in this town. People often forgo starters. And we have a perfectly good hotel dining room in La Cuisine. So don't push it.'

Today, this evening, was the credit card's first outing. Her boss was supposed to have been attending, no doubt to supervise, but Agatha's mother had selfishly suffered a heart attack that very morning, so at this very moment, Agatha was pacing the corridors of Cedars-Sinai, wishing she'd been cloned instead of born.

Emily sipped her champagne and smiled at her lap. There was gorgeous George: tiny bit too thin, bit of wattle under the chin, maybe not quite so gorgeous. Matt Damon: my, if that boy wanted to look like a film star, he should not stand next to Brad, and yet . . . Matt wore you down. He was a nice boy:

good-natured and cute. And Ethan Summers, oh my *God*, he made Johnny Depp look *ugly*. All the big stars had on their shiniest public smiles, although the calibre of guest meant that no one was going to jump them, or burst into tears and start kissing their feet – there were TV cameras.

She tried not to look at Ethan, but it was hard. The only thing she had against him was that, like a true action hero, he'd rescued Tim after the bomb had gone off in Paris. He should have let him burn.

She wondered if Ethan knew who *she* was.

He must do. *Entertainment Weekly* had once called her 'the thinking man's Paris Hilton'. Fuck off! She was, like, better looking to infinity. But maybe they just meant that she was the daughter of a hotel billionaire and notorious? That wasn't a bad thing. Ethan must know *of* her – she was still a Club Member . . . wasn't she?

She hated this self-doubt, when she had once been so certain.

When you were famous, you became a member of an exclusive club, and those inside welcomed you in. The thinking was: I am famous, and you are famous, so you must be OK and we might just hang out. That said, there were very particular levels of famous. Everyone in the entertainment business was finely ranked and it didn't do to get ideas above your station. Here, if an actress got a magazine cover before she was deemed to deserve one, she might be shunned by the industry for a while to remind her of her place. Well, if Ethan didn't know who she was, he soon would. All these people who dressed up for a living could shove over, because tonight, *she* was going to be the star of the show. Spend two thousand dollars max, Agatha had said sternly, even if it was for charity, in the name of Belle Époque. She should bid for something tangible, a 'modest artwork, nothing weird, hideous, or sexual, by a known artist, preferably local'.

Two thousand dollars indeed! Jack had already added

'celebrity-killer' to his distinguished title of 'disgraced billionaire', did he want to be known as tight, too? In the name of great publicity, Emily was going to buy something proper and big, and she was going to grandly, gaudily, pay top whack.

She flicked through the auction brochure. Private yacht trip around the Greek Islands? Flights to Vegas via private jet and a night at the Wynn? A Bentley Continental Flying Spur? *Yawn!*

It occurred to Emily that she hadn't had sex in months and despite her poverty-stricken existence, no yacht trip, no private jet, no flash hotel could thrill her. She wanted a man to play with and there just wasn't one in the brochure.

She'd forgotten. What was tonight again? Romania? Sanitary protection? Oh yeah. Orphaned babies in the Third World.

Lucky orphaned babies, touched by the sacred hand of Hollywood! Did those ungrateful orphaned babies know how privileged they were that all these gorgeous, famous, fabulous, powerful, special *godlike* beings had given up two hours of their Monday to help them? These people were about to give them cash out of their own pockets, when those babies had done nothing to earn it, except be orphaned. How fortunate, how blessed those babies were. If only someone would help Emily as they were helping those babies – her situation was almost as desperate.

Emily knew she should network, and once she would have done: she would have kissed air and talked small with ease and grace. But she didn't feel like making the effort. It was exhausting, finding out who did what so you knew who was worth speaking to. Anyway, she wanted to play it cool. Fox News was here and she didn't trust their camera angles.

So she sat, smoked, sipped her drink, hid behind her shades and admired the view (the stars on the ground – you could see the ones in the sky any time). She could have wolfed the entire tray of prawn tempura, not to mention the lobster wontons and the Kobe beef, but she briskly waved it all away. Paris might have been filmed having sex but to Emily's knowledge she had so far avoided the humiliation of having been filmed eating.

The live-auction host was one of Emily's least favourite actresses. It was the steely glint of naked ambition that put her off. In person, the woman was a cold, hard, flinty misogynist; it was bizarre that she had made her name playing cute, ditsy roles in romantic comedies, a habit that she'd continued, probably unwillingly, well into her forties. Often, when you met the *less* prominent actors, you realized they barely acted, that they had merely spent their career playing variations on themselves.

Emily wondered if Nanny would remember to give Molly avocado with her pasta, and if George would be forced to eat a bit of cucumber. Nanny was a no-nonsense Australian from Perth, happy to spot any celebrity, no matter how mad, minor, or niche. Every Sunday she was in awe of Ed Begley, Jr, hawking his All-Purpose Spray at the Farmers' Market; and if she spotted Jeff Goldblum in Wholefoods in his pink spectacles it was a major event. And yet, Emily knew – curious, not quite understanding how – it was just a diversion; these people meant nothing to her. Whereas to just about everyone else in LA, these people were *it*. Famous strangers mattered, more, Emily suspected, than family.

She loved this town but its priorities were screwed. She needed Nanny around, keeping it real.

She passed on a tray of skull-shaped chocolates and tried to pay attention to the host. She was having some trouble shifting the yacht trip. Didn't most of this lot have their *own* yachts? Emily stifled a yawn and gazed at the back of an Olsen twin – well, it was one or the other. The girl's posture sucked.

'Now, for those of you who don't realize, this yacht trip comes with a few extras. I'm throwing in a kiss with – don't argue, darling, you know it's for a good cause – Mr Ethan Summers! And I am not going to take less than ten thousand dollars; this man does not come cheap!'

Oh. My. *God*. The cheek of her! Trying to brown nose the star of the moment to make herself look good. Don't waste your time, honey; you haven't got that much left. But – piss off, Olsen twin, there are calories in saliva – this is worth bidding for. Emily's hand gripped the company credit card tight, and she knew, at once and with total conviction, that no one must win the kiss with Ethan Summers but *herself*.

And, if Emily had her way, she wasn't going to win just a *kiss*.

N. CRESCENT DRIVE, BEVERLY HILLS, JUNE 2005

Ethan

Ethan laughed. It was great, being Ethan.

He didn't understand the stars who got depressed. What could you possibly be miserable about when everybody loved you?

He guessed they were just sick with fear. Fear that someone else they knew was doing better and someone else they'd never heard of was about to break. Fear that someone else was getting that big script; fear that their pay cheque was a million dollars more, that someone else had a better body, a hotter chick, a slicker agent, more exclusive invitations; that tomorrow it would all be over and they'd be left with only millions of dollars, no friends and a few tapes.

Ethan didn't worry about shit like that. He knew he had the better life, and he loved living it.

It was crazy being famous, but you got used to it. Your ego swelled to fit the space. He liked it that people made an exception for him. He liked it that he was treated as special. He liked it that 99 per cent of people he met would crawl over cut diamonds rather than disagree with him. He liked it that others worked to make every moment of every day perfect. He liked it not because he was a complete dickhead, he liked it because it made him a *nicer person*.

Who likes being disagreed with? Who likes being told off? Who likes being treated like shit? *Then* you had cause to be a miserable bastard.

But being a Hollywood star you lived the dream. You lived the fairy tale. Your wish was their command. Like a spoilt child, you always got what you wanted. There was no excuse to be anything other than *delightful*.

Admittedly, he did find himself bristling with a silent 'Don't you know who I am?' when he wasn't accorded the red-carpet treatment – as he hadn't been yesterday when he'd driven the new customized Cadillac SUV the wrong way up a one-way street and come nose to nose with a cop car. There had definitely been a moment of stunned outrage at the guy's attitude – but then of course he'd taken off his baseball cap, smiled sheepishly, and the man had cried, '*Ohhhh!* God bless you, friend! You prosper and keep on being successful, Mr Summers!'

Afterwards, he'd giggled to himself for being so touchy. He had an answer for those who criticized the stars for taking themselves too seriously. They were stars *because* they took themselves seriously. You had to in this town or you wouldn't make it. But he could still laugh at himself for a sense of humour failure. Now that it was all OK.

Tonight, as with every night, he was feeling good. The interview with *Los Angeles* magazine had come out today, and it was a corker. They'd gone to the Natural History Museum and the journalist had been charmed when he'd paid for her ticket, saying, 'Anything else and my mother would slap me round the head!' You could always legislate for grateful amazement when you briefly brought yourself down to the little people's level.

He had carefully avoided talking about himself in the third

person, and he had convincingly laughed off the 'myth' that he used Fiji water to clean his teeth. They'd schlepped all the way back to the Hills and the chauffeur had dropped them at Mr Chow. While Ethan needed to order off menu (tuna tartare with lemon and extra chips), he hadn't noticeably revelled in the fuss and attention. He had greeted the valet by name, he had hugged the publicist, he had nodded his thanks for the secluded table: he had proven that he was an all-round decent guy.

And he was about to prove it again.

He stood up, reluctant, grinning, happy yet bashful to be the centre of attention when the true heroes of the hour were the orphaned babies in the Third World, and as the celebrated hordes clapped and cheered, he was bathed in that familiar golden glow, a sea of grinning faces oozing love. He could precisely recall the last time he'd seen a frown because it was such a rare occurrence.

'You go, girl!' said Clooney. He was such a wag! Ethan resisted the urge to give him a dead arm.

Outside he wore shades; inside, he had mastered the art of not making eye contact to avoid being pestered. The alternative was to take minders everywhere, which was great for kudos but a drag, like living in a baboon troop. Now, however, he removed his Tom Ford sunglasses and allowed his gaze to lock with various select females in the audience. There was Katie – ah, the untouchable, the gracious, the chocolate-cupcake-loving Mrs Cruise – he gave her his little-boy-lost look and she smiled back, maternal. And there was the newly single Emily Kent. Poor Emily, a shining product of bad parenting, but, Jesus, couldn't the girl tell a fruit when she saw one?

He shot her a wink. *Make my day.*

Then he stepped up beside the host, and smilingly suffered her to kiss him on the mouth, wondering if her publicist hadn't offered her a breath mint on purpose because she was such a total bitch. She routinely blanked other women and that was just plain rude. He wouldn't mind but she did it to her own employees, including her sister!

'So, my darling Ethan – oh my, get a feel of this guy's *muscles* – you know, suddenly I realize that ten thousand isn't going to cut it. Children, I think we are morally obliged to start the bidding at *twenty* thousand dollars. Now, ladies – and gentlemen! – think of those dear little orphan babies, and, more to the point, think of kissing Ethan Summers smack on the mouth! What do you say?'

Ethan grinned and declared, 'Man, I am going to be so pissed if Clooney doesn't bid!' It got a huge laugh, because famous people were just that extra bit funnier.

'Fifty thou, but I'm gonna insist on tongue!' shouted Damon.

Ethan laughed. Did he have a choice? He shouted back, 'This is blackmail! I'll double your money for a firm handshake!'

The host, unwilling to be prised from the limelight, cut in. 'The bidding stands at a hundred thousand if my math serves me right, and frankly, I'm not impressed. We're not doing wonderful. This man does not get out of bed for more than – I mean, less than fifteen million a picture. Come on, people!'

How *dare* she mention his salary – and she'd underestimated it! She was *underselling* him! He couldn't stand her.

She joined his list of unmentionables alongside that upstart George Eads from *CSI*, who'd nearly run him down on Mulholland last week in a silver Porsche. He'd told Mark, who'd got a funny look on his face. Ethan had just known that while Mark now hated George Eads on Ethan's behalf, he was torn. To be run over by a celebrity had its plus side. If you were seriously injured they'd be forced to visit your hospital bed (rather than leave it to their rep). You'd become friends ... gain access to their inner circle ... cosy dinners chez George. I mean, if you had medical insurance, what wasn't to like?

Mark's reaction had frustrated and delighted him. George

Eads was only *television*. He, Ethan, had starred in four of the top-grossing movies in the last three years. He could do no wrong. Right now, he was more powerful than *God*. The world was his.

He blinked, winningly, and smiled his whitest smile.

'Two hundred thousand for my dear friend Ethan – though I better make it an air kiss or people will talk!'

Ah, the lovely Patricia Arquette. She was a goddess. He adored her. He'd worked with her when he was just starting out; a nobody, still waiting tables, and she'd been so warm, so kind, so encouraging. Ethan never forgot how people had treated him when he wasn't Mr Ethan Summers. As he'd told *Access Hollywood*, years later, 'I felt so embraced.'

He blew her a kiss.

There was a clatter, and a husky English voice shouted, '*Five* hundred thousand – no, screw that – one million dollars!'

There was a stunned silence, then a murmur that became a buzz of excitement, as people started clapping and whooping and turning in their seats.

'Oh my good Lord,' cried the host. At least she'd managed to clean her potty mouth for the occasion. 'Hollywood's biggest hitter, Mr Ethan Summers, is going, going, *gone*, to the lady in last season's Hervé, for a grand total of *one million* dollars. I am so thrilled on behalf of all those little orphan babies, who I swear to God will be clapping their darling pudgy hands around now! Stand up, please, honey, so we all can have a good look at ya! Oh, Emily Kent! Honey, forgive me, I didn't recognize you. We haven't seen you in a while. Well, *what* a sensational comeback – isn't she adorable?! Ethan, how are you feeling right now?'

As opposed to yesterday?

Ethan twizzled his Tom Ford shades and gazed at his feet, then up at Emily, a challenge in his eyes.

She was smiling, her mouth half open, panting with the thrill of risk. Then she placed one hand on a slender hip, and pouted, looking straight at him. She didn't have that squeaky-clean Californian girl glaze. While she had a fragile beauty with a tanned, honed body, she was plainly a bad girl with a big mouth that got her in all sorts of trouble. This chick had a streak of pure filth. You got this babe in the sack, she wouldn't give a toss about messing up her hair, she'd ride you into the ground.

He smiled again and, without taking his eyes off Emily, he said, 'How do I *feel*? I'm stoked!'

The host squealed with delight. 'Oh, honey, you big spender, come on up!'

Slowly, Emily sashayed towards Ethan. She walked right up to him, until he could feel the heat pulsing off her. That dress, she was busting right out of it. *Jesus.* Their eyes locked and they understood each other.

There was dead silence, and she tilted her face, and he bent towards her. As their lips met, her hands fluttered and she gripped his shoulders. He pulled her close, pressing her body to his. It was as if the whole crowd had been teleported to the Valley and only the two of them remained. He felt her relax against him, and he knew, in that instant, she was his.

N. CRESCENT DRIVE

Emily

Sure, it was a thrill to be kissing the hottest movie star on earth. But the real thrill was to be kissing him in front of a million people. Emily always liked a chance to say 'ha ha' to the world – in particular her sister, her mother, the girls from school, all her ex-boyfriends, her husband, her father, and anyone who'd ever had a mean thought about her.

That only left about ten people.

As for the movie star himself, Ethan Summers was gorgeous, charming, rich and successful. His one flaw was his dating history: a hideous line-up of supermodels and Hollywood goddesses. As Emily was more intelligent than all of them put together in a sack and dropped off the Empire State, it would be insulting to compare badly as a sex object. She would stand out as special.

As their lips met, and a hundred cameras clicked, Emily's hand snaked down towards the crotch of his jeans, unzipped and squeezed.

She felt his lean muscled body tense with desire, and begin to tremble. Aha, the heat of lust!

Wait.

Was Ethan shaking with passion or was he . . . *laughing*?

She opened her eyes and saw that he was. Furiously, she pulled away.

Grinning, Ethan adjusted himself. And then whispered in her ear, 'I'm not that cheap.' He had a nerve. She'd paid a million dollars for this!

Or, rather, Daddy's firm had paid a million dollars for this.

There was his secretary on her mobile now. Those cameras must be live. Well, there was no way he could have a problem. It was for charity. Anyway, she had more immediate issues to deal with. The audience were starting to clap, uncertain, as if the kiss was over. This was not the plan at all.

She arched an eyebrow. 'That all you got?'

His grin faded. He gripped her arms and roughly pulled her to him, kissed her long and hard.

She felt dazed and weak with longing. She gasped lightly as he finally broke away. It was fate; they were meant to be together. Her gamble had paid off. It was the end of all her problems; the beginning of a twenty-first-century fairy tale.

Ethan stroked her hair and bent to whisper in her ear. Here it was. He was going to ask her out.

'Hey, babe, I didn't catch your name.'

'And how precious!' cooed the host who, despite extensive

370

surgery, looked at least forty and was now only ever cast to play grandmas or psychopaths. 'How romantic to raise so much money for all those little orphaned babies in the Third World. Thank you, Ethan darling, I'm sure it was tough. And thank you, Miss Emily Kent, for your hugely generous bid.'

The assembled Hollywood stars rose to their feet, clapping and cheering. Emily gave Ethan her best withering look, and said, 'I didn't give it to you.'

Then she turned her back. The man was so arrogant, he needed a snub British-style.

Her mobile rang again.

'Yes.'

'Good afternoon, Emily. I'm putting you through to your father now.'

Ah, crap. 'Daddy! My favourite. Hello!'

'Emily. You bore me. You are fired. Your desk at the hotel is cleared. You are twenty-three now, and a mother: finance your own mistakes. I am sick of seeing you in the papers, compromising the family name. We'll speak when you accomplish something. Until then.'

'Daddy, wait!'

She was speaking to dead air.

She shoved on her Gucci shades and strode away from the crowds to the quiet of the pagoda.

If she didn't have an income, she would lose the apartment. Tim would get the children. She felt sick. She stared down over the gorgeous sprawl of West Hollywood and its blue, blue sky, a line of ocean visible in the distance, but at that moment she saw only black.

'Do you support any other charities?'

Oh God. It was impossible not to smile at Ethan Summers when he was being cute, but she wasn't going to take off her sunglasses.

He paused. 'Jack wasn't so impressed.'

It was humiliating that he knew her situation. Of course he knew who she was. The kiss had been a mistake. It showed she was desperate. She didn't want pity. She supposed she wanted him to fall in love with her.

'He never is,' she said.

He raised a hand. For a moment she thought he was going to hit her. He gently removed her sunglasses. 'Now we're talking.'

She sighed. 'So now I have no job, and no way to pay the rent.' She smiled. 'I don't think even *Access Hollywood* are going to want a fifth interview.'

Ethan bent his head. Every move, every look, every word made her want to rip off his clothes. 'You could always crash at my place until you get yourself sorted. I promise I won't' – he waved a hand in the vague direction of her cleavage – '*interfere* with you.'

Yes, yes, *yes*. The hand down the trousers – told you – irresistible!

She made a point of hesitating. Ethan seemed to suppress a smile. 'That's a very kind offer,' she said. 'I'd like that. But I have a question.'

'Go.'

Emily gazed into his eyes. 'Do you ever ... break a promise?'

LOS ANGELES, A WEEK LATER

Emily

So *what* if her father had seen the news footage and sacked her on the spot? It was his loss. He had said goodbye to the best publicity genius he would ever employ. He had no idea. To him, she'd blown a million dollars of company money on nothing. What an idiot. Didn't he understand that publicity was all about perception? And, thanks to her and that kiss, millions of people, from New York to LA, from London to Paris, were perceiving the clip of Disgraced Hotel Tycoon's Daughter Kissing A-List Movie Star Ethan Summers for One Million Dollars in Aid of Charity.

Some stations had mentioned Belle Époque by name. Bookings would go through the roof. People were dumb. In their Neanderthal skulls, they would now link the exclusivity and desirability of Ethan Summers with her father's hotels: the silver sparkle of his Hollywood glamour, his youth, his sex appeal, would rub off on Jack's damaged empire like a sprinkle of fairy dust, for a mere million-dollar fee, when Japanese fizzy-drink firms paid ten times that amount, because other people knew that Ethan's name could rewrite a reputation and get the hard cash pouring in.

She hated her father, with a deep, dark, burning anger. She hated him for this, his latest crime, and she hated him for every other: that Claudia was the chosen one; that Claudia, though no blood relative, would inherit his billions, and not a penny to spare for Emily. She blamed her mother; she, Emily, was being punished for Innocence's sins. Maria had been the beloved geisha wife, and so Claudia, her daughter, was rewarded. And he was a shit grandfather. He was awkward, irritated, ratty around the children. The noise they made annoyed him; he thought they were rude and ill-disciplined. He expected them to act with the decorum of Prince Charles when, really, they were just children. They broke his Ming vase – well, of course they did, it was balanced on a pillar! They'd drawn an alien in purple felt tip on his Van Gogh. The implication also was that she, Emily, was a bad parent. Hello, pot!

It had all worked out, sort of, but no thanks to him. Jack had really upset her. He had screwed with her *life*. With no income, she couldn't afford the rent on the apartment; she couldn't afford to keep Nanny.

That was the worst of it – losing Nanny. She hadn't been half so upset when her mother had gone to prison. The

difference was, Nanny had been useful. Nanny had kept
Emily from losing control. Nanny had served as a buffer
between Emily and the children. Emily was still a child herself – like, she felt about *ten* – and the serious shit of being a
mother scared her to death. She was frightened of George
and baby Molly, those intense, powerful little people. As
Nanny insisted, she, Emily, was their sun and moon and,
truth was, she didn't feel worthy.

Nanny had been competent; she understood children. She
was the facilitator who stopped war breaking out.

Now that she was their sole carer, Emily felt terrified for
their welfare. Innocence had buggered off somewhere – perhaps Spyglass Island? She hadn't returned Emily's calls,
which meant that she didn't want to. In other words, the
bank was closed. Emily didn't even have the option of crashing at her mother's LA pad, as it was occupied by a Spice
Girl. One of them (Emily didn't care to know which) was
'working' out here and Innocence, a big fan of Zigazig Ha,
had offered her home as a base until the Spice Girl found
somewhere more permanent. Or until, as Emily hoped and
prayed, the US authorities declined to renew her visa.

There was always Claudia. But until Jack snuffed it,
Claudia was broke. In fact, she was such a martyr Emily
tensed her fingers into claws every time she thought of her
sister. Claudia was living a pious life of self-denial now that
that total fox Alfie had married that total *hound*. Basically, she
was in a sulk. Only Claudia could write for *Vanity Fair* and
make it seem unglamorous. When she was in the US, she
stayed in *other* hotels, and the rest of the time, she was holed
up in the Highgate flat. Apparently there were five flats in
this one house, and they had *parties*. Kill me now. Claudia
would have lent Emily cash, but Emily would have rather
hitched to Vegas and sold her body on the Strip. But Ethan's
people were helping out.

Oh my God, *Ethan*!

He had pretended to forget her name. That kiss was so hot

she'd almost forgotten her own name. Everyone had been *agog*. All those famous people were totally upstaged. It was one of the most satisfying moments of her life. The host, standing there like a botoxed lemon, had remarked that Emily had certainly got her money's worth, and Emily had murmured, 'Not quite.'

Then she'd taken the call from her father, via Ms Green: a total buzzkill. Dad would have been happy to let her starve on the streets of LA, feeding the baby in Taco Bell. It was just so amazing that Ethan had overheard the call and invited her to stay at his place. *With* the children. He was so sweet. She totally got why he was such a star. He had this wild charisma, this animal heat that people wanted to be around: it was like an energy source. She was desperate to fuck him. She could hardly walk straight for thinking about it.

The only trouble was, that creep Mark was always hovering. Lurch. She could tell that Lurch didn't approve. Well, tough shit, Lurch, *I've* got the fanny. In a way, it was good to have Lurch there as a live chastity belt. With Ethan she had no capacity to play it cool although she knew she should. She should be the one girl who didn't roll over and beg, but she wanted him *so bad*. Emily had always been the queen of mean, forgetting to return calls, postponing dates, showing men just how low they ranked in her fabulous life.

You didn't do that with Ethan Summers. She got the sense he didn't play games. This way was better.

She was full of hope. It was like a fairy tale. She was in distress, he was the conquering hero; he had swept her off her feet. He had rescued her, just as he had rescued Tim in the Paris bomb. She hadn't mentioned Tim – she doubted that Ethan even knew who Tim was – he'd just acted on impulse to help another human being. Tim was irrelevant. Now, it was all about her and Ethan and nothing would detract from that.

Her and *Ethan*.

Like, there were twenty websites devoted to this guy. The

clothes he was wearing, *today*, and where you could get them. On *Reel Clothes*, the khaki T-shirt he'd worn in *Parajumper* was on sale for $850. Today's headline in *People*, the most clicked-on image, was 'hot, shirtless: Ethan on the beach'. The quote of the day, on *ET*, was Ethan, on the paparazzi: 'What they're doing is illegal. Ten of them chase me down the street at sixty m.p.h. They're not trying to catch me doing a crazy thing. They're trying to *make* me do a crazy thing.'

A short quote given to *Variety*, about his forthcoming movie, *Hero*, had been picked meatless and regurgitated in every tabloid nationwide. 'Yes, I have a hero. My agent's daughter, Angie, is mentally challenged. She is my role model. She has cheerfully overcome more obstacles – learning to tie a shoelace, spell her name – than I ever will.'

His home was sick, way beyond anything in *Cribs*. She was used to this kind of space, where it took three minutes to cross a room. But his house seemed bigger than even her parents' homes, probably because Innocence was like a magpie – she couldn't stop filling her properties with *tat* – and Jack . . . well, she couldn't recall; she hadn't visited any of her father's homes for a while. Her father wasn't fun to be around.

He was depressed after Maria's death, and he was depressed that his injuries and the coma had aged him. He was still a good-looking guy, for a totally old person; he still had his hair. She hated bald men. They reminded her of clowns.

Ethan's main house was cool and white and chic. Each piece of furniture was a work of art; it was like a show home, designed to leave you open-mouthed with envy and awe. She *was* jealous of what he had – the land, the house, the stuff inside it; but most of all what these things together spelt: security.

She was jealous because she loved every bit of it: the polished hardwood floors; the whitewashed walls; the art (*Blood Head* by Marc Quinn – crazy! George loved gore and was transfixed – a translucent cast of the artist's head filled with his *actual frozen blood*); the gorgeous contemporary chandeliers (she loved the one that was made from hundreds of black and clear clusters of hand-blown glass baubles, like evil and good bubbling up). She loved, too, his luxury double armchairs of khaki-green nubuck where she could snuggle with Molly and George.

She loved the framed black-and-white poster of *Sick Day* with Ethan sexy and rugged, a shotgun slung over his shoulder; she loved the huge sleek kitchen of glass and steel – he never cooked but his chef was amazing; she loved the painting of the angel on his bedroom wall; she loved the wicker mannequin in *her* room and the little stone gargoyles on the roof; she loved the mirrored chest of drawers – the square bath in black ceramic – the model Dalek in the corridor – his bull's eye clock – the silver-grey fur throw on her enormous four-poster – and let's not even talk about the garden and the pool and the pagoda and the gym and the sauna and the steam room and the underground garage. Millions and millions of dollars had been lavished on this house to make it the perfect sanctuary and she wanted to cry with relief.

Secretly, she wanted to marry him and be rescued for ever, not just for a couple of weeks. Of course she'd told him that she would only stay until she found work. If it had to be PR, she'd probably send a résumé to her own mother. Meanwhile, there was now the possibility of earning a quick hundred thousand dollars. *Heat* – *Heat* was, like, a thousand times cooler than *Hello!* – would love to talk about her celebrity friend. But Ethan was private and she didn't want to betray him – or lose him.

He'd given her the run of the place and instructed his staff to be at her disposal, but he was working sixteen-hour days on *Transmission*. She'd barely seen him.

But he'd said that this weekend, they weren't shooting, and he would be all hers. 'All *yours*,' he'd said, and she'd felt

377

jittery with excitement. Maybe he'd whisk her off to the Malibu beach house where they would spend a romantic evening. Oh God, but there was a small hitch – *two* small hitches. Putting the baby to bed could take half the night. Emily could never resist the lure of the Two-Hour Late-Afternoon Nap. However, once the Two-Hour Late-Afternoon Nap was complete, baby Molly considered half the night's sleep done, and presumed she would be vigorously entertained until midnight. The truth was, minding a baby and a six-year-old was drudgery. Emily was pasty with exhaustion, shocked that Nanny had chosen this for a job. Working on a North Sea oil rig was less strenuous.

And Ethan's staff were morons. They were programmed to cater for the needs of a young, single male god. Had Molly been a puppy she would have been fussed over, fought over, her every requirement met, but human babies were unheard of in these parts, viewed as disgusting, unpredictable, unfathomable pests.

When Emily asked Cook, as Ethan had suggested, to prepare lunch for Baby, Cook had presented a lobster bisque followed by rare steak. Lurch's assistant had, again on Ethan's suggestion, purchased a few toys for Baby, one of which was a computer game, the other a tricycle. Emily looked around to see her child of sixteen months balancing unsupported on the tricycle on the granite patio while Lurch's assistant checked her hair for split ends.

Doors and windows were left open; the pools and the hot tub were all ungated so as not to spoil the *look*. Emily was used to issuing orders and being obeyed. It was a nasty feeling *not* to feel entitled, not to trust. Once, she wouldn't have noticed or cared – Quintin apart, she had always considered staff to be robots. Now, she was humbled, paranoid, her confidence shaky; the sullen glance, the slight flair of nostrils: no slight was missed. So Emily rose at six thirty to make the children's breakfast in case Cook saw fit to stir brandy into their porridge, then the chauffeur drove George to school in the black four-by-four, with Emily and Molly in the back, Molly in her regulation child seat. The chauffeur had reacted to the introduction of the child seat (let alone the child) as if it were a goat. Ethan's staff did her laundry, made their beds, cleaned their rooms, took her to where she needed to go, fed her, shopped for her, provided her with towels for the pool. They obeyed Ethan's orders with precision. But there was an air of snootiness, an aura of 'Who are *you*?' She didn't like to let Baby Molly out of her sight. It was a selfless act as she wasn't even sure that Baby Molly *liked* her. She suspected that Baby Molly was irritated, being in the hands of an amateur.

Even if Ethan *was* 'all hers' at the weekend, there might be zero opportunity to be *his*. George could be distracted with a small bowl of M&M's and *El Cid*. But Molly was a tougher call. The Two-Hour Nap was not guaranteed. At the sleeper's discretion, it could emerge without warning as a Ten-Minute Power Nap.

Also, Emily needed about a day to become a goddess. Ethan had a fearsome back catalogue of girlfriends: every one had topped the *FHM* '100 Sexiest Women in the World' list. Right now Emily looked a total hag by Isle of Dogs standards, let alone Sexiest Women in the World standards. What Emily actually required was that both children be removed from the premises for twenty-four hours. She didn't want this to be a quick bang. She wanted to start a relationship. She wanted to provide George and Molly with stability and a *father*.

Suddenly, after six years of remote parenting, Emily was at the coal face and she was flabbergasted. Who could know that having kids would change a person's fabulous, comfortable privileged life to an out of control mess?

Well.

She mustn't panic. It was going to work out. She just had to figure *how*.

MALIBU, THAT WEEKEND

George

You could wear shorts in LA. They called trousers *pants*! He could swim underwater now and fetch hoops from the bottom of the pool, and his teacher would shout, 'Good job!' and give him a high-five.

He liked Ethan's pool but he didn't like his house. He got lost a lot and there were too many people. He preferred when it was just him and Molly and Mummy and Nanny in the flat. When they were in Ethan's house, Mummy was always shouting, 'Don't touch that!'

He liked Ethan though. Ethan was cool. He was a super-hero. He was on TV. He was famous. He was on his mobile a lot and everyone had to shush. They'd gone to the zoo that morning, and Ethan had to go in disguise. Ethan had his soldier with him, who used to be in the SAS, but when George asked him 'Have you killed anyone?' he ruffled his hair and didn't answer.

And people still stared. And some of them came up and said, 'I *loved* you in *Hit Point*,' and he'd say 'Thank you' and his friend Mark would say 'Thank you,' and nod, and the SAS guy would nod too, and then the people would go away.

There was a lot of walking at the zoo, but he liked the tigers. And the most disgusting thing was, the monkey was eating *pooh*!

He got to ride on Ethan's shoulders, and Molly went in the buggy. Mummy looked very beautiful today, like a princess. He liked Molly now. She was a lovely chubby baby and he was her big brother. He was a very kind big brother. He was good with babies. He always noticed if she put something in her mouth. She put everything in her mouth, like a coin, but it was dangerous because she could choke. He wasn't allowed to pick her up. Mummy said, 'Children don't pick up children.'

Now they were at Ethan's other house on the beach and that had a pool with a slide. Ethan said that in the mornings you could see the dolphins playing. He liked dolphins but he preferred sharks.

On the way home from the zoo, Mark had got him a Krabby Patty from Fatburger. Mark was Ethan's servant, not like a mummy, a *real* servant. Molly was too little for a Krabby Patty, so Mummy had made her macaroni cheese (gross) and Ethan had helped. Mummy was a rubbish cook and Ethan didn't know how to cook and it took them a thousand years to make the macaroni cheese and Molly was screaming. It really hurt his ears.

But now she was eating it. He couldn't watch Molly eating because it made him feel sick, and once he had actually *been* sick. Mummy had been very cross.

Mummy was being as good as gold. *And* silver. She was laughing a lot and Ethan was making her laugh. They were pleased that Molly liked the macaroni cheese. He liked it when Mummy was happy. That was his best day. Mummy had promised that after lunch they would all go on the beach, and George could go surfing with Ethan, and she would help Molly to paddle, and they could all build sandcastles. It was cool that Ethan had his own beach. George wondered if he'd bought the sea, too, or just the beach.

'Mummy,' he said. 'Can you put on your swimming costume now? I think Molly's finished her lunch. She's throwing it all on the floor.'

Mummy laughed, when normally she'd be cross. She was *kissing* Ethan, and they were hugging. She was all pink in the face. He didn't mind. She didn't kiss Daddy any more – she wasn't his friend. Daddy was a stupid fuck, although we don't say fuck, we say bother. Daddy was a stupid bother. He did miss Daddy but Mummy was more fun.

'OK,' said Mummy. 'If Ethan thinks it's OK. If he's not too busy.'

Ethan smiled. 'Let's do it, buddy.'

He loved Mummy. She was the best mummy ever. 'Mummy, thank you *so* much. I love you to the sky!'

'I love you too, darling. Later, when we come back from the beach, you can watch a film, while Molly has her nap. How does that sound?'

'Oh, great! Can it be *Spiderman*? Are you in *Spiderman*, Ethan?'

'I passed on it, buddy.'

'Darling, let's get some sun block on you, and we'll have to smother Molly. Um, Ethan, sorry. It might take a few moments to get ready.'

'No worries. Is there anything Mark can do to help?'

'Oh, er . . .'

'Mark!'

'Hello.'

'Mark, can you hold the baby while Emily gets ready. We're going to the beach.'

'Oh! Are you sure you know how to . . . She's very strong. She wriggles, you'll need to get a good grip. Jig her a bit. Not too much. OK. Are you sure you've got her? OK. I won't be a second. Thank you!'

Mark looked cross. He was a rubbish servant. Now Mummy was out of the room finding their stuff for the beach, Ethan was laughing at Mark holding Molly. Mark wasn't good with babies.

'Don't you like babies, Mark?'

'Of course I like babies, George! I just happen to be wearing a very expensive T-shirt. I don't want her to – *shit*.'

'That's sick. Nanny says you can get it off with a baby wipe. Shall I find you a wipe?'

'Yes.'

George found Mark a wipe. 'There you go. What do you say?'

Mark said thank you, but in a cross way so it didn't count.

George smiled at Ethan. 'How good have I been?'

'Very good, George.'

'May I have a treat?'

'You're going surfing with *me*, buddy. That's the biggest treat in the world!'

'I mean a *chocolate* treat.'

'Later, buddy, OK? Here's your mom.'

The sand was boiling hot, too hot to walk on in bare feet. Malibu was nicer than Santa Monica beach. It was closer. You didn't get stuck on the 10 when you really needed to do a wee. Mark came with them to carry all the stuff, but then he went back in the house. George was pleased. Mark didn't like him. He knew when grown-ups didn't like him and Mark didn't. That was OK. Mark wasn't cool. He lived with Ethan in the guesthouse.

George was really excited to go in the water. Molly kept ripping off her hat. *He* had a baseball cap. The Green Bay Packers. He liked wearing it. Mummy took off her little shorts and top and she had a bikini underneath. The water wasn't that warm but it was fine. He didn't need his goggles. He jumped on the surfboard, lying flat, like Ethan, and paddled out. He looked back at the beach and waved to Mummy, but she was giving Molly her bottle and didn't see him. It was deep, now, but Ethan was right there.

He winked at George. 'Don't you worry, big man,' he said. 'I'll take care of you. So are we going to catch a wave, or what?'

George grinned. 'We're going to catch a wave!'

'All right!'

He was *quite* good at surfing but not as good as Harrison and Jesse in his class. They'd had more practice. Ethan was *brilliant*. We all have different talents, said Miss Gilmore, but Ethan was good at everything.

It was the best feeling when you rode the wave, but he hated wiping out and swallowing sea water. It made his nose burn, but you couldn't cry.

'Put your right foot there, bud, you got to balance, you got to *feel* it – it's like riding a bike.'

Awesome!

'Mummy! Mummy, did you see me?' He ran up the beach.

'Darling, you were brilliant! And you weren't bad either.'

'Mummy! Don't be rude! Ethan is a really brilliant surfer!'

'I was joking, darling. I was playing with him.' Mummy wrinkled her nose. 'I need to go back in the house for a second. She needs her nappy changed and I forgot the wipes.'

'Sweetie, don't worry about it. I'll get Mark on the radio. He can do it.'

'Mark can't change Molly's nappy!' Mummy burst out laughing. 'He'll die!'

Ethan laughed too. 'Sometimes,' he said, 'Mark gets a bit *LA*. It's good to remind him that he's a human being, like the rest of us.'

'Well,' said Mummy. 'Except *you*.'

They both laughed. Grown-ups were always laughing at unfunny jokes.

'Go on,' said Ethan. 'I dare you. Ask Mark to take Molly back to the house and change her nappy.'

'I can't! It wouldn't be fair.'

'Go *on*.'

Mummy didn't look pleased. But then she said, 'OK.'

She said 'OK' the same way she said it when George asked for ice cream for dessert *and* a biscuit *and* a lollipop, all together.

Mark ran out on to the sand as soon as Ethan called him on the walkie-talkie, and he didn't look pleased. But he nodded at all of Mummy's instructions. Ethan winked at George, but George could only wink if he held the other eye open.

'You have to clean in all the creases,' said George. 'And watch out for pooh on your hands.' George was *very* helpful.

Then Mummy and Ethan sat on the sand, and Mummy said why didn't George dig a hole?

He would have liked to do more surfing, but he liked digging holes so it was OK.

Mummy kept looking back at the house. And then Ethan kissed her, and she stopped looking. They were boyfriend and girlfriend. George had *two* new girlfriends: Amber and Lauren Rosenheim.

It was quite hard work, even with his spade. It was boiling, and he kept being thirsty, even though he drank lots of water. The sun got in his eyes unless he pulled the cap right down, like Ethan did. He didn't like wearing sunglasses, they got in the way.

'Darling!' said Mummy, and Ethan smiled in a cross way. 'Darling, why don't you go and check that Mark is all right with Molly? Please?'

'OK,' said George, sighing. 'I feel like your servant!'

'Thank you,' said Mummy.

George ran up to the house. It didn't look like a long way but it was. He used the secret way in that no one knew about, from the garden. It was spooky, being in there without Mummy. He couldn't hear any noise. Then he heard Molly make a baby squeak upstairs. He ran up. There was a sound of water running.

'Mark?'

'Yes, what is it? My hands are covered in crap. I'm disinfecting.'

'Where's Molly?'

'I've shut her in the bedroom.'

'Is she asleep?'

'I wish.'

'She doesn't like being by herself. She always cries and then you have to cheer her up by pretending to be a monkey. You go, "Ooh ooh ooh!"'

'Well, *I* don't hear anything. I'm sure she'll be fine for *one minute.*'

'Which bedroom is she in? Mummy says I have to check.'

'Jesus Christ. Fourth door on the right.'

George ran down the corridor. He was scared, more scared than he'd been watching *Star Wars*.

He opened the door slowly, in case Molly was right there. She wasn't.

'Molly! Molly!'

'*Ga!*' she always said, which was her way of saying 'George'.

But she didn't say *Ga* and George saw the curtains puffing in the breeze. He ran across the room. The doors to the balcony were open and so was the screen. 'Molly?' he shouted. 'Molly?'

Then he saw her, her fat little nappied bottom squeezing through the balcony bars, and he screamed. She disappeared and there was only air. He stopped screaming and a terrible noise filled his ears. He wanted to run down the stairs but his legs were jelly and he could only go slowly, one stair at a time.

'Mummy!' he screamed, and then she was there, screaming too.

'Where is she? Where is she?'

'She fell,' he said. 'She was trying to be a bird but it didn't work.'

He felt sick and ill. Molly would be dead and she would never see Mummy again.

'Oh my God, I can hear her.' Mummy ran outside.

Ethan was there, shouting 'Mark! Mark!'

George ran after Mummy. There was no one to give him a hug. She was crying and gasping as if she couldn't breathe and Molly was in her arms, all bloody, screeching in a fast, scary way, and there was blood on Mummy too.

Mark was there. *Stupid* idiot Mark, it was his fault. 'Oh, good God, I didn't know it was open. Is she all right? Thank God she fell on the grass. Should I get the arnica?'

'Call a fucking ambulance, you fucking fuck, she could have brain damage! Oh my God, what if she – Oh baby, oh baby, Mummy got you, it's OK, it's OK – oh God, why did I let him – get *off* me, Ethan. Don't just stand there, you bastard, call an ambulance!'

George was a big brave boy but sometimes you're allowed and he started to cry.

LOS ANGELES, THREE DAYS LATER

Emily

She was frozen. She couldn't cry. She kept playing the scenario back in her head, over and over, as if, the thousandth time, it might end differently. She was an unfit mother. Her worst fear had come true. She had failed to keep her babies safe. She had refused all medication. And yet she felt as if she were in a fog. She couldn't connect with reality, as if it were too unbearable for her conscious mind to allow it. Ethan had been useless, totally unlike his character in *Sick Day*, and it had shocked her. She had expected him to snap to the rescue, be the hero, walk the talk, and yet he'd seemed curiously relaxed, or maybe it was that she was so frantic that a normal human pace was far too slow. She wanted Molly to be seen by doctors *that second*; she wanted her *teleported* to the hospital.

She'd dialled 911, even though she couldn't catch her breath to speak. Finally, she'd puffed it out: my baby, fallen out of window. She couldn't believe she was forming those words; that it wasn't some hideous nightmare. She'd given the address.

The ambulance was as slow as a snail, or at least it felt like it. LAPD were faster. When she realized she wasn't going to be allowed to go with Molly to the hospital, she'd collapsed.

She'd been so naive. It was an accident, but they'd roped off the house as if it were a crime scene. The place was swarming with officers who addressed the guy in charge as 'detective'.

The paparazzi had gathered like vultures round a corpse.

People say dreadful things when they're in shock, but had Lurch *really* said to her, 'This is terrible for Ethan, I hope you realize'?

She hadn't been prepared for the questions, the endless interrogation. The guy was friendly but he didn't let up. Where had she been? Why wasn't she with the Subject? Who had left the balcony door open? Was she having marital problems? Did she think this was an accident? Did she know of anyone who would want to hurt the Subject? 'Molly!' she wanted to shout. 'Molly!'

All the while, she'd been desperate to get to the hospital. 'I want to see Molly,' she screamed. 'I want to see her *now*, she needs me, please.'

In England they would have given you a cup of tea for shock. Here, a can of Coke was put in front of her, as if she were a child. She was shivering uncontrollably. She couldn't touch it.

George, who was frightened out of his wits, had been shepherded into another room by a policewoman.

'Mummy!' he'd wailed, as he was taken off. She couldn't believe that they were going to interrogate a six-year-old.

She felt as if she might actually puke when she thought of the look on George's face. Last year, Nanny had been ill, and George had bounced into her bedroom at 5 a.m. – this after Molly had been awake on and off all night with a cold. 'Go back to bed,' Emily had hissed. He'd shaken his head. 'I'll get a man to come and take you away.' He'd scurried back to bed and she was at once ashamed and relieved: she was a terrible mother but one who would now get some sleep.

Now she would have stayed awake for the rest of her life if it meant that George and Molly could be back safely with her.

And then it had got worse. Bet it was something that idiot

Lurch had said in his statement, but suddenly DCFS were being notified – whoever the fuck *they* were. Department of Children and Family Services, it had turned out.

The DCFS woman was cold and formal. Like the detective, she punctuated her interview with long empty pauses and kept *staring* at Emily, making Emily feel she had said something incriminating. She felt dull and flat and empty and so desperate with agony, her answers were short and hostile. What did her relationship with Timmy and her parents and her sister have to do with this shit?

Perhaps, had she looked older, not quite so sun-kissed, had she not been wearing skimpy shorts over a bikini, had she sobbed and howled instead of being stiff with grief, it might have gone differently.

Her fingerprints had been taken by a guy with SID printed on his jacket. Another SID took photographs. It occurred to her that he could sell them to the *Enquirer* for a million bucks. A great rage welled up in her. 'Why are you doing this to *me*? You should be speaking to Mark. *He* was the one who left her. She was in *his* care at the time.'

It sounded like an excuse. He was at fault, but *she* was to blame. She was the mother. Then someone had said the words 'Child Abuse Unit'. It hit her like a blow to the head. They suspected that she had hurt Molly on purpose and there was a chance that her children would be taken away.

She had to fight, but her head was so groggy. Panic meant she couldn't find the words. They'd asked for her British social security number and she realized that they were going to check with the Metropolitan Police to see if there had been any prior 'incidents'.

She had been desperate. Surely that she was a friend of Ethan Summers counted for something? This was La-La Land and, in celebrity terms, he was the jewel in the crown. *His* word was sacred, even if hers was not. 'Ask Ethan,' she'd croaked, in desperation, 'he'll tell you I'm a good mother.' She hadn't expected the response she'd got.

The two officers had exchanged glances, one saying coolly: 'Mr Summers has given us a statement. Mr Summers was extremely helpful. Mr Summers did all he could to assist.'

Ethan would have told them how she'd made Molly the macaroni cheese, covered her in sun screen, given her a bottle in the shade, played 'Round and round the garden like a teddy bear', kissed the deliciously podgy bit at the back of her fat little neck. If you were an uncaring parent, you didn't do those things. Ethan might have even given them a free mug with *Sick Day* printed on the side of it.

So why didn't they let her go?

Finally, at last, she had been taken to the hospital, the DCFS worker there like a guard beside her in the cop car.

She had lost count of the hours they'd waited. She'd remained in a stupor until a doctor had entered the room and, with a strained expression, murmured in the ear of the DCFS woman. The woman had nodded, then informed Emily that Molly had suffered a broken leg, a broken arm and bruising, but the initial scan had revealed no apparent damage to the brain tissue, or the spine. There was no internal bleeding. She weighed only twenty-five pounds, and she had landed on grass, on her stomach. Those three facts had saved her from severe injury.

Emily had gone pale with relief. She could feel the blood drain from her face and her legs weaken. She'd nodded, silently, unable to find her voice.

They had misread everything.

She hadn't realized what was happening. People were speaking to her, but she gazed at the cold expression on their faces, and their words passed through her.

'Your children are being placed into protective custody pending a further investigation.' Case worker . . . foster home . . . District Attorney . . . court . . . Judge . . . expert witness . . . She couldn't take it in because she was too concerned that they were giving Emily the wrong milk. She hated American powdered milk. Emily had a British brand imported from the

UK. Would they give her *jar* food? She'd never eaten jar food in her life. And George, he was so sensitive, he wouldn't say, but he'd be sick with anxiety. He needed his mummy. He might be too shy to ask if he could use the bathroom.

She was permitted to see Molly briefly. It was so painful to see the tiny arm and leg in plaster, a tube up the tiny nose and know that it was *her* fault, that Emily could actually not stand to look at baby Molly and turned away. She saw the doctor and the DCFS bitch *look* at each other. She'd understood the look: this woman has a heart of stone.

Emily had been so focused on the little details that she'd ignored, or perhaps hadn't wanted to acknowledge, the terrible reality: a man was coming to take George away.

And when Molly was well enough to leave the hospital, she too would be taken, by a stranger, to live with strangers.

Then she had broken out of the trance and become hysterical. She'd lashed out, screaming, scratching, biting, sobbing. They'd handcuffed her. She had the right to appeal against the decision *if* the judge allowed it. It would depend on the evidence. *What* evidence?

'What evidence?' she'd screeched. 'What fucking evidence?'

They'd ignored the question, which is what they did when they didn't wish to give an answer. 'I want a lawyer,' she'd croaked. 'I want my lawyer, now.' She had been in such a state of trauma that, in the land of litigation, she hadn't thought to ask for her lawyer. Now, she asked for everyone: her lawyer, her mother. She wanted Innocence, because Innocence was as tough as old hide and Innocence would not let this happen. Her father – ach, her father was no use.

She wanted Ethan. She wanted his strong arms around her, soothing her, making her feel better, making it all go away. He would make it right. He'd get her babies back. At least she wasn't under arrest . . . *yet*.

She'd rung Lurch's mobile, in a daze.

'I'll send the driver,' he'd said. She'd felt her gut wrench with hatred, just hearing his voice. He was poison. *He* was the one who'd let Molly fall and not so much as a word of apology. She bet it was because he was scared of being sued. If he said 'sorry' he was admitting liability. He was a piece of shit. She'd get Ethan to fire him, and the interview she was going to give to *People* (free of charge) would ensure that Lurch would never work again.

She'd had to turn off her mobile in the hospital. There were missed calls from Innocence, from Claudia. The news was out. Claudia was flying out tomorrow. Innocence was already en route to LA on the jet. Too little too late, was Emily's reflex thought. She found she despised the shock in her mother's voice.

You could have helped me before, Mother, and now look. As for Claudia, half-crying on the phone . . . Emily felt her lip curl. How dare you appropriate *my* grief. As Emily stepped into the bright sunlight (normally she revelled in the heat but now it felt stifling and oppressive) a great mob of photographers and TV cameras surged towards her – 'Emily, Emily!' – with their horrible familiarity, as if they were her *friends*. She battled through them, trying not to cry with fear, as they jostled, sneered, taunted her to provoke the perfect sound bite, the five-hundred-thousand-dollar cover shot. She shook her head, covered her ears. Ethan's driver waited, impassive, by the side of the Bentley. He made no attempt to help. As she got to the car, gasping and trembling, he held open the door as if nothing were amiss.

The driver switched on the radio, and as the music played Emily curled into a ball, rocking silently on the back seat, her mouth open in a silent howl, all the way to the Hollywood Hills.

'Ethan!' she cried, rushing past the housekeeper. 'Ethan! Ethan!'

He appeared at the top of the stairs, freshly shaven, immaculate in a black T-shirt and khaki shorts. 'Ethan, oh God, you have to help me, they've taken my babies, they'll be so frightened, they need me, we need to get them back, today, *now*, please, I know they'll listen to you . . .' She sank to the floor in a heap and covered her face.

She expected him to exclaim in horrified disbelief, to race down the stairs, to stroke her hair, but there was nothing. He didn't speak. She looked up, and he hadn't moved.

'Come upstairs, Emily,' he said.

Slowly, she stood, and slowly, she walked up the stairs, with legs like lead. Her heart pounded. He looked so serious. Oh God, had he already tried to help? Was it bad news?

He nodded as she reached him, but when she went to hug him, he *flinched*.

She jumped back.

'Please. Come into my study.'

She felt shaken, confused. 'This is terrible for Ethan,' Lurch had said.

'I'm sorry, Ethan,' she blurted. Why was *she* apologizing to *him*, when *her* baby had fallen out of *his* window? 'I hope the press will leave you alone. I . . . I'll tell them it wasn't your fault.'

She expected him to tell her not to be ridiculous but he said nothing, just motioned for her to sit down on the red straight-backed chair. It was weird. She sat, and now the tears streamed down her face.

Ethan sat behind his desk and slung his feet on top of it. He nodded to a box of tissues. 'Emily,' he said. 'Congratulations. Wipe your nose.'

She felt her throat catch. Was he being sarcastic? '*Congratulations?* My children are in *care*.' She didn't quite dare add 'because of you', but the thought hung in the air.

He smiled. 'Because of me?'

She looked at her feet. Her breath was in her throat, in a hard lump.

He laughed, and a chill ran through her. Goose pimples prickled on her arms.

'You can say it, Emily. It is my fault that your little Molly and George are in care, in the hands of God knows who, having God knows what done to them, and you, their mother, helpless to protect or save them. What a bugger. Your family has had its fair share of bad luck. I say *fair*, because, sweetie, it is fair.'

She swallowed. What was this? It was . . . vile. Was he rehearsing for a part? 'Why are you saying these . . . disgusting things? What do you mean?' she whispered.

He grinned. 'Emily, I say congratulations because *you* can be the first to know. Oh, this is so exciting! Bear with me one sec!' He held up a finger. Pressed an intercom. 'Mrs Klout? Tea for two, please, and as it's a special occasion, why don't we break out a couple of KitKats? Smashing!'

She stared at him. Who was this person? He wasn't *Ethan*. He was like someone horrible pretending to be Ethan. This very morning, at four a.m., he had crept into her room and she had given him *head*. She had been half in love with this person. But . . . she had to get out.

She jumped as Ethan rapped sharply on the desk. 'PAY ATTENTION, BITCH! *Thank* you.' He smiled. He was mad. He was fucking nuts. This psychopath, he must have kidnapped the real Ethan and had radical plastic surgery or something. This was LA.

'What . . .' she croaked, '. . . what have you done with Ethan?'

He stared at her and burst out laughing. 'Oh, that's sweet! That's so cute! Sweetie, I *am* Ethan. Ethan is *me*. But, get this, I am an *actor*! But no, no, fair question. All right, how's this: Ethan Summers is the name on my Equity card, I have been Nathan Williams, and Nathan Alexander is my current name by deed poll – after my dear mother, God rest her soul – but my original name – perhaps it will ring a little bell? – was Nathan *Kent*.'

Kent? 'But that's . . .'

'*Yes*, Emily. It *is*. It is *your* father's name. *Clink!* Penny dropped? Talk about slow. Ah, thank you, Mrs Klout. The

Royal Worcester and the silver teapot. Marvellous. And my cotton gloves – excellent. I hate to see a print on silver, Emily, it tarnishes within the hour. Perfect. This really is the only way to drink tea. Your non-fat gluten-free orange blossom cookies too – you spoil me!

'Now, Emily. Let me tell you a story. A long time ago, your father adopted a little girl. Darling, perfect Claudia, oh, such a precious child. But Felicia, his wife, stupid bitch, too stupid to stay alive – sugar, Emily? – wanted a little boy to make the family complete. *Et voici!*'

She stared at him, this madman, unbelieving.

'Me, you fucking moron! *Me!* And then, when that stupid Felicia went and died, Jack couldn't hack it! Loathed me, apparently. *Me* – I mean, look at me! But no, not good enough for Jack. *Jack* took me back to the fucking shop! Wanted his money back! And do you know what happened to that poor little boy?'

Emily shook her head. She bit her lip to stop a whimper. The truth was, until now she had forgotten his existence. He had come and gone before she was even born. He was a vague memory, a snatch of overheard gossip.

Ethan laughed – a horrible sound. 'Oh, *everything*. Sex, violence, you name it! Pretty much everything that'll happen to *your* two, I should think. That George is a cute kid – he'll be someone's bitch before he turns seven.'

She jumped up. 'Stop it. Shut up! I'm sorry – I'm sorry for what my father did. Look, he's a crap father to all of us, not just you.'

'No,' he snarled. '*You* shut up. I haven't finished. I decided that it wasn't fair for Jack Kent to ruin my life. I have a finely attuned sense of what is fair, Emily. I decided that I would ruin *his* life. Of course' – he smiled – 'I have Mark to thank. He's been super helpful. He was my counsellor, back in the day. He was the one who left out my case notes for me to read; he allowed me to discover who was responsible for my shit life. Mark made me see that I didn't have to suffer, that I could make something of myself – that I deserved to be happy. And, now – ooh, you must try one of these cookies . . . *GO ON* – now I am so close to achieving my goal of destroying the Kent dynasty, making every one of you suffer as I suffered, I *am* happy.'

Emily tried to swallow a piece of biscuit. It seemed to have sucked all the moisture from her mouth. 'You're mad.'

'That old chestnut! No, Emily. Don't get mad, get even. I'm getting even. And the hilarious part of it is, anyone could have done this. Your family made it easy. You brought it upon yourselves. I just had to tweak fate a little.'

Was he going to kill her? She had to escape. Would Mrs Klout help? She should try to keep him talking.

'W . . . What do you mean?'

'I'm glad you ask! The hardest part of it has been not being able to tell. You know when you do something so brilliant you're just aching to share? Ooh, I just can't wait to tell you! So, here it is. Jack digs his own grave by marrying a gold-digger and screwing his dear friends and colleagues out of their money. Such a *mensch*! Meanwhile, Mark is kind enough to trace my real mother, silly bitch, and she is kind enough to provide me with a fine education and a nice inheritance.'

'She . . . died?'

'I killed her. Made it look like an accident. Mourned until probate was granted, buggered off to the Land of the Free. Hang on. I've got her eyeballs somewhere. Pickled. MAAAARK!'

Oh, Jesus. 'It's OK. I . . . believe you. Please . . . go on.'

'So, Mother paid for me to attend one of those exclusive schools with an excellent drama department – my King Lear was a *sensation*, the talent scouts just would not leave me be. I came over here. I waited tables for two weeks before my agent got me an audition. That was all it took. I only had to sleep with one person – the writer – ha! Only kidding. An industry joke, sweetie, don't worry about it.

'Mark came with me, Mary's little lamb. So I had a bit of

money, and now I had more. I had *power*. But the truth is, Emily, I'm no Lex Luther, I'm not claiming genius. An ape could have done it.

'Your family – you only have yourselves to thank. Take Claudia. After Mark left the file open for me, I wrote to Claudia, claiming to be a girl who'd met her at a party. Poor, pathetic Claudia was so desperate for a chum, she believed me. Mark gathered a little information on her, and got a PI to trace her parents. Took about three days. She was looking for a job, I directed her to journalism, to the paper where her blood father worked. The rest she did herself. I knew she'd fall for him – I do my research, Emily, because, as you now know, you must never trust to luck!

'Now here is the clever bit. It's proven, Emily, that blood relatives separated by adoption often find each other sexually attractive when reunited. My own mother . . . fucking gross. But I knew that dear Claudia would be different. Thanks to Jack being so goddamn useless, she was gagging for a father figure. She was desperate! All I did was prompt their meeting. I didn't force them to fall in love.'

She had to escape. But . . . she had to know. 'What else?'

'The bomb – yes, guilty as charged! Again, if your mother had been just that little bit kinder to her poor brother Gerry, he would have refused to help out. He would have said, "How *dare* you offer me three million quid and threaten my children, I wouldn't hurt my sister for all the money in the world." But you know what? He jumped at the chance, the old creep. Because she'd dropped him, just as Jack dropped me. *Family!* You people, you don't see the importance of family! Family is everything, love is all, but to you, it's nothing. You're obsessed with money, the lot of you. It's disgusting.'

'What about . . . ?'

'Timmy! Screaming iron! Girl, you need your gaydar tuned! But' – Ethan shook his head – 'money, money, money! You had to have that castle, didn't you? If you hadn't married Tim, *I* couldn't have led him astray. Well, not me personally,

I prefer snatch. But Mark has connections within the community. And someone's going to do it if the money's right. I paid for his luxury stay in Barbuda – oh, it's a gorgeous place, so romantic. Do you really think that tight arse the Earl would shell out after his son had married *you*? Again, Emily, you people don't pay enough attention to matters of the heart. People have feelings, emotions; they rarely act out of character. Where's your empathy, Emily? The Grand Old Duke of York: isn't that what the papers call him? Can't get enough dick!'

Very slowly, Emily looked around the study for a weapon. 'And my mother going to prison?' she said, as a prompt. The more he talked, the less he'd notice what she was up to.

'Ha! Pure luck! But let's face it, she's so crook – she was well overdue for a stay inside. But, again, serendipity! If she and Jack didn't hate each other's guts, I couldn't have pinned it on her. Still, she got out. She can thank her brother for that. His mouth was just too big. He had to go.'

Emily made all the right noises. 'Mm . . . Oh, yes . . . Ha ha . . . Definitely . . .' Maybe there would be a paperweight. No. No one except Timmy and small children used paper. The gold Buddha? The Oscar. *That* would be serendipity. To brain him with his Oscar. The Oscar was heavy, but the gold Buddha looked heavier. She wondered if she had a chance of overpowering him. He practised Brazilian Jiu-jitsu, or, as he called it, BJJ. Oh, she'd said. That sounds similar to what I practise! She shuddered. The thought of having gone down on this . . . madman . . . it turned her stomach.

'Emily, I hope you're listening. This concerns you.'

'Yes,' she said. She forced herself to stare into his eyes. They were beautiful.

'You're not going to get your children back.'

With a shriek of primal rage, she leaped at him across the desk, clawing at his face. He punched her once, on the nose. The pain was excruciating; she could barely see; the warm blood ran into her mouth, tasting of metal. She tried to pull at his hair, baring her teeth to bite. This time, he hurled her to the floor. Her head struck the stone with a great crack and an agonizing white-hot pain shot through her. She tried to speak, reach out, but she couldn't. Her vision was fading. She saw his handsome face, now blurred, in the distance, she saw him pull off his white cotton gloves with his teeth, and spit them – 'pah, *pah*' – on to the floor. She heard him whisper, 'Goodnight, sweet Emily, and flights of angels sing thee to thy rest,' and then, though she tried so hard to resist, the darkness came.

LOS ANGELES, SUNDAY

Claudia

'Claudia? Claudia? Is this Claudia?' The voice sounded panicked, almost hysterical, and vaguely familiar.

'Yes. This is Claudia. Who is this?'

'Claudia, you don't know me. I'm a friend of your sister. My name's Ethan. I'm so sorry. I have bad news.'

Ethan *Summers*. He of the box-office smashes and the non-childproof beach villa.

'I know about the children,' she said, hoping her voice sounded crisp. 'I'm at LAX. I'm in a queue. Tell Emily I'm taking a cab to the Hills. I'll call her from a landline as soon as I get there. Goodbye, *Ethan*.'

She cut off. She was a journalist; she was not going to ooh and ah over him because he was prominent in the entertainment business. She interviewed famous people month after month, and some were nice and some were not. Some had talent, some were lucky. Mostly they were like normal people, except with more money and bigger heads. She had no doubt that Ethan's head was the size of a pumpkin.

The news about George and Molly being taken into care had come out of nowhere. At first she'd thought it was some terrible mistake, but Sky News couldn't report on anything else. Of course, this story had it all: love, tragedy, violence, celebrity, a beautiful young mother – it was ratings gold. She'd booked her flight – Sunday morning was the earliest available. It hadn't occurred to her to call her father. Innocence had called *her* – she was on a business trip and tropical storms had delayed her flight. Tell Emily she'd be there the instant the weather permitted. Claudia had called Emily but she had never picked up. Claudia shuddered. The thought of those two gorgeous children being snatched from their mother . . . it was inhumane. She wanted to cry.

If they weren't returned to Emily within the next twenty-four hours – no, the next twelve hours – Claudia would embark on an international publicity campaign to have them returned. *Vanity Fair*, *Sunday Times Style*, *UK Vogue* would allow her this: she would write the first exposé of life as the daughter of Jack Kent and Miss Innocence Ashford. She would be brutally honest about what Emily had been, but also about who she was, and how she had changed on becoming a mother. Truly, those children were the blessings of her existence. They had been her focus, and her joy.

Admittedly, Emily had floundered at first, but she had grown to love them, and her confidence in herself as a parent had also grown. When Claudia saw her with her son and daughter, she often had to run upstairs to a bathroom to have a good bawl. It was a beautiful thing, strangely painful, to see the tenderness between them. Emily had no idea that she was such a natural, and now, because of this one terrible slip – it was so frightening that one slip was all it took to nearly kill a child – she would be forever punished; an unfit parent.

Emily was one of the few notorious people in the world whose reputation was actually a lot worse than the reality. Claudia would change the public perception and the social services would be forced to reconsider the case. Not because they cared, but because no one likes to be *hated*.

And, of course, the main point of her piece – or pieces, for she would write for anyone and everyone – would be that it was curious that *Ethan* had escaped blame. Not one paper or TV station had suggested that *he* might be culpable. She noticed that while reporters mentioned that the accident had occurred at a property 'owned' by the superstar, they also took pains to note that 'Ethan Summers was not present', when, according to *Claudia*'s sources, he was a few hundred yards from the house. Also, the journalists became vague when it came down to *who* had actually left the baby alone. 'The child's mother, Emily Kent, daughter of the disgraced billionaire, was lying on the beach when the accident happened,' according to one female newsreader with a severe bob and judgemental eyebrows. 'Ms Kent had asked an employee at the beach house, who was unqualified in child care, to change the baby's diaper inside the house. She was aware that the man had no official training.'

Claudia felt her face grow hot with rage. It was disgusting. Emily would never have risked Molly's safety – it was bizarre that she'd allowed this person to take the baby. Claudia wanted this employee interviewed – by the police, or herself. No doubt Ethan had the scarier lawyers.

Her lip curled. If her father had thought to give his younger daughter the full backing of his legal team, perhaps *Emily*'s name would have been handled with the same degree of care and reverence that the media had accorded Mr Summers.

Surely he was liable in some way. She'd even spoken to her mother's solicitors on Madison. There had been a case in California where a landlord was deemed liable for a toddler's injuries, sustained after falling from a window because: 'traditional tort principles imposed upon a landlord a duty to exercise due care for the residents' safety in those areas under the landlord's control.'

But then, oh God, he was Emily's new best friend. Emily's

famous new best friend. Emily wouldn't want to sue him. Suing Ethan Summers (and you might as well sue God) would not get Emily her children back.

If Claudia wanted to help, she'd have to focus on Emily. As it was, the media didn't fear Emily. She was young, naive; she was an easy target. She was indeed that poor little rich girl. The whole world could see that her parents were too wrapped up in their own lives to support her.

Well, her *sister* wasn't. Emily disliked her, she knew that. But she had never forgotten that one time when Emily had realized that her fiancé Martin was actually her father. Emily had been a saint. She had held Claudia up when Claudia could barely stand. Claudia knew that Emily loved her, even if Emily didn't. And Claudia loved Emily. She felt like a small flickering wax candle next to the bright, crackling, sparkling, fizzing firework that was her sister. She loved her passion and her spirit and her sharp wit, and it would be amazing if she, Claudia, could actually *do* something *for* Emily. If she could save those beloved children, return them to their mother, then she would die happy, knowing that she had accomplished one thing that actually mattered.

Her mobile rang again. 'Hello?'

'Claudia, it's Ethan again. I'm so sorry to trouble you but – it's not the children. It's Emily.'

Claudia felt a cold hand squeeze her heart. 'What about Emily?'

There was a stifled sob, then Ethan blurted, 'She's *dead*. She . . . killed herself. She . . . must have thrown herself over the banisters. My housekeeper found her. She was just . . . Oh God. I'm so sorry. I guess . . . the grief . . . those poor kids . . . those poor kids . . .'

People in the queue were turning to stare at Claudia. 'Are you OK?' She wasn't aware of having made a sound, but now she clung to a stranger. 'My sister,' she gasped. 'My sister . . . she's *twenty-three*.'

An official rushed her to the front of the queue; another

woman pressed her mobile phone into her hand. Someone else brought her hand luggage. 'Do you need medical assistance?' A bottle of ice water was put to her lips. In a daze she handed the customs official her passport. 'Are you sure you're OK, ma'am?'

She was crying now, howling, in the middle of LAX. It was a mistake – he must have got it wrong – that much vitality – it didn't just *go*. She fumbled with her mobile. The last number was withheld. When it rang again, she put it to her ear with a shaking hand.

'You're wrong, you're wrong,' she shouted. 'It can't be true – it's a mistake, she can't be. She wouldn't leave the children – she wouldn't do it. Please, check again, she's just unconscious.'

'It's been certified by a doctor,' Ethan whispered, his voice cracking. 'I can't believe it either. She was my great friend.'

Claudia screamed, 'You knew her a couple of weeks. She was my *sister*! Oh my God, Emily. Please don't go, oh please.'

'Claudia. I'm sending a car.'

'My mother – she doesn't know yet. My parents. I need to go to the Hills.'

'My driver will take you wherever you want.'

'W . . . where is she? I want to see her.'

'She's at the Cedars-Sinai Medical Center. I've spoken to the Chief Medical Officer. Claudia, I'm so desperately sorry.'

'Oh my God, what about her *kids*. George, she was his world. And baby Molly – oh my God.'

'Claudia. Please. It's going to be OK. I'll help you. Whatever I can do to help, I will do it.'

'Thank you,' she stammered. Dazed, red-eyed and disbelieving, she found her suitcase and wandered out to where a thousand grinning people awaited loved ones, shouting and laughing, because they didn't know that Emily Kent was dead and that little George and baby Molly would never see Mummy again. Claudia yelped as a suitcase wheel rammed into the back of her ankle. 'Keep moving, lady!' said a man. Only then did she realize she was standing still. She couldn't move. The world should stop turning. How dare it spin so blithely and merrily, so blue and green – it should be *black*, a cold, still, black sphere because Emily was dead and it was the end of the world.

'Claudia Mayer?' A hand briefly touched her shoulder. 'I'm Christian. Mr Ethan Summers sent me to drive you to your destination. I'm so sorry for your loss. Please allow me to take your luggage. Is this all you have?'

She looked up, nodded and permitted herself to be led away to a black SUV with blacked-out windows.

LOS ANGELES, MONDAY

Innocence

They have money, but they have nothing else.

Innocence sat in the hospital morgue and shivered in her sable fur.

All these years later, she could still hear the scorn in the man's voice. She'd pitied him, then. They had money. What else was there? Now she understood. When you had no love, when you had no children safe, warm, happy, *alive*, by your side: you had nothing. She and Jack had wanted Emily to suffer, because they wanted her to be strong, and what doesn't kill you makes you stronger. People were wrong to focus on the 'makes you stronger' aspect of that saying.

They'd wanted her to suffer because she'd enraged them by being a bad daughter, expelled, pregnant, divorced, heaping ever more disgrace on the family – and being bad for *business*.

Money was the root.

She couldn't believe it.

Emily's friend the film star had taken charge. Flanked by bodyguards, he had stood outside his enormous gated mansion and tried to ward off the slavering press: 'I beg you, grant Emily's loved ones their privacy at this difficult time.'

He had even called Jack. He was charming and kind and normally she would have killed for the chance to bond with Ethan Summers, but she was rigid, dumbstruck with grief. She realized she wanted him to go away. He wasn't *family*.

Emily's death – *my baby's death* – was the fault of the system. The police, the social services, the courts had made an example of Emily because she was on some level a 'public figure'. They had taken away her children. They had taken away her reason to live. They had blood on their hands.

Just like that.

Innocence sobbed silently, briefly into her hands. Then she gently stroked Emily's brow, wincing at the black bruising on her cold pale face, and bowed her forehead until it touched her daughter's arm. She was so very cold, in this thin cotton gown, lying on this hard cold metal tray. Innocence wished for a blanket.

'Forgive me,' she whispered. 'I failed you. I failed you as a mother.' She swallowed a sob, and said, through gritted teeth, 'But I swear, Emily, I will not fail you as a grandmother.'

LOS ANGELES, A WEEK LATER

Jack

What happened to the body when the weather was so *hot*?

Shut *up*. But the nasty little voice in his head chattered on, goading him, jabbing at the agony, twisting the grief like a knife turning in his gut, until he wanted to fall on the polished white coffin, prise it open with his fingernails, pull his daughter out of it and shake her alive.

He couldn't believe that this was goodbye. Emily didn't belong in the cold, hard ground, her place was *here*, with her kids. She had a great future ahead of her, decades of love and happiness; she was urgently required above to give the world its sparkle.

'Oh, she would *adore* it here,' one middle-aged woman in dark glasses and an ugly stretched face had drawled. 'She's in great company – Marilyn Monroe is buried here – and *such* a hot spot, bang in the middle of LA's prime real estate with Wilshire Boulevard just around the corner.'

He'd wanted to throttle the stupid old hag. He'd wanted to shout in her hideous surgery-ravaged face: Why aren't *you* dead, you old bitch? It's a travesty that she is young and beautiful and dead, and *you* are still alive and ugly and breathing *her air*. Emily doesn't give a toss about where she is. Marilyn Monroe should be glad to be in *her* company, not the other way round. Who's Marilyn Monroe to me, you stupid cow, I'm burying my *daughter*!

Innocence had reclaimed her long-lost Catholicism and the service had taken place at the Church of the Good Shepherd. Every one of the six hundred seats had been filled, and many more were standing. The young ones always attracted a big crowd. He was in so much mental pain that he could barely move. It was as if Emily's death had accomplished what a coma couldn't: complete physical shutdown.

And yet he had to shake hands; reply coherently to people's condolences; smile at their bungling discomfort. He was an accomplished public speaker, in fact he found it easier to address a thousand people than to address one, but today he couldn't manage it. To be alive when his baby was dead: it was so profoundly wrong. He literally couldn't stomach it, and had been sick, just before the service. Ms Green, a nanny to the end, had passed him a breath mint.

He hated the church. It was too bright, too sunny, the shafts of light filtered prettily through the stained-glass windows, casting a pink and red glow on those sitting nearest. It was more appropriate for a wedding.

He wished for an English church: chill, ancient, quiet in the subdued light of an early spring, Gothic awe-inspiring gloom. Or an orthodox synagogue: the one in Marble Arch was beautiful. Emily should have been buried in lashing rain as the heavens wept. Instead, here, with the sunshine mocking his pain, here, in the land of frivolity, the biggest deal about this funeral was not that he was mourning his 23-year-old girl, but that a movie star was giving a eulogy.

There were so many private security guards, so many ex-military, it was more like an army funeral.

He had fought with Innocence to give the day a little dignity.

He had refused the garish East-End-style 'EMILY' spelt out in flowers. Revolting. He had also refused Casablanca lilies – the scent of death. Innocence had wanted camera crews and he'd been furious – until he'd seen the tears in her eyes and watched her struggle to get the words out: 'Jack,' she'd said through clenched teeth. 'I need the world to take *note*.'

So television was the world's witness. In exchange, Innocence had agreed that no names would be spelt out in wreaths.

'Thank you,' he'd muttered.

She'd nodded, a tiny, agonized movement.

They'd fallen on each other, sobbing. She'd moaned in his arms, 'Why, Jack, why, she was our *baby*.'

The church was filled with clusters of tiny white spring flowers, a symbol of purity, because one didn't have to be pure of body to be pure of soul. Emily had been a good person and Jack hated and despised himself for how he had treated her. He found it hard to get close and so he'd stayed away – and yet, how did it still hurt?

He had remained aloof to protect himself, so that when he lost her, as he'd lost Felicia and Maria, he wouldn't feel so bad. But it was impossible to feel worse than this. He was

407

responsible, he knew, for this death. He had neglected her because he didn't want her to need him.

He'd wanted her to be able to stand alone. Only now was he beginning to understand that a child could only stand alone with confidence if she had been nurtured and protected and reassured from birth. Ability to survive in the world was a *learned* skill, finessed over the years. Now, of course, he saw all his mistakes with clarity, and he wondered for what had he been hoarding his money and his love?

And now his grandchildren were deprived of a mother. They had been allowed out of the foster home for the 'occasion', accompanied by some sort of *social worker*. He could barely look George in the eye, but he'd forced himself. George had been subdued and robotic until he'd seen Claudia. Then he'd become hysterical, lashing out, kicking, scratching, biting, screaming, 'I want my mummy! I want my mummy!' Jack could hardly control him. Finally, he'd subdued the child with a long hug. He'd made himself be pleasant to the chaperone. For the first time he had put his own feelings aside for the sake of those more important.

'I want to stay with Auntie Claudia,' George had whispered. 'Please. Molly doesn't like it there. She's scared of the dark. The food is disgusting. They make her eat slugs. No one gives her a hug. Please, Granddad, I'm begging you. I'll be as good as gold – and silver.'

He couldn't hear any more, his heart would break. It had crossed his mind to snatch the children – he couldn't quite believe they had to obey the decision of some halfwit parochial court judge – but this was the American legal system and a battle that would only be won through the correct bureaucratic channels.

'You will stay with Auntie Claudia,' he'd said fiercely. 'I am going to make that happen, George.' He'd paused. 'It might not happen immediately, because there are rules. But it will happen soon. I promise. You and Molly will stay with Auntie Claudia, very soon.'

That child had sat there, thin, silent, bewildered, clutching Claudia's hand, piteous in his navy suit. He had always hated dark colours on a child for this very reason. A child should not have to face *death*. He looked from George to Claudia and back again, and it was a horrible déjà vu; George became his little Claudia, sitting so small and helpless, wearing the same terrible expression, at her mother's funeral, all those years ago.

When Jack took the stand, he found he could barely form a sentence. He grasped the piece of paper handed to him by Ms Green.

'Today, I find that I have all this love for Emily in my heart,' he said. 'But it never reached her. She never knew it was there. Emily was an easy person to love and yet I found it so hard – I was so afraid of the power of love and the capacity it has to cause us pain. And so I squandered it. I am truly the poorest, the most humble, the most foolish man in this room. I was given the gift of love, the most precious blessing of existence – a *child* – and I *wasted* that gift. I pray that none of you in this room will ever make such a momentous error.

'Emily was my baby – *is* my baby, will always be my baby – and it is so very hard to believe that she is gone back whence she came. And, if I am honest, I cannot prevent the thought that if I had cherished her more, she would not have been taken. So I have a poem, a short poem, to read, for Emily. It's by a Scottish writer, George MacDonald.'

He looked up. A great blur of faces stared back. Timmy, that worthless skunk, was there with a handkerchief, and his father. The Earl looked subdued and solemn. What a hypocrite. Jack despised him for his grudging increase in warmth to Emily following the newspaper revelations about Tim. There was Elton, with that sweet boyfriend of his, in funeral purple. Who was that guy in the third row? He looked devastated and familiar. An actor? *Quentin?* Quintin – one of Innocence's people. Little Molly was asleep in the chaperone's arms after a jagged marathon of crying. He couldn't stand that she was already ravaged by loss.

He coughed. His throat felt as if it had been stuffed with wire wool.

'A "Song":

> *'Where did you come from, baby dear?*
> *Out of everywhere into here.*
>
> *Where did you get your eyes so blue?*
> *Out of the sky as I came through.*
>
> *What makes the light in them sparkle and spin?*
> *Some of the starry spikes left in.*
>
> *Where did you get that little tear?*
> *I found it waiting when I got here.*
>
> *What makes your forehead so smooth and high?*
> *A soft hand stroked it as I went by.*
>
> *What makes your cheek like a warm white rose?*
> *I saw something better than anyone knows.'*

He had to stop every few words, and found that he couldn't finish reading. Instead, he whispered, 'I hope Emily is . . . somewhere better.'

It was Innocence, majestic rather than ridiculous in a black veil, who helped him back to his seat. 'I know that Emily is somewhere better,' she told the congregation. 'Because wherever she is, is better.'

Everything felt obscene: to ride, flanked by security, in a shiny black chauffeured car, with butter-soft leather up-holstery – his every ridiculous vain whim and frivolity catered for – when Emily lay dead in a box. Now he understood the concept of sackcloth. When his jacket caught in the door, he pulled it so hard, in a spasm of rage, it ripped and he was so glad.

When they arrived at the cemetery it took him a full minute to summon the strength to step out and face people. He knew that if he met their gaze they would see all the way through to his soul and witness his deep shame. He was grateful, in a way, for the celebrity contingent – the presence of Ethan Summers had drawn out others, like salt acting on slugs.

It took the attention away from Jack.

He'd worn his dark glasses with relief, the sole reason not to curse the day's heat. It was a myth that LA was always hot. Their winters chilled him to the bone. He was never so cold in Britain, perhaps because he always expected to be. An extra day of winter for his little girl: was it too much to ask?

Ethan's speech made people cry. It was direct and simple: a waste of a good life, a beautiful person, inside and out, a mother who had so much more to give, a sister, a daughter, a friend. Perhaps there was nothing terribly profound, but delivered in his clear, rich, penetrating voice, his message caught at your heart. He was like a man of God – no, a *god* – preaching from the pulpit. Jack watched as the citizens of LA gazed at him in wonder. Remember, young man, Jack found himself thinking, remember who the star is today.

One tiny thing jarred, but he was bound to be edgy. Ethan said, 'We cannot argue with fate.'

What did he mean by *that*? It sounded as if he was saying that Emily's death was meant to be. As that would be inappropriate and grossly offensive, Jack had to assume that here was a young man, propelled to huge fame, accustomed to being agreed with, not quite – in the cold light of day – living up to his celebrated reputation. Like all of them, he must be exhausted and muddy-headed with shock. You had to respect the guy. As he'd said himself, looking directly at the audience, he felt sick with guilt that Emily had ended it under *his* roof, when he had intended his home to be her sanctuary.

Jack sighed.

The police investigation had been thorough but there was no suggestion of foul play. They had been kind, wanting to assure Jack that there was always the possibility it *was* an accident, that she had tripped, but the awful probability was, given the circumstances and her state of mind, that Emily had felt there was simply no hope and had thrown herself to her death.

Afterwards, there was a reception at the Bel Air Belle Époque. Its elegant sweeping drive was lined with trees from the Enchanted Forest. They had silver trunks and a classical *tree* shape. He had seen two great rows of them adorning Rodeo Drive and said, 'I want *those*.' He still had no idea what sort of trees they were, but they were fairy-tale perfect. Now their perfection mocked him. This world was lousy with beauty that Emily would never see.

He wanted to go home to his London residence, crawl into bed and tip a bottle of pills down his throat. It was repellent to see all these people stuffing their faces with salmon bagels with Emily still warm in her grave. How could they *eat*? His stomach threw up water. He'd heard people didn't eat in LA. Well, that was a lie. They were pigs.

He wondered if he could sneak away and go and lie down in the penthouse suite, where it was quiet and people's incessant idle chatter would not be able to worm its way into his head, making him want to rip it off. He wanted to howl and moan and throw himself on the floor and tear his clothes and all around him people were eating *cake*.

He couldn't stand it. People with chocolate crumbs around their mouths, tipping their heads back to drain the last drop of their free wine – they weren't even talking about Emily, they were networking, swapping business cards, bitching about other guests. He caught, 'Last thing he was in was *Teen Wolf*. . .', '. . . couldn't get a guest spot on *Entourage*.'

One of the girls her age – why her, why not *you* – was gazing up at a guy who had to be an actor (surrounded as he was by four stooges looking moody in shades) and she was resting her weight on one leg, her other knee bent as if she were modelling a swimsuit. The pose drew attention to her slender ankles and her sexy black-patent peep-toe shoes. He felt a surge of hatred. In a town where the kids would sell body and soul for a break yet couldn't be seen to be trying too hard, where all the wannabes pranced around in Juicy Couture tracksuits with yoga mats under their arms, people grabbed at any excuse to dress up and show off.

His daughter's funeral was no more than a fashion show. A pick-up joint.

He raised a hand – the sign for 'stay' was the same in body-guard as it was in dog language – strode to the bathroom and locked himself in a stall. He shut the toilet lid with his foot – bloody Innocence, her fear of germs – and sat down, his head in his hands. Oh God, oh God, he couldn't go on, it was too much. He was half muttering to himself, half in his own head, and so he wasn't immediately aware that someone had entered the room. He froze and held his breath. It was a silly fear that hung over from childhood: he hated hearing foot-steps when he was sitting on the loo, it could be a *predator*. It was the classic scene of male vulnerability in any film: caught with your pants down. It was one reason he hadn't used a public toilet for thirty years.

The person was washing his hands, and whistling. Now humming, now singing in a soft lullaby, 'Oh, how does it feel, to lose everyone you love? And I haven't finished with you yet.'

And then he felt the gust of a breeze, as the door to the bathroom closed. His shock-numbed brain took a while to react. He leaped up, ripped open the lock, skinning his knuckles, burst out of the bathroom, gasping, panting, look-ing wildly around. The voice was unfamiliar – foreign? He knew it – this was his *nemesis*.

He was sobbing now, with fear, panic, excitement. This was the architect of all his grief – this was the source of the evil that had dogged him for so long. None of it was imagined.

He knew without a doubt that this was the man who had killed his wife, had reigned over his world with a curse, and now he was gloating over Emily's death – *gloating*. How was he even *here*? How had he evaded security? It was as if he possessed some mystic power. He was unstoppable – but no, terror was turning him into a superstitious old woman. Get a grip. There had to be logic to it. Here was the enemy to fight – at last his fear had a focus. Here was a chance to end what had been started, if only he could work it out. Jack, *think*.

Jack gripped his head. It felt as if his brain were being pulled apart like an overcooked cauliflower. The migraines he'd suffered since the coma were unlike any headache he had ever experienced.

He leaned against a wall, screwing his eyes tight shut against the light that pierced his eyeballs like meat skewers, and slowly slid down until he was hunched on the floor in a flaming ball of pulsing pain. He pressed his hands to his temples as if to keep his head from cracking open. *Find him, kill him . . . You can do it . . . Get up . . . Protect the children . . .* said the voice inside. But instantly another: *Pathetic loser . . . He's won . . . he's invincible . . . They're doomed . . . You all are . . . It's over.*

BOOK FIVE

LOS ANGELES, A YEAR LATER, 2006

Claudia

It was odd to be draped in twenty million pounds' worth of diamonds when your normal accessories were silver stud earrings and a pink Casio watch. Claudia adjusted the tiara and touched the necklace that sparkled at her throat and gazed at her reflection.

This time tomorrow it would be for real.

'I am the bride.'

Instinctively, she thought of Alfie, how *he* felt about tomorrow. The news of his divorce had hit her like a sledgehammer. Funny, the way things worked out.

She wondered if her fiancé would be looking in the mirror and considering why he'd chosen *this* particular option.

She wasn't saying that she could have done better with her choice of husband, but she could have done different.

Did you ever really know the whole person? Did that matter? He didn't know every single thing about *her* – for instance, that she was having these silly thoughts. But that was why they called it pre-wedding nerves. You would be mad to enter into a lifelong commitment without having some doubts. Look. No one was perfect. And she wasn't saying he wasn't perfect. He was utterly gorgeous, an incredibly kind human being.

He *thought* about her.

She had resisted him at first. But he was gently persistent. He wore her down. She talked to him about her childhood and, surprisingly for a man like him, he listened and he *understood*. She'd told him about the attack on Spyglass Island, when she was little, and he'd expressed how she felt better than she could! It . . . *wowed* her.

'It turns the human body into something disgusting,' he'd said. Yes, yes, *precisely*. 'For sex, you need to get *out* of yourself.' Exactly, and she couldn't. She couldn't. If ever the opportunity arose, she was trapped in her disgusting body, doing disgusting things, with another disgusting body . . . no wonder her horizontal history was so short and awful.

He had talked her into bed. *His* body was not disgusting – it was God showing off. And his personality had just the right amount of wicked to turn her on. Add that to the fact that he understood her heart and soul absolutely and yet still loved her, when the normal consequence of full disclosure was to make any sensible man loathe and pity her: no wonder the sex was ridiculous.

She loved him for all these things, but mostly she loved him because if it weren't for him, the children might still be in care. He knew what he was doing; Jack and Innocence were all mouth and no trousers. *His* attorneys had guided her with wisdom and caution. While her parents seemed to think that the law of the playground applied, he understood the importance of working with the bureaucrats rather than antagonizing them. As a result, she was now the legal guardian of her niece and nephew.

Emily could rest in peace.

People surprised you in a crisis. They rarely acted how you thought they would. Money or misery brought out their true characters.

It had been a shock to watch Innocence crumble.

Claudia had expected her to be strong, unstoppable, but every time there had been a setback, she'd freaked out. One day, after the judge had rejected their initial appeal, Claudia had been sitting in the poolside cabana in the Hills, staring into space, when she'd heard a faint crashing sound.

It had taken her a full three minutes of running around before she located the source – Quintin, cringing, had pointed her in the right direction. Finally she had discovered Innocence in the ground-floor lounge, smashing china ornaments. Her pink hair was wild around her head like a fiery halo, and she was standing knee high in a litter of broken porcelain fauns, puppies, kittens, angels and fairies, about to hurl a large china blue tit out of its china nest to certain death.

'Stop this, now!' Claudia had shouted, surprising herself.

Innocence, also surprised, had stopped.

Claudia had snatched the blue tit. 'This isn't helping.'

'It's helping *me*,' Innocence had screamed. 'And why are you so calm?'

'Being angry doesn't achieve anything. And you were *told* not to speak to CNN. The case is under review. The DCFS is not going to be won over by that sort of behaviour and we need them to be on our side, to see that we are responsible. We're not supposed to talk to the press.'

'You *are* the press!'

'Innocence, you have been advised that it is in our best interests not to comment. So if you go ahead and ignore that advice, why are you surprised when it works against us?'

'I can't help it! I'm so *upset*! I'm UPSET! I have all this . . . influence . . . and I can't do one fucking thing to help my grandchildren – it's unbearable, it's unbearable, I can't stand it!'

Suddenly, without warning, Claudia was hugging Innocence, and her stepmother clung to her. The embrace lasted for under a minute, but in those few moments Claudia felt the tiniest green shoots of forgiveness emerge, like snowdrops breaking through a hard winter frost.

Afterwards she said gently, 'It's horrible not to have them with us, but we are working on it. You behaving like a lunatic won't help, though. All we need is this sort of thing leaked to the *Enquirer*, and—'

'You said they were supposed to be impartial, and disregard anything written in the press!'

Innocence had been impossible, like a spoilt brat. She *was* a spoilt brat. She was used to throwing money at every problem, and it was a shock that, in this instance, money solved nothing. Money could not bring Emily back from the dead, and money could not release her children from care. Innocence was stupid with grief. She was so distraught she could barely function. This was OK, because her staff did everything *for* her. But they couldn't stop her from throwing tantrums on television, which people found at once compelling and repellent. In the months since Emily had died, Élite Retreats shares had lost a third of their value.

Jack had been more successful, perhaps because he had managed to keep his emotions out of it. Well. He *had* no emotions! That was the key. He had been no comfort to his family whatsoever. At the funeral, Claudia had seen Innocence comfort *him*. He never did anything for anybody. He had squeezed Claudia on the shoulder and pursed his lips in regret. That was the sum of his fatherly compassion – his reaction to her losing her only sister. He couldn't comfort her, and she believed that he should. She supposed it was fear. He feared loss. He was scared that if he dipped a toe in the waters of grief, he would fall in and drown. Bloody hell – *everyone* feared loss! But his fear ruled – ruined – his life and his relationships. It was a weirdness that had its roots, as most weirdnesses do, in childhood. His own father had just left, when he was seven, and Ruth had told him, 'Your father is gone. Good riddance. I don't want to talk about it.'

Ruth had suddenly volunteered this information when Claudia was eight years old, playing the piano at the Primrose Hill house, JR crunching Rich Tea biscuits on the Persian rug. Ruth had also repeated *her* mother's wisdom: 'Only a hunchback will marry you if you're not a virgin.' The same conversation had also contained the invaluable advice: 'Never eat tulip bulbs, they give you terrible diarrhoea.' Now that Claudia thought about it, Ruth's doctor had possibly been experimenting with her medication.

Claudia was glad that Ruth hadn't lived to see the mess that her son had made of his life, but at the same time, she was a little bit annoyed – at Ruth, at Felicia – at these strong women who had loved her and left her. It was their fault, in a way. *You died and now look.*

If they had lived, a lot of bad things might not have happened.

She had to try and look forward, instead of back. She knew she shouldn't look back and regret, because there was nothing you could do about the past except make yourself miserable over it. And yet it was irresistible. You were drawn to it, in the way that people had to slow when they drove past a car crash.

'Auntie Claudia? Are you OK? What are you looking at?'

Claudia jumped, and smiled. 'Darling, I'm fine. I'm just thinking about the wedding. I suppose it's a bit like having a birthday party when you invite all your friends. You want everyone to enjoy themselves. I'm hoping that it will be fun. I'm sure it will be. Are you looking forward to it, George?'

She smiled, hopefully. All the adults were desperate to pretend that it was all OK for George. He made a good show of things, so as not to upset them. But she saw his terrible anxiety. He watched her so closely, he noticed the slightest mood change, and if she displayed irritation, he picked up on it, sucking up the negative energy and then erupting in a violent and uncontrollable rage. It was terrifying, and often over the slightest thing – if he was having trouble putting on a sock, or if he made a mistake drawing a picture. He missed his mother, he wanted his mother, he was sad and angry because his mother was dead and, worse, he had been *punished* – sent away to live with strangers. He had a right to be angry, but it was so hard to tolerate. It was unbearable to watch a child you loved display anger. Your reflex thought was: This reflects badly on me as a parent or a guardian. It was all new to her. All she could do for George was to be constant, patient, and loving, but God, it was tough.

He was nervous; he was clingy. His behaviour at school was impeccable. His behaviour at home was erratic, volatile and mostly dreadful. When he ran at Claudia, punching, kicking and biting, she was astonished and *frightened*. Already, aged seven, he was a match for her in strength. He was better behaved when her fiancé was around – did George respect him more?

Her therapist – she felt it more useful that *she* had the therapist rather than George, he didn't need the extra shit – her therapist had suggested that maybe George felt more secure with Claudia, more able to test her. It was a nice inter- pretation. So, however hard he pushed, Claudia vowed to herself that she would never reject him, ever. When she felt the impulse to shake the teeth out of his head, she had an emergency plan: switch on the Cartoon Network, leave the room, return in ten minutes. George would run to her for a hug, for reassurance that he was forgiven, still loved. By then, the anger she felt would have diminished, and she could return the hug with gusto.

'I'm not looking forward to you going away, but I suppose it will be fun with La-La. She said she's going to take me and Molly to Florida for a few days and we'll go swimming with dolphins. But I don't think she's actually going to get in the water. I don't think she really *likes* dolphins. I think they might wee in the water. Granddad said he might come too.'

'George, it will be great fun, and I'll be back in five days. And I'll speak to you on the phone, every day.'

'Thank you, Auntie Claudia.'

She paused, and let out a sigh carefully, quietly, bit by bit so he didn't hear.

Between George and Molly, and work, and organizing a wedding, she was frazzled to a crisp. Molly was two now, and had 'separation anxiety'. Claudia's back was sore from hauling Molly around. She couldn't bear to be put down. As you reached to place her on the floor, she clung to you like a koala, so, reluctantly, you hauled her up from the floor back to her permanent position on your hip. Her physiotherapist went *nuts* about it. She had, at least, managed to find Nanny and re-employ her. Innocence was paying for this.

She had said at the time – Claudia couldn't really bear to think about it – 'You'll get everything now. You did more for Emily – you deserve it. So when I pay for Nanny, *you're* paying – it's your money.' She'd said it in a blunt, terse way, which made it difficult for Claudia to respond.

In fact, when your stepmother announced that she planned to leave you her fortune – an estimated five hundred and fifty million pounds – it was hard to show gratitude in a way proportionate to the favour, so you ended up being awkwardly offhand about it, muttering, 'Oh, OK, thanks.'

It was too surreal.

It would be good for the children – that was the main thing – to secure their future. And there was a great peace in knowing that she would never have to worry about *not* having money, but it wouldn't change her actual life. She enjoyed her work, she needed purpose, and she needed *her own bit*. Writing was her self-expression, her creation. It was her achievement; it hadn't been handed down. Also, she had her flat in London, her condo on Woodrow Wilson, and there wasn't anything she didn't have that she madly wanted. Emily had once said, 'How can you be happy living such a *small* life?'

But she was. Because of Jack and Innocence, all the *stuff* was available to her if she felt the urge: to swim in an infinity pool in the Hollywood Hills, to fly to Vegas by private jet, to stay at a castle in the mountains of Mexico, to holiday in a beach villa by the Malaysian rainforest, to sunbathe on a luxury yacht off Cap Ferrat. Maybe that was the difference, that no one was saying, 'You can't have this.'

Also – though she hated to think like this – she was *marrying* a rich man. Before Innocence had coolly informed her that she would inherit everything, she had been quite embarrassed about the difference in their levels of wealth.

She'd even asked her fiancé if he wanted a pre-nup.

'Absolutely not,' he'd replied. 'Don't be ridiculous.' Then he'd grinned and added, 'I'm far too conceited to think you'd marry me for my money. I'm just *so* lovable!'

So now that *she* was the wealthier of the two, she couldn't possibly ask *him* to sign one – it would have seemed so churlish.

Of course, Jack had brought it up. 'I'm leaving everything to you, so a pre-nup is in *my* interest,' he'd said gruffly.

'Jack,' she'd said, because it was really too much now – for God's sake, how much money did a person need? – 'why don't you just put it in a trust for George and Molly? Please. I'd prefer that. Wouldn't it be more tax efficient?'

The carrot dangled in front of the donkey's nose.

He'd hesitated. 'I'll speak to my lawyers,' he'd said. Then he'd added, 'You're a good girl, Claudia. I'm proud of you.'

She'd nodded and turned away, so he couldn't see the tears in her eyes. It was too painful. When he was kind, it was too confusing.

She smiled now, at George. 'Well. It's nearly time for me to drop you and Molly at La-La's, so I can prepare.'

She winced inwardly at George's expression.

'But Auntie Claudia, there's nothing for you to do! You told me that every single thing is being done for you!'

'Well, George, you're right.' He *was* right. She felt like an observer, rather than the centrepiece. In a way, it was like marrying into the aristocracy. She compared it (in her head, of course) to Lady Diana marrying Prince Charles. Diana had had no idea what she was getting into, and Claudia was just beginning to realize what sort of life *she* had agreed to. There were precise expectations of how the wedding would be. Her only role was to sit and nod as the most prestigious wedding consultants in Los Angeles ran her through a neverending list of options, firmly steering her in the appropriate direction. She would have liked a chocolate wedding cake with white chocolate icing; somehow she got carrot cake – dairy-free because a lot of the guests would have allergies. Secretly, she supposed that those same guests would also have calorie allergies, so why worry about them, but she didn't want to cause trouble. The invitations, the guests, the gifts, the seating, the settings, the stills, the venue, the vows, the video, the ceremony, the car, the music, the menu, the drinks, the décor, the flowers, the bouquet, the rings – even the dress was not her decision. Roberto Cavalli had *asked if he might be permitted*: she couldn't complain.

There were some things she would have preferred to have done herself – such as her make-up. She had only ever been made up professionally once, and the woman had made her look like a clown. But *this* was the stylist (with a long, impressive CV of famous women she had styled, all so beautiful they didn't need make-up). But *she* didn't do eyebrows – please! Like asking the electrician if he could fix the toilet! For that, there was an – no, *the* – Eyebrow Lady, who had asked, in hushed tones, 'Do you even *pluck*?' The hair stylist (who, Claudia noticed, drove a Bentley) had shaken his bald head, lifted a lock of her hair and let it drop. 'Who *did* this to you?' he'd breathed, as if it were a war crime. The rest of the time they were deferential, but their horror that a person in her situation would 'abuse herself' was obviously too great to hide. There was a beautician, who had ripped just about every hair out of her body – nasal, knuckle, toe; there was a deep-tissue masseuse; an acupuncturist; a beauty therapist (the diamond-particle facial, the all-over body scrub); a tan guy; a manicurist ('Am I dreaming or do you *bite*?'); a pedicurist (who had been visibly shocked on first sight of the flaking skin on her heels and had been forced to take a long sip of Fiji water to regain composure). They were supposed to have made her feel beautiful, but by the time they'd all finished with her, she felt like the ugliest girl alive.

'You're right,' said Claudia again. 'I hardly have to do anything myself. But tonight, the night before my wedding, a very exciting day, I'd like some quiet time – to read, and be by myself. Do you understand that, George?'

The little boy looked at her. 'I think so. Is it because once you get married to Ethan he's not going to leave you alone?'

'Ha!' said Claudia. Oh, funny. Except – and she didn't quite know why – not *that* funny.

MARINA DEL REY, LOS ANGELES, LATE AFTERNOON THE FOLLOWING DAY

Ethan

Ethan stood in the Rose Garden of the Ritz-Carlton before three hundred major Hollywood stars – and God – and kissed the bride. He particularly liked that Claudia was a nobody.

You had to be a fool to marry a supermodel. If you were that desperate you could hire one.

And only the insane would marry an *actress*. He truly could not think of a worse torture. You would have to employ a second husband who could pick up your slack. One man alone couldn't possibly cope with the necessary barrage of reassurances and compliments that would be demanded from dawn till dusk then all through the night on perform-ance – scene by scene, moment by moment, line by line, word by word; on face – exquisite, camera totally besotted, young like a *teenager*, skin is the secret; on body – lithe, toned, perfect Pilates shape, but *genes*, can't compete with what's God-given; on interpretation – genius; on scene-stealing – poor creature didn't have a hope next to you, like holding a candle to the sun; on coping with inferior talent of co-star – you were *kind* to her. Dismissal of fears – fat? What! Where? No, not a wrinkle, no, not a wobble; affirmation of talent – utterly convincing, breathtaking, Oscar-worthy; denigration of competition – ageing so badly, shoddy work, original nose

426

better, no waist to speak of, cellulite plain as day, devoid of charisma, zero chemistry; slagging off of rival series – second rate, embarrassing, network on verge of dropping it . . . Ethan always thought of that Arquette guy and laughed his head off.

Claudia didn't frighten the fans. She was pretty, not beautiful; she wasn't a threat. They couldn't imagine that she was a great fuck.

As it happened, she wasn't bad. She liked it, but she hated herself for liking it, which made for a great screw.

He couldn't *wait* for the wedding night. She was in for a treat.

She'd pissed him off, actually. She hadn't quit about the children. Literally, hadn't shut up, and he had realized that she wouldn't stop whining until they were out of care. It was a real bummer.

He'd wanted that pair of brats to rot in the system. He wanted them to suffer. It was poetry, how the mere thought of their unhappiness had a destructive effect on the entire family. They'd changed.

But he was cool. He was flexible. You had to adjust. People were so annoying and selfish and stupid, they didn't consider that someone else might want a different outcome. But no matter! It had all worked out brilliantly. His work securing their release had helped persuade Claudia that she was in love with him. That had been slightly harder than anticipated – picky cow.

He had been the hero. It always amazed people when reality imitated art. The world was so simple, it adored symmetry. He had made sure that *he*'d led the legal campaign that brought George and Molly home to Auntie.

There was always another way.

In the last three months he had been like a father to the brats. It was perfect. When a stupid bitch like Claudia made things difficult, you simply had to think out of the box. And then he had realized that she had offered him a priceless opportunity. It was one thing, to have agony inflicted by a stranger. But in a way, later, as an adult, you could rationalize that: it wasn't personal, it wasn't to do with any flaw of yours, this could have happened to anyone.

Now, thanks to Claudia's pig-headed stubbornness and the fact that she hadn't shut up about it for one goddamn ear-melting minute, the kids were hers – and because he was seducing Claudia, they had spent time with him, they'd *bonded*. They loved him. And, as he knew so well, it was far, far more powerful, the wound was so much deeper, if you were hurt by someone you loved.

'We're *married*, Ethan!' she giggled in his ear. 'We're married!'

She was so full of *love* – love for Emily, love for the kids, love for *him*. It annoyed the crap out of him. Funny, because it had annoyed him that this family had no respect for love. As the great Nicolas Cage had decreed in some rag (Mark read everything), 'Don't look down on love.'

Ah well! Claudia just couldn't win!

Gravely, he bent and kissed her hand. If he had to kiss her on the lips even one more time he would shoot himself in the head. She reminded him of his mother. Not a great quality in a wife.

Then he smiled, and their audience stood, cheered, clapped, showered them with rose petals. Little Molly clung to his trousers, alarmed by the noise, and he wanted to shake her off, boot her into space. Her thumb glistened with drool and her nose was running. Jesus, these kids, it was thirty degrees! There was always some *leak* from some fucking *orifice*.

He breathed deeply and calmed his nerves by focusing on the glorious surroundings. The palm trees tall and solemn against the deep blue sky; the Grecian-style pagoda; the pink rose petals strewn at their feet, the hotel – a quiet poke in the eye for Jack. But this wasn't a fucking PR stunt, the father of the bride could damn well shell out for a nice do at a *proper* hotel, not his crappy Past Times themed guesthouse.

He felt uncomfortable about making eye contact with Jack. The moment that Jack realized who Ethan was – the most satisfying moment of Ethan's life, that orgasmic, *pinnacle* of a moment – would be when Ethan declared his true identity, as he stabbed Jack in the heart with the wedding knife that had cut the cake. Cute, but not too cute – Ethan did not wish to go down in the history books as mawkish.

But there was no denying he was getting sentimental. He'd picked *that date* for the wedding. He couldn't help it. He wasn't a machine. He had feelings. He'd wanted to test Jack. Just to see if there was a spark of memory, if this was a date of any significance. It was pathetic really. Like an unloved housewife, not reminding her husband of their anniversary, then presenting him with a lavish gift: slyly trying to force the guilty man to acknowledge his love crime.

But there had been nothing. Not a glimmer. Claudia had informed her father of the date on a video conference call from Ethan's media room. Ethan had watched eagerly for his reaction. He'd waited for the eyes to flicker up to the left, a recollection, a memory. *Zilch.*

Ethan had wanted to raise the stakes. It was simply no fun baiting an impassive victim, you wanted your prey to struggle and fight. There was no fun in torturing someone who was brain dead. Since he'd taunted Jack, in the bathroom at Emily's funeral, it had heightened the tension.

Jack was suspicious, jumpy, but he wasn't *sorry*. He had gone to the police; he'd heightened his security; he had spoken to the media. *Time* had run a story on it, detailing the curious catalogue of disasters that had befallen the Kent family, under the headline 'Hunted or Cursed?'

There was no way that Jack suspected *him*. This was good, but also infuriating. Ethan wanted contrition. He wanted remorse. But Jack was acting as though *Jack* was the victim!

It killed Ethan that Jack was so untroubled by his crime

that he'd forgotten it. He was so oblivious that it hadn't occurred to him to look back into his past, his *private* past, and confront his old sins.

The breathtaking truth: he didn't think he'd committed any!

He had no idea that Ethan was anything other than a regular guy. And yet, *still*, he wasn't friendly. In fact, the last thing he'd said to Ethan before the wedding was, 'You change voice a lot.'

Fuck off! Ethan was an expat; he was the finest actor of his generation; he was the River Phoenix who lived. It was his prerogative to borrow, like a magpie, bits and snippets of language that appealed to him, from here, or there. He had no ancestors, no family, no identity, he was *no one*. The soul of him was patched together from imitating other people.

He liked that he could talk and no one could place him.

But maybe Jack was simply exhibiting the distrust that a father shows to any young man who is fucking his daughter *and* who is bold enough to force him to celebrate the outrage. Ethan couldn't stand it. The crazy thing was, having waited over twenty-eight years, his patience had run out, less than a day before the deadline. So he'd said something. It wasn't much. After the ceremony, Jack had wandered over with that sharp-nosed PA of his, and gruffly congratulated him. 'Lovely weather for your special day,' he'd said. Duh.

Ethan had retorted, without too much venom, 'Today has always been my special day, but it's your special day too, Jack, remember?'

Jack had replied, 'Of course, a daughter's wedding day is always special for a father.'

He was just too obtuse to get it, and Ethan should stop knocking his head against a wall. He was the unloved housewife, pointlessly douching, wearing lace knickers on her fat arse, pinching the flab on her waist and kidding herself that she wasn't repulsive. Ethan felt his face burn with humiliation. 'Hey, guess what, *punk*,' he wanted to spit.

'Twenty-eight years ago *this day* you quit on me as a father, slammed the door in my little angel face and sent me to hell. Well, now I'm back and you're my father again. Hello, *Dad*. And this time, I am going to send *you* to hell!'

Ethan turned away and focused his energy on schmoozing up to Innocence. He needed to be soothed. She was blinded by vanity, the fuss, the status, the outlandish attention that the world gave to a pair of adults signing a contract to love each other, and the great thrill of her family marrying into *fame*.

It was disgusting, the way people worshipped celebrity. Half of the stars he knew were total losers. Clooney. God, he loathed Clooney. Clooney, and his fucking perfect career, his perfect choices, his still adoring ex-waitresses, his dazzling personality, his *integrity*, his palazzo on fucking Lake Como, the way he filled out a suit, his quick wit, his 'old-star quality' – yeah, *old* being the operative word – his universal popularity. *Hate*.

'Claudia, you look stunning. *Mazel tov*. Though you threw yourself away on this Summers guy!'

'Thank you, George! It was so sweet of you to make it. I'm so sorry about the motorbike accident. How's your shoulder?'

'It's a scratch. You worry about yourself, young lady.'

Yeah, well. Clooney had never spoken a truer word. Twat.

Ethan accepted a goblet of champagne and allowed himself to be swarmed over by well-wishers. These people: they'd step over him in the street if they only knew. These people, with their compassion for the poor, the unprivileged, the misunderstood: all that he had been and all that he was, they despised, and they didn't even know it. They were afraid of what he was, inside – and that hurt. Even as he suffered their hot kisses, their clammy hugs, their bacteria-ridden fingers to stroke his face and their white-smiling mouths to shout joy in his ear, he felt rejected and loathed. He looked around for his Mark, the only person in the world with real *empathy*. Mark understood him. Mark had been delightfully corruptible. Ethan was the love of Mark's life and Mark would do anything, forgive *anything*.

He'd miss Mark.

He needed to go inside. The whirring of the paparazzi helicopters overhead was getting right inside his skull, making his ears itch. To make the day easy on himself, he was simply playing a part in a romcom. He loved romcoms – not to act in, but to watch. Even so, it was hard going. He wanted night to fall.

He posed for pictures. They had agreed to release one shot to the media in return for privacy. Of course (he glanced skyward), they'd broken their half of the deal and it was lucky for their editors that Ethan was a focused professional. Claudia – she did insist on keeping that ridiculous *box* of a condo on Woodrow Wilson – had been surprised by a pap that very morning as she collected the paper at the bottom of her drive. 'Why are you running?' he'd taunted as she'd scurried back up to the house. 'Are you scared?'

Ethan didn't care that they were disrespectful of *her*, but he cared that they were disrespectful of *his property*. A lesser man would have been hiring hitmen to pick them off at the intersection. Ethan didn't work like that. He was like a sportsman. Nothing could distract him from his goal.

He slung an arm round Jack, just to see how it felt. It took all his willpower to keep his hand on the man's back. His instinct was to rip it away, screaming, as if he'd touched the surface of the sun. Jack had stiffened and Ethan realized that seeking physical contact had been a mistake. Humans were animals, although base, stupid, inferior, and they retained a tiny residue of instinct that alerted them to danger. Would Jack recognize this?

Happily, Molly distracted him. There were a lot of distractions at weddings. His speech would smooth his way until tonight. Also, he had gifts for the family. Mark had sourced an 18-carat white-gold bracelet with 1,604 diamonds from H. Stern in New York, over half a million bucks of wedding present for Ethan's dear wife. She would, he thought fondly, wear it to her grave. For his mother-in-law, Mark had ordered a silver metal open-backed dress from Versace. It was brash, short, quite revolting – she'd love it. Also, Jack would be needled as there was something not *quite* kosher about this present – men never stopped being possessive about women they'd slept with and this was a few steps away from presenting the mother of the bride with a vibrator.

Innocence was looking hot.

Mark had a fashion radar. He'd just look a person up and down, and a laser print of who they were wearing and how much would whirr out his ass. Her shades were identified as Mask, $1,000, by Oliver Goldsmith Couture, available by special order at City of Angels. The only trouble with stealing style tips from acquaintances was that afterwards you couldn't allow them to live long. Ethan would not wear an identical item to another person, it screwed with his sense of self. No one appreciated that sense of self was an *issue* for adopted people.

His speech was a masterpiece.

'I've always known what is important: love, and family. Some people believe that good parenting is essential for a person to be a good husband. I disagree. As you may know, for the first twelve years of my life, I was raised by my grandmother' – Mark had conceived of this fairy tale; it was genius as there was no one alive to corroborate it and, try as they might before the lawsuits were slapped down, those grubbing hacks just couldn't disprove any of it – 'as my own mother, who was young when she had me, couldn't cope. For a few precious years, I enjoyed a loving relationship with my mother before, God rest her soul, she passed away. But I will always regret what I missed – and what *she* missed – and I think that when you miss something, you cherish it more. No one values love and family more than I, and I intend to love and cherish Claudia for the rest of her life.'

Claudia smiled up at him and squeezed his hand. He squeezed it back, then glanced at his watch. That meant a full eight hours of love and cherishing – or longer. Up to her really. He got wolf whistles and a standing ovation.

The one advantage to being the groom was that the adoration reached fever pitch. Though all these people were right there staring at him – it reminded him of that stint on Broadway. He wasn't wild about theatre. Fuck the craft. He preferred remote worship, for his face to be on a screen, adored by millions, while he was elsewhere, alone, unobserved.

But there were worse things. And his honeyed words had pacified Jack. He'd pursed his lips, nodded, lit a cigar. Vile.

The bride also received a lot of attention, but it was inevitable in that snowstorm-in-hell of a dress. Innocence was also resplendent in white, which struck him as inappropriate. She really was one selfish bitch. Hadn't it occurred to her that this was Claudia's day to shine? That said, Claudia had lowered the tone by inviting a bunch of her no-mark friends from Britain.

As Mark had said, on spying a pair of high-street slacks, 'My life just got five per cent less glamorous.'

Claudia's most heinous crime, however, had been to introduce him to that posh twat Alfie Cannadine. This was the guy who'd saved her from the pervert when she was a kid. Claudia hadn't said a word (sly) but he knew immediately there was something between them. Alfie looked at her *that way*. It was the expression of a man in love, and Ethan wanted to puke. As for Claudia, she blushed as she said his name. Ethan suppressed the urge to hit her across the room.

A few moments' polite chat established that the guy was divorced – young, free and single. Ethan realized his great luck. This berk hadn't wanted to contact the love of his life because he'd read in *Harper's Bazaar* or *Posh Twats' Weekly* that she was in a relationship with Hollywood's young hero. Jesus, grow some stones! This cretin had no idea what Ethan

434

could see now, *at his own bloody wedding*: Claudia would have dropped the great Ethan Summers for this bumbling goofball in a second. Thank fuck for chivalry!

It would be a real pleasure to slice this braying waste of space into a lot of small pieces. 'Do excuse me! I'm using the steak knife. Forgive me. Once I've shucked out the brain, I'll switch to the vegetable knife. Oops a daisy, my grip is all wrong!' But no, he would not harm Alfie. He'd leave the guy alone to live his worthless life. It was hard, very hard, to control one's urges, to refrain from a spontaneous killing spree, but it was a question of *intelligence*. It was the difference between failure and success.

Ethan's lip curled as he considered the disorganized serial killer. 'Disorganized'. That said it all. They couldn't control themselves. Fucking *babies*. They made a mess and got caught.

Ethan was a superior, unparalleled operator because he had patience, precision; he understood the importance of sticking to a plan, rather than being dumbly distracted.

Now he was all riled up.

Céline Dion made it better, though she made you pay through the nose. She was worth it though. He'd nearly cried when she'd kissed him hello. She was his type of woman. He preferred her image – in person, she was actually *sweet* – she had a look that could kill a man at ten paces. He supposed he was influenced by 'My Heart Will Go On'. He'd watched *Titanic* an embarrassing number of times. Ethan Summers's shameful secret was that he couldn't stand to watch a film rated 18 – which precluded *Sick Day*. He'd had to have emergency hypnotherapy before the preview.

Jack had kept his speech short – was he rude, thoughtful, or merely brain-damaged? He had praised Claudia as a 'wonderful daughter' – as if *he* knew; he had mentioned Emily – respectful silence; and the children – oohs and aahs; and he had declared that he'd always enjoyed Ethan's work, and that it was great to finally 'have some talent in the family'.

435

Everyone laughed. Damn. Had people laughed at *his* speech? Was Jack's speech funnier? His was more poignant.

The food looked spectacular (Oliver was cooking), crunchy raw beet salad with feta and pear to start. It wasn't bad. The hotel hadn't been thrilled about their kitchen being taken over, but it had been a toss-up between allowing Oliver to cook, or losing the booking. He'd covered their 'loss' – people were all about money. They had no sense of occasion, no soul, no grasp of *decency*. He tried not to drum his fingers to speed up time.

'I can't eat,' said Claudia. 'I'm too excited! I can't focus. It's all passing me by in a blur. I can't believe we're married, Ethan.'

'Nor me,' he'd replied, injecting his voice with great enthusiasm. 'I can't wait for us to be alone.'

She giggled. 'How early do you think we can leave?'

'After the first dance?'

They were staying at the Malibu house before, in theory, jetting off to the beach of Costa Careyes, in Mexico.

He could feel the heat off her; his nose tickled with the scent of her perfume. It made him want to run to the ocean to breathe fresh air. The first dance was 'Satellite of Love' – nothing more than a moving hug. He wasn't about to put on a big fancy show. This was a wedding, not *Dancing with the Stars*.

You had to know when to keep it real.

'I have a surprise for you back at the house, Mrs Summers,' he murmured.

'Ooh,' she murmured back. 'Is it a *big* surprise?'

'Oh yes, honey,' he replied, softly kissing her hair for the benefit of the crowd and camera. 'It's *huge*. It's the surprise of your life.'

HOLLYWOOD HILLS, 11 P.M.

Claudia

It was terrible to be thinking 'if only' as a white Hummer limousine sped you towards your wedding night.

She loved Ethan. She did. But marrying him was a rational decision, it wasn't a call of the heart. She'd done it because the children loved him, and he loved them, and he'd been a dear friend of Emily, and he'd been so incredibly sweet, and he was the safe bet: he was here, in LA, an important fixture; he was *known*; he wasn't going to disappear.

Why hadn't Alfie *said*? It was so stupid, such a waste. Now it came out that the marriage to Polly had fizzled a while ago – 'a duty marriage' according to the *Daily Mail*; she had looked it up on Google – he had been a single man for *six months*. He hadn't even given her a hint of it. And no one had told her.

She couldn't stand it. She had to say something. While Ethan was talking to his agent – a man who reminded Claudia of a velociraptor – she'd cornered Alfie and asked him. She had nothing to lose. His reply had stunned her.

'Your father warned me off. He said you were happy now, and to leave you alone.'

What?

She felt a great anger rise inside.

Alfie had added, 'He was trying to protect you, Claw. He was trying to do the decent thing. I know about Martin. I'm so sorry.' She'd paled. 'He just didn't want you to be hurt again.'

'But . . .' she'd said, and the rest of the sentence had remained unspoken: *you wouldn't hurt me because we love each other.*

They had stared at each other helplessly. She felt suddenly ridiculous in her big stupid white dress, and a great heavy ring on her finger, while *his* ring finger was newly naked. She had a crazy thought of running away. She gazed into his eyes and, very gently, he shook his head, and kissed her. Ah, so soft, so full of regret, of missed opportunity.

She smiled to herself, then realized that her husband was caressing her neck.

'We're here,' he said. And then, a little sharply, she thought – but then, didn't most men find the wedding day a grinding chore? – 'You won't mind if I don't carry you over the threshold.' It was a statement, not a question. He paused, and so did she. 'I don't want to strain my back.'

'That's fine. I can walk.'

It was weird. They were both oddly flat, and it felt awkward. How ridiculous! She felt a curl of fear. Oh God. He hadn't seen how she was with Alfie? She felt ashamed. It was really low – emotionally unfaithful. She'd make a big effort for their wedding night – oh dear, was that bad, to think of making an *effort*? The truth was, while he was beautiful, and chiselled, and muscular, and tanned, with piercing eyes and even features, he wasn't her *type*. She was attracted to him, but she didn't find him attractive in the *primal* way she was drawn to Alfie. If you had to draw up a scientific checklist, Alfie was the uglier by far – a biggish nose, broken several times from playing rugby, hair like straw – but she preferred quirky to perfect.

She was exhausted.

She had all this flimsy, lacy, flirty underwear, but at heart she couldn't be *bothered*. She wanted to curl up in thick brushed-cotton pyjamas, read a trashy magazine, sip a mug of hot chocolate – Ethan's air con was polar, they disagreed about temperature and it was irritating. She wanted to stretch out in a king-size bed, *alone*. But it was her wedding night, and a girl was expected to perform. Ethan, she knew this already, did not tolerate failure. Even if he was comatose from tiredness, she knew he'd want to have sex, because he wouldn't be able to exist comfortably knowing that he was one of the sad 43 per cent of not-passionate-enough couples who *didn't* fuck on their wedding night.

He kissed her, briefly, on the lips. 'Go make yourself nice, I'll be with you in a minute.' He winked, was gone. He was oddly secretive, but then, as a public figure, the paparazzi forever prying into your business, a little privacy in your personal life was surely essential to keep you from madness.

She hurried upstairs – to *his* bedroom. It was laughably enormous; it was a workout just to reach the bed. She had her overnight bag; she would have a quick shower. Ethan liked a woman to be 'clean'. It gave her a funny feeling when she recalled him saying that, as if women were naturally *unclean*. Now and then, she allowed herself a fantasy about Alfie, and they didn't mess about wasting time with showers, they just *did* it. Well. Here she was. Mrs Summers: the envy and hate object of millions of women all over the globe.

If only they knew the mundane reality. She couldn't reconcile herself completely to a man who had had his teeth whitened. Not that a man should have yellow teeth, but *bright white*? It was a bit much sometimes. She understood that he had to beautify himself for his job, but somehow, all this unabashed preening and pampering felt unmanly. It was more the American way than the *British* way.

Ethan's bathroom cabinet doors ran the length of the vast room and were mirrored mosaic; crazy-paving-style shards rather than neat little squares. It was a beautiful yet disturbing effect; it reminded her of Gaudí, the Ice Queen, a smashed window, all at once. Every cupboard was stocked with expensive male grooming products. She had a hunch that Alfie used Head & Shoulders and a bar of soap.

This was ridiculous. She'd feel better after a good sleep.

But duty called.

She shrugged out of her wedding dress, struggling with the buttons at the back – *he should be doing this* – and turned on the bath taps.

She peered closely at herself in one of the shards of mirror. Here she was, alone, unconnected. It was a feeling that had tailed her all her life, but you didn't expect to feel alone a few hours after a minister had pronounced you man and wife. Carefully, she removed the tiara and the diamond necklace. It had been kind – surprising – of Innocence to lend them to her. They had a good relationship now, for them.

Oh my God, a *hair* on her chin. How could it have been missed? She looked like a witch. At least, her husband would think so. When you married a man who'd had love scenes with Angelina and ex-girlfriends who populated the Pirelli Calendar, you had a lot to live up to.

He must own a pair of tweezers. She pulled open a mirrored cabinet door, then another. A thousand fragmented Claudias did the same. She felt uncomfortable surrounded by so many broken reflections of herself.

There were an endless number of lotions and potions. But no tweezers. Maybe higher up. Electric toothbrushes. Cut-throat razors. She'd try that door at the top. If she stood on the edge of the bath, she might just reach it. She mustn't slip. Felicia had died in the bath. A heart attack, and she wasn't a blood relative, but sometimes you got superstitious.

Nothing. It was empty.

Fine. It would be a silly place to keep tweezers anyway. Wouldn't you keep them nearer to hand?

She carefully stepped down and scurried, naked, to his bedside cabinet. Also mirrored. She pulled open the bottom drawer. Ah, there we go. Tweezers. It was full of magazines: a *Vanity Fair* supplement with Bill Murray on the front dressed as a rhinestone Elvis. Someone had doodled 'fatty' across his face in Biro. There was a ripped-out newspaper report – a quote from Morgan Freeman, on presenting Ethan Summers with an award, 'Very occasionally, there is a crossover between a great actor and a great film star.'

What was *that*? It looked like two furry-looking gob-stoppers floating in a screw-top jar of brown liquid. Props from a film set? Gross. There, in the corner, was a little red velvet bag. She had a vague sense of memory associated with it. A déjà vu. She picked it up, and, slowly, opened it. Inside was a bracelet, a thin gold chain with a fat little gold heart hanging off it. Her heart was beating fast, and her hands trembled as she turned it over and found, yes, a small dent in the metal – a bite mark from a five-year-old girl who had broken a tooth trying to establish if there really *was* chocolate inside the heart as that bad boy Alfie had promised.

How did *Ethan* have it? How was that possible? It had been stolen when she was ten or eleven years old. Her legs felt like jelly. It had been a present from Felicia and it had been stolen. She still remembered crying under the bedcovers that evening, the sound of her own sobs drowning out the boom of the music, and then, suddenly, horribly, being aware of a much closer sound – realizing, with a lurch of fear, that some-one was in the room, an intruder. Wanting to throw off the covers and run screaming away but not daring – waiting – sobbing – fearing that Orinoco had escaped from prison and come back for her to finish what he'd started. Would he shoot her dead through the bedclothes or would he rip off her pyjamas first? Hearing him come closer, angrily rifling through her bedside drawers, and then, amazingly, in-credibly, he was gone, caught, and it wasn't Orinoco after all, it was some little thief, a *kid*. She hadn't realized he'd stolen the bracelet until months later. The cold creep of fear entwined itself around her as her mind screamed its warning: *So how did Ethan get your bracelet?*

'I bought it for you, as a wedding gift.'

She shrieked and jumped. Ethan was right behind her. 'God, you scared me. I . . . was looking for some tweezers. Sorry.' She felt uncomfortable, being naked when he was fully clothed. 'But . . . how did you know it was mine? It was stolen. How would you possibly know?'

There was a strange expression on his face. Why wasn't there anything to cover herself with – a blanket, a robe?

'Well, darling, when it was stolen there was a photo of it in the paper and—'

'But, Ethan, it was never *in* the paper. I never told anyone. I was afraid of getting into trouble.'

'Oh FUCK IT. You know, if you're that afraid of getting into trouble, Claudia, why do you always go looking for it? You had to *push* it, didn't you? You had to uncover the truth. Well, here's the truth, darling. *I* stole it. Me. Yes, *me*. I was the thief in your pretty pink bedroom, listening as you snivelled under your covers. You were irritating then, and you are irritating now. Do you know, I nearly stabbed you, purely to make the noise stop?'

His look was one of polite enquiry. She stared at him, terror welling up inside like a cyst. In one second, she knew. He had killed Emily.

'Why?' Her voice was a croak.

'Don't move.'

She swallowed. 'You have everything now. You've done . . . so well. You've . . . bettered yourself.'

'*Bettered* myself? You patronizing cow!'

'No . . . no! I meant . . . I'm sorry. I'm sorry if you went to prison . . . but it wasn't personal. You had' – she got the feeling she should shut up – 'you had broken into our house.'

He was standing – too close – the picture of civility in his white dinner jacket. 'It wasn't personal,' he repeated, laughing. 'It wasn't personal, she says.'

She couldn't look at his face. The world's favourite movie star was a psychotic killer. And, somehow, she was his *wife*.

'Claudia, you are so right. It *wasn't* personal. But it should have been. Look at my face! LOOK at it!'

Trying not to flinch, she looked.

'Well?'

She couldn't give him the answer he wanted. She didn't *know* the answer. She wanted to cry, but she didn't want to be stabbed. 'I don't know,' she whispered. 'Please, can I put on some clothes?'

'Claudia! It's our wedding night. Don't you want to have naughties?'

She jerked her head forward, one tiny movement.

His hand caressed her neck, and she shivered. His other hand went to his pocket. A gun? A knife?

A lighter. He was going to set fire to her hair, watch her burn. She bit back a whimper.

He lit a cigarette, then shoved the lighter back in his pocket. 'You nearly fucked your own dad, and now you're fucking your brother! You like to keep it in the family, eh girl?'

'What . . .' She could barely speak. This was rubbish. It had been a one-night stand. Martin had never seen her mother again. Ethan, whoever he was, was not her brother. 'Ethan, I don't . . . I don't have a brother!'

He slapped her, hard. She gasped. Her cheek stung with pain.

'Not Ethan, *Nathan*! I'm Nathan, you callous bitch! I was your brother! I am your brother! You're disgusting! You disgust me! You're worse than Emily! *You* were there! She wasn't born yet, but *you* were there. How *dare* you forget me! How dare you! How could you?'

He was shaking her, violently. Her neck would snap.

'Stop! Eth— Nathan! Nathan – oh God. Of course I remember you, of course I do!'

He let her go. She was still shaking. 'You remember?' he said quietly.

Slowly, as if she were approaching a feral cat, she reached out and forced herself to stroke his cheek. Her head was spinning. She nodded, and staggered to stop herself falling over.

Abruptly, he turned and walked across the room. Jesus. What now? He returned, smiling, with a white waffle dressing gown. 'Here.'

Trembling, she put it on. He sat down on the bed and patted it. She sat beside him, clearing her throat. 'I have this image in my head. I am a little girl, standing in a big hall, with a herringbone-wood floor, and I am watching a carrycot being taken out of the front door. And I feel so, so sick and alone.'

She looked at him. Tears were rolling down his cheeks. Maybe it would be OK. He would cry in her arms. He would fall asleep. She would call the police. He would be taken to a . . . mental institution. A nice one.

'Go on.'

'That's it.'

'Nothing *more*?'

'No one ever talked about it again. But I thought a lot about that carrycot going out of the door. I was scared to ask people – I didn't know if it was a real memory, or a dream. I am so sorry, Nathan. Was it . . . awful, after?'

He nodded, leaning against her. She wanted to push him away, and run, but she gritted her teeth and pulled him to her. 'Poor you.' She paused. 'I know it's no consolation . . .' Oh, tread carefully, Claudia. '. . . but he was not a good father. He was neglectful . . . useless really. He didn't know how to relate to children. My childhood was miserable, really. You didn't miss a great time, I swear.'

He sat up. Every new second, she feared for her life. But now, he was smiling.

'Claudia, I'm glad you say that. Not because it makes me feel better, only the Kents' total annihilation could make me feel better, but because it gives me hope.'

'Hope?' she whispered.

'Yes, ma'am. One second.' He pressed a buzzer. 'Mrs Klout? The champagne, please. Knock once, then leave it outside the door. Thank you.'

Mrs Klout was silent and dour. *She'd* be no use.

Minutes later, Claudia was in the ludicrous position of being curled up in bed with a killer, incidentally her *spouse*, drinking vintage champagne while her teeth chattered so hard she was afraid of biting off a chunk of glass.

'*So*. My plan was always to destroy the Kent family, in the same way that they destroyed me. Because, Claudia, while I

444

might resemble a fine figure of a young man, the truth is, I am a husk.'

She was afraid to agree; she was afraid to disagree.

'I am empty. I make my living by slipping into the bodies of others.' Oh God, was he talking about acting or some fetish to do with killing people? 'I am sad, Claudia, because while rationally I can understand the circumstances in which I was rejected by Jack, *emotionally* it is impossible, and I am scarred to my soul by a feeling of worthlessness. And that is so *wrong*, and it is all Jack's fault. I want to make him pay – and I will make him pay, and you will help me, because he hurt *you*. Oh, I know you wouldn't help if he had only hurt *me* – people always think of number one! So, of course, the first thing, we take all their money – obvious really, a cheap dig, taken as read. You inherit everything when Jack and Innocence die. So, we kill them. A plane crash, a helicopter crash. Something dull. That can be arranged. But the money thing isn't the big deal – I only take their money because it hurts. I think you're the same as me – you aren't hypnotized by money, you don't worship it as they do. It's so' – he wrinkled his nose – '*common*.

'That's *one* possibility. I'm thinking off the top of my head here. Obviously, I'd prefer the personal touch: a knife in the heart, shortly after an explanation. You understand, you're a journalist. It's the satisfaction of getting a byline, as opposed to a pseudonym. You want to take credit! If we did it the helicopter way, there would have to be a tape. But it's clumsy. I prefer the stabbing. The only disadvantage is it's *messier*. And – it's a shame, because I'm terribly fond of him – I'd have to kill Mark. You know, frame *him* for the bloodbath. You'd back me up, of course.'

Claudia put down her champagne glass. 'Nathan,' she said. Her voice was firm – she hoped. 'Nathan. I understand your rage, but . . . I don't think it's a good idea. You would be caught. You would go to prison.'

He stared at her. 'No, I wouldn't. You'd back me up.' He grinned. 'And even if I did, it would be worth it.'

She took a deep breath – her last? 'Nathan. I resent my father. And yes, you're right – I *have* wanted to punish him – punish them for how they treated me. But . . . no parent is perfect. And I have a nice life. So do you. You have an amazing life. You are living well. That's the best revenge. So, you move on.'

'BULLSHIT!' he screamed. 'A stab in the heart is the best revenge! Fucking hell, I knew you'd be like this. Fine. OK. Well get *this*. Maria, yes? *Your real mother*. Jack was fucking your real mother. She traced him – you. And he never had the guts to tell you – it never occurred to him that you might need to meet her, that it might help your sense of self-worth, your fractured identity, to reunite with the woman who gave you life. As ever, he thought only of himself, and so it was *your* blood mother he married, and it was your blood mother blown to smithereens in the Paris bomb. Yes, *my* work, collateral damage, boohoo, but Maria was the one who found out about Martin – my little whimsy. Yes, Claudia, *I* was your mysterious pen pal who suddenly moved to . . . South Africa, was it? God, you were gullible. You don't *think*, Claudia. None of you do. I have spent all of my life thinking, plotting, imagining brilliant, twisted ways to make all of you suffer the same unimaginable hell that I did, and the annoying thing is, you all have the presumption to think it *COINCIDENCE!*'

She stared at him.

He raised an eyebrow. 'Changed your mind?'

Maria.

Maria.

Eventually, she found her voice, subdued, tiny, but resolute. 'I might hate Jack. And I . . . hear what you say about . . . Maria. But I would never kill. You mistake me. You don't understand, Nathan. You don't understand the nature of love. I hate him, but I love him also. And so do you. That is why it hurts so much.'

She paused.

He said nothing.

She shrugged. 'Give it up, Nathan. It's over.'

'No, it's *not*. It's not *over*. Don't try and psychobabble me into submission! Jesus. I've been married five minutes and already it's driving me *nuts*. I knew you'd be difficult. Christ almighty. MARK!'

He was screaming now, into a radio. 'Mark! Bring them in!'

She felt her heart shrivel. Even though she knew the answer, she had to ask the question. 'Bring who in?'

He smiled at her, and it was a look of pure evil. 'Well, Mrs Summers. You're going to die, and I still want my naughties! You can't expect me to abstain on my wedding night.'

'Ethan . . . Nathan . . . I'll do anything . . . please.' Now she was sobbing, begging, on her knees.

'Mark! Bring in the children.'

MARINA DEL REY, 11.30 P.M.

Jack

Jack sighed into his drink. 'Ms Green. Claudia has married a wanker.'

Ms Green pursed her lips and inclined her chin to her chest. People always talked too much around Ms Green, because she said so little. She was always remarkably well informed.

He felt hostility from the guy – it glowed off him like phosphorescence. He was used to other men bristling with inferiority, but Summers was a big deal, so why?

Jack didn't like him; *that* was why. Egos like his were used to adulation. Did the guy honestly think that he deserved admiration from Jack? His daughter had died in his house. His granddaughter had almost died. Somehow

Emily had been painted as the villain. He resented that.

There was no *quietness* in this man, no reflective sorrow. Everything bounced off him. His investigators had hit a lot of brick.

They were still working on it. Not fast enough.

And now he had taken Claudia.

Jack had never been a father-in-law. Did it always feel like two magnets fighting over gravity?

He lit a cigarette and nodded to his detail. The happy couple had gone; most guests were still partying. Innocence was in a corner, harassing George Clooney.

He needed a moment.

His special day.

That was a dig.

The guy was taunting him about the loss of his daughter. *Which?*

Hadn't she arrived only yesterday? That blissful *click* of connection as their eyes met – who would think that such a fat little chunk of humanity could blow your whole world? It was the first baby you remembered. After that it became a blur. The first baby redefined the nature of love.

How had it gone so wrong?

'Ms Green?'

'Sir.'

'Remind me. When did we get Claudia?'

He didn't have to edit himself with Ms Green. The clumsiness of his words did not mirror the nature of his emotion and she understood this. He didn't remember dates and it was her fault for remembering everything.

She paused. 'Nearly thirty-two years ago, sir. Twenty-first of February. It was a Friday.'

He smiled at her. The funny thing was, Ms Green wasn't even *working* for him when he'd got Claudia. She was still the Cannadines' nanny back then. Inwardly, Jack shuddered, as ever when he had this thought. Stealing Nanny Green to be his PA was probably what had marked the start of his moral

448

collapse. And yet he didn't regret it. There had been mitigating circumstances – his wife had just died. Harry had forgiven him, even if the old boot still bore a grudge.

'How do you remember that it was a Friday?'

'The rhyme, sir. Its words applied to all your children – both of your children. Emily was born on a Monday.'

There was a buzzing in his head. 'What rhyme?'

She cleared her throat:

> 'Monday's child is fair of face,
> Tuesday's child is full of grace,
> Wednesday's child is full of woe,
> Thursday's child has far to go,
> Friday's child is loving and giving . . .'

'All of my children?' he said. His head was thick.

He looked at Ms Green. She looked down at her neat brown lace-up shoes. Very softly, she said, 'Wednesday's child is full of woe.'

MARINA DEL REY, 11.30 P.M.

Innocence

It was a dilemma. The primal urge to boast about your grand-children to . . . *George Clooney*!

She liked to believe that nothing was impossible, but the odds were thin. That waitress was hanging around like a cold sore on a lip.

'Nanny!'

'Yes, Miss Ashford.'

Australians. 'Nanny, where are the littlies? They haven't gone to bed without saying goodnight?'

'No, Miss Ashford, they're with Claudia.'

'Why on earth would they be with Claudia?'

'They're putting rose petals on the bed.'

'Excuse me?'

'It's an English tradition? When you get hitched, the kids decorate the honeymoon suite for the wedding night?'

'Are you asking me or telling me?'

'Mr Summers said it was a surprise for Claudia.'

'It's a surprise for *me*, because I didn't— George, you're going? – I suppose it is late, but *do* call if you – Yes, goodbye, darling – Spyglass Island – Goodbye.'

Now she *was* in a bad mood.

'Nanny, what's going on? I've never heard of such a tradition – and now that I do, I don't like the sound of it. A *two-year-old*, what were you thinking? And look at the time. It's nearly midnight, they'll be exhausted. This is ridiculous. How are they getting back? Why on earth didn't you ask my permission?'

'Mr Summers – I thought – Mark said he'd drop them—'

'Out of a window? Are you *crazy*?'

'Miss Ashford, I'm so sorry – I . . . Mr Summers is going to be their *father* now, so I assumed if he said it was OK, and that *you'd* OKed it—'

'Stop talking. Be quiet. You're annoying me. Go away.'

Her head felt full of white noise. It wasn't Nanny's fault, not really. Ethan was persuasive and important – no wonder she'd agreed. It was a sweet gesture; he knew how Claudia adored those little ones. Presumably, Mark wouldn't drop them back to the hotel – they might as well sleep at the Malibu house. The newlyweds were jetting off the next day – Nanny could pick up the kids in the morning.

There was Brad. She might have another glass of champagne.

Jack

At the moment of clarity, he saw his life as if he were looking down from the sky on a stupid little ant.

It was amazing that you thought you were intelligent and yet you only saw what you wanted to see. You thought you were a harsh judge of yourself, but in fact you were a favourable critic. That kid had obsessed about you ever since you had shut the door on him and *forgotten his existence*.

It didn't matter though, if the monster had been born or created. He had – oh God – murdered Emily, and Maria, now he had Claudia. There was no time to think, no time for self-hatred and regret, he had to *act*. He had to do something. He had to save his daughter.

He leaped up, the blood pulsing hard and hot. 'Innocence,' he shouted, 'Innocence.' He pulled at her shoulder, spilling her drink. She turned, furious; her face changed when she saw his expression. 'I know. I know who he is – it's *him*,' he said. 'It's the boy.'

She shook her head, not understanding.

'Nathan – the boy who went back. *Ethan*, he's the one, he's psychotic, he's the guy – he's got *Claudia*.'

Her face paled. 'He's got Molly and George.'

His legs turned to rubber. He wasn't the man, in a town of make-believe heroes; he couldn't even pretend. He was terrified. He was terrified that he wouldn't be able to save them. Because *he* had to do this – the police – he couldn't take the chance. Ethan was a Hollywood god. He didn't have the time to convince people who might not be inclined to believe.

He could send in his security to do it for him. They had guns.

Jack was a powerful man, a man who could pay anyone to do anything for him – almost.

No.

Ethan wanted him.

And, fuck it, *he* wanted Ethan. He wanted to look that bastard in the eye as he knelt on his chest, put his hands round his neck and squeezed the life out of him.

It was his time.

He had to step up.

Innocence saw it in his eyes. 'Let's GO,' she hissed.

He clenched his jaw. 'Let's go,' he said.

Innocence

Oh, crazy. What did he *want* from them? He could have it all – she would give him every dollar, every cent.

'It's not about money,' said Jack. 'I wish it was.'

He turned off the engine, drummed his fingers on the steering wheel, and they looked towards the house. It was in darkness.

She was quiet. Didn't every feel-good movie end with a kiss and a pot of money just so you felt *comfortable*?

She felt a cold, creeping anger mingle with the fear. He had turned off the engine. They were sitting in the car, helpless. Their plan to 'break in' seemed foolish. Ethan Summers would not have stinted on security. He probably had armed guards stationed at every entrance, with instructions to shoot intruders dead on sight.

Jack had driven like a maniac (through panic, or lack of practice, she wasn't sure which) but now what? She had forbidden him to tell his security the situation – the guy would want to call for back-up. Ethan would not react well to a direct threat of violence. She couldn't take the risk.

Suddenly, the car was bathed in a harsh white light. She gasped. Flashbulbs, popping, again and again. They were surrounded.

'It's the in-laws!' one of the snappers yelled. 'Come to

check she's still a virgin!' The photographers swarmed around the car.

'*Fuck!*' screamed Jack. 'Shut up!'

For a second, she was speechless with shock that this could happen. These morons had ruined everything. Now Ethan knew they were here.

Of course he did!

Who was she kidding? If Ethan didn't want them here, *he* wouldn't be here. The kids would be in Mexico.

'Get out of the car,' she told Jack. 'We're going to walk right in the front door.'

Smiling, Innocence opened the car door. 'Good evening. Yes, guilty as charged! We've come to collect our grandchildren so the newlyweds can get some peace, if you know what I mean, and I think you do. Hello, Charlie, hello, Max – did your wife? . . . A girl, congratulations. Now don't be too hard on poor Jack. He's terribly afraid of all you big men – not you, Curtis, you need to go back to school and finish your education. We won't be long. You can have one nice family shot, and then we can all salvage a night's sleep, how about it?'

She looked at Jack. 'We'll see,' she added.

She pressed the buzzer at the gates.

Nothing.

She pressed again.

Slowly, very slowly, the gates whirred open.

She felt like a fly walking into a web. The worst thing was, she knew this was Ethan's finest hour. This was what he had been working towards for *all his life*. He would kill them all, and if he had to die with them, he would. That indifference was his real source of power.

When they finally reached the main door, it was pulled open. 'You're just in time,' said Ethan with a smile. With a lurch, she saw the gun. 'It's only taken you twenty-eight years! Please take off your shoes; we don't want you walking dirt on the carpet. And if it's not too much bother, kindly allow Mark to bleep you! A concealed weapon – oh, Jack, did that big Mary lend you his gun? How sweet. Thank you, Mark, although I'm tempted to give it back to him. I can't imagine he knows how to fire it. Anyway, do come up to the bedroom. I'm about to get George acquainted with the birds and bees. Do you like to watch?'

She was resolved to say nothing, do nothing, react to nothing until the children were in her sight. Until that point, any action was futile. She swallowed her nausea.

'You evil f—'

She didn't have time to tell Jack, no.

He launched himself at Ethan with a roar. Ethan took a neat step back, hunched his shoulders in a wince, and shot Jack in the foot.

Jack screamed and collapsed, gasping, writhing. He was on the floor, choking in agony, his eyes wild with terror. Don't cry, she told herself, don't make a sound. She wanted to gibber like a chimp but she wouldn't. Biting her lip, trembling, she slowly pulled off Jack's tie, wrapped it around his foot, trying to staunch the gushing blood. Her hands were covered in fresh red blood, and the soft sound of Jack's moans made her want to vomit, more so than the wound itself, a neat round hole where the bullet had gone in. The exit wound near his ankle was bigger, messier, and the skin around it was torn and raw.

'*You* made me do that!' Ethan shouted. 'I didn't want to but *you* made me!' There were beads of sweat on his forehead. 'You should have taken off your fucking shoes!' He glared at Mark. 'Just . . . drag him up!'

Claudia

It was a gunshot. It was definitely a gunshot. Please let Ethan be dead.

'George,' she said, sucking her bruised lip. 'Ethan's just playing a game.'

'No, he isn't,' said George. 'He's a baddie. He's hurt you. He's made Molly cry. I want him to untie you. What was that noise?'

She had to be strong. 'Molly, darling, you need to make a den. George, see this blanket on the bed? I want you to put that in that big wicker basket there, and Molly, you snuggle up inside it, and it will be your pirate den. Quickly, George. Help her. They'll be back in a minute.'

It was not exactly a plan, but Molly was exhausted and scared. It might work.

'No! *No*. Don't want to go in basket! I frightened of basket! Want to stay with you!'

Jesus.

'That's fine, Molly. You stay with Auntie Claudia. I'll look after you. Snuggle up. George. Can you see anything – anything sharp to cut this rope? *Ouch*.'

She had shifted her weight – on to the tweezers. Tweezers did not cut rope.

'What is it, Auntie Claudia – oh, I see . . .'

George picked up the tweezers from under her.

The door swung open. 'We're back and look who is joining us for the show!'

Ethan's voice had a manic lilt to it, and the hope died in her chest as she saw Jack dragged in by his hair. His foot was wrapped in plastic – red plastic – or was that . . . *blood*?

'Don't look, George. Oh God, please . . . it's enough. How can you do this, they're *children*!'

'Don't criticize me. How dare you tell *me* about how to treat children! Your family don't *know* how to treat children – do you, Jack? Do you, Jack?'

'La-La!' sobbed George, running over to Innocence and throwing his arms around her.

'You big brave boy,' said Innocence. 'You big brave boy.' She looked over at Claudia and nodded. What did the nod signify? Claudia could only hope. Well. She was nails. Still wasn't scared of looking death in the face – although, as Emily would have said, she *was* older.

'We'll see about *that*,' said Ethan. 'Want to see him squeal like a girl?' Roughly, he pulled George by the arm. 'Take off your clothes, George.'

'No!'

George was trying to bite Ethan's hand. Ethan hit him on the head. 'Oh, quit whining, that was *nothing*. You're still conscious.'

Claudia struggled against the rope. 'Please, Ethan. Please, you can do anything to me, anything, I mean it—'

'My bride, I *will* do anything to you. Patience. But after, yeah? Mark, fetch some towels. I don't want blood on the carpet.'

Mark nodded. 'I will be *one* second, so no one try any funny business.'

'Shut up, Mark, just go. I think the Glock and I can handle it. Oh, and bring more rope to tie up Sharon Marshall.' He grinned, insultingly, at Innocence. 'Never be ashamed of who you are.'

Innocence hung her head.

If anything could be done, now was the time to do it. But Claudia's hands were tied behind her back so tightly George had been unable to unpick the knots. It wasn't like in the films, where the kidnapper was careless and the rope easily came loose. Jack was slumped on the floor, white with pain. Once, when they were little, Emily had tipped all the water out of the goldfish bowl because she couldn't understand why fish didn't drown. Claudia had come into the room and seen the goldfish flapping and gasping on the floor. Looking at Jack now brought the memory flooding back.

She couldn't bear to see him like this. Even Innocence looked cowed and frightened, as if she had surrendered all hope. Ethan kept the gun trained on her. There was silence in the room, apart from Molly, who was crying, and crying, and crying. The noise was like a drill hammer, juddering into your brain.

'JESUS,' shouted Ethan. '*Shut UP!* My head feels as if it's about to explode. Someone do something. I tell you, if that brat doesn't stop crying in three seconds, I am going to shoot her in the mouth. One . . . two . . .'

Innocence

'If you bring her to me,' Innocence said quietly, 'I'll comfort her.'

Ethan gave her a suspicious look. 'She can sit with Claudia.'

He picked Molly up by one arm and threw her on to the bed. Whimpering with fright, the little girl scrambled to Claudia and buried her face in Claudia's lap. She was tiny, just bigger than a doll. Innocence felt a rip of white-hot rage. George was standing in the corner, head bowed. She would die before anything happened to these kids. The trouble was, there was a good chance of this event actually occurring, which would be no use to them at all.

'It's OK, baby,' whispered Claudia to Molly. 'It's OK.'

'Jack,' murmured Innocence. 'Jack.'

Jack gazed at her feebly, dozily; his eyelids were lowered, his eyes were bloodshot. She felt another bolt of anger. This was no time to play the victim. If she'd had a gun at that moment, she'd have shot him in the other foot.

'You,' Ethan said to Innocence, his head snapping around. 'Get away from him. Over there.'

Innocence screwed up her face. 'I'll need a second, if you don't mind. My ankle is twisted from when you pushed me to the ground.'

'Bullshit,' snapped Ethan. He strode over to her and hauled her roughly to her feet. She felt his hand grip her upper arm. He yanked her towards him. 'Move!'

'Oh,' said Innocence as she stumbled and clutched at Ethan

for support. She watched with interest as his mouth opened in a howl of pain, and she smiled, gritting her teeth as she twisted the tweezers, jamming them harder, deeper into the soft fleshy part at the base of his spine. As he arched in agony, she tripped him, sliding her foot behind his, so he fell on his back like an upended beetle, clawing desperately at the source of the pain. She grabbed for the gun, but he was too quick. She cringed, instinctively, until she realized he wasn't aiming at her. His target was George. 'No,' she screamed as he pulled the trigger. 'George, get *down!*' George screamed, and Ethan started to laugh. She was grappling for the gun – she couldn't look, she didn't dare – at least, at least it had been a quick death, a quick death for a seven-year-old boy.

Jack

A one-man Mexican wave from a cripple, thought Jack, and wanted to laugh. It was weird how the mind worked: instinct first, the primal bit; then analysis, the civilized part, obliged to comment on your actions, to make sense of it, so that you understood why. Jack didn't need an explanation from the rational part of his brain about what he had just done, although, yes, you could see it as a man leaping in joy, though you could also compare it to a dolphin leaping out of the water. He had acted on his instinct to protect his grandson. The strength had come from nowhere, and the punching, oozing heat in his chest, the breathlessness, the red blood pulsing on to his fingers told him that he had been success-ful. He had taken the bullet meant for George and there was his joy. The pain infused every part of him, merging with the agony of his injured foot, reaching to his very core, until he was no longer human, only a pulsing ball of white-hot agony. It was funny, what your mind entertained you with in your final moments – one of the few human secrets that would never be revealed. He remembered those dolphins, trailing phosphorescence, the very first night he had set eyes on the woman before him . . . He steeled himself. He had to reach her, had to drag himself forward on his belly like a wounded snake . . . Yes, thank God, she had the gun . . .

'Mark,' he said hoarsely. The man had crept noiseless into the room like a cat.

Innocence turned as Mark ran at her with a kitchen knife. She shot him in the chest.

'*Bitch!*' screamed Ethan as Mark fell, curiously silent. Ethan staggered to his feet, grabbed the knife where Mark had let it drop, and pulled George to him. He lifted the cowering boy's white shirt and put the blade to the soft swell of his stomach. 'Give me the gun or I'll rip him apart,' he screamed.

Slowly, Innocence bent in surrender, to push the gun across the floor to him. A tear glistened on her cheek.

'You little faggot,' said Jack, forcing the breath to give sound to his words. It took a great force of will to speak; his strength was steadily trickling away. 'You miserable coward – so full of hate, too weak to take the blame for your own evil. *Everyone* has bad luck, you're not special. You want to be a victim, it drives your twisted soul; you want to spread suffering because you can't bear that other people are loved, unlike *you*, so weak, worthless and alone . . . Your fans don't *love* you, they don't *know* you, no wonder your own mother gave you away. She must have sensed the evil curled inside you like a maggot. Rejecting you was the best decision I ever made—'

With a screech of rage, Ethan hurled George to the ground and lunged at Jack, stabbing him frenziedly in the heart, again and again.

He could hear Claudia's screams, far, far away, Molly's squeals of fear, and George sobbing.

Pain on top of pain; it made no difference now. It was like watching another person being thumped; he was drifting away from his rag of a body. He felt Ethan's hot breath scorch his skin, 'I hate you, I hate you,' repeating it over and over, like a child, until there was a bang and his face suddenly split like a smashed pumpkin, shards of brain splattering Jack, warm and wet, and he slumped forward, a dead weight, on top of him.

'Jack! Jack, oh God . . . George, baby, it's all OK now . . . Ethan is dead . . . he can't hurt you . . .'

The cries of his women blurred into one, as if in a dream, and there were sirens and men shouting, 'Four nineteen!' He was vaguely aware of Innocence, wiping her forehead, the gun still in her hand, of Ethan's body being pulled off him and a gentle voice, a face leaning over him, 'Jack, please, it's going to be OK,' and as the light faded for the last time, the pain lifted and he was filled with a sense of great peace, because he knew it was true.

SANTA MONICA BEACH, LOS ANGELES, TEN MONTHS LATER

Claudia

'Look what I found.' Molly thrust a delicate pink shell, like a unicorn's horn, under her nose.

'It's beautiful, darling.'

Carefully, Molly squashed the shell on to the side of the sandcastle. She was wearing a pale red swimsuit and when she bent over, her podgy little legs ramrod straight, she reminded Claudia of Winnie the Pooh stuck in a rabbit hole.

Alfie and George looked up from digging the moat. George was tanned and his legs were covered in a fine dusting of sand. She loved to see him like this: hair tousled, face serious, intent on the business of childhood. When she hugged him